McCOY PRESSED A BUTTON THAT WOULD START THE PREPROGRAMMED STIMULUS SEQUENCE.

Impatient, he counted to ten. Now this *should* have an immediate effect. McCoy glanced up at the monitor.

Nothing.

"If there's no physical cause," he said, increasingly worried, "then what's slowing his brain down?"

"Infection?" suggested Brent. "Virus?"

"Can't be," McCoy said, "he hasn't been off the ship. The only recent possibility of infection is C-15's anatid flu, but biofilters would stop that from getting aboard."

"Blood analysis?" Chapel asked, grabbing an empty hypospray.

McCoy nodded. "Worth a try—but we need to treat him immediately. This man is dying." Desperate to try anything, he adjusted his hypospray. "Ten cc's should do the trick."

Still no reaction. He didn't understand—what could be causing this? By all appearances, there was nothing *wrong* with the man.

You have no idea what to do, do you?

STAR TREK®

A CHOICE OF CATASTROPHES

Michael Schuster and Steve Mollmann

Based upon *Star Trek*
created by Gene Roddenberry

POCKET BOOKS
New York • London • Toronto • Sydney
New Delhi • Mu Arigulon V

Pocket Books
A Division of Simon & Schuster, Inc.
1230 Avenue of the Americas
New York, NY 10020

This book is a work of fiction. Names, characters, places, and incidents either are products of the authors' imaginations or are used fictitiously. Any resemblance to actual events or locales or persons, living or dead, is entirely coincidental.

First Pocket Books paperback edition September 2011

POCKET and colophon are registered trademarks of Simon & Schuster, Inc.

For information about special discounts for bulk purchases, please contact Simon & Schuster Special Sales at 1-866-506-1949 or business@simonandschuster.com.

The Simon & Schuster Speakers Bureau can bring authors to your live event. For more information or to book an event, contact the Simon & Schuster Speakers Bureau at 1-866-248-3049 or visit our website at www.simonspeakers.com.

Text design by Esther Paradelo
Cover design by Alan Dingman

Manufactured in the United States of America

10   9   8   7   6   5   4   3   2   1

ISBN 978-1-4516-0716-1
ISBN 978-1-4516-0723-9 (ebook)

To the people who believe in me,
to the people who have given me a chance to prove myself,
and to the people who are there for me when I need them.
—M.S.

To Bradley Knipper, Patrick Maloney, Christopher Tracy,
David Poon, James Sand, and Adam Johnson.
You were the best crew a captain ever had.
Tally ho, you blokes—it's tea time!
—S.M.

MISSION ROSTER

U.S.S. *Enterprise*, NCC-1701

Bridge Staff

Lieutenant Hikaru Sulu, *acting captain*

Lieutenant Nyota Uhura, *chief communications officer*

Lieutenant John Farrell, *navigator*

Lieutenant Manjula Rahda, *helm officer*

Lieutenant Esteban Rodriguez, *science officer*

Ensign Ali Harper, *engineer (subsystems monitor)*

Petty Officer (second class) Tina Lawton, *duty yeoman*

Medical Staff

Doctor Leonard McCoy, *chief medical officer*

Ensign Christine Chapel, *head nurse*

Ensign Zainab Odhiambo, *nurse*

Ensign Cheryl Thomas, *nurse*

Lieutenant Clifford Brent, *medical technician*

Ensign Magaly Messier, *medical technician*

Chief Petty Officer Robert Abrams, *medical technician*

Miscellaneous Staff

Lieutenant Vincent DeSalle, *assistant chief engineer*

Lieutenant David Galloway, *security*

Lieutenant Ryan Leslie, *security*

Lieutenant (junior grade) Hayden Singh,
    engineer (auxiliary control)
Ensign Homi Padmanabhan, *spatial physicist*

Shuttlecraft Columbus, NCC-1701/2

Captain James T. Kirk, *commanding officer*
Lieutenant Commander Salvatore Giotto, *chief of security*
Lieutenant (junior grade) Niall Rawlins, *geologist*
Ensign Pavel Chekov, *science officer*
Ensign Karen Seven Deers, *engineer*
Petty Officer (first class) Fatih Yüksel, *exobotanist*
Crewman (first class) Y Tra, *security*

Shuttlecraft Hofstadter, NCC-1701/3

Commander Spock, *commanding officer*
Lieutenant Commander Montgomery Scott, *chief engineer*
Doctor Jabilo M'Benga, *medical officer*
Lieutenant Karl Jaeger, *geophysicist*
Lieutenant (junior grade) Mariella Kologwe, *security*
Ensign Antti Saloniemi, *archaeology & anthropology officer*
Petty Officer (third class) Cron Emalra'ehn, *security*

PROLOGUE

"You can't be serious!" Leonard McCoy didn't care one bit whether his reaction was appropriate. "Captain, tell me you're joking."

James Kirk shook his head. He was occupying his usual seat at the table in the *Enterprise*'s primary briefing room, leaning back in his chair and taking in the reactions of the senior staff members he'd summoned. "Do I look like I am, Doctor?"

McCoy couldn't—*wouldn't*—believe it. "Anyone with a medical degree could do this. Hell, anyone who's ever held an anabolic protoplaser in their hands could do this. You don't need me."

Spock cut in. "According to Starfleet regulations, transfers of medical supplies rated class-3 or above must be supervised by the chief medical officers of both locations. Your presence is required to facilitate the transfer."

McCoy had to keep himself from reaching across the table and throttling the Vulcan.

The others in the room—Sulu, Scotty, and Giotto—looked astonished at the doctor's reaction. They could afford to; after all, they didn't have to personally oversee the transfer of two hundred forty containers of medical supplies to Deep Space Station C-15. They didn't have to stand there inspecting every damn one, then witnessing its dematerialization on the pad of *Enterprise*'s cargo transporter. It was a tedious job, and McCoy didn't want to do it.

Why did the people on C-15 have to come down with the anatid flu right now? Why did it have to spread to the nearby settlement of Tomogren? The station had exhausted its med supplies, requiring the Federation to arrange for a replacement shipment. This being a relatively uncharted and unsettled region of space, the *Enterprise* was the only ship in the sector. The crew was interrupting their mapping mission to pick up the supplies from the automated production facility on Phi Kappa.

The *Enterprise* had only six more weeks to explore this sector, with one week allotted to Mu Arigulon V, a planet so far surveyed solely via automated probe. This medical detour reduced the week to three days. As a result, the *Enterprise* crew needed to rework their plans, much to McCoy's annoyance.

Spock was clearly intrigued by indications that Mu Arigulon V had been abandoned by its inhabitants. He'd quickly come up with a plan: drop off two shuttles, fully crewed, on the *Enterprise*'s way from Phi Kappa to C-15. The shuttles were uprated models, equipped with warp drives and phasers. After delivering the supplies, the *Enterprise* would rendezvous at the planet, reaching it two days after the shuttles. They'd then have three more days to finish the survey.

The problem was that McCoy had been looking forward to the mission to Mu Arigulon. The first two weeks in this sector had mostly been tedious charting of stars with only barren rocks for company. There had been nothing interesting, and now that there was, he was being kept away from it.

"Doctor," Kirk said, "what Spock means is that we don't have any leeway. Regulations. Besides," he added, making an effort to appear conciliatory, "it's not as if there's anything on the planet that won't be there when you join us. The ruins won't disappear." The captain grinned. "We'll just be scrambling through dirt all week. Mister Sulu, since Spock, Scott, and myself will be on the shuttles, you'll be in command for the duration."

"Yes, sir!" said Sulu.

"Mister Spock and I will release a full roster for the landing party within the next day. Is there anything else, gentlemen?"

Giotto leaned forward. "Sir, I'd like to be in the landing party."

McCoy could see Kirk's surprise. Giotto was the *Enterprise*'s chief of security, but he rarely served in landing parties. "Any reason, Commander? Can't your people handle it?"

"Of course they can," said Giotto, "but under normal circumstances I can beam down if things get hairy. That won't be an option on this mission—I want to be there from the start."

Kirk nodded. "Understood. I want two security personnel per shuttle; send Mister Spock your picks for the other three." He looked around at the crew. "If that's all, dismissed."

McCoy couldn't remember a mission in which Giotto had participated and he hadn't. The doctor just wanted to be busy. Today was his third anniversary as chief medical officer of the *Enterprise*, and he needed to get his mind off that fact. He'd gone into space to get away from his thoughts, and now he was being left alone with them. Since joining Starfleet, he had never held a post this long, and it unsettled him. He needed to be moving, otherwise he began thinking, began wallowing.

As the others filed out of the briefing room, Kirk and McCoy remained seated. The doors closed behind Sulu, the last to leave. Immediately, Kirk leaned forward and rested his arms on the tabletop. "What's gotten into you, Bones? You're tearing into me for something I can't do anything about. It's not like you. What's going on?"

The doctor thought about it for a moment. But would Jim understand? This was a man for whom space was a passion—for McCoy it was an escape. How could Kirk understand that McCoy felt he didn't belong here and never had? "Nothing," he said.

"Stop being so pigheaded," Kirk said. "You always get me to tell you what's eating me. Let me do the same for you."

"Jim, I'm fine. Stop projecting."

"Bones." Kirk shook his head. "Whenever you're this prickly, there's something gnawing at you. I can't help you if you don't tell me."

McCoy opened his mouth to reply but found he didn't know what to say. He just wanted to *go*, to plunge into the depths of space and leave everything behind. But that wasn't healthy.

So he said nothing, but stood up and walked toward the door. He was out of the room before Jim had a chance to add anything further.

The last time McCoy had felt like this, he'd signed up for

a six-month survey mission on a primitive planet near the Klingon border to get his mind off things. Where would he have to go this time?

Ten Days Later
Stardate 4757.2 (0452 hours, ship time)

James Kirk loved the first sight of a new world. No matter how many planets he'd seen, each one was different from the one before it. There was no substitute for that moment when the ship came out of warp and there, suspended before him in the infinite darkness, was a small bastion of life.

The feeling was more intimate right now in a shuttle-craft—just him, the six others, and the unknown. With a crew this small, the captain took the controls.

"ETA to Mu Arigulon, Ensign?" Kirk asked the woman sitting next to him at the navigation controls of the shuttle-craft *Columbus*.

"Two minutes, Captain." Karen Seven Deers was older than Kirk, having elected to join Starfleet after a success-ful career as a mechanical engineer on Centaurus. She had only recently completed training and been posted to the *Enterprise*. Kirk remembered being a green ensign ner-vously following Captain Bannock's orders on his first land-ing party. Seven Deers, by contrast, was positively blasé.

"Stand by for warp deceleration." Kirk's hands ran across the console in front of him, setting the engines. He could feel the power of the craft humming beneath his hands. "Signal the *Hofstadter* for verification."

Seven Deers tapped a control. "*Hofstadter* signals ready, Captain."

Not wanting to miss his first sight of Mu Arigulon, Kirk

looked up to check that all three of the viewport covers at the front of the *Columbus* were open.

"Is everyone ready?" Kirk spun his chair around to take a quick look at the remainder of the *Columbus*'s crew. Lieutenant Commander Giotto was sitting right behind his captain, of course. The silver-haired security chief—also older than Kirk—gave the captain a curt nod. Next to him was one of his security team, Crewman Y Tra, a male Arkenite with the distinctive large cranium typical of his species. He nodded even more curtly.

The two scientists, Rawlins and Yüksel, offered quick "ayes," but Kirk heard nothing from the shuttle's seventh and final occupant. "Mister Chekov? Are you ready?"

The young Russian looked up from the data slate he'd been engrossed in. "Aye, Captain! I have been refreshing my knowledge of the history of this sector. Did you know that Station C-15—"

"Thank you, Mister Chekov," said Kirk with a smile. "That'll be all for now." The ensign was serving as the *Columbus*'s science officer for this mission. Spock had personally selected him, and Chekov had perhaps been overdoing it to live up to the Vulcan's standards.

The captain noticed Giotto studying the ensign. During the long journey to Mu Arigulon, the security chief's attitude toward Chekov had seemed to waver between amusement and frustration. Kirk chalked it up to boredom, but he knew they'd all be able to do something soon, which should improve everybody's mood. The four-day flight had seemed even longer, since the crew had spent the time gradually transitioning to the planet's long day/night cycle, disrupting everyone's sleep patterns.

Kirk checked the spatial plot, in the console between

him and Seven Deers. They had just cleared the outskirts of the Mu Arigulon system and were rapidly approaching the fifth planet. "Point of deceleration in five," announced Seven Deers, "four . . . three . . . two . . . one."

Kirk throttled down, and with a gentle hum the *Columbus* dropped to sublight.

All of a sudden, right in front of him, he could see it: Mu Arigulon V. It looked vaguely Earth-like—blue ocean and green continents—but the clouds, which covered the planet in large, rapid swirls, had a dusky gray tinge. "There she is," he said. It truly was a glorious view.

"Captain, we should signal the *Enterprise* now," Seven Deers said.

Kirk nodded. He knew that, of course, but he was pleased to see that the ensign was already becoming familiar with ship's procedure. "Take care of it, Ensign. Bring the *Hofstadter* into the linkup, too." According to his instruments, the other shuttlecraft had also safely decelerated from warp and was already settling into standard orbit. Spock hadn't wasted any time. Kirk set the *Columbus*'s controls to do the same.

"Link established," Seven Deers reported. "Bringing it up now."

"*Enterprise*," Kirk said, "*Columbus* is in position and ready to begin landing procedures."

"*Hofstadter* *is also in position*," said Commander Spock on the other shuttle. "*We are preparing to begin our orbital survey.*"

"*Acknowledged,*" Lieutenant Sulu said from the bridge of the *Enterprise*. "*Captain, you have fifty-four hours on your own before we join you. I'm sure you'll make the best of it.*" Kirk knew from previous communications that the

Enterprise had transferred the supplies from Phi Kappa to C-15 without incident.

"We will, Lieutenant, we will," Kirk said. "Mister Spock is already getting antsy. He can't wait to set foot on the planet."

Spock spoke up. *"I must correct you, Captain. I am not getting 'antsy.' That peculiar adjective implies impatience, something I do not experience. However, I must admit to considerable scientific curiosity as to the fate of the inhabitants of Mu Arigulon V."*

"I withdraw my remark," Kirk said, grinning. "Everything all right on the *Enterprise*?"

"Absolutely, sir," came Sulu's immediate reply. *"Mister DeSalle assures me that the engines are in perfect order."*

"They'd better be," said a new voice that Kirk immediately recognized as belonging to Commander Scott, who was with Spock on the *Hofstadter*. *"I dinna want to come back and find my wee bairns fried."*

"Don't worry, Mister Scott, I'll make sure that doesn't happen," Sulu said. *"Captain, I hope the planet's as interesting as it looks."*

"So do I," Kirk said. "Sixteen planets charted so far in this sector, and every one of them has been completely unsurprising. I'm hoping for something different this time."

"I'm sure you'll find it, sir," Sulu said. Kirk thought that the young helmsman sounded at home in the big chair.

Still, he could do with a little ribbing. "Thanks for your confidence. We'll contact you again in a few hours. Try not to miss us too much."

Sulu chuckled. *"We'll do our best, sir.* Enterprise *out."*

"Mister Spock, are you ready to proceed?" said Kirk.

"Affirmative, Captain. Initial orbital surveys have already

revealed that the planetary ruins are relatively intact. I esti-
mate that this planet has been abandoned for a period of one
hundred to one hundred and fifty years."

The first probes of the Mu Arigulon system had shown
that this planet had metal alloys and other traces of techno-
logical and industrial development—but no active energy
signatures or life signs. Whoever had lived there was long
gone. "Any clues as to what happened to the inhabitants?"

"*I hesitate to indulge in wild speculation, Captain. I
need more data before I can begin to formulate a reasonable
hypothesis.*"

"Of course, Mister Spock. I wouldn't want to rush the
scientific method."

"*Very admirable, Captain. I take it that you will be landing soon?*"

"As long you don't mind being left behind."

"*Sir, we did agree on this at the mission briefing. However, if you would prefer for* Columbus *to wait while Hofstadter makes the orbital survey, that can be arranged.*"

Kirk smiled. His sense of humor was frequently lost on
Spock—or so it appeared. The captain had never been able
to solve the mystery of whether Spock merely pretended to
misunderstand. If he did, were his retorts attempts at wit?

"Never fear, Mister Spock. I won't disrupt your careful
plan." A smile tugged at the corners of his mouth. "We'll
land just as soon as you tell me where."

"*Transmitting coordinates now, Captain.*"

Kirk looked at Seven Deers, who nodded. "We've got
them, Spock. See you on the surface when you're done up
here."

"*Yes, Captain. Hofstadter out.*"

"Course laid in, Ensign?"

Seven Deers checked her controls. "Aye, Captain. The landing site is outside the largest metropolitan area in the northern hemisphere."

"Well," said Kirk, looking around at the crew of the shuttle, "what are we waiting for? Let's go."

ONE

Two days after leaving C-15, McCoy was still restless. Together with Christine Chapel, the *Enterprise*'s head nurse, he was organizing the medical supplies that they'd gotten from Phi Kappa. Tedious but necessary work. They'd been at it for a while, and just as the doctor had feared, it was allowing his mind to wander.

Maybe it was time for him to move on. He'd heard that Starfleet was beginning to put together crews for the next generation of ships to succeed the *Constitution* class. If he managed to finagle himself onto one of their duty rosters, he'd be able to go *really* far out, blazing new trails in frontier medicine.

The problem was, he'd be disappointing his captain and his friend. Not only would Jim have to search for his third CMO in four years, he would take McCoy's desertion personally. Either way, McCoy would be miserable, but it was a feeling he was already intimately accustomed to.

He and Chapel were interrupted in their work by the arrival of Lieutenant Kelowitz. He claimed to be a patient, but insisted that he would talk only to McCoy. "That's never a good sign," McCoy whispered to Chapel. He took the young man into his office, sitting down behind his desk while Kelowitz stood, his hands flapping around uselessly.

Kelowitz was a little shorter than the doctor, and his hair a little lighter. They'd been on a couple of landing parties together, but McCoy knew virtually nothing about him apart from the fact that he was a tactical officer.

McCoy nodded toward the chair, and the other man sat down, though he still didn't know what to do with his hands, folding and unfolding them repeatedly.

"Now, tell me what's the matter, son." Whatever Kelowitz might reveal, it would be hard to embarrass McCoy after twenty years of medical practice, so he used his most reassuring tone.

"Doctor, I was wondering if you could give me some advice."

"Advice?"

"You've, um, helped out others before, and I was hoping you could do the same for me."

"You'll have to tell me what this is about first."

Kelowitz avoided looking directly at him. "It's personal. You see, I've been working with Mister DeSalle recently, and— He's kind of—"

McCoy was beginning to get a pretty clear idea of what the young man was really here for. "Lieutenant, I'm just the ship's doctor . . ."

"Um . . . sorry, sir. But Demick told me that Brent told her that you told him that when he—"

McCoy breathed in deeply. Clifford Brent, one of his med techs, had landed a secondary assignment on the bridge, and the doctor had given him advice on how to handle the senior staff, especially Spock. The thought that his advice was a sought-after commodity evaporated his bad mood. McCoy stood up and sat on the desk, adopting a casual air. "Okay, tell me what the problem is."

Ten minutes later, McCoy had sent Kelowitz on his way, no longer fidgeting. Chapel gave him an amused look as he emerged from his office. "What was that about?"

McCoy shook his head. "Just a young man needing some advice." He looked at the tray of tri-ox cartridges in front of him, waiting to be sorted, and just like that, his bad mood was back. *He* could use some advice.

Hoping to keep his mind from lingering on painful thoughts, he started counting off cartridges, but lost track in the low twenties. He grumbled, "Why do I have to be stuck here while Kirk and Spock are having fun? M'Benga should be *here*, and I should be *there*."

Chapel had put up with his complaining the past few days, but this time she surprised him. "So you've said repeatedly, Doctor." Her gentle tone didn't quite cover her annoyance.

McCoy snorted and restarted his counting.

"What's the matter, Doctor?" asked Chapel at last.

He lost track in the upper fifties this time. "Dammit, Christine! I was almost done!"

"Sorry, Doctor." She turned her attention back to her slate.

"Nothing's the matter." He was unable to stop himself. "Why should something be the matter? I *like* counting tri-ox capsules and supervising cargo transfers and being trapped on a boring starship on a boring mission while Kirk and Spock gallivant around the galaxy."

Chapel didn't look up, but even so, McCoy realized that maybe he was going a little too far. His volatile nature was sometimes difficult to manage, especially when he felt he was doing work that didn't make use of his experience. Well, Chapel had taken worse from him before; she was certainly used to his occasional dark moods.

McCoy reached for the first tri-ox capsule, to start yet again, when the deck under his feet moved abruptly and he was knocked forward. In an instant, the lights went out and all the displays shut off. His hand hit something large and flat, which shot away and crashed onto the floor—it must've been the tray.

"What—" Chapel began, but she cut herself off when the lights all whirred back to life. No sooner had McCoy regained his bearings than he felt the deck shift again. Nowhere near as badly as the first time, but longer. What in blazes was going on?

"I'll check the situation monitor," he said, heading back to his office. The deck moved underneath him yet again. The doctor almost fell, but he made it to his computer. Nothing. Even intraship was down.

He returned to Chapel, who was preparing for casualties. Their first one came in barely a minute after the mysterious incident: Jacobs, a security guard, whose limp indicated to the doctor that he'd twisted his ankle.

McCoy hated being left in the dark. With Jim in command, he was accustomed to barging up onto the bridge whether he was needed or not, but with Lieutenant Sulu?

To hell with it. "Can you handle things, Nurse?"

She already had the hobbling Jacobs on one of the beds, and she nodded at McCoy, who headed out. Even though she'd never admit it, Christine was probably glad to get rid of him.

When Pavel Chekov was a teenager, he had been fascinated by the massive raised highways that crisscrossed Russia. Built in the twentieth century to support wheeled vehicles, they had become redundant with the invention of the hovercar and then the transporter. Yet no one had ever torn them down, and Chekov had hiked through the reclaimed countryside on six lanes of concrete no vehicle would drive again.

It made human endeavors seem pointless. The structures had outlasted the needs they were designed to fill. He doubted the inhabitants of Mu Arigulon V had designed this complex array of metal frameworks and roadbeds to support a diverse panoply of plant life.

"What do you think this is, sir?" asked Fatih Yüksel. The Turkish exobotanist was older than Chekov by several years. Chekov felt uncomfortable giving orders to someone who'd already been in Starfleet when he was still in elementary school.

"It looks like a support structure for a launch facility," said Chekov. He gestured back behind them as they pushed their way through the bushes. "It reminds me of the old Plesetsk Cosmodrome. I am picking up tanks that must have once held some kind of fuel or reactant."

"No spaceships." Yüksel was scanning the area with his tricorder. When the *Columbus* landing party had split up, he had requested this part of the city, pointing out that it had the highest concentration of plant life. Chekov had been assigned to go with him.

"But was there ever a spaceship?" Chekov knew that for every planet that made it into space and made contact with the interstellar community, there was another whose space program had collapsed, preventing the inhabitants from discovering warp drive. "I want to get a closer look at the launch pad. Maybe the locals left the planet."

"Well," Yüksel said, "what I really want to get a look at is the flora ahead." He pointed to where the bushes gave way to thick vines descending from the gantries above.

Chekov checked his tricorder. They were supposed to stay together, but the two locations were within a kilometer of one another. If anything happened, each would be able to come to the other's aid. "Okay," he said. "We will split up." As the senior officer, it was his call to make.

The botanist smiled. "Good move, sir," he said. "We'll have this planet surveyed in no time."

"Good luck, Mister Yüksel." Chekov pushed off into the bushes. When he glanced over his shoulder, he saw the petty officer vanishing into the green draping vines. Shortly, the only sign of him was the rustling noise that was slowly fading away as they parted from one another.

Petty Officer Fatih Yüksel continued to push his way through the dull green flora. Bits of machinery he couldn't identify lay unused and rusting, covered in what seemed like a moss. Let Chekov and the others try to figure out what had happened to the inhabitants; he was interested in what had taken their place. The plants in this area would have adapted to an urban environment over the past century, and would make a remarkable study.

The complex had been open once, but was now a tangled mass of plants. Yüksel was trying to reach its center, where his tricorder indicated a tree—the largest one in this area. He wanted to take a core sample that could be analyzed, revealing past climates and possibly indicating what had caused this planet to be abandoned.

He pushed his way through an overhanging set of vines and came upon a small building in the middle of the complex, about ten meters tall and four meters wide. This structure, like all the ones they'd seen from the *Columbus*, possessed no flat surfaces. With its irregular but continuous walls, it looked like something that had been grown. There were no obvious windows, and no door that he could recognize. But it was inside the building that his tricorder was picking up the tree's signature, so he began to circle it. As he reached the other side, he discovered that a wall had crumbled in.

Or rather, had crumbled *out*. Within the building grew an enormous tree, similar to a Terran one but a dull green. It had no leaves, but sported fat, bulging buds all over its branches. One of its branches had extended past the confines of the building, knocking out part of the wall, through which Yüksel could barely make out the trunk.

Yüksel scrambled eagerly over the bits of wall between him and the alien tree and stepped inside. Everything was bathed in a light green glow. The roof had collapsed, allowing light to stream in. He had no idea what the structure had been designed for; now it was entirely occupied by this tree, which was two meters thick and taller than the building.

Yüksel realized that its base wasn't on this level—the floor had a hole in it, through which the tree had grown. The standard site for taking a core sample was 1.3 meters up from the base, so he would need to get down into the lower area. There was a small gap between where the floor ended, torn and crumbled, and where the trunk began, but he couldn't see down there—too dark.

Yüksel slung his backpack off his shoulders and pulled a flashlight out, shining it into the depths of the structure. The floor, he estimated, was two meters below; he could hang off the edge and drop. Determined to get his sample, he stowed his tricorder and tossed the backpack down first, followed by the flashlight, providing him enough of a view to know where to land. He carefully dangled himself over the edge and let go.

When he hit the floor, his foot hit a piece of rock, but he quickly regained his footing. Glad that he'd made it down unhurt, he recovered the flashlight and moved its beam around the room, a basement with large semicircular shapes set into the wall. But that wasn't what interested him. Awed by the immense sight that was the alien tree in front of him, Yüksel grabbed the sampling kit out of his pack and began to activate the core sampler. He couldn't wait to see what the results were. Preliminary meteorological analysis by Lieutenant Jaeger on the *Hofstadter* indicated a recent period of global warming, and that—

A scraping noise from behind Yüksel disrupted his concentration. What was that? An ancient piece of machinery coming to life?

He turned around, casting his flashlight in the direction of the sound. Nothing. What could have caused the noise?

He had heard *something*.

Yüksel dropped the sampling kit and unslung his tricorder. He continued to shine his light all across the room, but what had moments ago seemed mysterious and exciting was now gloomy and foreboding. Strange shadows crisscrossed his vision.

Something scraped again, behind him. *Lanet olsun!* He'd better call Chekov.

His hand reached for his communicator. Before he could activate it, there was a loud snap, and then something thick and flexible hit him in the back, like a giant whip.

It threw him off balance. Yüksel landed on his hands and knees, dropping his flashlight. He had no time to get up. Out of nowhere, a weight pressed down on his back. As its pressure increased, Yüksel was forced to take in smaller and smaller breaths. In moments, he was pinned to the floor.

The beam of his flashlight hit the wall, now useless.

McCoy had always been impressed by how calm the *Enterprise*'s bridge was, even in a crisis situation. When you had Jim Kirk in the command chair, with his nerves of steel, and Spock at his side, steady as a rock, there seemed to be no better choice than to follow their example.

This morning, the bridge was filled with chatter, with subdued conversations. Sulu was at the helm controls; a young woman in a command uniform, Lieutenant Rahda, was standing next to him. Crew members at the upper stations looked a little frantic. Sulu carefully adjusted controls on the console, trading information with Farrell at navigation. The ship rumbled again as they worked, causing Sulu to run his fingers over the controls.

McCoy stepped over to Lieutenant Uhura at communications. She was listening to reports on her earpiece and manipulating her own panel. Intraship was back up again, evidently. "Copy that, damage control. I'll relay that information to Lieutenant Sulu." She looked up as McCoy approached her and smiled, but didn't say anything as she continued to handle all the requests coming through her board. "You'd better send that on to physics section, they'll know what to do with it."

He watched her work for a few more moments, then she pulled her earpiece out. "Hello, Doctor," she said.

A number of message lights were still blinking. "Don't you need to answer those?" McCoy asked.

"Part of being a good communications officer is knowing when *not* to answer," she said, gesturing at the few lights that were still on, all of them amber. "I handled everything important. Those are low-priority."

He smiled. "What's the situation up here? We didn't hear anything down in sickbay."

"We've encountered a spatial distortion," replied Uhura. " 'Run aground' is what Lieutenant Rodriguez said. Subspace is too rough and unstable here for the ship to move through."

McCoy spared a glance at the science station, where Rodriguez was writing notes on a data slate as he peered into the scope. "What about the shuttles?" he asked. "They didn't hit this, did they?"

Uhura shook her head. "The captain reported that they reached Mu Arigulon early this morning with no problem."

"Yet two days away, and we hit . . . something." McCoy gestured vaguely toward the viewscreen, though this section of space looked no different than any other. The deck vibrated beneath him, but this time the sensation was barely noticeable.

"Gotcha!" Sulu's triumphant cry drew McCoy's eye back to the helm console, where the lieutenant was standing up. "She's all yours, Lieutenant Rahda."

The woman obligingly took her seat back. "All systems normal," she reported. "We are maintaining position, one-point-oh-five light-years away from Mu Arigulon."

"Situation report," ordered Sulu as he settled back into the command chair, turning to face Rodriguez.

The lieutenant picked up his slate, peering at his notes. "The ship hit a spatial distortion," he said. "A bump in space-time. It's not been previously charted in this sector."

"How large?" asked Sulu.

Rodriguez tapped on the slate nervously. "I'm not sure. I don't detect anything other than what we just cleared—but then, we didn't detect the distortion until we hit it. It's very subtle."

"It didn't feel very subtle to me," McCoy muttered to Uhura.

"Warp six was probably too fast under the circumstances," said Sulu. He turned his chair to face Uhura. "Lieutenant?"

"Intraship's functioning again, sir. Some static on the subspace channels, but that's normal for this sector," she said.

"Send a transmission to the shuttles, reporting what's happened here. Advise that we are continuing toward Mu Ari at a reduced rate." Uhura nodded and placed her earpiece back in position. Sulu turned his attention to McCoy for the first time. "Crew status, Doctor?"

"No casualties apart from a sprained ankle," McCoy replied. "This ship's had rougher rides."

"That's for sure," said Sulu, turning to face the officer at the engineering subsystems station. His baby face made him look like he was fresh out of the Academy. "Damage report, Ensign Harper?"

"Nothing substantial," the young man said. "There was that shipwide power outage when we first hit the distortion. Lieutenant DeSalle is investigating it right now. Other than that, all systems are now normal."

Sulu nodded and turned back to face the viewscreen. "What speed would you recommend, Rodriguez?"

The science officer scribbled some calculations on his slate and checked the scope. "Warp four."

Leaning forward, Sulu clapped his hands together. "Lay in a course for Mu Arigulon at warp four, Lieutenant Farrell."

The navigator did as ordered. "ETA is five days, twenty-three hours, sir."

"Take us forward, Lieutenant Rahda," Sulu said. "Slow acceleration."

As the ship began to hum with the power of the warp engines, McCoy moved forward to place his hands on the railing that circled the center of the bridge, leaning down over the command chair. "Listen," he began, "are we going to . . . 'run aground' again?"

Sulu looked up and smiled. "Relax, Doctor. Everything should be fine. We'll see it coming this time." He seemed at ease, but McCoy didn't buy his casual attitude. The helmsman had to be anxious about being in command of over four hundred people.

"Current speed?" Sulu asked.

"Warp three-point-five," Rahda replied, her hand slowly pushing forward the speed control. "Everything—"

This time, as every light shut off, McCoy swore that he didn't just feel the deck buckle, he felt it ripple, throwing him forward. He gripped the railing as hard as he could, keeping himself on his feet—but then a second ripple threw him backwards.

The doctor reeled and hit the communications console with his hip, only narrowly avoiding Uhura. He heard her cry out as she fell off her chair. McCoy reached out with his hand, hoping to catch her and help her back up.

Everything was suddenly dipped in blood red as the emergency lights came on. McCoy had always thought that color choice was unfortunate, but right now he didn't give a damn. Now he could see. As he guided Uhura back to her seat, everything tilted sideways, sending both of them flying to port as they futilely held on to each other for support.

"Stabilize!" Sulu shouted.

"Working on it!" came Rahda's voice at the exact same time that Farrell shouted, "Aye, sir!"

McCoy's feet scrambled for purchase on the deck, and he almost had it—was almost safe—when the bridge recoiled, tilting the other way, knocking him straight onto the floor. Uhura managed to stumble back into her chair and grip her console.

The main lights switched on, and McCoy squinted until his eyes adjusted. Gravity was back to normal, as were the inertial dampers. The deck had stopped lurching. Most of the crew were resuming their positions, except for the young yeoman forward of Rodriguez. She'd somehow ended up clear on the opposite side of the bridge, clutching an unoccupied port station.

"That spatial distortion of yours has a helluva kick." McCoy had trouble suppressing a pained groan. Damn, that had not been good for his back. He had to use the railing to pull himself up. "I don't—"

"Doctor McCoy," Uhura interrupted him, "sickbay is signaling. Nurse Chapel needs your assistance."

"Tell her I'll be right down." He nodded at Sulu, but the lieutenant was only paying attention to Rodriguez, who was explaining something about spatial physics.

McCoy sprinted for the turbolift. In a crisis situation he knew where his place was. His patients came first.

As Montgomery Scott put on his silver EV suit, he remembered all the memos he'd sent to the quartermaster pointing out that if the things weren't so damn uncomfortable, people wouldn't complain so much about extravehicular work. He'd never received a reply.

This excursion had been his idea, and his alone. Nevertheless, that didn't keep him from muttering under his breath while checking all the seals on the suit.

"Thanks, Doctor," Scotty said as Doctor M'Benga handed him the large helmet he'd just pulled out of the storage unit of the shuttlecraft *Hofstadter*. The physician had made himself useful by helping Scotty get ready for the work awaiting him outside.

Scotty checked the shuttle's force field. With the hatch open, the thin energy barrier would be the only thing keeping the air in. The force field was fully operational. Scotty fidgeted with his suit's controls as the shuttle pulled closer to the satellite, checking the tether line.

He glanced over at Petty Officer Cron Emalra'ehn, the Deltan security guard who'd volunteered to go with him. Scotty was, quite frankly, gobsmacked by the man's decision. "Are you sure you want to do this, laddie?"

"I *like* to get away from it all," Emalra'ehn said. "Too much *stuff* in here, if you know what I mean."

Scotty didn't see how anyone could think that a G-class shuttle had too *much* stuff in it. On the other hand, he could understand wanting to get outside after four days of low-warp travel. "We're almost there." Scotty looked up toward the controls of the *Hofstadter*, where Spock was making final adjustments to the shuttle's course. "Right, Mister Spock?"

"Correct." Spock looked backward just for a moment. "I suggest you put your helmets on."

Scotty lifted the bulky thing up over his head, and

M'Benga helped him activate the seals. Everything checked out: he was ready to go.

Ready, yes, but not overly enthusiastic.

While this had been his idea, Scott found he didn't want to go through with it. The actual step through the force field into free fall took a lot of gumption. He'd never been one for extreme sports like orbital skydiving.

Ah, sod it, he thought. There was no time to whine now.

"Velocity matched." Spock's voice sounded through the suit's comm. *"Ready?"*

"Aye, sir." Scotty nodded and tugged on the cable from his waist to the anchor point by the hatch. Emalra'ehn did the same.

"Opening hatch."

The door swung up in front of the two men, revealing the expanse of stars—plus a small metal object only a few meters away. It was a satellite built by the missing inhabitants of Mu Arigulon V, one of a thousand orbiting the planet but no longer active. Antennas projected from the side of the sat, which was a cylinder a meter and a half tall and less than half a meter wide. A misshapen dish sat on top.

"Lieutenant Kologwe, please monitor their activity," ordered Spock. The security officer, sitting in the seat nearest the door, turned on a tricorder.

"Time to go." Scotty stepped forward, the atmospheric shield fizzling around him.

Simply being in zero gravity was always disorienting, but stepping into it was even more so. One second, Scotty was in a world with up, down, left, right; the next, there was nothing but the limited confines of his own suit. He was drifting slowly forward, carried by the momentum of his step over the shuttle's threshold. Glancing to his right, he made out Emalra'ehn behind him.

The sat appeared motionless. However, Scotty knew that both the little metal ball and the shuttle were moving at 15,000 kilometers per hour relative to the planet, but with their velocities matched, it seemed like neither was moving.

Scott understood the mechanics of low gravity perfectly from a mathematical standpoint, but his stomach never had. While Spock and other scientists worked on the orbital survey, Scott wanted to study the alien satellites. However, Spock had not wanted to spare the shuttle's limited sensor time to analyze them in detail. Scotty's idea of bringing one on board so he could study it had been deemed an "adequate" solution. Effusive praise from the Vulcan science officer.

Scotty tapped some controls on his suit, causing its tiny thrusters to fire. Soon he was close enough to the satellite to touch it. Its purple metal surface was pitted by over a century of micrometeorite impacts but otherwise intact. Emalra'ehn had moved to the opposite side, all the while making sure that the tether didn't get caught on one of the antenna spikes. After Scotty made a quick scan to verify that the satellite was inert, they moved to grab hold of it.

"Got it?" asked Scotty, keeping his eyes on the satellite to avoid vertigo.

Emalra'ehn, on the other hand, was glancing in every direction. "*Yes, sir,*" he said. "*Pity to go back inside already. It's nice to get out.*"

Scotty raised an eyebrow. "Lieutenant Kologwe, bring us in."

"*Aye, Commander,*" came her voice over the comm. The

cables on Scotty and Emalra'ehn's suits began to retract, reeling them over to the shuttle. Scotty let his eyes wander over the satellite, wondering what lay beneath its surface. Was it for communications? Scanning? Mapping? Or something more malevolent? Many early-spaceflight civilizations used satellites for housing rudimentary nuclear weapons.

Ah, well. He'd have enough time to speculate later. Taking great care not to lose himself in the infinity of space, he directed his gaze toward the small gray-green orb some Berengarian astronomer had christened "Mu Arigulon V."

As they came within a meter of the shuttle, the comm came on again. *"Stopping the cable."*

Scotty turned toward Emalra'ehn, but he moved his head too quickly. The stars began to spin. Cursing himself, he quickly focused on the satellite. "Fire your thrusters," he said. They needed to slow the sat down.

Scotty and Emalra'ehn activated their thrusters at the same time, reducing their speed to a gentle drift just as they came within a meter of the hatch. Scotty steeled himself—as disorienting as it was to go from one *g* to zero *g*, the opposite was worse. Scott positioned his feet a few centimeters above the deck just before he felt the crackle of the atmospheric force field.

The sudden weight of the satellite caught him by surprise, and he almost lost his grip, but Kologwe was waiting to brace it from inside the shuttle. Emalra'ehn was fine, of course.

The three of them moved the satellite to the back of the shuttle as Doctor M'Benga resealed the door. The two scientists—Jaeger from geophysics and Saloniemi from archaeology and anthropology—looked up from their tricorders, but not for long. They had data from the sensor sweep to occupy their attention.

Scotty pulled off his helmet and slung it onto the deck of the shuttle. "Well, that was exciting."

Emalra'ehn shrugged. "I've had better."

As Scotty took off his suit, he gave silent thanks that he'd put yet another EVA behind him. Above all, the thing Scotty didn't like about spacewalking was that it made him realize how small he was compared to the rest of the universe. It made him feel unimportant and useless. Unsettling, that.

Well, there was one good way to combat that feeling. Scott smiled at the thought of studying this piece of alien tech. The sooner he could figure out what this satellite was for, the better.

Lieutenant Commander Salvatore Giotto had to admit he'd been on more challenging missions. He wasn't bored—and even if he had been, he would have had no right to complain, considering that he'd volunteered—but from a purely professional point of view, Mu Arigulon V was rapidly shaping up to be what security officers called a "haunted planet."

Haunted planets had one big danger: the lack of excitement led you to become complacent and inattentive. As a junior officer on the *Lantree*, he had participated in a similar survey, only to be caught unawares by local predators that had gravely injured Captain Gees. With twenty additional years of experience, Giotto felt he was the perfect man to look after James Kirk. The captain could be a challenge. At least on this dirtball there was little chance of him getting into a fight with local aliens—if the scientists' readings could be believed.

It paid to be wary of first results, another lesson bitterly learned. More than once, Giotto had witnessed how quickly a boring mission could turn into a deadly trap with little hope of escape. For a long time he'd kept the scars on his back to remind him of this, but he'd eventually realized how foolish it was and gotten rid of them.

The *Columbus* team was exploring the northeastern edge of a once-thriving metropolis. They'd split up—Giotto was with the captain and Ensign Seven Deers. He liked the engineer; nearly as old as Giotto, Seven Deers had raised two kids, making her more practical as well as more taciturn than other crew members.

He squinted in the bright light of the midday sun. The captain was picking out a path through the city, trying to take in as much of it as he could, occasionally asking Seven Deers what she thought the purpose of different structures might be. Giotto would have preferred point, but Captain Kirk would never allow it, so he followed behind, keeping his eyes open to assess where danger might arise.

Toothpick-like towers, barely wider than the *Columbus* was long, pierced the sky, their tops disappearing in the clouds. Ahead, the thin towers gave way to a squat building, round in general shape, but with many bulges on its outside, like a fat, warty toad. The road system was obviously designed around this mound.

"Ensign," Captain Kirk began, "do you have any idea what those bulges are?"

Seven Deers looked up from her tricorder. "Dense machinery of some kind, Captain, but I can't make out what. I'd like to get closer."

"To do that," Kirk said with a grin, "we're going to have to figure out how to open the doors."

Several large semicircles a little taller than Giotto were set into the ground floor of each building, but the landing party had yet to identify a way to open them. Without even knowing what these aliens had looked like, they couldn't know how they opened their doors. The thing Giotto didn't like about new species was that you had no idea how they thought, and if you didn't know how they thought, you couldn't anticipate what they were going to do.

"I have—" Seven Deers began to speak, but she was cut off by the chirp of their communicators.

They all reached for the devices, but Kirk had his out first, flipping its antenna grid up. "Kirk here."

"Captain, there's somethi—" Yüksel's voice rang out, but something cut off the end of the transmission. All Giotto could discern was rising panic.

"Yüksel!" Kirk barked into the device. "Where are you? What's happening?"

"—eneath the surfa—"

They waited expectantly for the signal to kick back in, but after a couple seconds, there was nothing but hissing static. Kirk looked to Giotto.

"He was with Ensign Chekov," Giotto said, "in the northwest quadrant, sir."

"Let's go," Kirk said, and immediately began moving at a quick jog, taking point. "Commander, keep trying to contact him."

Giotto had already taken the rear and drawn his phaser; he flipped open his communicator. "Yüksel, do you read me?" he called. "Yüksel!" There was only static.

Kirk was continuing to give orders. "Get a fix on that signal, Ensign!" he called to Seven Deers, who was between the two men. "I want to know exactly where he is." He held his communicator up again. "Kirk to Chekov."

A moment passed while Giotto considered what could have happened to the exobotanist. On this planet for only four hours and already—

"Chekov here, sir."

"Ensign, where's your teammate?"

"He was off looking at some plant life, sir."

"You split up?" Kirk sounded incredulous.

Giotto's anger was rising. What had they been thinking? You could expect a bit of airheadedness from a scientist like Yüksel, but not from an officer like Chekov. He continued to call for the specialist into his communicator.

"Did you get that transmission?" Kirk was asking. "He was obviously hit by something."

"Yes, sir." There was a small pause. *"We thought it made sense to cover a greater area. We were exploring a launching complex of some kind. I will meet you where we split up, sir."*

"You do that, Mister Chekov," Kirk said, snapping his communicator shut. He fell back to draw even with Giotto. "Commander, contact Rawlins and Tra. Make sure they're safe."

Giotto switched channels. "Aye, sir." Kirk sped up to exchange some words with Seven Deers about tracking Yüksel's signal as Giotto made contact. "Giotto to Tra."

There were a few moments of silence. *"Tra here."* The security guard sounded fine.

"Crewman, did you receive Yüksel's signal?"

"Yes, Commander. Rawlins and I are fine; we're looking at what we think is graffiti."

"What's your location?"

"*We're in the southeast quadrant of the city. There are a lot of small buildings.*"

"We're converging in the northwest area to look for him. I'll send you the coordinates. Keep your eyes open." They didn't need more people to go missing.

"*Always do, sir. Tra out.*"

Giotto slipped the communicator back onto his belt. Tra would keep Rawlins safe.

"How are they, Commander?" Kirk yelled over his shoulder, having taken point again.

"They're fine, sir."

"Good."

In his early days on the *Enterprise*, Giotto had had great difficulty getting used to Kirk's command style. It was nothing like how things had been done on the *Lantree*. Captain Gees had always brought his security chief with him on landing parties, and when there had been fighting to do, Giotto or Commander Mauracher, the executive officer, had handled it.

It was difficult to say exactly why Kirk was so different. It could simply be that Gees was an older man, but there was more to it. The captain felt he couldn't ask his men to place themselves in danger unless he did the same himself. Sometimes, Giotto thought there must be some underlying issue, but he had to admit that Kirk's style got results. The captain always got the job done.

Giotto regularly walked the path of danger; it was difficult to complain about getting shot at when you put on the red shirt. It went with the territory.

TWO

Stardate 4757.4 (0924 hours)

In sickbay, well over a dozen people had come in for various injuries from the repeated jostling the *Enterprise* had taken. Chapel had called in Nurse Thomas, along with med techs Brent and Abrams. Additional help was required while the other duty nurse, Zainab Odhiambo, worked on burns. McCoy's patient was an engineer who'd suffered multiple fractures of his arm when he'd unexpectedly been knocked off a catwalk. Simple enough to treat with a bone knitter, but time-consuming.

McCoy had been worried that the aftereffects of the distortion would continue, but it seemed as though they'd gotten the ship under control, letting the doctor work without interruption.

He was about halfway through the bone repair when Brent and Abrams came up to him, startling him. He was about to grumble at them, but their somber expressions stopped him. Something bad must've happened. McCoy switched off the regenerator. "What is it?"

"Coma," replied Abrams, his trademark scowl deeper than normal. Brent nodded wanly. They worked together frequently, but McCoy had always thought them an odd pairing. Clifford Brent was a skinny, black-haired man who more often than not looked worried, whereas Robert

Abrams was a stouter man, with thin, brown hair, whose face seemed molded by perpetual displeasure. Whether Brent was worried because Abrams was unhappy, or Abrams was unhappy because Brent was worried, McCoy had never been able to discover.

"How . . . never mind. Nurse!" McCoy shouted across the room. Both Chapel and Odhiambo turned toward him, looking expectant. "Zainab, please finish up here." He turned to the injured engineer, who looked understandably dejected. "You'll be in good hands."

That done, he joined Brent and Abrams at the end of the ward, where a tall, thin man in a gold command uniform lay on a biobed. The face looked familiar—McCoy had passed the man in the corridors. . . . Bouchard. Wasn't he from Neu-Stuttgart?

A glance at the life-sign monitor above the bed told McCoy all he needed to know: each indicator was depressingly low. The periodic bleeps that indicated respiratory and cardiovascular function were too widely spaced. "What happened to him?"

"We don't know, to be honest," Abrams said. "Apparently he just fell over."

McCoy glared at him, but it was Brent who explained. "We really don't know, Doctor. He works in phaser control, and his fellow officers brought him in just now. They said he collapsed in the middle of the room."

"When we hit the distortion?" It wouldn't exactly be difficult to do that, as McCoy well knew.

"Seems likely," said Brent.

His colleague shook his head. "No, I don't think so. They acted surprised; it couldn't have been that."

From the corner of his eye, McCoy spotted someone in

blue approaching him—Chapel. McCoy was glad to have Christine and her insights at his side. He touched a control on the side of the monitor to skip to more specific readouts of the man's brain. "Well, he's definitely in a coma. Readings don't point to any physical trauma." He switched back to the summary display, about to give an order for a more detailed analysis when he noticed something wrong. "Neuron activity is dropping. He's dying." But not if he could do something about it. "I need a hypo of dalaphaline and a neural stimulator."

The med techs ran off without more questions, and he inspected the monitor again. Without knowing what was actually wrong, he couldn't bring the man out of the coma. All he could do was slow down Bouchard's decline. If he was lucky.

What he needed right now was information—as much as he could get. He asked Chapel for the man's medical records.

"Olivier Bouchard," she said, reading off a data slate, "assigned to phaser control since transferring here. He's been in sickbay twice before. Routine physicals. Nothing out of the ordinary. He's never even been in a landing party. No previous brain injuries."

A low grunt escaped McCoy. "I'm not surprised. It would've been too easy."

The monitor bleeped loudly. Bouchard's levels were now dangerously low. McCoy turned to demand where the devil Brent and Abrams had gotten to, and found that Brent was already hurrying over, hypospray in hand. "Dalaphaline," he said, delivering it to McCoy.

In one swift motion, McCoy set it for five cc's and injected it into Bouchard's jugular. The drug would boost his nervous system and help his brain keep going. He looked up at the monitor, though he knew the change wouldn't happen instantly. The readings stopped plummeting only for a few seconds before resuming their decline.

Chapel came up to him then, holding a whole tray of devices suited for brain analysis and repair that she'd taken over from Abrams. "Thank you," McCoy said, grabbing the neural stimulator. Lifting Bouchard's head gently with one hand, he slid the arc-like device underneath and positioned it around the man's parietal bone. After a few seconds, it squealed to indicate a connection with the brain's regulatory centers, and small lights on it began to flicker accordingly. The doctor pressed a button that would start the preprogrammed stimulus sequence.

Impatient, he counted to ten. Now this *should* have an immediate effect. McCoy glanced up at the monitor.

Nothing.

"If there's no physical cause," he said, increasingly worried, "then what's slowing his brain down?"

"Infection?" suggested Brent. "Virus?"

"Can't be," McCoy said, "he hasn't been off the ship. The only recent possibility of infection is C-15's anatid flu, but biofilters would stop that from getting aboard."

"Blood analysis?" Chapel asked, grabbing an empty hypospray.

McCoy nodded. "Worth a try—but we need to treat him immediately. This man is dying." Desperate to try anything, he adjusted his hypospray. "Ten cc's should do the trick."

Still no reaction. He didn't understand—what could be causing this? By all appearances, there was nothing *wrong* with the man.

You have no idea what to do, do you?

McCoy shook off the thought. The problem was that the dalaphaline took too long to work through the bloodstream. If injected into the brain—

It was insane. It was dangerous. He could remember reading journal articles about how terrible an idea it was.

But all he needed to do was give Bouchard a little nudge. He set the hyprospray for just two cc's and reached out to place it against the man's skull, where the frontal and parietal bones met.

This time, Chapel grabbed his hand. "Doctor, what are you doing? You can't increase the dosage again," she whispered sharply. "You'll kill him!"

"He'll *die* otherwise." McCoy gestured up at the readouts with his free hand. They were as low as they could be without Bouchard being dead. "I've never seen this outside of one of Spock's healing trances."

Chapel didn't let go. "He's *not* Spock. No human being can take that much neural stimulation."

"I do this, or he dies," McCoy said, hoping to drive home their lack of options. With a short but vigorous shake, he freed his hand. Before Chapel could react, he had jabbed the hyprospray through the tangle of Bouchard's thick hair and into his skull.

The monitor began bleeping alarmingly. A few of the level indicators shot straight up. Over the course of his career, McCoy had probably done crazier things, but nothing with so uncertain an outcome.

"His brain's going into overdrive." Reproach coated Christine's words.

And just like that, the bleeping stopped. The levels slid back down to where they were before—but no lower. They weren't decreasing.

He'd done it! McCoy allowed himself a small smile. "Well, look at that. Perfectly fine."

Chapel's look was more than enough to indicate how she felt.

"Well, not *fine*," McCoy admitted. "But stable. That'll give us time to figure this thing out."

Chapel locked eyes with him. "Yes, Doctor."

For a young ensign fresh out of the Academy, a posting on a *Constitution*-class ship operating on the edge of explored space was a plum assignment. It still amazed Chekov that he'd been picked for the *Enterprise*, a ship with a name that went back centuries.

As a new officer, he'd worked in multiple departments to familiarize himself with all areas of the ship's operation, intending to develop a specialization later. So far, he'd alternated primarily between the sciences and operations. Today, he was not only serving as the senior science officer of the *Columbus,* but also security backup.

As soon as the call from Captain Kirk had come in, Chekov had began running toward the part of the complex Yüksel had set off for, phaser in one hand, tricorder in the other. *Chyort poberi!* How could he have done something so stupid? He couldn't get a fix on Yüksel's communicator, nor did his tricorder detect any human life signs. There was a small amount of interference, but he didn't think it was blocking all scans. There was nothing here to find.

He found himself becoming tangled up in vines, barely able to move. Captain Kirk's voice interrupted his thoughts. "Mister Chekov!" He couldn't see the captain, but he sounded close.

"Over here, Captain!" he called back.

There was some rustling off to Chekov's side, and moments later, Commander Giotto emerged from a bush, Captain Kirk and Ensign Seven Deers right behind him. Giotto immediately began surveying the area, while Kirk walked over to Chekov.

"Ensign," he said, looking stern, "report."

"Yüksel was looking at this part of the complex, while I was inspecting the launch pad."

"Have you detected anything unusual?" asked the captain.

"No, sir," said Chekov.

"You split up?" asked Giotto.

"Yes, sir," said Chekov.

"Ensign, what did we say when we landed?"

"I know, sir. I am sorry, sir."

"You might be sorry, but he's—" Giotto cut himself off when the captain shot him a look.

"Right now," said Kirk, "we need to focus on finding Yüksel. It sounded like he said 'beneath the surface,' so check for ways underground. Tricorders out, phasers on stun. Commander, you're with me. Chekov, you and Seven Deers stick together."

Chekov nodded. "You can count on me, sir. We'll find him."

"I hope so, Ensign," said Giotto.

Did he have to rub it in? Chekov elected to ignore Giotto and took a look at his tricorder screen instead. "There are two areas of dense plant life ahead, sir. I believe that he would have gone to one or the other if he was—"

"Good thinking, Mister Chekov," said the captain. "Giotto and I will take the far one. You and Seven Deers wait for Tra and Rawlins, then take the other."

■   ■   ■   ■

After about an hour, most of the casualties had been discharged, though McCoy had retained a couple to monitor their injuries. He'd ordered Odhiambo, Brent, and Abrams to get something to eat—Chapel too, but she said she wasn't hungry. He didn't believe her, but he had enough to worry about.

In his office, McCoy sat down with the readouts of Ensign Bouchard's brain scans. It was a damned puzzle: no trace of a current infection, nor any other plausible cause, and yet the man was dying. What could be wrong? Since Chapel was so intent on helping, he had her check with phaser control to find out exactly what had happened.

He skimmed through a few dozen pages of data before a whiff of a very subtle perfume reached his nose. Chapel had returned and was standing in his office doorway. "Go ahead and sit down, Nurse." She deserved some time off her feet; she looked at least as tired as he felt—and of course her shift had started quite a while ago. "What did you find out?"

"According to three witnesses, he fell over *after* the distortion. Everything was steady and clear. Bouchard was crossing the room when he suddenly collapsed."

McCoy nodded. "That fits with his injuries. Some bruising on the shoulder from where he hit the floor—but nothing else."

"Nothing in the cranial region at all?"

McCoy spun his monitor around to show Chapel Bouchard's readouts. With M'Benga off on Mu Arigulon, McCoy didn't have another physician to discuss medical conundrums with, but Chapel had been a promising bioresearcher before enlisting. He would have consulted her even if M'Benga *had* been on board. "Symptoms, but no *cause*," she said. McCoy refrained from saying anything, letting her work through the issues herself. "No hemorrhaging, no brain injuries. Blood sugar normal, carbon dioxide normal. And yet he's down to level four on the Glasgow scale."

McCoy just nodded. "I don't mind a good mystery, but this one's a bit too much for my taste. The only medical problems listed in his record are things that happened to the whole crew, like the spores on Omicron Ceti III."

"How could he come down with something this serious that affects no one else on the entire ship?" asked Chapel.

Doesn't affect them yet. McCoy brushed the thought aside—no sense worrying about something that hadn't happened. "There's only one thing that stands out about him, and only in the context of a brain injury." He was about to flip through the pages of medical data when the intraship squealed. Annoyed at the interruption, he jabbed the button. "Sickbay here."

"Doctor, this is the bridge," the voice of Lieutenant Uhura replied. *"Lieutenant Sulu is taking the ship back up to warp speed."*

McCoy asked, "Could there be another of those space sandbars out there?"

"We're proceeding forward at warp one," said Uhura. *"It'll take a while to clear the zone of spatial distortion, but we should get through smoothly enough to avoid any ill effects."*

McCoy could hear the slight uncertainty in her voice. "Or at least that's the theory, right?"

"Sulu decided it was the safest option. There are distortions both ahead and behind now."

"What does *the captain* think of this plan?"

"There's a lot of subspace interference, and I haven't been able to punch through yet. Expect warp speed in another thirty seconds."

"Well, good luck to Mister Sulu, then," McCoy said as he flipped off the comm. "And to all of us."

"You're worried," said Chapel.

"I'm always worried when one of my patients is dying from something I don't know how to treat. And this time it's even worse because we keep getting tossed about like a toy in a hyperactive child's hands. Forward into unimaginable danger, that's the Starfleet way."

And your way, too, to be fair, even if for different reasons.

As if to mock him, the deck plates vibrated slightly, indicating that the ship had begun the transition to warp speed. All too aware of how the last warp jump had gone—McCoy's back still hurt from the fall on the bridge—he gripped his desk as the ship accelerated . . .

And nothing happened.

"Well, that went better than last time," he said, letting go—but slowly. "Maybe Sulu does know what he's doing after all."

Chapel gave him a disapproving look. "Doctor—"

"Yes, Nurse?" He wondered if she'd actually say it. He'd welcome it, certainly. Sometimes he needed someone to tell him to stop grumbling and get to work, and Jim wasn't here to do that.

"Nothing," she said. "Let's get back to Bouchard."

"Right." McCoy pulled back the monitor, retrieving the page he wanted. "Take a look at *this*." He turned the screen around to show her.

"Aperception quotient of twenty over a hundred and one, and a Duke-Heidelburg score of two hundred sixty? He's an esper."

"Right. Overall ESP rating of eighty-seven."

"I don't have much experience with human telepathy."

McCoy turned the screen back around. "According to the report, he's not powerful enough to be reading anyone's mind on a conscious level, but he can pick up on things. This says it was first noticed because of his skill at board games in school. Always knew what his opponents were going to do, but never quite why."

"Good attribute for a phaser officer."

The typical human was no more telepathic than your average rock, but extrasensory perception had been scientifically documented in human beings in the early twenty-first century, and the number of recorded human espers had risen steadily ever since. Even so, they were still fairly rare.

"Could that be it?" asked Chapel. "Have we come into contact with any psychic phenomena?"

"Not that the science section has noticed," said McCoy. "Just these spatial distortions." The deck hadn't moved at all this time, thankfully. It looked like the warp field was going to stay stable. "No energy fields, nothing. Our best hope is to keep him at his current level until we get to a starbase with better medical facilities."

"I wish Mister Spock were here," said Chapel, a little wistfully. "He could tell us if something was out there."

McCoy snorted. "I doubt it. Vulcans are touch telepaths. He'd be just as oblivious as you and me."

"He could do a mind-meld," Chapel pointed out, almost stubbornly. "Go straight to the source."

"And I bet he could also play us 'Pop Goes the Weasel' on his damned Vulcan lute!" McCoy snapped. "We need to focus on what we can do, not what we wish we could do."

"Right now, we can't *do* anything!" Chapel forced the words out abruptly.

McCoy stared at her for a moment, not sure of how to respond. She was right, but he wasn't prepared to admit defeat just yet. With a stab of his finger, the doctor snapped the monitor off, then stood up. "I'm going to go get something to eat. Biopsy Bouchard's brain and get the sample to Harrison in the lab," he said. "And when Thomas gets back, consider yourself off duty. Get some rest, Christine. That's an order."

She said nothing, giving only a hint of a smile.

They both headed out of his office, Chapel a few steps ahead of McCoy. His destination was the recreation room on this deck, which wasn't far. McCoy walked slowly, wanting to spend some time alone with his thoughts. With the ship on Red Alert, most of the crew were at action stations, and those who were in the corridors were on urgent errands. Something must have damaged the power conduits in this section, because the lights were dim, giving everything a dusklike feel.

The doctor 's conscience was rearing up: he knew he'd been short with Chapel. Tired and stressed, McCoy was taking it out on her. And she—as usual—accepted it and did her duty.

No surprise—she's out here because it's her choice. Not because she feels this need to keep on moving, like you do.

Chapel had initially gone into space to find her missing fiancé, Roger Korby. *Enterprise* had located Korby two years ago, discovering that he'd been dead for years. And yet Christine had stayed on board, never once expressing to McCoy a desire to move on, or even to return to her career in bioresearch. She seemed settled in a way that he wasn't.

He resolved to apologize to her once he got back to sickbay. Maybe he'd even bring her a sandwich.

After a few minutes' slow walk deep in thought, he reached the rec room. It was almost noon. Normally the room would be full of officers and crew talking, eating, playing games, even singing. Today, there were a scant dozen in here, silent as they wolfed down their food. Eat and run.

Run. Ha! The *Enterprise* couldn't afford to run. It did little more than crawl at warp one. McCoy hoped that they cleared this spatial distortion soon; at this speed it would take months to get to Mu Arigulon.

As he made his way to the food slots, the doctor passed a lieutenant with a familiar face whose name escaped him. Sitting at a table by himself eating mashed potatoes, the sandy-haired man nodded at McCoy, who nodded back. The man had been assigned to sickbay for a rotation. *Connors.*

McCoy continued to the slots. With something in his stomach, he might just be able to find the inspiration he needed—

The whole deck rose beneath his feet, vaulting him into the air, and the lights chose that moment to fail again. Before his mind could fully process the absence of gravity, McCoy plummeted back down, accompanied by the sounds of things crashing hard. His training kicked in, and he pulled his legs up to his chest in a tuck as he made contact with the deck once more. A jolt of pain ran through him. Doing his best to ignore it, the doctor rolled backward and then on his side.

He still couldn't see, but the noises around him were terrible. Crashing, shattering, groaning.

Lots and lots of groaning. People in this room needed his help. No time to moan about his hurting backside; he had to get up and get going.

Spock was intrigued. Having finished their orbital scans, the *Hofstadter*'s crew had taken the shuttle into the atmosphere, to a large continent in the southern hemisphere. The inhabitants of Mu Arigulon V had vanished. Evidence to date ruled out a violent extinction, either natural or artificial. There were no signs of war or civil unrest, nor was there anything amiss in the environment, aside from a low level of atmospheric toxicity.

The absence of remains of any kind presented a puzzle. A mass exodus, while possible, required a planetary space industry that Mu Arigulon V lacked. There were no stations in orbit, no space elevators, no vast spaceports, nothing with the capacity to process the millions, if not billions, of beings who must have lived on the planet.

With all the knowledge at his disposal, Spock could not devise a theory that made use of all the available facts and explained where the natives had gone. It was a challenge, and he looked forward to discovering what had happened.

Karl Jaeger, a geophysicist specializing in meteorology, was seated behind Lieutenant Kologwe at navigation. Spock turned to face him. "Mister Jaeger," he said, "do you have an explanation for this planet's atmospheric toxicity?"

"I do, sir," Jaeger said, handing Spock his data slate. "If you look at the readings we've taken, you'll see that a major climatic shift took place about two centuries ago, perhaps a little longer, causing the temperature to rise." Jaeger turned to M'Benga and the others seated behind him. Spock listened while studying the data. "Evidence of this can still be seen everywhere. Levels of heavy metals and atmospheric pollutants, especially polyaromatic hydrocarbons such as compounds of the benzopyrene family, are just below toxicity threshold for most humanoids. Several decades ago, this place must've been deadly. Thankfully, the air's clean now and the planet's cooled down again. Sir, if you require a detailed breakdown of what happened, I'll have to analyze precipitation layers at one of the polar ice caps."

Spock considered this. "Thank you, Mister Jaeger. I'll add it to our list of objectives."

"Sir . . ." Jaeger hesitated for a moment. "There's one other thing."

"Yes, Lieutenant?"

"Windspeeds are picking up, and cloud formations are growing across this entire continent. All indications are that we're in for a storm."

"I am aware of this, Mister Jaeger."

"But it doesn't make any sense. We're talking about a big storm—one that could cover this part of the southern hemisphere. But when we were in orbit, there was no sign of it: no low-pressure system, no inversion layer. There *still* isn't. But now it's on its way."

Spock momentarily considered that Jaeger was not accounting for the idiosyncrasies of the weather of a new planet, but he immediately dismissed the idea. The lieutenant had too much experience. "Thank you, Mister Jaeger." Spock was confident that the shuttle's shields would minimize the effects of any adverse weather.

He added the weather dilemma to his internal list of conundrums, tasking a small part of his mind to its resolution. "Mister Scott," he said, rising from his seat, "report on the satellite we recovered."

The engineer was hunched over the strange mauve-colored device at the back of the shuttle, having unsealed a panel to access its innards. "There are some highly sophisticated electronics in here, Mister Spock." He pulled his hand out of the device, dislodging several wires. "Plus a fusion reactor only as big as the palm of your hand."

"Have you determined the device's purpose yet?"

"Aye. Projecting energy," he said, picking his tricorder up off the deck, "but I canna tell what kind of energy. It's been inert for at least a decade. The only bits I can be sure about are its thrusters; it's got a powerful reaction control system."

Spock nodded. The satellite could be nearly anything: a weapon, a shield generator, a tractor emitter, even a surveillance sensor. "Would it be possible to activate the device?"

"Aye." Scott peered back into its innards, his eyes jumping between the device and the readout on his tricorder. "Everything seems intact inside." His facial expression transformed in a way that Spock knew humans called "lighting up." "I'd like to take a crack at it if you don't mind, once we land. Wouldn't be safe in here."

"Indeed, Mister Scott. Once our aerial survey comes to an end, you may proceed."

Scott leaned back to sit on the deck, against the aft wall of the shuttle. "Mister Spock, shouldn't we be helping find Yüksel?" His face distorted in a portrayal of what could only be termed exasperation. "The poor lad is out there somewhere."

"The captain has ordered us to continue our survey for now. There is little that a second shuttlecraft could do that the first cannot."

Scotty nodded and began looking at his tricorder read-outs once more. Spock recognized that he was not entirely satisfied, but knew better than to press the issue. He returned to the pilot's seat to examine the surface beneath the *Hofstadter*. It was a large expanse of wooded land dotted with mountains that grew larger the farther the shuttle flew. Rivers cut patterns into the terrain, a flood plain of times long past, and they eventually converged into one wide torrent that rushed on toward a high cliff.

A light began bleeping on Kologwe's controls. "Incoming transmission from the *Columbus* party, sir."

"On speakers, please, Lieutenant."

The voice of Captain Kirk crackled from the speakers. *"Spock, do you read me?"*

"Perfectly, Captain."

"Do you know anything about this interference we're starting to pick up?"

Spock checked his controls. There was indeed static in some of the scan results, though it was not pronounced enough to trip any alerts. "A negligible amount was reported by the initial probe of the planet, but I have only just detected the increase myself, Captain. Is it impeding the function of your tricorders?"

"A little. Could it be related to the distortions that Uhura reported?"

"Unknown, Captain." Several minutes after Yüksel had sent his distress call, the landing parties had received a transmission from the *Enterprise*, indicating that it had encountered a spatial distortion, but would be continuing to Mu Arigulon at a slightly slower pace. "The data that the *Enterprise* sent were not comprehensive."

"Raise them again."

"Captain, do you want us to come and help you look for Yüksel?" broke in Scotty.

"Negative, Scotty. Right now I want to know more about this planet. And what happened to its inhabitants."

"Understood, Captain," said Spock. "I will contact you if we acquire further information."

"Good. Be careful."

Spock raised an eyebrow. It seemed an unnecessary reminder. "Of course, Captain. *Hofstadter* out."

He readied a transmission to the *Enterprise* and sent it, but there was not an immediate response. If the level of subspace interference was higher near the starship's position, there could be a time delay of up to six minutes. He returned his attention to the *Hofstadter*'s path.

The shuttle followed the river until it shot over the cliff edge, thundering down in a waterfall so high that when it arrived at the bottom it shattered into an all-enveloping mist. Ignoring the expressions of awe coming from the others, Spock took the shuttle in a slow descent down to the lowland, still following the river. The former inhabitants of Mu Arigulon V appeared to have needed or wanted access to water; they had constructed their population centers near bodies of water. This much the survey probe had established.

"Mister Spock," Kologwe said, turning to him. Her normally smooth and expressionless features evidenced excitement, indiscernible to any but him. "I'm getting a reading here."

"What kind of reading, Lieutenant?"

"There's an energy source dead ahead of us. It's weak, but definite."

Spock was surprised to pick up an energy signature,

after having spent the better part of half a day first in orbit and then in low-altitude flight with sensors constantly in active mode. "Intriguing. Well done, Lieutenant. We shall investigate." Spock altered the *Hofstadter*'s course, simultaneously increasing speed.

Attempting to retrace the route Yüksel would have taken, Kirk and Giotto had followed the readings of freshly broken vegetation, following the trail to a gigantic tree growing in the middle of a structure. Giotto helped Kirk drop through a hole in the floor into the basement, made possible by years of collapse and decay.

Kirk grunted as he stood up. "Careful, sir," Giotto called down. "I don't want you disappearing, too."

The captain smiled. The security chief was perhaps overzealous sometimes, but he got the job done. "Give me your flashlight!" he shouted back up.

Giotto dropped it right into Kirk's hands. The captain waved it around the room. There were large pieces of machinery, but none of them seemed to be on. The walls were lined with the same large semicircles as they'd seen on the surface. He began walking around the base of the tree, keeping an eye on the walls of the chamber. The dirt crunched beneath his feet.

"Sir?" Giotto called down into the hole. "Do you want me to come down there?"

"Hold on, Comm—" Kirk was interrupted by a glint of bright silver metal near one of the walls. He pointed his beam right at it.

It was a Starfleet-issue flashlight. "I've found something!" he called. "Yüksel's light." He began picking his way over toward it.

"I'm coming down." A few moments later, Kirk heard Giotto hit the dirt and walk in his direction.

Kirk squatted on the ground next to his find, the only sign that Yüksel had been here. He picked it up and turned it over in his hands, but aside from scuff marks from landing on the gravel floor, there was nothing about it that told him anything. "'Beneath the surface,' his message said." Kirk looked over at the large semicircles on the wall. "Those are doors, right?"

Giotto had his tricorder out. "Yes, sir. There are long tunnels behind each of them."

Kirk handed Giotto his light back and turned Yüksel's on, walking over to the semicircle to get a closer look at it. Its surface was black and featureless, completely smooth. "What happened down here, Commander? If he was attacked—what did it?"

"We haven't even seen any signs of large animal life." Giotto was slowly turning, shining his light on every corner of the room. "If only Chekov had stayed with him—"

"Then we'd likely be missing two men now instead of one," interrupted Kirk. He flipped open his communicator. "Kirk to Spock."

"Spock here, Captain."

"Any word from the *Enterprise* yet?" The easiest solution to this problem would be using the starship's powerful sensors to probe the planet from orbit. If Sulu brought her up to maximum warp, she could be here in just over twelve hours, not two days.

"The only signal I have received is my own, approximately six minutes, thirty seconds after transmission. An unknown phenomenon is reflecting all subspace communications."

"Dammit, Spock," hissed Kirk, "I need the *Enterprise*. What's Sulu doing to my ship?"

"*Unknown at present, sir. We have, however, located a powerful energy source and are en route.*"

"What is it?"

"*Also unknown, sir.*"

"Well, find out."

"*Affirmative. Hofstadter out.*"

Kirk turned to Giotto. "I'm not wasting any more time trying to find a way to open those things. Half-power should do it."

Giotto nodded, and both men drew their phasers from their belts, turning the dials up. Kirk momentarily felt a twinge at the idea of destroying an ancient alien artifact. The captain stepped back from the semicircle he was examining, and Giotto stepped over to join him, training his weapon on it.

"Fire!"

Bright blue beams lanced out from their phasers, striking the center of the door and sending sparks flying. The light burned brightly, but the door remained the same black color.

"Full intensity!" Kirk twisted his dial all the way up, and the pitch of the phaser increased drastically, as did the light it produced. But despite the fact that the noise made him clench his teeth, nothing was happening.

Kirk released his finger from the trigger. "That's enough. I'm calling Chekov and the others down here— we're finding a way in."

THREE

McCoy untucked his legs, reaching tentatively out with his arm. Finding metal, he put his weight on his hands as a prelude to standing up, only to find the metal slipping away. He fell right back to the deck. Another tray.

He waited a couple of moments, and realized that he could make out shapes now. His eyes were adjusting, the emergency lights providing just enough illumination to see. Apparently even they were affected by the damned space distortion's effects. He'd have to exchange a few words with Scotty about them when he got the chance. Now, he had other problems to worry about. Time for another attempt at getting back on his feet.

Not a good idea. He'd landed pretty hard, and now he was discovering exactly how hard. His eyes widened in reflex at the new pain that momentarily took away his breath. But viewed objectively, he'd been hurt worse.

McCoy looked around, trying to make out who was there, but without much success. A moan rose from nearby, causing him to call out, "Do you need help? It's Doctor McCoy."

Somebody answered, but from elsewhere in the room. "I'm fine. But I'm afraid to move . . ."

"It'll be all right. Keep talking, I'm coming over." McCoy advanced tentatively toward the voice, trying not to stumble, and worried that the deck would rumble again at any moment. Were the lights coming back to full power or what?

His left foot came down on something; it snapped. What had he done?

"What was that?" asked the voice.

"That's what I'm trying to figure out." It had been an object, not someone's body part. He leaned over, and his eyes finally picked up what had been a three-dimensional chessboard.

"What's the deal with the lights?" demanded a new voice, in a far corner of the room.

The emergency lights shouldn't be so dim. Something had to be wrong with the backup power systems.

"I need help over here!" called another voice, quivering with pain. "I think my legs are broken."

This was bad, but more worrying to McCoy were the number of people who *weren't* calling out. There had been about twelve other people in the rec room before the distortion had hit.

"Count off!" he called out as he looked around, trying to orient himself. "One!"

"Two!" That was the voice he'd heard earlier, the man who'd said he was fine.

"Three." Another man.

"Four." A woman's voice, the one with the broken legs.

There was a long pause.

"Five." Another woman.

No more? Hell. "Anyone else?" called McCoy.

Someone moaned, but no one answered. The deck

chose that moment to rumble once more under McCoy's feet, but nowhere near enough to do any harm, merely a gentle reminder of the straits the ship was in.

"How close are you to the intercom?" asked Two.

McCoy turned around. His eyes had adjusted enough that he could probably make it safely. There was one next to the food slots, and he'd almost made it there before the distortion had hit. But the intercom wasn't as important as what was next to it: the emergency kit. All large public areas on the ship had a cubbyhole in the bulkhead that contained medical supplies and other emergency paraphernalia.

Stepping cautiously to avoid fallen hazards on the floor, McCoy worked his way to the speaker grille of the intercom. He hit the activation switch. "McCoy to sickbay."

There was no response.

"McCoy to bridge."

It wasn't even hissing with static or interference, it was just dead.

"Intraship's out," he called to Two. "You don't happen to have a communicator on you, do you?"

"Not today," Two replied. Not good, because neither did McCoy.

McCoy felt to the left of the intercom, locating the release for the emergency pack. He gave it a hard push, and a panel sprang open, revealing an inset in the bulkhead, faintly illuminated by an emergency glowstrip. He grabbed the medical kit and slung it over his shoulder.

Next to it was a flashlight, which McCoy grabbed and flicked on immediately—promptly sending blinding light right into his face. Blinking, he turned it around and cast it over upturned tables and toppled chairs, until he saw someone. A lone man sitting at a table by himself, the same one that McCoy had seen eating mashed potatoes just before this whole mess had happened.

"Hey, Doctor," the man said. McCoy recognized him as the voice of Two. "Watch where you point that."

"Sorry." McCoy dipped the light to illuminate the man's body, not his face. "Who is that?"

"Lieutenant Leslie, sir."

That's who he was! Ryan Leslie had done a rotation in sickbay as an emergency med tech, though McCoy had repeatedly mixed him up with a navigator named Connors. Judging by his red shirt, he was now in security, or maybe engineering.

"Okay, Leslie, I hope you remember your medical training, because we've got a lot of work to do here."

Leslie swallowed visibly, but gave a confident nod. "I think so, sir."

"Doctor!" called out another voice, a woman's. Four, McCoy thought. "Over here." McCoy swung his light across the room to find a woman with her legs stuck beneath a collapsed table. "I think my legs are broken."

"Don't move and stay quiet. You'll be fine soon enough." McCoy turned around and found another flashlight in the emergency compartment.

Leslie held tight until McCoy made it to him and handed him the second flashlight. "How are you doing, son?" He kept his voice quiet, so that no one else could hear him.

"I'm fine," said Leslie, but he still seemed nervous.

McCoy narrowed his eyes. "You don't sound it. Really, how are you?"

"I hit something when I fell. Hurt my arm."

"Show me," McCoy said.

Leslie held up his left arm, which even in the unsatisfying light was visibly bloodied. The sleeve's fabric had torn above the elbow, and the skin showed a gash halfway down the forearm. It looked bad, but that was due to the amount of blood. All McCoy needed was an autosuture, and thankfully there was one in the medical kit. Working quickly, he rolled up the torn sleeve to be able to use the device. As he moved its beam slowly over the wound, the affected tissue was stimulated into healing quickly. Within a couple of minutes, there was no trace of any damage except for the drying blood.

"*Now* you're fine," McCoy said. "Right now I need your help, son. There were about a dozen of us in here. We need to find the seven who didn't count off before we do anything else. We can't afford the chance that one of them is bleeding to death while we help someone else. Got it?"

Pale and visibly shaken, Leslie said nothing; he merely nodded.

"Then let's get to it."

They fanned out, taking opposite sides of the room. McCoy's search was aided by his tricorder, which led him to a man slumped underneath a table. He recognized him as Ensign Rix, from the communications center. A quick inspection, coupled with tricorder readings, showed that he had a concussion, but there would be no lasting damage.

Leslie called him over to look at a noncom who'd been flung into a bulkhead with extreme force. Externally, she looked fine, but McCoy's tricorder showed massive internal bleeding. He injected her with a drug to slow it, but she needed to be taken to sickbay, and soon.

In a back corner, they found the patient McCoy had been dreading. A tall Saurian with numerous injuries. He didn't say anything, even when the flashlight's beam hit his face, but he wasn't unconscious. A large shard of something had gotten lodged in his gigantic left eye. It was probably taking all the fellow's willpower to keep from blinking.

McCoy handed Leslie his flashlight while he went to work on dealing with the eye. He might not be able to save it, but if he waited until they got to sickbay, it was a loss for sure.

The odd thing was, despite everything, McCoy felt better than he had all day. Oh, he was sore and hungry and rapidly getting tired, but he was *doing* something. He was solving problems.

"Hey!" came the voice of Four once more. "What about me?"

"Are your injuries life-threatening?" McCoy shouted.

There was no answer.

"Then let us do our job. I promise we'll get to you as soon as we can."

Leslie looked up from his work. "Shouldn't we see if she needs help?" he asked.

"We'll get to her, don't you worry," replied McCoy. "There's only the two of us. We can't heal everybody at once."

"Yes, but . . ." Leslie let the sentence trail off.

"But what?" McCoy asked. "The best we can do is treat one patient at a time." *And maybe not even that.* He just barely kept himself from swearing: the shard had penetrated too far into the Saurian's reptilian eye. "I'm not going to be able to get this out without taking this man to sickbay."

He finally made his way over to Four. Though she was indeed trapped underneath a table, her legs weren't fractured. No ruptured arteries, either. McCoy knew she was in considerable pain. Wasting no time, he motioned Leslie over, and together they lifted the table off her. A damned heavy bit of furniture that could have done much more damage—Four didn't know how lucky she was. "There you go," he said as he gave her a dose of pain-killers, "you'll be fine. We'll send somebody to get you to sickbay."

"Thank you, Doctor," she said in a small voice.

He'd helped another person—but what worried him now was Three. They hadn't heard from him since McCoy had had everyone count off. A check of his tricorder revealed another life sign, very faint, in a corner of the room. When he moved his light there, a hard-to-define shape turned into the body of someone slumped on the floor. McCoy hurried over.

It turned out to be a man, unconscious. No, not unconscious—comatose.

The man's foot had been injured in the distortion, but there was no brain damage that McCoy could detect.

And just like that, McCoy felt himself deflate. What was wrong with the man? He'd obviously been fine enough to talk in the immediate aftermath of the distortion. Like Bouchard's, this man's readings were getting weaker by the moment. McCoy checked the emergency medical kit, but there was no dalaphaline in it.

"Lieutenant!" he called, shining his light across the room. Leslie looked up from where he was working on the Saurian. "We need to get this man to sickbay right away. Help me open the doors."

It likely won't matter, even if you hurry. This man is dying before your eyes. And you have no idea why.

■ ■ ■ ■

Scotty eyed the sky warily. The clouds were thick and dark now, but the shields were keeping the *Hofstadter* safe as it moved closer to the energy reading. A light rain was starting to pelt the shields, but thanks to the thick, insulated hull, it was almost silent.

But Scotty couldn't shake the feeling they were moving in the wrong direction. "Mister Spock, that poor lad could be out there in this blasted weather."

Spock's steady hands held the shuttle as level as possible, given the forces that were hitting it, and he did not look away from his console as he answered. "Negative, Mister Scott. The cap—"

A loud clang of thunder reverberated through the ship's hull. Scotty noticed that the view outside the shuttle was completely obscured. The rain had picked up immensely, and all he could see was pouring water. The shuttle rocked back and forth as the winds redoubled, but the commander did not flinch.

A chirping alarm drew Scotty's eyes to the displays in front of him. "Shield status is impaired," he said. "The weather is hitting us harder than it should."

"Is the weather the cause of the impairment?" asked Spock.

Scotty began checking the circuits, but he already knew the answer. "No, sir. It's something else."

"Mechanical fault?"

Scotty knew that Spock was simply being thorough, but he couldn't restrain himself. "These shuttles can take whatever you throw at them, Mister Spock! I've been over every circuit my own self. It's some kind of interference."

His eyes narrowed as he traced the interference's progression through the circuits. "The pattern is the same as what's affecting our sensors."

Spock nodded. "Weather report, Mister Jaeger."

Scotty swiveled his chair around to see that the geophysicist was peering into his tricorder. "I still don't know what's causing this," Jaeger said. "It has the marks of a hurricane, yet it's forming over the land, not the water. There's no warm front that I can see. But all signs indicate that the farther we head south, the worse it gets."

"Thankfully, we are almost at the source of the energy reading. We will land the *Hofstadter* in a sheltered area and proceed to its source on foot."

"On foot?" Scotty repeated, incredulous. "It's worse than a gowk's storm out there!"

"That is why we are equipped with ponchos, Mister Scott." Lightning flashed through the shuttle's viewports, momentarily casting the Vulcan's severe features in a fierce, bright light. "Please locate an area of shelter near the signal. I wish to land immediately."

Scotty looked down at the scans of the surface. The problem with the first officer wasn't his unflappable logic, it was that his unflappable logic was always *right*.

McCoy and Leslie improvised a stretcher out of a table and lifted the comatose man—a transporter operator named Gaetano Petriello—onto it as quickly and carefully as they could. Soon they were waddling down the dark hallway, Leslie walking backward and taking the front, McCoy at back and directing. Progress was painfully slow when they needed speed. It didn't help that McCoy had to use his teeth to hold the flashlight because he needed his hands to grip the table. The beam wavered wildly, giving them only a rough idea of what lay strewn about.

Once they got a few dozen meters down the corridor and turned the bend, they got to an area where emergency power was on. The dim, red lighting helped McCoy see, but at the same time worsened his mood. Seeing Petriello bathed in red from head to toe only seemed an omen of what was to come.

Thankfully, the rec room #3 was on the same deck as sickbay, and they soon made it. The doors slid open to reveal a madhouse. As they carried Petriello inside, McCoy had a hard time processing just how full sickbay had become. All the biobeds were occupied, even those generally reserved for routine physicals. In fact, there were more beds here than usual; McCoy was pleased to see his staff had reacted quickly and put up additional beds in between the others. And yet, despite all that, people sat on chairs or leaned against walls, waiting to be treated.

Working unaffected in the middle of all was Nurse Chapel. She was standing next to a female patient, sealing up a gaping wound in the woman's stomach. McCoy spotted a number of other medical staff buzzing around from patient to patient. Chapel didn't even look up, just kept on running the device over the patient to help stem the bleeding and bridge the gap. Her arms were covered in blood, and her hair had fallen into disarray.

They stood on the threshold for only a moment before McCoy gave the table a shove, sending Leslie toward the center of the room. If these distortions went on for much longer, they'd quickly run out of space if they were unable to discharge any patients—but then McCoy spotted Nurse

Odhiambo helping a man off bed 5, and he ordered Leslie to move Petriello over to it. "One more heave, son, then we're done." Together, they lifted Petriello off the table onto the bed.

The monitors flicked on immediately, showing what McCoy had feared—the man was going the way of Bouchard, all his vital signs slowly sinking. McCoy quickly went to the supply cabinet and loaded a hypospray with dalaphaline. He turned to Leslie. "If you still remember your turn in sickbay, get me a neural stimulator. Or ask somebody to give it to you." As Leslie went to get one, McCoy injected the drug straight into Petriello's skull. After a few moments, the crewman's vitals weren't falling quite as fast, but they were still sinking.

His brain was giving up. Why? McCoy pulled up Petriello's medical records, which included this interesting morsel of information:

ESPER RATING: 085
APERCEPTION QUOTIENT: 20/97
DUKE-HEIDELBURG QUOTIENT: 255

He was not very surprised. Two similar cases of sudden coma had to be linked somehow. Granted, Petriello wasn't quite as powerful mentally as Bouchard, but he was still an esper. They both had to be suffering from the same kind of cerebral problem.

And if the two cases were related, that meant more data. Maybe he could get somewhere.

Grateful that you have an extra patient? Some doctor you are.

Leslie returned, handing McCoy the stimulator. Quickly, the doctor slipped it under Petriello's head and adjusted its settings. The effect was far from immediate, and not at all satisfactory: the vitals stopped dropping, but they leveled out dangerously low. He had the unpleasant feeling of merely having staved off the inevitable. It was all he could do for now. Others needed his help.

Taking a deep breath, McCoy surveyed the room. It wasn't often that it was so full of people in need. From the look of it, Chapel and Odhiambo had gotten to some of them, but not all. To be fair, the two of them did their best, but even so, they were only human. They needed assistance. Where were the med techs?

Ah, yes. Messier sped about like the tiny whirlwind she was, taking notes about the patients' injuries, while Abrams was at the far end of the room, peering intently at the monitor readings of . . . who? If he wasn't mistaken, the person lying on the bed looked uncannily like Brent. What had happened here?

"Doctor?" said Leslie, breaking in on his thoughts. "Do you need any help?"

McCoy turned around to face the lieutenant. "Do I?" he said. "Lieutenant Leslie, you're damned right I do. I need somebody out there with the necessary experience. First thing I want you to do is go back to the rec room. Get those casualties—especially the Saurian fellow and the internal bleed—in here immediately. Find someone to help you."

Leslie nodded, his face serious. "I'll get on it right away, sir." And with that, he was gone.

McCoy cleared his throat. "Abrams."

The med tech looked up to see who had called him. Displeasure was etched into his face deeper than normal. "Sir?"

"What happened?"

"Brent was looking after a patient during the last disruption. Lost his balance and hit his head on the bed." Abrams almost sounded angry, but McCoy knew it wasn't directed at him. "Can you take a look, sir?"

Moving over, McCoy saw that the man's vitals were safely in the normal range. Thankfully, this was not another coma case. A simple head wound like this was easy to treat.

Resolved to get the injured med tech back on his feet, McCoy inspected the wound. It wasn't severe, and most of the repair work had already been done—probably by Chapel. McCoy would finish it up, and then Brent would have to rest for a few hours. Afterward, however, he'd be perfectly healed, which was a big relief; with M'Benga gone, McCoy needed every pair of hands he could get.

Directing Abrams to get back to work, McCoy made the rounds to familiarize himself with the injured and start triage. There were people with broken bones, crushed hands, major cuts, head abrasions, burns, and everything else he could think of.

Life-threatening injuries first. Second, injuries requiring treatment that could be delayed. Third, minor injuries that did not require immediate and extensive care.

From what he could tell, most of the patients fell into the second category, and he and his staff would tackle them one at a time. Almost all of the rest were in the third category.

However, there were two patients that needed to be treated instantly. Odhiambo was already working on one, a man with a severe skull fracture, while Chapel was trying to stabilize a woman in obvious pain. Biobed readings told him enough: the woman, Ensign Haines, had three broken ribs and a collapsed lung.

Chapel was about to deal with the pneumothorax, ready to treat the affected lung to let the trapped air escape. She was doing her best to look confident and unflappable, but to McCoy's practiced eye she looked dead tired. "Christine," he said, giving her an encouraging smile. "Let me help you."

She returned the smile, but up close, the tiredness was even more evident. "Thank you, Doctor. Are you all right?"

"Of course. Why—" Oh. He looked down at himself, noticing for the first time since the lights went out in the rec room how bedraggled he looked, covered as he was with blood spatters and a variety of other stains. "Yeah, I'm okay. You?"

She said nothing. The look she gave him spoke volumes, however. Quickly, he grabbed a bone knitter off the well-stocked cart next to the bed and began working. "What happened?" he asked, his mind in two places at once, as he continued to contemplate the coma patients. As his eyes followed the curve of the patient's ribs, his ears listened for Chapel's response.

"Inertial dampers failed in most sections on this deck and a few others," she answered. "Most of the ship was fine. I was in the corridor, coming back from the lab." McCoy remembered that he'd sent her to give a brain tissue sample to Harrison, the med tech who was working in the medical lab. "When I got back here, Brent had been knocked out."

At the worst possible time. McCoy could only hope that the situation didn't deteriorate any further. He didn't dare think about what would happen if they received additional patients without being able to discharge at least as many.

Haines moaned loudly, startling them both. McCoy quickly checked her vitals, discovering that Chapel had already given her the maximum dose of painkillers. She shouldn't be feeling any pain—certainly not enough to make her react this way. "It's a good thing we're almost done. Christine, I trust you can finish her up?" he said, flipping off the knitter. With the woman's ribs mended, he had time to update his triage list. He checked off Haines. Next up was Lieutenant Lewis, with a spinal injury.

When he put the slate back onto the cart, he couldn't help but glance down at his uniform shirt to study the abstract pattern of red, black, and brown that almost resembled a Neoanarchist surrealistic painting. He'd forgotten to change into his medical smock. When working in sickbay, he much preferred the short-sleeved surgical uniform made of nonabsorbent nanoweave, but he hadn't worn it today, expecting to be doing nothing more than counting supplies. Eager to feel clean again, he hurried into his office, pulled his soiled shirt off, and began looking for his surgical one.

Can you actually handle surgery today? Sure, you can seal up a broken bone, so what? Even Nurse Chapel can do that. Hell, even Leslie. But what about those two men in comas, almost dying?

Pushing the niggling voice aside, he headed back into sickbay. It was time to get to work.

As he worked on Lewis's spine, Leslie returned with a couple of other security officers, bearing the injured Saurian and the female officer suffering from internal bleeding. McCoy grabbed Leslie and asked him to take his fellows and continue to bring people in from the other areas of the ship. With his medical training, he'd be a good man to have out there as the sickbay staff worked its hardest.

McCoy just hoped it would be enough.

■ ■ ■ ■

Chekov stared at the semicircular surface set into the cavern wall. They'd seen many of them on the buildings above, but so far, they'd been unable to find a way to open them. The problem was that they weren't made of any ordinary metal.

"The molecular bonds have been enhanced, sir—a phaser cannot break them," he said to Kirk. "Some kind of hyperbonded matter."

The captain had been pacing the periphery of the chamber, as if that would somehow help find Yüksel, and had just made his way back to Chekov's position. "What about a phaser rifle?" asked Kirk.

Chekov shook his head. "Even its power would be insufficient." He looked at the readings on his tricorder, which showed the energy level of the bonds. The material was very cleverly made. "With some tinkering, I might be able to disrupt the bonds somehow—"

"Try it, Mister Chekov." Kirk walked off to talk to Seven Deers, who was trying to open the doors mechanically. Chekov looked at the tricorder display screen and wondered if he would ever see the botanist again. He'd tossed off the idea somewhat unthinkingly, just to have something to say so the captain wouldn't think he'd lost Yüksel *and* couldn't help get him back. It was possible to loosen the molecular bonds, but all the ways he could think of required resources from the *Enterprise*.

Footsteps signaled that Giotto had walked over to join Chekov. "What about a phaser on overload?" the security chief asked. "Would that have the power?"

"We did not come all this way to this planet to sack it," Chekov said. "We are not Cossacks."

"Mister Chekov, once we lost a crew member—" Giotto

didn't say *because of you*, but Chekov felt it was understood. "—this stopped being a survey mission and turned into a rescue mission."

Feeling his face grow hot, Chekov lowered his gaze and inspected his tricorder screen. "It might do the job," he admitted, returning to the security chief's previous question, "but the damage could be catastrophic. Too *much* power."

"I was afraid of that," said Giotto. He looked over at the captain, who was listening to Seven Deers explain that she could not find a release mechanism for the doors. "But I'm sure we could improvise something."

Unfortunately, without the *Enterprise* their options were limited. They'd brought no photon grenades or other explosives, and they could not dig their way into the tunnels from above because they had no excavation equipment.

"Everyone over here!" Kirk ordered. Chekov looked up to see that the captain was now talking to Crewman Tra, the security guard, by the base of the large tree that dominated the chamber. Rawlins and Tra had joined Chekov and Seven Deers after being recalled by the captain, and they'd made their way to this place together.

Chekov and Giotto scrambled through the darkness to where Kirk, Rawlins, and Tra were staring at a tricorder. Chekov noticed Seven Deers shoot the captain a questioning look; he shook his head, and she continued to work on the door.

"Share your report with everyone, Mister Tra," ordered the captain.

The Arkenite man nodded, holding his tricorder out so that everyone could see its screen, showing strange squiggles and swirls on the sides of buildings. "We found a large amount of what we think is graffiti on the surface. Most of it seemed to be incoherent scrawls—"

"No underlying linguistic patterns," chimed in Rawlins.

"Exactly. When we were called back here, we took quick scans of everything we could see, and I've been sifting through it, and I found this." Tra pressed a button, and an image of a group of creatures standing under a curved black line appeared. They resembled furry octopi as drawn by a preschooler, and each one was labeled with some kind of alien text. "It's the only thing we've found that clearly represents something."

"Are these the inhabitants of Mu Arigulon?" asked Giotto. "Could they have taken Yüksel?"

Even though the wall graffiti wasn't very detailed, it at least gave the landing party an idea of what the inhabitants of Mu Ari V might have looked like. An elongated body with a large "head"—actually not so much a separate body part as a bulbous top, crowned with what could be horns, ears, or eyestalks—formed the center of the creature, and five differently proportioned limbs extended from it in all directions, making it difficult to get an exact idea of the aliens' anatomy. The color was washed out from decades of being exposed to the elements and covered in dirt.

Assuming this was an accurate depiction of a typical native sapient, it could be extrapolated that the planet had been inhabited by sentient invertebrates.

"Mister Tra," Kirk said, "forward these scans to the *Hofstadter*. I'm sure Mister Spock will be fascinated. I want Mister Saloniemi to work on this also."

"Aye, sir." The text was the first instance of the alien language they'd encountered, too.

There was just one thing that troubled Chekov. "How do we know these are the aliens, sir?" he asked. "I used to draw dinosaurs on my bedroom wall." He'd hate for them to get all excited over what might well turn out to be a made-up creature.

"Good point, Mister Chekov. We'll keep that in mind."

"They're inside a dome or building," said Rawlins. "And the writing looks like dialogue to me. I mean, I'm not an art expert, but—"

"Anthropomorphic animals," Chekov pointed out. "They might simply be figures of—"

"Captain!" Seven Deers's voice interrupted them as she ran up to the group.

"What is it, Ensign?" asked Kirk, the graffiti apparently forgotten.

"I think I found a way to open these things up."

FOUR

An emotional being might say that he "disliked" the rain. But for Spock, it was a matter of efficiency: a dry, still environment presented fewer obstacles than one where vision was limited, and even his sensitive hearing was impaired by constant noise. The landing party pressed forward in the pouring rain, into the alien town.

Spock had landed the *Hofstadter* next to a large, flat building, interposing the structure between the shuttle and the source of the wind. He left Ensign Saloniemi to work on analyzing the graffiti sent over by the captain's team, and assigned Petty Officer Emalra'ehn to stay with him for protection. Spock had then set out into the rain with Commander Scott, Lieutenant Jaeger, Doctor M'Benga, and Lieutenant Kologwe.

Their destination was a tall, spindly structure 310 meters ahead, not as impressive as the needle-like towers the *Columbus* had discovered in the other city. Scans revealed it to be 55.7 meters high and 20.6 meters wide at its base, tapering to 3.1 meters at the top. Its façade lacked the rough surface of the other buildings. Instead, it was covered in tiles of a reflective and slightly translucent material that looked like glass, even through the rain.

Once the landing party gained access, they would attempt to locate the source of the energy reading. This was the only sign of *active* technology they had thus far encountered. Could it have something to do with Yüksel's disappearance? Unknown, but even a single dormant computer with an active information store could prove invaluable.

The group moved along an extensive, straight stretch of road, made from a concrete-like substance that was covered in cracks with plants growing out of them. The conspicuous absence of vehicles on the roadways led Spock to theorize that the worldwide disappearance of the Mu Arigulon sentients had occurred in a relatively ordered fashion. Had the circumstances been chaotic, there would be abandoned vehicles.

The buildings were widely spaced, and the wind buffeted the landing party as it swept across the flat surface. Engineer Scott reeled, his poncho protecting him from the water but not the wind, but he managed to draw even with Spock.

"Mister Spock!" he shouted to make himself heard above the howl of the wind. "I want to know how come we havna seen any bodies? The sensors dinna pick up anything, there's no trace of remains anywhere." Wiping the rain from his eyes, Scott continued. "If there had been a planetwide catastrophe at some point, surely there'd be bodies still lying where they dropped."

"Indeed, Mister Scott. I have been considering the same questions. So far, I am not able to offer any theories."

"I just hope that whatever took them didna take Yük-sel." The engineer fell silent and continued to walk beside Spock.

"What happened to the population depends on how

fast the atmosphere became toxic," Lieutenant Jaeger explained. "It takes time for anything to spread over an entire planet. If they had enough time to think of measures to save themselves, that could explain why they're gone."

"What caused the toxicity?" Lieutenant Kologwe asked.

"There are a number of possibilities, but I think the natives did it to themselves," Lieutenant Jaeger answered.

As they had seen during their orbital survey, the inhabitants had spread out across the face of the planet. Even though the native flora had begun to reclaim what had been taken from it, the scars left by extensive deforestation were still plainly visible. However, Spock could not rule out natural disasters such as volcanic gases, solar flares, or asteroid impacts.

"It must've been very bad," M'Benga said. "We can consider ourselves lucky that the air's breathable now."

Jaeger nodded. "For us, it is. There's no telling if the same would be true for the natives." He wiped a hand over his face, futilely. "For all we know, they'd have to wait another two or three centuries before they could live here again."

"Idle speculation will not help us in our search for answers, Lieutenant," Spock said, needing to curb the geophysicist's imagination, "especially since we have very little reliable information."

"Aye, 'tis true." Scott had stopped under an unusually shaped building that jutted out and provided some shelter. "I canna wait to get my hands on whatever's making that reading."

Spock stopped to let the others regain some energy. He remained in the open, surveying the area with his tricorder. Thanks to the pervasive growing interference, he had not yet been able to lock down any data on the energy reading. "You will soon have the opportunity to do so, Mister Scott," he said. In Spock's estimation, they would have to walk for seven minutes to reach their destination if they continued at their current pace. "I am aware that we are operating on a considerable number of untested assumptions. However, I trust our situation will soon change. If Ensign Saloniemi succeeds in interpreting the visuals discovered by the captain, we will be able to gain access to a wealth of information."

Scott looked at him with an uncertain expression. "I just hope that doodles help us find our man."

"All information is valuable, Mister Scott."

Deciding that the brief respite had been enough, Spock gave the order to resume moving. Ahead of them stood the spindly tower, barely visible in the sheets of rain that continued to pour from above.

"It's very interesting, Captain," Seven Deers said, motioning at the now-open semicircle. It revealed a smooth and featureless tunnel, curving as it progressed. "It looks like there's no way in, but it's just camouflaged. I discovered it accidentally—I leaned against the wall."

Kirk had to smile at that. "Good work nevertheless. How does it work?"

Seven Deers pointed at a dark blotch on the wall, at hip height and very inconspicuous, next to the semicircle. "This is a touch-sensitive button, sir. Press this, and the section of the wall retracts."

Kirk wondered if it was subtle for aesthetics, or for another reason. The captain peered into the depths of the tunnel. The walls seemed to be made of the same hyperbonded material as the doors. They were unlit, but his flashlight revealed only a continuous surface.

They would have to go in one of these tunnels if they wanted to find Yüksel. Lacking any better option, Kirk decided to try this tunnel, the one he'd found the botanist's flashlight in front of. He ordered Tra to relay their discovery about the doors to Spock's team.

"Let's go." Kirk pulled his phaser out, and Chekov followed behind him, waving his tricorder in every possible direction. Giotto assumed the rear.

Every footstep the group took sent echoes up and down the tunnel, and Kirk had trouble differentiating them from noises that might genuinely be coming from the end.

Once they were out of sight of the original chamber, they came across another door, which was easily opened. This led into a smaller chamber, unlike anything Kirk had seen before. During his time in Starfleet, he'd visited many alien planets and seen many strange civilizations, but this was something else. The small room's walls—all rounded—were dotted with holes leading into small tunnels.

"Be careful," said Kirk. "We still don't know what happened to Yüksel."

With Chekov's tricorder to guide them, they began to crawl into one of the tunnels. Kirk went first, his phaser in one hand and Yüksel's flashlight in the other. The only noise was a low hissing sound. "Is that some kind of machinery, Mister Chekov? Pneumatics?"

Chekov fiddled with his tricorder for a moment before admitting, "Unclear, sir."

Suddenly, Kirk lost his footing and tumbled forward onto the ground. His elbows and lower back ached slightly where he'd landed, but he ignored them and came up into a crouch. Cautiously, he waved his phaser back and forth, but there was nothing. He'd fallen into a small room. The hissing noise was a little louder, but there was nothing else in there.

A moment later, Chekov and the others entered the room behind him. They quickly ascertained that it had four more tunnels leading off in various directions—including one that was a straight vertical ascent.

"Whoever built this," said Kirk, shining his light up the hole, "must have been very limber."

Chekov nodded but said nothing, focusing on his tricorder. The captain realized that he was trying to make a good impression, trying his best to find their missing crew member.

"What way now, Chekov?"

Chekov shrugged. "I can find no life signs, Captain."

Kirk considered for a moment. If they wanted to explore this place efficiently, they'd have to split up. The buddy system would be safest, even if it was a risk. "Tra and Rawlins, you take that one." He pointed to the leftmost tunnel. "Seven Deers and Giotto, up the right one. Chekov, you're with me." He looked at the vertical tunnel above their heads. "We'll have to wait for a champion rock climber to handle that one," he said with a smile. "I want everyone to maintain a constant lock on each other's life signs, and above all," he added, "stay together." The groups headed off.

Continuing through the tunnel, Kirk and Chekov soon realized that there was no smooth surface; instead it appeared as though they'd entered a large sponge. Holes and tunnels dotted this subterranean lair, some large enough for Kirk to step into without having to duck, while others were barely big enough for a child to crawl through. There were no flat surfaces anywhere, no angles, no hard edges.

Kirk moved into each new section of the tunnel with his phaser drawn, but there was never anything but that omnipresent hissing noise, not even lights. Finally they entered a room that was slightly larger than normal, with hollow bowl shapes set into the floor.

"What is this place?" Chekov asked. "It reminds me of the old government buildings in Moscow. Laid out to be as confusing as possible."

"To make it difficult for people to get what they wanted?"

"We Russians invented bureaucracy, Captain." There wasn't a hint of irony in Chekov's voice.

Kirk bent to take a closer look at objects that had been heaped in the hollows. He grabbed one at random and inspected it up close. It was soft and colorful and looked like the graffiti creature—a child's doll?

Chekov's tricorder chirped. "Sir, Commander Giotto and Ensign Seven Deers are headed this way."

The captain nodded and continued turning the doll over in his hand, looking at the other similar ones on the floor. Had beings like this taken Yüksel? A few moments later, a noise caught his attention, and his head jerked up toward the other end of the chamber. Giotto and Seven Deers had squeezed themselves through a narrow hole.

"It's easy to get turned around in this place," said the engineer. She was staring at her tricorder, bewildered.

Giotto was holding a bright red cylinder. "Sir. It's some kind of scroll." He pressed a button on the end, and a screen popped out. "It's got text, but even with the universal translator, it doesn't make any sense."

"Give it to Mister Chekov. I want scans sent to Saloniemi."

Giotto handed the scroll to Chekov, not saying a word. Kirk knew that Giotto was taking his frustration at Yüksel's disappearance out on the ensign. It had been over four hours since they'd received the interrupted message. It had been the scientist's first time on an initial survey, and he'd been so excited. Kirk dreaded what would happen if they didn't find him. *Dear Mr. and Mrs. Yüksel. I regret to inform you that your son Fatih was lost on a planetary survey mission in the Høyland 5900 sector . . .*

"Any sign of him, Commander?" asked Kirk.

Giotto shook his head. "I don't think anyone's been in here for a long time."

Damn. With a dozen of those doors set off the basement of the tree chamber, they'd be searching a long time. The botanist could be behind any one of them, never to be found.

"Let's head out and rejoin the others."

They were going to find him.

She would *not* close her eyes even for a moment. The temptation was great, but she wouldn't give in—didn't dare to. Christine Chapel knew her body—she would try to stay awake, regardless of how tired she felt. People depended on her, patients as well as colleagues.

The situation in sickbay was beginning to come under control. The number of people coming in for treatment had trickled down to one during the past fifteen minutes. That injury had been minor: a broken nose, whose owner had had the misfortune of walking into a door that failed to open. It was easily dealt with, and a once again cheerful

Lieutenant Riley walked out of sickbay, his nose showing no evidence of any recent mishap.

Despite the medical staff's work, sickbay was still full of people who required intensive care. Crew quarters on the same deck were being changed into post-surgery recovery units, or PSRUs. Messier and Brent were out there, arranging the transformation. According to their latest status report, they were about to finish the last two rooms. The entire undertaking had taken only a short time. The medical drills Doctor McCoy occasionally ran were well worth the hassle.

Chapel turned her attention to checking on the skin patch that covered most of Crewman Polk's right arm. Focusing on the task demanded her full attention. Her thoughts were a total mess, trying to draw her away from her work. It was an indication of how tired she was. However, she'd kept up her resolve not to use a stimulant. That was her final option; if the situation deteriorated enough that she couldn't function without a hypo, she would have to think about the patients first, and herself second.

Chapel found herself thinking about her past—the people and things she had left behind for a career in space, her teenage ballerina phase that was over after the third lesson, the months of blue-eyed hope after her fiancé's disappearance and the profound change that followed. It was all so long ago, but—

"Christine!"

She turned to see Cheryl Thomas approaching her. The younger woman had done sterling work today, unfazed by the confusion. "Yes, Cheryl?"

"How're you holding up? You look like you're going to fall asleep any moment now," the nurse asked, her bun losing its ornate curl—evidence of long, demanding hours.

"I'm fine," Chapel said. "And you're exaggerating."

"Look, you've done all you can to help these people; the least you can do now is look after yourself."

"I'll rest when there are no more patients that need to be treated."

"Uh, right. So you want to stay up indefinitely, is that it?"

"No, of course not. I—"

"Nurse!" Doctor McCoy's voice rang out across the ward. Chapel turned her head, glad for the interruption.

Yes, you're glad because you know you'd lose the argument. How very responsible of you.

Chapel was angry at herself, because her inner voice was right. "Yes, Doctor?" she said to shut it up.

"Could you do me a favor and finish sealing this man's lacerated eye?" He motioned at the supine figure on the bed next to him. It was Chief Yocum, the Saurian that had been in the recreation room with him during the most recent . . . shockwave, or whatever the cause of all this was.

It was simple work, perfect for her current state. She didn't dare show McCoy how tired she really was.

"Christine," he said softly. "Don't make me tell you again."

"Doctor?"

"Get some rest. We're just about done here, anyway. A few hours of sleep'll do you a world of good."

He knew her too well.

The sound of the main sickbay doors swishing open saved her from having to reply. A group of security guards, led by Lieutenant Leslie, trooped in, bearing three red-shirted people on stretchers. They swiftly moved them onto empty beds.

"What's up?" McCoy asked, his short-sleeved arms crossed over his chest.

Leslie sighed, weariness evident in his face. The situation was taking a toll on everybody, in every department. Over the past few hours, security had been instrumental in getting those people to sickbay who couldn't get there on their own. "Unknown," Leslie said. "All three were off shift when the distortion hit, and should have reported to damage control. When they didn't, Lieutenant DeSalle sent Galloway to see what had happened."

David Galloway was the tall, strong-looking security officer standing next to Leslie. "I thought they were sleeping," he said. "But it's obvious they're not."

Their monitor readings corresponded exactly to those of Bouchard and Petriello. Doctor McCoy said somberly, "They're in comas."

"Sir?" asked Galloway, his forehead wrinkled in confusion and obvious worry. "The inertial dampers were fine on their deck. They didn't even fall out of their bunks."

Leslie shook his head. "We've already had two coma cases today. The doctor can't figure out the cause there, either."

"Not *yet*, Lieutenant," the doctor said pointedly.

Nurse Chapel leaned over slightly to glance at the nearest unconscious figure.

"Okay, people," Doctor McCoy said. "Y'all know what to do. We have three more cases of sudden-onset coma without apparent cause and rapid deterioration of brain functions. I need a steady supply of dalaphaline and three neural stimulators. What're you waiting for?"

Chapel started toward the drug cabinet, her fatigue now

a thing of the past. It was just as well; there'd be no chance for any of them to rest for a few hours.

Gaining access to the tower was simple once Tra had explained the procedure. The strange, semicircular door lifted, and the *Hofstadter*'s landing party went in. They were straining their necks to take in the interior.

It was breathtaking and unsettling at the same time. Scotty had expected a large space inside, like a hall of sorts. Instead, he was looking at something his mind was busy seeking comparisons for.

There were similarities to what he thought an anthill must look like inside, with tunnels and caverns. Or perhaps, if you happened to find yourself in a large block of Swiss cheese. The door had opened into a reasonably spacious cavern. A number of tunnels led into darkness. The only light they had available came from the open door and their flashlights.

After a quick security sweep by Mariella Kologwe, Spock gave them the go-ahead to search for a route to the energy source, which was near the apex of the building. Unfortunately, the structure was a labyrinth—there was no direct route. Spock, wanting to avoid further disappearances, split the landing party.

Scott and Doctor M'Benga set off to their assigned tunnel. Heads bent, they squeezed into a dark shaft leading gently upward from the entrance chamber. It was low, but wide enough to let them move side by side.

Their flashlights illuminated the passage ahead. Its sides were warped and twisted, creating nooks that could hide anything. Scotty kept glancing at his tricorder to check his surroundings. M'Benga, reticent by nature, kept pace quietly beside him. Scotty listened, hearing at first only their footsteps, but then . . . a whispering?

It was like someone talking very quietly, out of earshot. Scotty couldn't pick out individual words—not even alien ones—but he knew language when he heard it.

"Do you hear that?" Scotty stopped and turned to face M'Benga.

The doctor's face was more confused than fearful. "Hear what?"

Scotty grabbed his arm. "Dinna move," he said, whispering. "You have to be very quiet." M'Benga nodded and stopped where he was, waving his flashlight back and forth.

Nothing. Had his worried mind enhanced some small sound? A piece of ancient machinery stirring to life? Or had he imagined it entirely?

Or had the whisperers just fallen silent, hearing their approach?

"Let's go," Scott said at last. The silence was more unnerving than the whispering. "Are you picking up anything?"

M'Benga tapped some controls on his tricorder. "Nothing."

"Aye," said Scotty, "but I bet that's what Yüksel thought too."

After a few more minutes, during which the whispering never resumed, M'Benga suddenly stopped and moved his flashlight around. They'd left the shaft behind and now stood in a chamber. Scotty added his light to M'Benga's to get an idea of where they were.

The chamber was roughly circular, and it was impossible to say where the floor ended and the walls began, because everything here was sloped and merged into something else. Even the furniture—at least, Scotty assumed it was furniture—was a part of the floor. Unlike the entrance chamber, this one was packed with items of different sizes and shapes. Scotty couldn't even begin to guess what they'd been used for.

"Are any of these the source of the energy reading?" asked M'Benga.

Scotty checked his tricorder readings. "No," he said. "It's farther up. We have to find that energy reading—this can wait."

They stepped into another tunnel, which rapidly changed from a gentle slope to a tight spiral. Scotty led the way, noticing that the intensity of the reading was growing. "We're getting close!" he called behind him.

Scotty's ears strained to hear a reply, but what he heard was more whispering, louder and clearer than before.

"I'm coming!" The doctor's shout obliterated the whispers.

But they had definitely been real. They were too distinct to be the products of an overactive imagination. The engineer paused his clambering to get out his communicator. "Scott to Spock."

"*Spock here.*"

"Commander, we're getting close. And I keep hearing something—whispering or the like."

"*I have locked onto your current position, Mister Scott. We will join you shortly. Spock out.*"

Scotty resumed climbing. They could be only a couple more minutes away at most.

"What are you doing?" asked M'Benga. "We should wait."

"I want to see what's up there," replied Scott. The first working technology on a new planet! Maintaining his engines was Scotty's passion, but getting to examine an ingenious contraption created by another culture was a close second.

"Mister Scott, I can hear it now. The whispering."

Scotty listened for a moment. The sounds were more distinct, but they didn't resemble words. The engineer had heard enough alien languages not to let that fool him. "Keep your phaser ready." Difficult while climbing. He wasn't getting nabbed by whatever was up there.

Scotty moved quickly up the last several meters of the spiral. He emerged into a large spherical chamber whose walls were covered screens displaying alien glyphs. A compact bronze-colored gizmo, roughly spherical, stood in the center of the room.

The whispering was everywhere.

Scotty cast around for its source. And there it was—a hole in the metal paneling, near floor level. He drew closer and saw that the noise was coming from damaged wiring inside the hole, which sparked and flashed. That was the source of the sound, not a group of aliens.

Scotty had holstered his phaser and was scanning the alien apparatus by the time M'Benga caught up. "What is it?" the doctor asked.

"Power generator," Scotty replied. "Not a fusion one, like on the satellite, but a matter/antimatter reactor."

"A warp engine?" asked M'Benga.

"Aye, but a very small one," said Scotty. This was the first indication that the inhabitants of Mu Arigulon were a warp society.

"What's it for?" asked M'Benga.

"That question," Spock said from the chamber's entrance, "has a surprising answer."

Scotty turned to see Kologwe and Jaeger follow Spock into the chamber. "Sir?"

Spock ran his own tricorder over the generator. "Our explorations initially took us downward, where we discovered a massive underground power conduit. This structure is designed to generate power, but all of it is carried somewhere else, seemingly far away."

"Where?" asked M'Benga.

"That is what I am attempting to ascertain, Doctor," Spock said. "I see little need for the entire landing party to stand here while Mister Scott and I do technical work. Please join Lieutenants Kologwe and Jaeger in exploring the tower."

M'Benga nodded and left with the other officers, while Spock resumed scrutinizing the generator.

"Annoyed, Mister Spock?" Scotty asked.

Spock glanced up from his work, but only for a moment. "That would be an emotional reaction, Mister Scott. I merely desired a less cluttered working environment."

Scott smiled to himself—he knew annoyance when he saw it. He held up his tricorder, letting it take in the images on the wall. The universal translator could tell they related to energy levels and power distribution. But it still couldn't parse the information; it needed more for a baseline.

The engineer dropped to the floor to examine the pedestal that the warp generator sat on, and quickly located a recessed panel. He tried to pry it open, but it wouldn't budge. "Mister Spock, can you lend me a hand?"

In a matter of seconds, Spock had the panel open. It clattered onto the floor. Inside, Scotty could see a power conduit descending into the depths of the tower.

"Here, Mister Scott." Scotty turned to see Spock examining the panel. The back had a diagram of a dilithium crystal, and labels on various lines going in and out of the image. He held the tricorder up to the diagram, and it began to beep as it recognized what some of the labels represented—physical measurements like the crystal's stress level, goniochronicity factor, fourth-dimensional permeation, and so on. The tricorder matched those measurements with the crystal inside the pedestal, then combined them with the text in the graffiti and the information from the other displays, and soon the rest of the data cascaded into place and the tricorder had enough of a baseline to translate any text in the room.

"Sending the UT program to your tricorder, Mister Spock. Have you seen a master display anywhere?"

"Over here." Spock directed him to a screen displaying the planet, with several lights set into it. One of them was blue, the rest red. Gray lines connected the red lines to the blue one. The blue light was lit, as were most of the red ones.

Spock ran his tricorder over the image. "Our current position corresponds to this red light," he said, pointing. "It is labeled 'generator nine.' "

"The red lights are power generators." Scotty's finger traced the line between their red light and the blue one. "What would need an output of almost a dozen warp engines to power it?" asked Scotty. "And why scatter them all over?"

Spock consulted his tricorder again. "It is labeled 'main projector.' "

"What does that mean?"

"Mister Scott, we must find out."

Scotty nodded in agreement. "Aye."

Having retreated to his office, McCoy stared at the medical readouts of the three comatose security guards who had just come in: Salah, Fraser, and Santos. They were all espers—less powerful than Bouchard and Petriello, with ratings in the low 080s and high 070s, but that was still above the human norm. Out of curiosity, McCoy had looked up his own esper rating for comparison, and had found it to be 046, about as average as you could get.

Spurred on by a sudden insight, McCoy then pulled the esper ratings of the rest of the crew. The computer displayed the results as a list, in descending order of esper rating.

Some doctor you are. The first thing you should have done was figure out who could be susceptible to this!

Cron Emalra'ehn, a Deltan in security, was a full-blown empath, but he was off on the shuttles surveying Mu Arigulon. The next highest rating after the five victims was in the 060s, but that was well below the threshold of what was considered esper.

Six espers in a population of four hundred was an unusually large percentage. Three years ago, before McCoy's time, all of the *Enterprise*'s espers had been killed on a mission. The doctor was determined not to lose these espers.

Being determined isn't enough. You need results . . . and you're not getting any of those.

He'd looked over the notes Mark Piper, the *Enterprise*'s previous chief medical officer, had recorded. A "negative energy" the ship had encountered had killed all of the espers on contact, except for two. They had been transformed into dangerously powerful beings. There was no apparent connection between that case and the current one.

McCoy brought up the displays of the five espers. Their decline had slowed, but they were still sinking. If he wasn't able to find a solution soon, every one of them would die. The doctor was stumped, much as he hated to admit it. He rubbed his eyes. The sound of approaching feet made him look up. It was Chapel. "How are you doing?" he asked.

"Nearly done," she said.

"No," he said. "How are *you* doing?"

"All right. I've been worse."

She didn't look all right, but McCoy didn't press the point. He probably looked awful, too, but they still had work to do. "Anything I should handle?" he asked, flicking off his monitor.

Chapel glanced at the list. "There's Ryerson. Zoology specialist, first degree burns on his torso. Nurse Odhiambo's treated him, and he's okay physically, but I feel he might like to see a doctor. Do you think you have a moment to settle his mind? All you'd need to do is tell him he'll be out of here in a little while."

McCoy smirked. "I should be able to do that. Not that I'm capable of doing much else."

Self-criticism? How novel. Funny what you come up with when you have enough time for reflection. Normally, you just keep on moving, moving, moving, leaving yourself no time for anything substantial. You push the past away from you and try to forget it, not because it's good medicine, but because it's what you've always done to avoid the pain. That's not doctoring, it's cowardice.

His thoughts were interrupted by the whistle of the intraship. "Sickbay here."

"Bridge." It was Lieutenant Uhura again. McCoy hoped she wasn't calling to say they were going back to warp speed. That was the last thing he needed now. *"Doctor, can you send someone up here? We've got a few injuries."*

A few injuries! The incident had been three hours ago. "Why did you wait so long?"

"We've been busy," said Uhura drily. She sounded tired.

In three hours, a lot could go wrong, especially when the injured didn't receive any medical attention. McCoy wondered what could possibly have been so important that they hadn't found time to notify sickbay. "I'll be right up."

"Thank you, Doctor. Bridge out."

"Let's hope it's nothing serious," Chapel said.

McCoy gathered up his gear, saying, "Academy graduates don't have an ounce of common sense. Trying to keep a stiff upper lip, while their arms fall off because they think it'll impress their commanding officers."

Sulu's forehead was covered with a raised purple bruise, the result of an impact with the deck. His cheek and chin were bloody, and his lower lip was split. He looked like he'd been attacked by a *mugato*. McCoy ran his tricorder's Feinberger over the lieutenant's forehead, checking for any kind of internal damage.

"We have a crisis, Doctor," Sulu said in defense when McCoy asked him to explain his state. "I needed to remain in command. I intend to bring this ship back to Captain Kirk in one piece."

McCoy's anger evaporated as he was suddenly struck by the impossibility of trying to live up to the image Jim always projected. Jim wouldn't have reported to sickbay under these circumstances. McCoy knew that if Sulu didn't bring the *Enterprise* back in himself, he'd feel like he'd let down the captain.

He shut off the Feinberger, watching as its analysis streamed into his tricorder. "How do you feel?" he asked.

Sulu shook his head, grimacing slightly. "I'm fine."

Right. "I'd like you to come down to sickbay nonetheless. Everything looks all right, but it's better not to take any chances where the brain is concerned."

And this is a brain problem where you'd actually know what to do, after all. Unlike poor Bouchard and the rest.

Sulu squinted at him, dubious. "So nothing's actually wrong?"

"No," McCoy had to admit, "but there's no sense in—"

"In that case, Doctor, I will remain in command of the *Enterprise* until the crisis abates. Please give me something for the pain."

McCoy loaded up a hypospray but didn't inject it yet. "Mister Sulu, I strongly advise that you come with me to sickbay and let us check you thoroughly."

"Is that an order, Doctor?" Sulu was usually an open book, but McCoy was finding him hard to read.

Dammit. Under extreme circumstances, the chief medical officer *could* order a commanding officer to stand down if their ability to command was compromised. McCoy had threatened it on more than one occasion, but he'd never actually gone through with it.

"No," he said at last, and jabbed Sulu's arm with the hypo, injecting its contents into his bloodstream. "No, it's not. But if you pass out up here, it will be."

McCoy began working his way around the bridge, double-checking that everyone else was fine. He started with science, where Lieutenant Rodriguez was working to coordinate the results from several different labs analyzing the phenomenon. He kept repeating to someone on the comm, "That shouldn't have happened. It doesn't make any sense!" He looked harried and didn't even say anything to McCoy other than a muttered "I'm fine."

The yeoman on the bridge was Tina Lawton. McCoy didn't know her well, but this had to be her first time in a crisis. She was handling it with aplomb. The incident had left her with a small gash on her forehead that was easily healed. As so often happened when he talked to young women, McCoy found his Georgia accent becoming a little bit more prominent. She seemed flattered by his attentions, and McCoy enjoyed it.

You would like it, wouldn't you? Keep your mind on the job.

Rahda and Farrell at helm and navigation were taking readings. The *Enterprise* hadn't advanced since hitting the last distortion. McCoy looked at the spatial plot between their consoles, but other than the fact that it was covered in squiggles, which must represent spatial distortion, he didn't know what to make of it. The unsettling thing was that there were just as many squiggles in front of the *Enterprise* as there were behind it.

Ensign Harper's red shirt was soaked with sweat, and McCoy injected him with an antiperspirant, telling him it was a stimulant. No sense embarrassing the man. Harper seemed to have his hands full running the damage control teams, their biggest problem being the power losses that had affected the ship with every distortion. There was no evident cause; none of the *Enterprise*'s energy systems had taken any damage.

McCoy had set up his journey so that he'd end with Uhura. Sulu was having an animated discussion with

Rodriguez and Farrell about what route they should take. The doctor used the opportunity to get information. "Any word from the shuttles?" he asked quietly.

Uhura shook her head. "Every subspace signal we send into the zone of distortion comes right back to us about five minutes later. It's like something is absorbing them and retransmitting them."

"We were in contact with the landing party before, though." McCoy frowned. "What changed?"

"The farther we've moved into the zone, the worse the distortions have become. Not just ahead of us, but behind us. We can pick up some really rough ones behind us, but if we'd hit them we wouldn't be here."

"So going backward isn't an option?" McCoy asked.

Uhura took her earpiece out. "No more than going forward."

"We're going to continue forward," said a deep voice close to him. McCoy looked up and realized that Sulu was now standing with the two of them.

McCoy glanced around the bridge, taking in the crew's frantic discussions and the chirp of instruments. "I hope you know what you're doing."

"We can't stay still," Sulu said. "We have no way of getting a signal out. It could be weeks before another starship gets out here to look for us." Only the very fringes of this sector were charted; there was no Federation presence beyond Deep Space Station C-15.

"We could send out a probe," said Uhura, "but I'm not convinced it would survive long in the distortions."

Sulu nodded. McCoy was struck by how calm he looked despite the giant purple bruise across his forehead. "That's what I thought."

It became clear that the young officer was looking for validation. He wanted someone to confirm that he was making the right decision. "Well, moving forward seems like our best bet to me," McCoy said. "I'll tell sickbay to brace for more casualties."

Sulu's spine seemed to straighten up at that, and he looked slightly more authoritative than a moment ago. "We shouldn't hit any more distortions," he said. "They're only in subspace, so as long as we stay out of warp, they can't affect us." He glanced over at Rodriguez, who was listening to their conversation. "Correct?"

Rodriguez moved slightly closer to their impromptu conference around the communications console. "Yes, sir. More importantly, we won't be able to affect the phenomenon. We think they're feeding on the space-time distortions our engines create." He rubbed his hand against his face. "It's not my area of expertise, but Padmanabhan and Bellos in spatial physics are fairly certain . . ."

Sulu moved back to the command chair and sat down. "Course set, Mister Farrell?"

The navigator checked the plot to the left of his console. "Yes, sir. We are laid in for Mu Arigulon."

"Maximum impulse, Mister Rahda," Sulu ordered. McCoy was impressed by how quickly his deep bass voice had regained its authority, given how uncertain he had sounded a few moments ago.

You always mask your own uncertainty in complaints and crabbiness. Sulu masks it in authority and carries it off. Give him time and he'll be as good as Jim. But everyone will always see straight through you.

"Maximum impulse, aye," Lieutenant Rahda said. "Engaging engines."

As she pushed the controls forward, McCoy imagined he felt the ship's power throb through the deck beneath his feet. He quickly moved to the railing above the command chair—he didn't quite trust Sulu and Rodriguez's assertion that nothing would happen, and he wasn't going to be tossed around again like last time.

As the *Enterprise* crept up to a significant fraction of light speed, McCoy tried not to let himself relax. He was afraid that whispering voice of self-doubt would creep in when he did.

FIVE

The shuttlecraft *Hofstadter* sat forlornly in the rain.

Ensign Antti Saloniemi was inside, reading and reread-
ing the text on his data slate. It was almost impossible to
concentrate: Petty Officer Emalra'ehn had left the side hatch
open a crack when he'd gone on a quick patrol, and the
whistling of the wind across the gap was driving him mad.
He'd been warned against closing it by Emalra'ehn, who'd
wanted to be able to get back in the shuttle quickly in case
something came up.

"Visualization: orange vegetable of mysterious provenance," he read aloud. *What is this?*

The UT baseline provided by Mister Scott had turned
out to be an excellent starting point, though it was naturally
better with more technical language. Right now he was trying to read the scroll found by the *Columbus*. It had come
out scrambled. Best as Saloniemi could tell, it was a children's book. Strangely, the language didn't seem to have any
verbs, which meant that the translations were hard to parse.

"Impairment of orange vegetable's forward motion."

His eyes zipped back and forth across the curvy lines
on his slate: waves, circles, dots, curls. He found it helpful
to examine the original text so he could get a feel for it. On
the surface, the squiggles bore a marginal resemblance to

Old High Vulcan script, with their curls and crossed lines, but you might make the same connections between old Terran cuneiform and written Klingonese. Making base-less assumptions was one of the worst things you could do when studying new languages.

"Intersection with blue fruit. Collision! Chaos! Exclamation of—"

The hatch came open the entire way, letting a blast of wind and rain into the shuttle. Saloniemi jumped as he looked up, but it was only Emalra'ehn stomping in, his poncho leaving cascades of water all over the deck. The hatch shut behind him.

"Find anything?" the Deltan said.

Saloniemi shook his head. "I could ask you the same thing."

"Nothing. Just plants. And water."

"Doesn't that make your job easier?"

Emalra'ehn took off his poncho and deposited it on an empty seat. "It makes you complacent. Slow and stupid. If nothing happens for a few hours, you start to think it's like that all the time. Then, when something does happen, it comes as a surprise and kills you. You don't want that."

Saloniemi couldn't help but laugh. "No, I definitely don't want that."

The security guard's face was deadly serious. "I'm not joking."

"I know that. Believe me, I do. But the way you said it . . ." He let the sentence trail off, rather than say anything that would make the other man angry or feel insulted.

"Ah. I get that a lot."

"You do?" Saloniemi regarded him with surprise. "What, exactly?"

"People think I'm funny. I'm not."

"Ah."

In a quick move that startled Saloniemi, Emalra'ehn crossed the distance between them and extended his hand. It took the ensign a moment to realize this was an offer, not a threat. "Call me Cron."

"Um. Thank you." He shook the man's hand, then fell silent. "I'm Antti, by the way."

"Yeah. Wet day, isn't it?" By way of demonstrating this, Emalra'ehn shook his head, splattering Saloniemi with rain.

"Um, I guess so."

"I quite like the rain. Helps me relax."

"Ah," was all Saloniemi said. He heard a distinctive beep emanate from his controls. "The computer's found something. I'd better check."

"Yeah." Emalra'ehn moved to the back of the shuttle.

Saloniemi didn't believe it. The computer had found a few phrases matching the Mu Arigulon language in an Orion database the Federation had picked up used in a deal with the Haradin. The Orions had traded with the representatives of a distant world for some rare metals. They hadn't known the location of the planet, but they had known it was somewhere within this sector, and they had also known its name: Farrezz.

He reached for the communicator to call Mister Spock.

Chekov and Kirk were exploring another subterranean structure. Chekov's preliminary readings—interference made getting a full picture difficult—indicated that the network of tunnels they'd found extended underneath the entire city. They'd already gone up one of the tunnels to find themselves in a building on the surface.

Thanks to the airtight seals, there was no dust. If something had taken Yüksel down one of these tunnels, it was impossible to know which one.

There were pictures on the walls down here, round pieces of unknown material with very realistic renderings of landscapes and machinery. No natives, however—at least none they'd seen so far.

Taking a tunnel that angled down, they made good use of their flashlights and proceeded at a decent pace. No traces of artificial lighting, no light shafts to let the sun in. The natives either had very good eyesight, or they'd all carried their own personal light source with them. Or, it occurred to Chekov, maybe they didn't even *need* light.

After a number of curves and bends, they emerged into a large chamber, the largest yet, but all it contained was a round metallic structure, cagelike, in the center. A platform in the middle of it covered most of a hole in the floor. The cage was taller than they were, almost reaching to the ceiling, and large enough to accommodate ten humanoids.

The ensign wondered, *Could this be an elevator?* Or was he applying familiar functions to alien tech? As Captain Kirk walked up to the device and began running his hands over it, Chekov pulled out his tricorder and began scanning down the shaft.

The shaft led down about fifty meters and emerged into a large cavern so vast it took his breath away. "*Bozhe moi,*" he whispered, unable to contain his amazement. From the look of it, the cavern ran beneath both the city and the spaceport complex. Could this be where Yüksel had been taken. The exobotanist *could* be down there somewhere! "Captain, I have found something!"

Kirk turned around. "What is it, Mister Chekov?"

"An underground cavern beneath a large part of the city, sir. Enormous, but scans aren't detailed enough to tell exactly how big it is."

"Good work, Ensign." Kirk smiled for a brief moment, then pulled out his communicator, summoning the rest of the *Columbus* party.

Chekov continued to scan. It wasn't easy to get decent readings of the cavern, with the rock around them impeding his efforts. This wasn't the only shaft; similar ones dotted the entire area, the closest about half a kilometer in either direction.

Seconds later, Giotto burst out of the tunnel, with Seven Deers, Rawlins, and Tra behind him.

"Report, Ensign," the captain ordered.

Chekov explained what he'd uncovered to the rest of the team. "Yüksel could be down there."

"Don't assume, Ensign," snapped Giotto.

With a mix of disappointment and frustration, Chekov could see that nothing he could do would please the security chief. "I suspect that many of the tunnels lead here eventually," he said. "Besides, sir, it is the only lead we have."

"I know that," said Giotto brusquely. "I'm just suggesting you don't pin your hopes on it."

Seven Deers was taking a closer look at the machine. "This contraption might still work," she said.

Kirk seemed skeptical. "It's a miracle it hasn't rusted through."

Seven Deers shook her head. "Oh, this wouldn't rust, Captain. It's made of the same hyperbonded material as the doors and tunnel walls."

"Can you get it to work?"

The engineer hesitated only slightly before nodding. "I can give it a shot, Captain."

"That's all I'm asking," Kirk said, smiling.

"Are we going down, Captain?" Chekov was eager to put right what he'd messed up.

"That's right, Mister Chekov. Even if we don't find Yüksel, I want to see what's so important these people built this massive cavern for it."

Doctor McCoy was about to leave the bridge when Vincent DeSalle arrived. The ship's assistant chief engineer looked uncomfortable. It was plain he felt his damage-control report had to be delivered in person.

"Lieutenant, your report," Sulu said.

"Most of the damage we sustained is impact-related," DeSalle said. "From the unplanned transition from subspace to normal space."

"What about the power systems?" asked Sulu. "Why do we experience that cutout every time?"

DeSalle was standing over Ensign Harper at the engineering station, who looked nervous in the presence of his superior. The lieutenant hit a couple of controls, replacing the unmoving stars on the viewscreen with a cutaway diagram of the *Enterprise*. "I've highlighted power conduits in yellow," he said. "If you watch this . . ." The yellow lines disappeared and reappeared. "Every one of them shuts down for a split second when we hit a distortion. It took a while, but we eventually traced the cause—the computer systems shut down and had to reboot."

"Why," asked Sulu, "if they didn't take any damage?"

"We're looking into that," said DeSalle. "We've got some ideas."

McCoy moved closer to the viewscreen, looking at the diagram. "There's no apparent cause?" He felt the need to emphasize the point.

You do that because you recognize when someone's trying to hide complete ignorance.

"No," DeSalle grudgingly admitted. "I've got the computer section checking and rechecking every duotronic circuit, but so far they've found nothing."

"That's three unexplained problems," McCoy said. "Call me old-fashioned, but I don't believe in coincidence."

"Three problems?" asked Sulu. "The distort-zone, the computers, and . . . what else?"

McCoy briefly outlined what had happened to the espers. "I can't find a cause for it in any of them."

You actually admitted that out loud? You're braver than I thought.

He tried to shush his inner voice, but it was getting harder and harder.

"What could connect a computer failure to comas, though?" asked DeSalle. "That doesn't make sense."

"Nothing about this makes sense," said Sulu. "Any suggestions, Lieutenant Rodriguez?"

The science officer had been listening to and quietly responding to someone via his earpiece and hadn't been paying attention. "Sorry, sir. I was just talking to Padmanabhan in spatial physics. He's on his way up with a report on the distortions."

"Very well, Mister Rodriguez." McCoy could sense the disapproval in Sulu's voice. Being the science officer of a starship was a difficult task; there were a lot of disciplines you were required to be conversant with. The Spocks who had mastered all of them were few and far between.

"Do you know of any link between the computers and the espers?" Sulu asked.

Rodriguez shook his head. "No, sir."

The turbolift doors hissed open, discharging an Indian man—almost a boy, really, McCoy thought—in a blue sciences uniform. He had a data slate in front of him, which he was scribbling on even as he stepped onto the bridge. He continued using it as he passed McCoy to join Rodriguez at his console, handing it to him as he arrived. "Here you go, Esteban," he said.

"Thanks, Homi."

McCoy wasn't the only one watching the pair interact; Sulu had oriented the command chair toward the sciences console and had an expectant look on his face. "Report," he said finally.

Padmanabhan straightened up and faced Sulu. "Sir, we've been trying to map the extent of the distortions—that is, Bellos and I have been trying—me being Ensign Padmanabhan, sir—and we were having problems—difficulties that would arise—"

McCoy caught Uhura's eyes, and she smiled.

Sulu, on the other hand, was becoming impatient. "We don't need every detail of the investigation, Ensign," he interjected. "Skip ahead."

"Sorry, sir. The interiors of the distortions are infinite—they're bigger on the inside, you might say—not just ripples or bumps in the space-time continuum, but holes to another universe. They're spots where another universe is pushing its way into ours."

Sulu nodded in apparent understanding. "What kind of universe?"

"This is a realm entirely separate from our own—floating around in the higher dimensions, with its own stars, its own planets—maybe not, though, if its physical laws are too different."

"Wait," said McCoy. "I thought the universe was infinite. How can there be other universes out there?"

Padmanabhan looked back at Rodriguez helplessly. Sulu graciously stepped in. "A sheet of paper could be infinite, Doctor, yet since it is almost two-dimensional, there could be other infinite sheets of paper out there, within the three-dimensional world. Our universe has the same relationship to the higher dimensions."

"Exactly!" Padmanabhan chirped. "And if you had *two* sheets of paper—well, probably you have more, but let's just say two—then they'd intersect in some places, and that's where *we* are. At an intersection."

"Does the other universe have different physical laws?" asked Sulu.

"We think so," said Padmanabhan. "These distortions—'holes' would be more proper—are places where our universe is being rewritten by the other one. Well, parts of our universe—subspace, to be exact—the overlap seems to be confined to that."

"I might just be a simple country doctor," said McCoy, "but that doesn't sound good."

"It is!" Padmanabhan looked around excitedly, then immediately backtracked. "Well, it sort of is. It is from a physics perspective—it could be absolutely *fascinating*—"

Obviously this boy had been spending too much time around Spock.

"—but it's not good for us—seeing as how we come from *this* universe—and its laws."

"Could this account for our computer problems?" asked Sulu, turning to face DeSalle.

"It's possible. I'll look into it," he said.

"And what about my patients?" McCoy asked. "Is the other universe affecting them?"

Padmanabhan gave him a quizzical look. "Patients, sir?"

"I have five people in comas, Ensign, with no apparent cause. Can these intersections be causing that?"

"Sorry, sir. I'm a physicist, not a medical doctor."

"Ensign, I want you to send all the data you have to Lieutenant DeSalle and Doctor McCoy. And gentlemen, please pass whatever you have to the physics labs," Sulu ordered. "If there's a connection, we need to pool our knowledge to find it."

Watch a group of Spock's number-crunchers figure out this problem before you can. That'll satisfy the pointy-eared intellectual.

"I'd better head back down to sickbay," said McCoy.

Like that'll help.

Could he put that self-doubt aside for just a moment?

McCoy began moving toward the turbolift as Sulu hit a button to clear the power diagram from the viewscreen. "Distance from Mu Arigulon?" the lieutenant asked.

Farrell checked his panel. "Point-nine-seven light-years," he said.

McCoy paused just before the lift and turned. "We won't be moving at impulse that entire distance, will we?" he asked.

"Hopefully not," said Sulu. "The distortions only extend a few days ahead of us."

"If we stay out of warp," Rodriguez added, "no new ones should form, and once we're far enough away, we can go to warp again."

And what would happen if they weren't able to find a

way around this? McCoy was not at all happy about the thick layer of uncertainty that coated everything. It made getting a definite answer impossible. "If this other universe is too different from ours, it can't be good if these holes in space stay open, right?"

"Correct," Sulu said gravely. "Depending on the power of the force, *Enterprise*'s destruction could be the first in a series of disasters."

Great. "I knew I shouldn't have asked. The more you tell me, the more I think I should've stood in bed."

Sulu put on a smile that was doubtless intended to be encouraging, but it failed to have that effect on the doctor. "Of course, that's only a worst-case scenario. They might stop growing once we're destroyed. Then Starfleet would only have to quarantine this sector."

"Thanks, Sulu." McCoy's sarcasm was only thinly veiled. "I'm feeling much more confident now."

"We'll be careful, Doctor, I promise." Sulu had grown more serious the further this talk progressed, the very image of a man born to be in charge. "We'll probably be about four days late, but at least we'll still be whole."

McCoy thought about Kirk, Spock, M'Benga, Scotty, and the others in the landing parties, stepping onto that new world, no doubt fascinated by an unending stream of new discoveries. "Well," he said, "I'm sure they'll relish the extra time." He envied them, as a matter of fact. Unaware as they were of the *Enterprise*'s troubles, they were no doubt having the time of their lives.

"Weather report, Mister Jaeger."

Upon returning to the *Hofstadter*, they had found that conditions had lessened to a mild drizzle, and Spock had taken off immediately. Wind continued to blow, but even with the weakened shields, continued flight should be safe in the current conditions.

"The winds are increasing. The level of rainfall has to be abnormal," Jaeger insisted. "I've been looking at visual data from the orbital survey, and there's a large number of dried-out lake beds, especially next to metropolises. And I can't figure out why—many are fed by active rivers."

"Is the upper atmosphere safer?" asked Spock. Given that the shuttle was a spacecraft, entering orbit to avoid the storms might prove the safest option.

"If anything, it's worse. Close to the ground seems to have lower-force winds." He flipped back and forth between reports on his slate. "I just don't get it."

"Interesting," said Spock. "Continue your investigations." He would continue to apply part of his mind to the task of solving the problem. In the meantime, he was still pondering what had happened to the inhabitants of Mu Arigulon, and what the warp reactors were sending their power to, which was the *Hofstadter*'s current destination.

Perhaps useful information could be found in the data Saloniemi had uncovered. He pulled up the A&A officer's report on the central console and began reading. "I see that the Orion databases confirmed that the doll the captain found represents an inhabitant of Mu Arigulon V."

"A 'Farrezzi,' sir," interjected Saloniemi.

Spock nodded. "Have you discovered any other information of value?"

"The Farrezzi were definitely involved in interstellar markets around two centuries ago, but abruptly withdrew." He shrugged. "The Orions seemed disappointed, but unconcerned. Is it possible they just left the planet?"

"Perhaps," replied Spock, "but there is still no evidence of the large-scale space industry such an exodus would require." He turned to face the rest of the shuttle crew. "I wish to journey to whatever 'projector' is at the hub of the reactor network. I will contact the captain momentarily, but I expect he will approve my decision."

"Sir," interrupted Jaeger. "My projections show higher wind intensity ahead."

"Is that safe?" asked Scott.

"I estimate only a six percent chance that the *Hofstadter* will suffer damage, Mister Scott, and any damage will be within your abilities to repair."

Scott smiled slightly. "Thank you, Mister Spock. I'll do my best."

Why an emotional species always felt the need to say this was a mystery Spock had long given up attempting to solve—or even commenting on. He set the *Hofstadter* to accelerate, plunging into the windy depths of the storm ahead.

It was getting late. Chekov hadn't yet fully adjusted to the thirty-three-hour day here, and even though the sun hadn't even set, his body was telling him that it was night. Not even the discovery of an alien elevator shaft was enough to keep him from yawning.

Ensign Seven Deers had been inspecting the elevator for the past few minutes, while the captain had talked to Spock on his communicator. Seven Deers hardly said a word, but she looked confident.

The captain shut his communicator and walked over to the hole in the floor, his arms crossed as he peered down it. "What do you think, Ensign?"

Seven Deers looked up. A strand of her long, brown

hair had escaped its clasp and hung over her face. She casually tucked it behind her ear. "Well, sir," she began, "I'm certain that it's an elevator, that much I can say. As for how it works, I *think* this is the control lever." She pointed at the object in question.

The captain nodded. "Do it." He joined her to get a better view.

When Seven Deers pulled the lever down, a rumble started, the sound of metal banging against metal, and the platform moved, slowly but surely, down into the shaft. After a few seconds, she pushed the lever back up, and the platform ascended again.

"Excellent, Ensign," the captain said. "Let's see what's down there." He glanced back at Chekov. "Material strength satisfactory, Ensign Chekov?"

He'd been caught off guard but recovered quickly. "Aye, sir."

"Just what I wanted to hear." Kirk moved closer to the elevator and gripped one of its vertical bars. "We'll need to split up into two groups, however. There's no need to push our luck. Ensign Chekov, can we tell what's down there? Does the tricorder have an idea?"

"Scans are better here, but still not optimal, sir. All I can tell you is that the space below is potentially as large as this city." He fiddled with the tricorder settings, trying to penetrate the interference. "There seem to be many rows of almost identical items, and—" Chekov fell silent, unable to believe what the tricorder was telling him.

"Ensign?"

He looked up at his commanding officer. "Captain, the items are highly sophisticated devices, and they're still active!"

The faces of the others displayed surprise to varying degrees. Commander Giotto was pulling a face that showed how unhappy he was about this development. Crewman Tra was mimicking his superior. Seven Deers's and Rawlins's faces were mirrors of Chekov's, full of stunned disbelief. And the captain . . . well, the captain was smiling, evidence of his satisfaction.

Understandable reactions. Finding this much working technology after all this time of neglect was unexpected. Too bad Commander Scott wasn't here—Chekov knew the chief engineer would be having a field day. All Chekov needed to do now was find Yüksel, and he'd redeem himself.

Right now, both Kirk and Giotto were looking at him, likely expecting him to elaborate, but anything further would be guesswork, and he didn't want to resort to that. "I'm afraid I can't tell you anything more specific, Captain."

"Well, it appears we have no other choice," Kirk said. "Commander, any reservations?"

With his tightened jaw and his grim face, Giotto looked even older than his salt-and-pepper hair made him out to be. "As a matter of fact, yes, sir. Since the ensign's unable to provide better information, we've no idea what to expect. I must point out the obvious danger involved. And then we don't even know that what's down there has anything to do with Yüksel."

Kirk nodded. "Thank you. I understand your concerns. However—" He paused for a moment, leaving Chekov to silently hope. "—we're going down there. Chekov and I will go first. If everything is fine, Commander Giotto, you'll bring the rest of the landing party with you."

"Are you sure you don't want security backup, Captain?" asked Giotto.

"I have one, Commander." Chekov thought he could detect a slight charge to the captain's voice. "Mister Chekov."

Giotto just nodded. Chekov wanted to know why it was so hard to please this man, considering that he'd even managed to impress Spock enough that he now served as backup science officer. He moved onto the platform, drawing his phaser. Kirk joined him.

"Ready, Captain?" asked Seven Deers.

"Ready?" asked Kirk. "Ensign, I'm looking forward to it."

Seven Deers pulled the lever, and they began their descent into the darkness.

McCoy's self-preoccupation was momentarily dispelled when he returned to sickbay and saw Nurse Chapel still moving about when she should be off duty. Nobody knew how long the quiet would last—she should be making the most of it.

"Christine," McCoy said, watching her inspect the settings on a patient's biobed.

"Doctor?" Chapel looked up, startled.

"How long have you been working without a break?" Part of it was his fault, he knew. He'd been the one who'd gone off to the rec room, retreated to his office, and visited the bridge. She'd been down here, working the entire time.

At least someone is pulling their weight here today. She can actually take care of problems, unlike you.

His attempt to suppress the thought didn't work very well. The voice in his head seemed to grow more distinct with each passing moment.

"Not since I came on shift," she said, blushing just enough for him to notice it.

"That's eight hours!" McCoy exclaimed. "Have you even eaten?"

"I grabbed a salad from the food slots a few hours ago," she said. "Have *you*?"

"Yes—" he began, but stopped himself. He hadn't, he suddenly realized. He'd never made it to that sandwich on his trip to the rec room. But he didn't even feel hungry. "I'll be fine," he said. "You need to sit down. I'll take over here."

You're just trying to avoid a problem you know is too difficult. You're in your element when you're doing these small, manageable tasks. It lets you feel accomplished. But if you take a look at the espers, you'll never get anywhere, and you know it.

Damn it! He hated it when the voice was actually *right*.

Chapel shook her head at his suggestion. "I can handle this."

"Maybe. But you do need a break, Christine," he said.

"Any thoughts on our coma patients?" Chapel asked. Like him, she was good at changing the subject when it became uncomfortable. "It could be weeks before we make it to a starbase."

"No, not yet," he said, pulling a face. "I'll get back to it."

He retreated to his office, nodding at Brent as the med tech passed him. The lieutenant looked a bit the worse for wear, but at least he was back on his feet again and able to do his job, which was the important thing right now.

Once he'd seated himself at his desk, McCoy quickly called up the medical records for all five espers: Bouchard, Petriello, Santos, Fraser, Salah.

Can you even do this? Do you have the expertise to save these people?

Of course he did. He'd seen and overcome stranger diseases and ailments. Hell, he was the man who'd cured the Gamma Hydran hyperaging syndrome!

That wasn't science, that was a lucky break. If Chekov's adrenaline rush hadn't happened to protect him at the moment of infection, you wouldn't have known a thing about what was going on. And you know even less about espers.

That was true, he realized with painful clarity.

You always like to call yourself "a good old-fashioned country doctor," and that's what you are. But that's not what this situation needs. This situation needs someone who trained to go into space, not someone who did it because they were running away.

Well, that might have been true to begin with, but he'd risen above that, hadn't he? He'd embraced all aspects of being a starship surgeon. There were few things he liked more than going to a new world and surveying a whole new biology, or spending time with physicians from a new civilization and learning their medical practices.

Well, sure, you like it. That doesn't actually translate into being good at it.

That wasn't even remotely true. Right? He pushed the thoughts aside by calling up a comparative analysis of all five espers' brain patterns. The fact that they'd been affected in roughly the order of decreasing extrasensory ability pointed to a strong link between the unknown phenomenon and their powers. The more sensitive the mind, the harder it had been hit—but by what? What was out there doing this to the minds of these people? Was anything even out there at all?

The doctor located Spock's reports from the *Enterprise*'s encounter with the negative energy field that had killed the nine espers at the beginning of the ship's five-year mission. Sensors hadn't been able to detect it, but Spock had noted a complete lack of energy, a presence of something that somehow gave off no readings at all. But here, there wasn't even that. Just these . . . bumps in the fabric of space. Starfleet records were no help at all, he found. Plenty of spaceships had encountered patches of subspace rougher than this without there being any kind of psychic phenomena. However, those hadn't led to other universes with totally different physical laws.

He wished he knew more about spatial distortions, or extrasensory perception. Despite his early-career success with partial grafts of neural tissue, he had a generalist's knowledge of the human brain and its abilities, and a specialist's was required here. He wished M'Benga wasn't off with the landing party; he'd interned in a Vulcan ward, and knew about telepathy.

Hell, he wished Spock was here. Although . . . maybe he didn't need him, just the medicines his people used. Vulcans had to have experience with disorders of the telepathic mind. It stood to reason that they knew how to treat them.

McCoy checked the medical database for information. Maybe there was something in the Vulcans' arsenal that would let him suppress the espers' abilities, allowing him to reduce the stress on their brains. He navigated through directories and subdirectories, occasionally reading an article only to find out that it wasn't at all what he was looking for. But Vulcan telepaths had to have gone through similar ordeals; the doctor refused to believe they didn't have anything that could help.

He'd keep searching for answers, even if that meant he wouldn't get much sleep. His own needs were the least important right now.

Anything to save these patients.

Anything except actually being the capable, experienced doctor they need. Ever since you joined Starfleet to avoid your problems, you've been moving. You stay somewhere too long, and you move again. You've served in so many different places, always just for a short time. And then you started to feel comfortable here. You liked Kirk, you liked Chapel, you liked Scotty, you even got invited to Spock's wedding.

He tried to push the voice aside and focus on the data in front of him, but he couldn't. The voice insisted. It kept on speaking. He knew it somehow; it was familiar.

You stayed here too long, and now it's caught up to you. Your ignorance, your lack of training, everything. You're a ship's surgeon not because it's the right thing to do, you're a ship's surgeon because it lets you ignore all your other problems. Until now, that is. Now you've hit a situation outside of your abilities—and five innocent people are going to die as a result.

I hope you feel good about this, at least.

McCoy suddenly recognized the voice.

It was his ex-wife's.

SIX

Leonard McCoy sits in the back of Doctor Ducey's philosophy class and complains a lot. He doesn't think he's complaining loudly—just loud enough for Kotchian next to him to laugh at every one of his jokes. However, four weeks into the class a girl three rows in front of him turns around and says, "What is your problem?" She is a bit shorter than Leonard, with shoulder-length brown hair and a round face. Pretty cute.

"My problem," Leonard says, "is that I have to take Introduction to Extraterrestrial Philosophy. If I wanted to know what *The First Song of S'task* was, I'd buy the album." Leonard hopes she's not a philosophy major, because then she's only going to become more annoyed with him.

"It's not that kind of song!" she hisses back. "It's a long-form philosophic poem that tells—"

"And if I'd wanted to know all *that*," replies Leonard, "I'd be paying attention instead of complaining."

Kotchian taps Leonard on the shoulder, nodding toward the front of the class, where Doctor Ducey is staring pointedly at him. He clams up for the rest of the class, but the next time it meets, he moves down a couple of rows, sitting right behind the girl.

"What are you doing?" she asks, turning around. She acts exasperated, but there is a twinkle in her eye.

"Since you seem so interested in extraterrestrial philosophy, I figured I'd see if some of that could rub off on me." Leonard hopes he's right about her. Meeting someone in class seems to be his best bet, given how little time he has for socializing these days. He hasn't been on a date since his freshman year.

"Good luck with that," she says. "It's plain you're not interested in hard work."

"I work hard every night," he replies. "On things that are actually important and interesting. It's not my fault that zh'Mai and Shran of Andor are so blasted dull."

"And what *do* you find interesting?" she asks. "Crabbing and Whining 101?"

"You, my dear," he says with a wink.

She rolls her eyes and turns to face forward with a sigh, but Leonard continues to sit there every class. In two weeks, they're "study buddies"—in another two, they're dating.

Her name is Jocelyn Darnell.

Stardate 4757.7 (1604 hours)

Kirk watched the smooth walls of the elevator shaft move past them, slowly picking up speed as the open cage made its descent. "How long until we enter the cavern?" he asked Chekov.

The ensign was studiously peering at his tricorder. "Thirty seconds, sir."

The captain nodded and checked the setting on his phaser. With the level of interference they were getting, there could be anything down there. He knew Giotto thought Yüksel was dead, but Kirk was not going to leave this planet until they found him. With the *Enterprise* delayed by unknown forces, they were on their own.

The mottled gray rock of the shaft edge suddenly vanished, and Kirk found himself looking into a vast cavern from above. Thanks to a soft blue glow that seemed to come from everywhere, he could see thousands—tens of thousands—of cylindrical objects, roughly three meters high and one meter wide. They dotted the floor in the same confusing spiral patterns as the city streets above. The platform continued its rapid descent, and the capsules had already grown bigger, enough that he could make out details.

Chekov's tricorder was beeping busily. "They are all powered, sir," he said, reading the scan results. "And I believe I am picking up . . . life signs." He looked up, a smile forming. "Something is alive down here!"

Kirk nodded. "Careful, Mister Chekov."

They had nearly reached the floor of the cavern, and Kirk could finally see the capsules up close. They were silver, a blue light emanating from their insides through transparent paneling all around their circumference.

Inside each one was a tall octopus-like creature, resembling something out of a particularly imaginative child's nightmare. Each sleeping alien had a fat body with protrusions on top, limp tentacle-like appendages serving as legs, and possibly as arms, too. Difficult to say more, since they didn't move, calmly standing in the blue light, immersed in a transparent liquid—maybe water.

With a loud *clang* the platform hit the ground of the cavern and stopped. "Are those things cryopods, Mister Chekov?"

"Yes, sir," said the ensign. "The creatures' life signs are slowed down. They are in suspended animation."

Kirk put his hand on the gate of the cage. "We're going out there," he said. "Behind me, phaser and tricorder out. Send the elevator back up. I'm calling the rest of the landing party down here."

The *Hofstadter* shook and rattled, the wind from above buffeting it time and again. Scotty sat in the navigator's seat and sent course corrections to Spock as they attempted to continue their journey south, toward the hub of the reactor network. Scotty's scans were frustrated by the ever-worsening interference.

"Commander," Jaeger's voice came from the back, "my projections show there's a high danger of lightning up ahead."

"Thank you, Mister Jaeger," said Spock, not looking up from his controls. "Please feed the data to Mister Scott. Mister Scott, please locate a safe landing site."

"Aye." Scotty grimaced as the data came in. The storm kept on growing larger; it now covered half the southern continent. They had to go to ground now—the interference to the shields was increasing.

A shock of white light filled the cockpit of the *Hofstadter*. A second later, the entire shuttle jolted to starboard, nearly knocking Scotty out of his seat. "Mister Scott," Spock said, unflappable as ever, "a safe location, if you please."

"I'm working on it!" The Vulcan might be ineffably calm, but it was almost impossible for Scotty to concentrate. He hadn't had to do his own navigation in conditions like this since he was a young lieutenant. Finally, he located a nearby metropolis with a number of low buildings that would shield them from the wind, worked out a course, and submitted it to Spock's console.

Spock nodded in acknowledgment as the data flooded in. "Thank you—"

The world exploded then, and Scotty was flung forward. His eyes and ears were overwhelmed, leaving him in a light daze. It took him precious seconds to react; his hands flew out barely in time to stop his face from smashing into the console. The controls hurt his palms, even as his mind wondered why the inertial dampers weren't working. He struggled to move back into his seat, but the shuttle was careening out of control in the wind and the rain. The *g* forces were pulling him down, whirling him out of his chair and onto the floor.

On all fours, he barely managed to turn his head to look for Spock. Like himself, the commander had been knocked to the floor of the shuttle, but he managed to pull himself up slightly against the overwhelming force. However, even with his Vulcan strength he was only able to peer at his readouts. "Lightning strike!" he shouted, barely loud enough to be heard over the roar of the storm and the straining of the engines. "Main controls have shorted out."

Scotty reasoned fixing that problem was more important than reaching the navigation console, so he stopped trying to get to his feet, and instead began crawling aft. Most of the shuttle's crew had also been knocked out of their seats, and as Scotty passed Lieutenant Kologwe, he tapped the security officer on the shoulder. "Take navigation!" he shouted above the din.

"I can't get up there!"

"Do it! Spock needs your help!" Thankfully she was professional enough to shut up and go, inching forward by gripping the bases of the seats as she passed them. He did the same in the other direction.

M'Benga and Jaeger had been fortunate enough to remain in their seats, but they had a hard time holding on to them, looking as though they might get thrown off any moment. Onward—no time to gawp. The engineer was making progress, but he had to use up his last reserves of determination and strength. Eventually, he reached the aft wall of the compartment, where he'd be able to gain access to most of the shuttle's controls. The access panel he wanted was near deck level, easy to reach from his position. It opened without a hitch, revealing a twisted mass of cables and circuits that let off a whiff of burnt connections.

Behind him, Scotty was aware of more shouting from Kologwe as she and Spock attempted to get the shuttle under control. Saloniemi yelled something indiscernible.

The transtators beneath the access plate were burnt out, leaving Scotty no choice but to yank them all out as fast as he could. They went flying over his shoulder, now useless. There was no time to replace them all; he needed to bypass them in order to get the signals to the correct junction.

Where could he get a spare transtator now? Yes! Grinning, he yanked his communicator from his belt and pushed the release that opened the back of the device. Its innards were arranged around a transtator. Carefully, he unhooked it and slotted it into one of the empty spots.

"You should have engine control now!" he yelled. Well, some control, anyway. Enough for the moment. Scott briefly wondered if the others could even hear him, but then he felt his chest lighten, the painful forces no longer threatening to squash him. The shuttle had stabilized.

Losing no time, he pulled himself to his feet. Forward, Spock was once again seated at the pilot's controls as if nothing had happened, with Kologwe next to him. The noise of the straining engines had eased off, leaving only the storm to shout over.

"Excellent, Mister Scott," said Spock, loud enough to be heard clearly. "Can you restore full engine control?"

"Aye. I'll have to bypass the mains six ways from Sunday."

"I would prefer that you did not wait until Sunday, Mister Scott. Speed is of the essence, given that shields now seem to be completely inoperative."

Scotty wanted to know how the interference could have grown so much worse so quickly, but he needed to focus on the matter at hand. He ran some quick mental calculations. Even leaving some leeway for unexpected difficulties, it would take him about ten minutes to finish the job.

"Half an hour, Mister Spock."

"Hold her steady, Lieutenant."

Hikaru Sulu winced. Had he really just said that aloud? There was no order a helm officer hated more. It wasn't as if Lieutenant Rahda needed a reminder to do her job.

"Aye, sir."

This was his first time in command during a crisis since the Klingon war, and that had been over a year ago. When Captain Kirk and Mister Spock were off ship, Scotty was usually in command. Sulu wanted to show that he was up to the challenge. He wanted a command of his own.

Flying the ship was what he did best. But he knew better than to try to fly the ship and command.

Lieutenant Rahda was doing an excellent job. The *Enterprise* was moving forward at maximum impulse, and hadn't encountered a single problem. Without the warp drive active, the ship was in normal space.

Smooth sailing.

Yeoman Lawton crossed from her console to hand him a data slate—fuel consumption reports, damage requisitions. Even in the middle of a crisis, there was still paperwork to be pushed. He skimmed the reports, his eyes drawn to that line at the bottom. "COMMANDING OFFICER, *U.S.S. ENTERPRISE*." Someday, that would really be—

A quiet beeping from the front of the bridge drew his attention. The red warning light between the helm and navigation consoles was blinking insistently. "Report," he said.

Farrell at navigation pressed some buttons and inspected the spatial plot. "I'm not sure, sir."

Sulu turned his chair to face the science panel. "Rodriguez?"

The science officer looked at the display on his console. "Distortion ahead, sir." Rodriguez gulped noticeably as he studied the readout. "*Real-space* distortion ahead, sir."

"Full stop!" Sulu called out the command before Rodriguez had even finished his sentence, but it was too late.

The deck dipped forward, knocking him into the chair's armrest. Holding on to it, he could only watch as Rodriguez tumbled and fell.

A moment later, the science console fizzled, gentle sparks flying out in every direction. All its screens went dark. The briefest of moments later, it exploded, fragments of metal and plastic pelting Rodriguez, who was lying on the deck, moaning.

Sulu swiveled forward to discover with horror that both Rahda and Farrell had been thrown face-first into their consoles by the phenomenon's force. Farrell was slumping backward in his chair, apparently unconscious. Rahda's face was resting on her controls, a bright stream of blood trickling down them.

Sulu vaulted out of the captain's chair and pulled Rahda upright in her chair. Her body was limp, her face covered in blood.

As he hurried to cut all power to the forward engines, another loud explosion from the front starboard corner of the bridge overpowered his senses for an instant. Very quickly, smoke filled the air. Lawton had been thrown from her station, and the console was on fire.

"Stay away from all the controls!" Sulu shouted. "Harper, get Farrell!"

As the engineer moved, Sulu finally succeeded in canceling forward thrust, but it didn't look like it was going to be enough. He put the ship into reverse, building up the power as fast as he could. The *Enterprise* needed to get out of this distortion before—

The navigation console sparked and then belched out an enormous gout of smoke. Sulu hadn't noticed Ensign Harper grab Farrell, but the navigator wasn't there anymore, thank goodness. The force of the explosion knocked the unconscious Rahda out of her chair, and Sulu had to hold on tight to maintain his footing.

The *Enterprise* was pulling out of the distortion, but it was careening out of control now. He had to stabilize it, had to stop it from spinning off into space and even more trouble.

His hands sped over the controls as fast as they could. He didn't have much time. The explosions had worked their way across the bridge from starboard to port.

There was a sudden flash of light and a loud noise. And then Lieutenant Hikaru Sulu didn't see or hear anything at all.

■ ■ ■ ■

Despite the stunning sight before him, Jim Kirk was frustrated. Their discovery of a sentient species cryogenically hidden from prying eyes would redefine the *Enterprise*'s mission of exploration in this sector, but that didn't help them find their missing crewman.

Tricorders picked up thousands of Farrezzi life signs—Chekov estimated there were thirty-four thousand cryopods in this chamber alone. Who knew how many more of these chambers were hidden away beneath the planet's surface, but there were no human life signs. None at all. Part of Kirk wanted to wake one of the aliens up and yell at it, demanding the location of his missing man. But, rationally, he knew that would be absurd.

"Captain." Chekov's voice rang out from around the other side of a row of pods. The landing party had fanned out, but Kirk had ordered everyone to stay in visual range of one another.

"Over here, Mister Chekov," he answered. "Not too loud, remember." Giotto had advised caution until he and Tra could ascertain that they were truly alone.

The ensign squeezed between two pods to join his captain. Barely able to contain his excitement, Chekov pointed at the pod in front of him. "Captain, this is remarkable. These beings are perfect pentamerian organisms!"

"Excellent, Mister Chekov." Kirk waited a beat. "Now assume I don't share your expert knowledge of biology."

He had kept his voice light, but it still looked like the ensign was actually turning red. "Sorry, sir. They are radially symmetrical, in five roughly equal parts, like many species of Earth starfish, for example. That's why we can't pick a front or a back side, sir. There's little about sentient pentamerians in our scientific literature, but what's there leads me to think the Farrezzi can move in any direction without changing their orientation."

"Remarkable." Completely nonhumanoid sentients were rare. Kirk peered at the alien closely. "I don't see a mouth."

"That's because we would expect it at the front, which doesn't make sense from an anatomical standpoint."

Chekov was clearly enjoying himself. Maybe the ensign would stop beating himself up over what had happened to Yüksel.

Chekov explained, "If you have five limbs and can move in any direction, the only parts of you that stay more or less the same regardless of where you're facing are the upper and lower ends of your torso. If you look closely, you can see a . . . an aperture, there on top. Given that it is ringed by five eyestalks, I am tempted to say this is the Farrezzi's mouth."

The captain had a closer look, and he could see what Chekov was pointing at. The protruding eyes were closed, but it was clear what they were. Looking almost like the eyestalks of a crab, only many times bigger and equipped with eyelids, they were placed equidistant around the central torso. There was no clearly definable head, at least none that the captain could make out, since the torso, almost as long as Kirk, started out wider at the top and grew thinner at the bottom. The five limbs were attached below the torso's halfway point. He imagined they could serve as both arms and legs.

"Good work, Ensign. Continue your scans. I'm going to talk to Ensign Seven Deers."

A minute's walk brought him to where Seven Deers was investigating a pod. However, she was more interested in its machinery than its inhabitant. Tubes ran along the floor of the chamber, connecting to each pod, and she was crouched on the floor, scanning them. "Report."

"These are complete environments, Captain," she said, not looking up. "Supplying the Farrezzi with water, air, and nutrients."

"Air?" Kirk asked. "Were they designed to protect them from the planet's toxicity?"

She nodded. "I think so. They slow the body's metabolism through a chemical means. The system also seems to need a constant supply of water. All of the pods are connected to a system drawing water from elsewhere, probably subsurface."

The entire population had fled underground to avoid their planet's environmental collapse. It was a risky move, but Kirk had seen civilizations that had destroyed themselves. "Impressive."

"One more thing, sir," Seven Deers said. "It looks like the control mechanisms for this facility are at the north end of this cavern, the area beneath the launching complex. If Yüksel is down here—"

"Then he might have headed—or been taken—in that direction." Kirk flipped open his communicator. "All hands, this is the captain. Converge on my location. We're heading to the part of the chamber beneath the launching complex. If Yüksel is down here, that's where he'll be."

"*Who would have taken him, sir?*" asked Rawlins. "*Everyone down here is asleep.*"

"Good question, Lieutenant." Kirk mulled over the possibilities. "My instinct is that it's some Farrezzi, who stayed awake to guard this place. Yüksel may have set off some alarms." The captain looked at the rows of pods, the bluish light illuminating the life-forms within them. Too bad this survey had to turn into a manhunt. "We can explore this place after we get him back."

McCoy didn't understand how the *Enterprise* could have encountered another of those space-time ripples at sublight. Nevertheless, he'd made sure to keep himself safe this time, clinging to his desk at the first sign of trouble. This quick reaction meant, of course, that he was ready to spring into action once the bucking stopped.

One minute after the *Enterprise* hit the distortion, he ordered the nurses to go through sickbay and discharge anyone remotely fit for duty, anticipating more casualties. Thank goodness they'd already sent quite a few of them to their quarters early on. His comatose espers would have to wait. As McCoy changed into a clean surgical smock, he briefly considered what effect yet another delay in finding a treatment for their affliction might have, but pushed the thought aside.

Easy to ignore problems you're not capable of handling, isn't it?

There was Jocelyn's voice. What was wrong with him? He'd been in stressful situations before, but he'd never heard voices.

I told you—you're out of your depth this time, Leonard.

He'd have liked nothing more than to shut the voice up, but finding out how would have to wait. For now, he needed to get to work. McCoy rounded up the med techs and told them to double-check every cart and every tray, and if there was some item missing, they were to replace it. He couldn't afford to waste time during emergency surgery.

Two minutes after the *Enterprise* hit the distortion, the first casualty was at his door: Petty Officer Carriere, who'd been flung by an exploding computer console. What the hell was going on out there? Dozens of lacerations all across the face, where little bits of metal had buried themselves with enormous force.

This was going to be ugly.

Burns, broken arms, cracked ribs, concussions, the gamut. McCoy was fairly certain that there wasn't a single type of crash injury he hadn't seen today. Injury reports kept on coming in over the comm, but they were having trouble just keeping up with what was already in sickbay.

Ten minutes after the *Enterprise* hit the distortion, he was examining a bruised lieutenant from the history department. She was sitting in a chair in his office, since all the biobeds were full—even those in the examination room. The incident had left her with a nasty cut on her forehead, but he'd have that healed in no time.

"So, Lieutenant Watley," he said as he moved the regenerator over her wound, "anything else you feel the need to report?"

The young woman regarded him with a quizzical expression. "What do you mean, sir?"

"Oh, I don't know," he said, even though he did, "anything out of the ordinary. Are you hearing voices, for instance? Imagining things? Memories suddenly come to life, that sort of thing?"

Her expression grew confused. "Uh, no, sir. Should I? I mean, it's only a minor head wound."

"Are you a doctor, Lieutenant?" he said, though the accompanying smile took the edge off his words. In fact, McCoy was asking her these questions not because he believed her injury could cause her to hallucinate, but because he was unsettled by what was happening to him.

"No, sir," she said, suitably chastised. "I haven't heard or seen anything unusual. Sorry, sir," she added when she saw his face.

"Don't worry about it. Routine questions in head wound cases. Everything can be a symptom of something, and I'd hate to miss it because I failed to ask a stupid question."

Maybe he *was* losing his mind, then. For now, the only thing he could do was keep on working.

Sixteen minutes after the *Enterprise* hit the distortion, Ryan Leslie returned bearing an injured comrade. His guards were bringing injured personnel here. It was Abrams who suggested going with them to either treat people on the spot or get them to sickbay. McCoy couldn't spare many of his staff, but he also couldn't afford for injured personnel to be lying out there, helpless, so he sent Abrams and Thomas out with the security people, telling them to cover the ship from top to bottom, checking names against the crew roster and making sure nobody was lying alone and helpless in their quarters, in need of immediate medical attention.

Only those who really needed the help were coming into sickbay, and many of them had been given first aid by their comrades.

Twenty-two minutes after the *Enterprise* hit the distortion, Uhura and Harper came hurrying into sickbay, the body of Lieutenant Sulu slumped between them.

"Uhura! What happened?"

Sulu's face was covered in first- and second-degree burns, his uniform shirt partially blackened. A massive bandage on the back of his head was evidence that he'd apparently been thrown backward onto the deck. McCoy handed the dermal regenerator he was using on a crewman to Messier and went to give the two of them a hand. Together, they lifted Sulu onto a biobed that had been vacated only a few minutes before.

Uhura was covered in soot but seemed physically unharmed. "The distortion we hit was the biggest so far." She was breathing heavily. "Normal space. Most of the bridge consoles . . . exploded from some kind of energy surge."

McCoy was listening, but his mind was focused on the readings on the monitor above Sulu's head. If he worked quickly, Sulu would be fine. But the doctor couldn't afford to waste any time at all.

Uhura was now telling Harper to go back up to the bridge and get Rodriguez to help with Rahda and Farrell.

"What about Lawton?" asked McCoy, as he began loading up a set of hyposprays.

"She's fine," said Uhura. "Completely shaken, but physically okay. I told her to help out in the physics lab."

"Good," was what McCoy meant to say, but it sounded more like a grunt. Uhura's breathing had slowed back down, and she seemed fine. But poor Sulu. So much for bringing the ship back to Mu Arigulon under his own command.

A realization hit him. "Wait a blasted minute! Who's in command, now?"

Uhura thought for a moment that struck McCoy as uncharacteristically long. "Lieutenant DeSalle—he's in auxiliary. I'm going to relieve him."

"He'll have his hands full in engineering," said McCoy.

Uhura began to walk away, toward the exit.

"Wait!" McCoy grabbed a hypospray from his tray. "You should have thought of this yourself." He jabbed the hypo into her arm. "You'll need a stimulant. It's been a long day, and it's only going to get longer."

Her eyes brightened almost immediately. "Thank you, Doctor. I'll be in auxiliary control if you need anything."

McCoy watched her go, her upright frame indicating her confidence. She would handle the situation to her utmost abilities.

If only you were capable of the same.

He ignored Jocelyn's voice and went back to working on Sulu.

Thirty-four minutes after the *Enterprise* hit the distortion, he lost his first patient.

SEVEN

Jocelyn's a logistics major, and she too isn't happy about taking a philosophy class—she's just better at hiding it. Their "dates" are typically extended study sessions in McCoy's dorm room or, more commonly, hers. They help each other focus. Leonard needs the help. A junior at Ole Miss, he always feels like he's drowning in work. He knows it's only going to get worse.

They're both from Georgia, albeit from opposite sides of the state. She's from Waycross, while Leonard calls Forsyth home. Over summer vacation, Leonard spends his weekends and the odd weeknight with her, while working at his father's practice. Spending most of the week separated is awful for them both, and they talk to each other incessantly.

Thankfully, the summer is soon over and they're back at school for their senior year. Leonard still lives on campus—easier to study at the library. Jocelyn has an off-campus apartment, which is great. Really great. He tries not to spend *too* much time with her—he's trying to stay at the top of the class and he's applying to medical schools.

As winter break nears and Leonard's applications are sent, he asks Jocelyn about her post-graduation plans. She's cagey, saying they "depend." Leonard wonders what they depend on.

The day before they go home for the holidays, he takes her on a walk around campus. In Doctor Ducey's classroom, he gets down on one knee and looks up into those brown eyes. Leonard extends his hand, a simple diamond ring in his palm. "Jocelyn Abigail Darnell, will you marry me?"

She says yes.

Stardate 4757.8 (1803 hours)

As the *Columbus* landing party worked their way across the chamber, the blue light gave everything a cold, dismal glow. Everyone's skin looked washed out, especially Tra's, whose Arkenite skin was pale to begin with.

Chekov checked his tricorder, puzzled by the readout. His analysis of the gas being pumped into each cryopod indicated that it almost matched the atmosphere of the planet. There were still trace elements of toxicity in the atmosphere, but according to his scans of the Farrezzi, they were well within the aliens' tolerance. Why hadn't they woken up?

The Farrezzi should already have returned to the surface. Chekov wondered if he could persuade the captain to wake up some of these aliens and ask them what had happened. His scans explained the near-dry lakes and rivers they had seen near every population center: the water was being diverted into the pods.

Answers could wait until after they found Yüksel. The captain was determined to locate him, but Commander Giotto was still saying that taking the entire landing party was an unnecessary risk.

"No risk is unnecessary if it gets one of our men back, Commander," the captain had snapped.

The chamber had appeared to be one large room in the initial scans, but it had turned out to be subdivided into smaller sections by thin clear walls, with the same semicircular doors. They made their way into the next section of the chamber, where Chekov's tricorder registered another thirty-four thousand cryopods. It was hard to scan down here; the Farrezzi had hidden themselves well.

Chekov's tricorder began to let off a steady beep. "Energy reading ahead, Captain."

Kirk looked back at him. "Human? Or Farrezzi?"

"Farrezzi, but—" The ensign found himself fumbling for words. "This is a different signature. Not the same as the cryopod readings."

"Okay, Mister Chekov," the captain said, "guide us toward it." With the captain and Giotto on point, and Chekov right behind them, Y Tra was bringing up the rear, following Seven Deers and Rawlins in the middle. Their tricorders actively absorbed every bit of data.

The ensign guided the landing party through a spiraling maze of pods. After two minutes, Giotto held up a hand.

"Do you hear that, Captain?" he asked.

Chekov could barely make out an irregular noise. It sounded like something metallic being pulled over a stone floor.

"Something is moving, Captain."

"Chekov, can you tell what it is?"

Chekov shook his head. "No, sir. I *think* I am picking up active life signs. It could just be a tight cluster of cryopods."

"Guards?" asked Kirk. "The ones who took Yüksel?"

"Or killed him," murmured Giotto, so quietly only the captain and Chekov could hear.

Chekov's tricorder bleeped, overly loud in the relative silence of the cavern, so he slipped it into silent mode. "Captain, I am picking up an unusual life sign to our right. Not Farrezzi, but I cannot tell what it is."

"Human?" Kirk asked.

He shook his head. "Unclear. It is in suspended animation."

"Mister Chekov, you and Tra check out that new reading. The rest of us will continue ahead."

Chekov nodded. "Aye, sir."

"Make sure you stay out of trouble," the captain said with a small smile. "If this is a first contact, I want it to be a smooth one. Don't let them know you're there, if you can avoid it."

"Keep him out of trouble, Tra," Giotto added.

"I'll do my best, sir." Tra took point, squeezing through a gap between two pods. Moments later, darkness enveloped Chekov once more.

Luke Hendrick died while McCoy was operating on him.

After finishing with Sulu, McCoy had moved on to a new patient with severe internal bleeding—a young woman in a maintenance coverall by the name of Golaski-Lawrence. When she was secure, her internal bleeding stopped and her biosigns stable, McCoy rushed over to the biobed where his next patient had just been laid.

Nurse Chapel was already there, looking grave. The man had serious abrasions covering most of his skin. His uniform shirt sported a central patch of still-wet blood. As McCoy approached, Chapel turned to face him. Her mouth had turned into a thin line, and there was a look of grim determination about her. She shook her head sadly.

McCoy studied the man's readouts. "What happened?" he asked.

"He was thrown from the observation station in the shuttlebay," Chapel said. "Extensive damage to the spinal cord and vertebrae, as well as four fractured ribs. One of them pierced his left lung."

McCoy glanced at the data slate she offered him. "I hope whoever brought him here took great care," he grumbled. Spinal injuries were a damned difficult business, if you didn't know what you were doing.

"They did. Messier was with them."

Ah, good. One of his most capable med techs, Magaly Messier wouldn't have let anybody mishandle a patient.

All right, then. There was no time to lose. "Get me an emergency cart!" he shouted in the direction he'd last seen Brent disappear in. Mere moments later, the cart was delivered, and Brent stood next to him, waiting for further instructions.

"Nurse, you'll have to assist me," McCoy said. This was a very delicate operation that needed two pairs of hands.

McCoy couldn't avoid feeling a little uneasy; despite the almost miraculous nature of most modern treatments and surgery techniques, a damaged spinal column wasn't easily healed. You needed to be well trained and highly experienced, especially when the patient had suffered a horrific fall like Hendrick.

You're not that good a doctor, not today. Probably won't ever be. Just an ordinary country doctor, way out of his depth.

The self-doubt that Jocelyn's voice put into words stopped him from beginning the operation. After a while, he became aware of Chapel looking at him expectantly.

He shook his head in a futile attempt to dislodge the phantasm and breathed in deeply. "Right," he said, "let's get on with it."

McCoy lost himself in the operation. It occupied the entirety of his mind, left no room for Jocelyn to interrupt and insult him. Before long, the vertebrae showed no sign of ever having been broken, and he'd taken the first steps in splicing together the ends of the spinal cord that had been separated by the impact.

When the alarm rang out, he almost dropped his instruments.

"What the hell is it now?" he said, fearing the worst. A look at the monitor didn't improve matters: all the readings were dropping. The indicator for neural activity was approaching zero—brain death was imminent. "How is this possible?"

Not only was the man's brain shutting down, he was going into cardiac arrest. McCoy had no idea what could cause this, but there was no time to guess—he had to act. He tried everything he could think of. Nothing. Not even a high dose of cordrazine could get the man back.

"No, no, no!" This shouldn't be happening.

Luke Hendrick drew his last breath.

"There's no reason he should be dead, goddammit!" McCoy said, almost shouting. Giving in to his anger, he slammed his fist on the medical monitor. He wanted to hit something, hit it hard. "Time of death: 1819 hours, Stardate 4757.8. Name: Luke Hendrick, senior chief petty officer. Cause: unknown complications, possibly due to spinal injuries. Exact cause to be determined." He gazed down at the still form of the man, who should still be alive.

"You did everything you could," Chapel said.

McCoy sighed and turned away from the body, forcing himself to accept that he hadn't been able to save Hendrick. Moving on to the next patient, he stopped after a few steps and turned around.

Chapel had been just a step behind him. "What is it, Doctor?" she asked, worried.

McCoy stood there, watching her. He could hear all the sounds around him—people talking, machines beeping, whirring, thrumming. Precious seconds passed before the doctor shook off the feeling of detachment. There was no time for woolgathering; he needed to get back to work. "Brent," he said at last, "please take the body to the morgue."

Once a patient is dead, you're done. I should hardly be surprised. You abandoned me before I died.

What? Jocelyn wasn't dead—

With a rush that made him dizzy, the doctor realized that the voice wasn't his ex-wife's. It had morphed into another one—that of his father. The father he'd let die four years ago now, taking him off life support rather than letting him continue to suffer.

And what did you do then? Jocelyn's voice asked. *Signed up for duty on Capella IV, to get as far away from Earth as possible. Running away from your problems and your pain. Absolutely typical.*

No, no, no! He couldn't afford this now! McCoy was usually at his best under pressure—he needed to stay focused. The voices had faded when he was occupied. If he threw himself into his work—

As always.

—he could stop them. Or at least quiet them. Time to get back to work, then.

There was little time for McCoy to think about anything

other than the problem in front of him—rebuilding a shattered knee, closing a deep gash. The doctor did wonder when the stream of new patients would stop. He kept worrying about the espers, the mystery behind their comas.

Damn it all. He'd forgotten one of the most important lessons he'd learned from his father—and the one he'd found most difficult to accept—don't let the work get to you, keep some distance from everything. McCoy liked to complain about the loss of compassion in modern medicine. But secretly, he agreed that a level of detachment was necessary.

And you've become too attached, to this ship, this crew. You never were attached to me. It scared you. That's why you always moved on. You left me behind, you should leave these people behind too.

He'd never left Jocelyn behind! What was the voice even talking about?

I'm not Jocelyn. Don't you recognize me?

Joanna. His only child, born out of a crumbling marriage. He'd wanted custody of her, but hadn't gotten it.

By your own choice!

They still talked, exchanging messages. Joanna was in high school, and she'd mentioned something about going into medicine.

There's a way to practice medicine . . . and what you do isn't right. You're not a doctor because you believe in it, you never chose the life you live. What you chose was escape.

No, that wasn't true! McCoy ignored the voices as best he could and focused on what he was doing. He couldn't afford to have his concentration slip.

"Yeoman Zahra," he said as he gently held her right arm and ran his trusted connector over the broken bone, "how are you feeling?"

She smiled weakly. "All right. The last shake caught me by surprise. I've gotten enough bruises to last me a lifetime, but others weren't so lucky," she added, glancing around the room. "I don't want to take up so much of your attention."

"Oh, don't worry," McCoy said, waving her concerns away. "You're my patient now, and you have my full attention. Tell me something: have you been . . . experiencing anything out of the ordinary?"

Zahra looked up at him, displaying the same lack of comprehension as the other crew members he'd asked. "Such as?"

"Well, anything, really. Perhaps hearing voices?" McCoy was concerned that he was the only one suffering from this problem. If M'Benga was here . . . But he wasn't. The *Enterprise* was wounded, her crew needed him.

Zahra bit her lip, then shook her head. "No, sir. Why do you ask?"

He took a deep breath, more to buy time than anything else. "Those folks are in deep comas," he said, motioning with his head. "I'm trying to find out if something is affecting the minds of the crew." There, that sounded almost believable. "And now, Yeoman Zahra, I won't keep you any longer. Your arm's fully healed, but try to be gentle with it."

The most beautiful smile he'd seen in a long while lit her face. "Thank you, sir."

"Off you go, then." He put on his grumpy face. He enjoyed his reputation as a soft-hearted man in a misanthrope's guise.

With Zahra gone, he only had a few patients left. He'd deal with them, then get some rest. Refreshed, he'd continue his research, while telling himself that he wasn't going insane, that what he was experiencing was just a side effect of stress. Yes, his body was simply telling him—albeit rather creatively—to slow down a little. However, over an hour later, McCoy was still hard at work, Odhiambo lurking over his shoulder.

"Doctor," Nurse Odhiambo said. "You're needed in auxiliary control."

"Is someone hurt?" McCoy asked. With the *Enterprise* immobile, they hadn't hit any more distortions, but who knew what could have happened. What if another computer console had exploded? If Uhura had been injured, then this ship was going to be in even more trouble.

Odhiambo shook her head. "No, sir. Lieutenant Uhura wants a report."

"Nurse, please tell her that I'll report to her as soon as I finish here." He didn't wait for her reply but instead returned his attention to his patient. He wouldn't admit it, but he was afraid. Afraid of not being able to help the espers, afraid they were going to die.

The closer they got to the energy reading, the louder the noises became. Kirk could hear squeaking as well, which reminded him of the Guidons, who had the highest-pitched voices he'd ever heard. As the landing party drew closer, the captain realized there was a deeper component. Each squeak seemed to carry three or four tones at once.

The rows of cryopods were coming to an end, and Kirk could just make out the wall of the chamber in the dim blue light. Large shadows moved across it. "Ensign," he asked Seven Deers, taking care to keep his voice low. "Are those Farrezzi?"

"Aye, Captain," she whispered back. "A large group of them—active and moving."

"Sir," Giotto said, "if they took our man, we don't want to just barge in there."

Kirk nodded, having arrived at the same conclusion himself. "Agreed. Seven Deers, find us a spot where we can observe them safely. All equipment to silent."

Seven Deers checked her tricorder, then led them behind a row of pods, where they could get a good look.

A large group of Farrezzi—awake Farrezzi—were moving in front of a gigantic, blocky metal structure that filled the end of the cavern. Fifty meters wide and almost as high, it was embedded in the rocky wall, so the captain couldn't tell how deep it went. The block was lined at its base with more of the semicircular doorways, and the Farrezzi were pushing cryopods through them. They were talking to one another, and now translation would go even faster because the UT could use its scans of their brainwaves to aid its analysis.

"Mister Rawlins, any readings on what's in that structure?"

The geologist shook his head. "Machinery of some type, Captain. I can barely get a reading through the hyper-bonded metal."

Kirk nodded. Was it a facility for reawakening the Farrezzi? Were they getting ready to reclaim their planet?

It took a few moments for him to notice that his communicator was blinking—the UT was ready. At a level he could barely make out, a voice began emanating from the device. "Attention! Order: damage avoidance. Alternative: fatality!"

"Remorse." The translator rendered both voices androgynous. "Speed increase attempt. Obedience."

"Order: silence! Arrival intruders on planet, high-speed necessity for avoidance load-theft."

Kirk shared a glance with Giotto, who asked, "Intruders? They have to be talking about Yüksel. But what did they mean by 'load'?"

"Not-we knowledge of planet location nonexistent. Statement inclusion Orions. Load-theft impossibility."

"Contradiction! Orions commerce contact time abundance then/now, century-plus. Intruder resemblance, exception: skin color."

Orions? Saloniemi had said he'd found a reference to Farrezz in Orion records. Were they trading with the Farrezzi, after all this time? Were they here?

"Desire: completion loading process. Nonpossession: knowledge of waking procedure failure."

Kirk had been watching the Farrezzi, trying to figure out which two were conversing. Finally, he managed to pick them out, by virtue of their moving, trunklike appendages. One was pushing a cryopod with two of its limbs, waving the others in agitation, as another stood next to it, slightly taller, and waving three limbs in reply.

"Attention: avoidance of merchandise damage!"

The captain didn't like the sound of that, not in connection with Orions. "Merchandise," he repeated, careful not to raise his voice. "Seven Deers, double-check that."

The ensign entered commands into her tricorder.

"They definitely said 'merchandise,' Captain," she said. "Ninety-two percent certainty. They are calling those cryopods 'merchandise.'"

"Does that mean what I think it means, Captain?" asked Rawlins.

"It means the Farrezzi inside those cryopods are slaves," Kirk said. "These people are slave traders."

■ ■ ■ ■

A Vulcan mind is a disciplined one, able to concentrate on many different tasks at once. At the moment, Spock had to keep the *Hofstadter* under control, analyze the mysterious storm, work on the conundrum of the Farrezzi, and navigate to a safe location. Had he been human, he would have been relieved that Scott had succeeded in bypassing the burnt-out circuits in only 7.3 minutes. However, Spock was well aware of the engineer's tendency to exaggerate his repair estimates and had expected a quick solution.

Lieutenant Jaeger's report on the storm indicated that it had reached unexpected levels of power in a very short time. The air over the southern continent was continuously being agitated by an unknown phenomenon, which was the cause of the hurricane-like effects they were experiencing. With the shields impaired by interference, the storm was already dangerous to fly in.

Spock was flying low over a Farrezzi metropolis, speeding toward a building lower than the others, with a radius of over forty meters, possibly a storage facility. "We must land."

"Aye, sir," said Lieutenant Kologwe, who continued to man navigation. "Quickly, in order to avoid another one of those lightning strikes." She pointed at her navigational plot, which displayed a massive swirl of meteorological activity across the entire region.

As Spock initiated the descent, his mind actively returned to one of the other problems he had been considering since the lightning strike. The shuttle's autopilot did most of the work for standard landing maneuvers, enabling him to examine the mysterious interference. It was not present in the initial probe surveys, or the *Hofstadter's* orbital sweep. Therefore, it had to derive from an outside force. Something had been added to the equation. They would have to perform another detailed survey of the planet.

Spock brought the *Hofstadter* down in front of the squat building. There were items strewn all about, resembling crates and shipping containers. The building possessed semicircular entrances, but large enough for the shuttle to pass through. Spock sent Kologwe and Emalra'ehn outside to open one, and once they had, he moved the shuttle inside and shut it down. Scott immediately set to work on repairing the shuttle systems.

The landing party moved out in order to take stock of their temporary refuge. A few items of uncertain function littered the ground, as well as more of the containers they had seen outside. Kologwe and Emalra'ehn examined their shelter with flashlights and drawn phasers, the others with their tricorders. Having achieved a temporary reprieve, Spock turned his mind to their present situation. A check-in with the captain was due. Spock activated the shuttle's communication systems and signaled the captain's communicator.

No connection. During their last contact, Captain Kirk had reported that his landing party was about to enter an underground chamber, and Spock assumed that they must be out of range. He signaled the *Columbus*. Receiving no reply, he recorded a succinct report to be stored in the shuttle's memory.

Outside, the storm continued to howl, fierce bouts of rain reverberating as they bounced off the roof of the structure. Spock restrained an emotional desire for the dry skies of his homeworld.

■ ■ ■ ■

Finally, they'd caught up. McCoy ordered Chapel to rest, while the med techs moved out to check up on the people who were recovering in quarters.

The biggest problem still remained: What was causing the comas? If he applied himself to it, without interruption, the voices wouldn't take over.

Vanishing your own inner demons isn't really an admirable reason to practice medicine.

McCoy willed Jocelyn to shut up. But it was pointless—every time he began to think about *anything*, there was one of the voices, whispering in the corner of his mind. Part of him knew he should relieve himself of duty. With M'Benga off the ship, he was the only doctor.

And that's not very much as it is.

The most recent addition to the list of perplexing facts was that the espers' readings had taken a sudden dip around the same time the *Enterprise* had hit the last distortion. They'd risen slightly when the ship had pulled out of it, but not to where they'd been before. There had to be a connection between the distortions and the espers' comas.

The medical computer was already poring over and analyzing every scrap of data on the comas. McCoy sat down at his office desk and called up every report the spatial physics lab had generated on the distortions and added that to the mix. Then he added in a treatment he'd thought of: shutting their brains' higher functions down and letting the neural stimulators take over. While theoretically possible, it was exceedingly risky.

Depending on a machine to do your job for you? Very good medicine, son. I'm glad you got that MD so you could stare at a screen.

That was not what he intended to do!

If you were any good at what you were doing, his father continued, *you'd have figured this out already. Should have been a general practitioner in Georgia, like me. Do what you're somewhat good at, not what you have to fake your way through. No McCoy ever went into space until you had to run away from everything.*

His father was right. All he'd ever wanted to be was a doctor, but if he'd stayed on Earth, he'd have been too close to Jocelyn. Too close to everything—

"Making any progress?"

McCoy raised his head to see Chapel standing at the entrance to his office. Had she slept? How long had he sat here wallowing in doubt? "Not really," he admitted. "No physical injuries, and if they've been infected by a virus or bacteria that somehow only affects espers, it's nothing we can detect."

"So it has to be the distortions."

"That's the logical conclusion, as a certain pointy-eared hobgoblin might say. But that doesn't really help us. How does a hole into another universe send someone into a coma? If only we knew more about how telepathy worked."

"I thought it was a universal psionic field," said Chapel, "tapped into by the brains of telepaths."

McCoy shook his head. "That's the Bormanis Theory, but it's never been proven. It doesn't explain human espers; we don't have a paracortex like some telepathic species. There are theories about quantum consciousness, projected electrical energy . . . all sorts of things."

"If we could just move the ship—" Chapel offered.

"That doesn't seem likely," said McCoy. "Until they come up with a way to move this ship without shaking it apart, we'll have to solve this one ourselves."

"You should go to auxiliary control, see if anything has changed."

"I need to keep working here." McCoy leaned back in his chair.

Chapel closed the distance between them, leaned forward, and said, "Go. You can't keep yourself holed up in sickbay."

But you'd prefer it, if it let you avoid your problems, wouldn't you?

McCoy grabbed his medical kit. Now, he hoped Uhura was going to tell him what they were going to do.

Initially, Chekov had found the hibernating Farrezzi fascinating, but now they were beginning to unnerve him. He imagined that everyone he passed was staring at him. And how would he know? Without backs or fronts, they could see him coming from any direction. Chekov told himself they were all unconscious and had been for over a hundred years.

"How close are we?" Tra whispered. The Arkenite security man seemed completely unperturbed by the whole affair. He was staying just ahead of Chekov, phaser in hand. His uniform shirt looked almost purple in the blue light.

The ensign checked his tricorder. "One more row of pods." He pointed in front of them. "Once we squeeze through there, we will reach the source of the life sign."

"Can you tell what it is yet?" asked Tra.

"It is definitely not Farrezzi." He tapped some controls. "I cannot penetrate the interference in here."

"We need to see what it is and get back to the captain and the others."

Chekov nodded.

Tra squeezed between two pods, and he called back sotto voce, "Clear." Chekov came through behind him. He was getting tired of forcing himself between these things.

On the other side, he could see a small, curving row of cryopods that came to an end right in front of them. Most of the pods were empty, no blue light emanating from their interiors, all the water drained out. But the last pod was still on—and it was where the life sign was coming from. Chekov pushed past Tra, who was advancing cautiously, and almost let out a cry when he discovered who the life sign belonged to.

Fatih Yüksel was almost unrecognizable, his face frozen into a shriek of pain, his eyes open and unblinking. The Turkish exobotanist was bobbing slowly up and down in the middle of the chamber, looking tiny in the pod designed for a Farrezzi. Tubes ran from the walls of the pod into his wrists. Blood was mixing with water where they'd been attached, coloring the pod's interior pink.

"Damn," Chekov gasped. No wonder he hadn't been able to get a lock on the type of life-form inside—they were keeping him alive to Farrezzi specifications, muddling the readings. Chekov didn't know what the treatment would do to him, but there was no way it could be good.

"Can we get him out?"

Hesitating, Chekov scrutinized his readings. "I don't know," he admitted. "We could kill him if we just try to turn this off. I need Doctor M'Benga."

His tricorder vibrated in his hand, a silent alarm. "Farrezzi life signs approaching from the end of the chamber," he told Tra, pointing toward where the row they'd just passed through curved out of sight. "Three or four."

"I'll scout them out," Tra said. "You stay here and see

what you can do for him. But if a Farrezzi comes, get out of sight."

"Right," said Chekov, watching Tra slip off. The ensign bent down to look at the power feeds on the cryopod. Could he cut them off? Was that even a good idea? If he came all this way only to kill Yüksel—

That machine *was* killing him. Slowly, but it would do it.

Chekov pored over his readings. It looked like Yüksel was in rough shape even before they'd put him in here. There was a bruise on the back of his head, and his face was scraped. They must have knocked him out and thrown him in.

His communicator vibrated, disrupting his train of thought. Chekov pulled it off his belt and flipped it open, its volume low. *"Sir, get out of there,"* hissed Tra. *"There are four coming right at you."*

Chekov could hear them. They were talking to each other in a weird multipitched way that reminded him of Mongolian throat singers. He hoped his tricorder could offer him a safe route back to Tra's location.

"Query: not-I reason desire biped alive then?"

Chekov almost jumped out of his skin before he realized that the voice was emanating from his communicator, translating the squeaks of the approaching aliens, albeit somewhat poorly.

"Ignorance. Indifference. Nature of orders: biped transfer to capsules there."

"Query: biped weakness, lack of size? Labor unsuitability."

"Query stupidity! Order reason: not-labor!"

"Confusion. Query: statement not-I, ignorance indifference not-true? Possibility: Villach desire biped sale to Orions, inclusion in capsule complement."

"Correction: Orions bipeds. Labor sufficiency among Orion abilities."

The language left too much room for misinterpretation. However, the Farrezzi were almost certainly gathering up the cryopods to transport them somewhere, possibly under the orders of somebody named Villach, to sell them into Orion slavery. He hoped he was wrong. What kind of beings would sell their own kind into slavery?

If they took Yüksel's pod away, the exobotanist might be lost for good, and it would be Chekov's fault. He had to get the man out of the pod, and he couldn't afford to waste any time. He started using the tricorder to map the power cables feeding the pod, trying to figure out a safe way to disconnect it.

"Admission: comprehension inability. Bipeds lack of size, lack of strength—"

"*Sir.*" The ongoing translation was cut off by Tra's voice. "*What are you doing? I can see you from here, and they'll be on top of you in fifteen seconds. Get moving!*"

"No!" Chekov hissed into the communicator. "I'm getting Yüksel first. I don't want to lose him again."

"*I'm coming to get you,*" said Tra.

"No," Chekov said. "Get back to the captain and the others and tell them what's happened. I'm staying here, and I'm getting him out of here. That's an order." He flipped the communicator shut and put it on his belt.

Kneeling in front of the pod, he began examining the wires and tubes that connected to its base. It was a pity he didn't have Commander Scott's engineering prowess.

"Admission: surprise, not-I/I agreement. Reason: biped transfer not-labor. Reason: information extraction—"

A new voice cut in. "Explanation!"

With a sense of dread, Chekov glanced up from the machinery he was hiding behind. Four Farrezzi had just come around the bending row of cryopods and into sight. One of them was pointing a tentacle at him. The others began moving in his direction—faster than Chekov would have thought, given their size.

He stood up and aimed his phaser at them.

"Biped! Query: reason presence?"

He took a deep breath, bracing himself for what was to come. "Greetings."

One of them started to lunge at him, and he fired—but the Farrezzi absorbed the beam as though it was nothing at all and kept on coming. The stun setting evidently wasn't strong enough.

Before he could adjust the phaser, a Farrezzi's tentacle whipped out and knocked it from his hand. The weapon clattered to the floor, out of reach.

The other three Farrezzi drew in around him, blocking off his possible escape routes.

Ensign Chekov swallowed, thinking of something to say. There was no other choice.

"Take me to your leader."

EIGHT

They get married after the end of their senior year. It's a week before Jocelyn's twenty-second birthday. She's already agreed to go wherever he goes for medical school. They end up in Georgia, since Leonard's been accepted at Emory.

He and Jocelyn share a small Atlanta apartment, and while he studies, she works at an interstellar shipping firm downtown. She likes the work, but it's not very difficult—as opposed to his studies. His senior year was hard, but this is worse. Rare is the moment when he's not thinking about something school-related. As an undergraduate, he made a point of never doing schoolwork on Saturdays; as a medical student, he doesn't have that luxury.

He's doing something he loves, and he's with the woman he loves. How can that not be fantastic?

By the beginning of his second year, his exuberance over medical school has faded . . . as has his exuberance for Jocelyn. He loves her, but things have become strained. They don't spend as much time together, and Leonard's studies are to blame.

"You spend too much time studying," Jocelyn says to him one night as she goes to bed, leaving him sitting at the computer terminal. "Plenty of your classmates get by on less."

It's after midnight and he's been up since six—and he's heard this complaint before. "I'm not my classmates," he snaps.

It's hard for both of them, especially when Jocelyn's job demands so little of her, but somehow they make it work.

In his third year, Leonard is doing clinical work at Emory University Hospital, and that only makes things worse, now that he's working long hours. The only relief he gets is when he does four weeks of off-world experience, on the colony world of Dramia II. Leonard and Jocelyn can't talk in real time, and the messages they exchange are positive and encouraging, if a little banal. Part of Leonard wonders if he's running away from his problems, but he resolves that when he gets back to Earth, everything will be better.

Stardate 4757.9 (2034 hours)

Auxiliary control was a small, cramped room that contained a medium-sized viewscreen and one large console with three terminals. To either side of the viewscreen, two chairless consoles were set into the walls.

When McCoy entered, Uhura was sitting in the central chair. DeSalle was hunched over the control panel on the port wall, while the chair to Uhura's right was occupied by a man in an engineering coverall. McCoy recognized him as Lieutenant Singh, who was usually responsible for manning the room. With Padmanabhan, the excitable spatial physicist, standing next to Uhura, it was already rather crowded.

"Good to see you, Doctor McCoy," said Uhura, cutting off the science officer. "You should hear this, Doctor. You remember Ensign Padmanabhan, from spatial physics." She looked at the young man and gave him a nod. "Begin, please."

Padmanabhan took a deep breath and looked back and forth between Uhura and McCoy before launching into his explanation. "The distortions in this zone of space are places where another universe's laws are extending into ours, rewriting the way our universe works. The farther we travel, the more that other universe intrudes into ours."

"It's pushing into normal space," McCoy said slowly. "That's why the hits keep on getting bigger."

"Yes, sir," Padmanabhan said. "There could be distortions where our physical laws have been completely overwritten. The last one *barely* pushed into our universe, only twenty-five percent permeation."

"We think that explains the computer difficulties," began DeSalle. "Damage control says the problem is that quantum superposition ceased entirely."

"Oh, wow." Padmanabhan looked astounded for a moment, then began scribbling something down on his slate.

Even Uhura looked impressed. "The effects of that would be terrible."

"Look, I'm just a simple old country doctor—" McCoy began.

You've got that right. Out of your depth again.

"—so I'd appreciate some help."

Padmanabhan obliged. "Quantum superposition is when a system simultaneously exists in a combination of the states the system can potentially be observed to take—"

"Dial it back a little, Ensign," said Uhura. "I think that'll just confuse the doctor further."

Heaven knows we don't want you to be any more *confused. Things here are bad enough as it is.*

"Is this information even necessary?" asked DeSalle,

crossing his arms in annoyance. "I don't see how the ship's surgeon can help with the computer systems."

"The ship's surgeon is standing right here, thank you very much," said McCoy, more than a trifle annoyed. "The ship's surgeon has also discovered that there's a link between five patients in comas and the distortions in space, and he thinks that stopping personnel from dying is what he's here for."

Uhura glared at DeSalle. "Quantum superposition is when one particle occupies multiple states at the same time," she said. "For example, in our computers, an electron can have an up-spin and a down-spin at the same time."

Padmanabhan had been standing there impatiently, obviously unable to restrain himself. "Quantum computing is the basis of the duotronic revolution," he burst in. "Well, technically the marriage of quantum computing and classical computing—hence *duo*tronic, since we use both systems. In old-style computers, each bit was either on or off—one or zero—but in quantum computing each *quad* is a combination of up-spin and down-spin—not just one or zero, but every fraction in between, which lets us put the same amount of data in a smaller amount of space."

"I bet you and Spock get along famously," said McCoy drily. "But I get the idea."

"So," said DeSalle, "when we hit that last distortion, the laws of this other universe didn't let the quads exist in multiple states at the same time. The quantum waveform collapsed and was released as heat, the volume of which exploded the transtators."

McCoy couldn't help but wonder if this was Starship 101. There were a lot of things he wasn't required to know.

That's true. You could never be as good at your job as these people are.

"A universe with no quantum physics—that's amazing," whispered Padmanabhan, close to rapture. "I don't even see how that would work. I suppose there could be *different* quantum physics, ones we couldn't recognize. Can you have your people send that information to the science labs?"

"I already did, Ensign," the engineer said.

"Doctor, could this have any relation to what's affecting your patients?" asked Uhura.

McCoy thought for a moment. The word "quantum" had actually been ringing a bell. "Maybe," he said. "Lieutenant Singh, can I look something up in the library computer?"

Singh looked startled that someone had noticed his existence. "Of course, Doctor." He hit some keys and said, "All yours."

McCoy sat down on the empty chair to Uhura's left and began doing searches for "telepathy." They appeared on the main screen, replacing the sensor readings.

This is a familiar sight. He couldn't always identify which voice was speaking, but that one was definitely Jocelyn's. *You hunched over a computer, reading intently.*

What point was she trying to make? He tried to ignore her as he read an abstract of an article by a Vulcan researcher named V'v. When he realized it was primarily about touch telepathy, he moved on.

It's basically what you did for the entirety of our marriage, isn't it? Hunched over a computer and ignored me.

He'd been trying to survive medical school. Jocelyn should've been aware of that. He'd been working hard for both of them, to make sure they had a good life they could look forward to. He selected another article, the work of a Doctor Harding-Cyzewski: "The Universe Within: Neurological Quantum Effects in Telepathic Brains." Now this looked more like it. . . .

Well, I suppose you weren't always hunched over a computer terminal. Sometimes you spent the entire day and night in the ward.

He was not having this fight again, he absolutely was not. He'd had it too much in reality to play it out again in the confines of his own mind.

"Anything, Doctor?" somebody asked, disrupting him. It was DeSalle, looking impatient.

"Lieutenant, I'm sure you don't want me to miss vital details."

"Nobody wants that, Doctor," Uhura said.

He nodded and resumed his study of Harding-Cyzewski's article. When he reached its conclusion, it had confirmed his suspicions.

I suppose that's why space was so perfect for you. If you just kept on moving, you never got to know anyone well enough for it to be a problem. Who'd care if you ignored them if you just left after a year, before you could even become friends?

McCoy spun his chair around to face Uhura and the rest. "No one quite knows how telepathy works," he said, "especially human telepathy, which is too rare and too weak to study. But one theory is that it's a form of quantum entanglement. The theory is that once two particles become linked, they stay linked, no matter the distance between them. Particles in my brain are linked with some in yours, and information can pass between them instantaneously. Some species can access this better than others."

"If we've hit a universe with no quantum physics," said Uhura, "then it would affect our telepathic crew."

"Yes," said McCoy grimly.

"This is amazing," Padmanabhan muttered, frantically making more notes on his slate.

Uhura asked, "What can we do about this?"

"You say the other universe is pushing into ours?" asked McCoy.

Padmanabhan nodded.

"Well, when most people get pushed around, they push back."

You pushed back at me, all right. Great way to handle a marriage.

No, that wasn't how it had been.

"Push back?" asked Padmanabhan.

"The warp engines can generate a bubble of subspace." Uhura was suddenly excited. "But can they generate a bubble of real space?"

Everyone looked to DeSalle. "It'll be difficult," he said, looking thoughtful, "but it should be possible. I might need Ensign Padmanabhan's help with checking the math."

"Hop to it, gentlemen," Uhura ordered. Padmanabhan joined DeSalle at his console, data slate at the ready. She looked up at McCoy, a smile on that beautiful face of hers. "Thank you, Doctor."

The doctor returned the smile. "All in a day's work. Now if you'll excuse me, I need to get back to my patients."

Take that, Jocelyn.

Captain Kirk and the landing party hung back, watching the Farrezzi moving the cryopods into the block-like structure. Kirk hated to just watch, but he had his reasons.

The first, he wanted a better idea of what was going on. The other reason was the Prime Directive.

If slavery was a normal Farrezzi practice, Kirk had no right to put a stop to it. The Farrezzi were trading with the Orions; perhaps they picked up the practice from them. In that case, Kirk could act, and argue that he was restoring the Farrezzi to their norm.

Or he could just take action and deal with the consequences later.

"Captain," said Giotto, being sure to keep his voice down. Absorbed in their task, the Farrezzi slavers had not yet noticed their hiding place. "I recommend we reunite with Tra and Chekov, get back to the surface, and contact the *Hofstadter*. We can't handle this ourselves."

"I'm tempted—" began Kirk, but he was interrupted by footsteps from behind. Both of them looked around together to see Y Tra coming up in a hurry. He was alone.

"Where's Chekov?" Giotto barked.

Tra looked uneasy. "The Farrezzi got him. I'm surprised you haven't seen him yet. He was kicking up quite a—"

"Captain." Rawlins pointed at the moving Farrezzi. Three Farrezzi were pushing a cryopod with a human into the blocky structure. Kirk couldn't quite tell, but the figure could have been Yüksel. A fourth alien was coming up behind them, a human man in a gold uniform shirt squirming in its limbs. Even from this distance, Kirk could tell that it was Ensign Chekov. As he was dragged along, Chekov occasionally yelped in pain.

"Order: end of resistance, alternative: pain! Long agonizing pain!" the Farrezzi holding Chekov said. It was dragging the ensign up to the Farrezzi who had been issuing orders. "Discovery: biped here."

"Confusion, annoyance. Query: biped intrusion imminent?" The Farrezzi did not have to change direction to focus on Chekov. The captain found its radial symmetry disconcerting. "Order: declaration of name, purpose of presence?"

"Aah! I am . . . a tourist. I came here . . . to visit your beautiful planet," Chekov said, pain evident in his voice. "I heard you had nice beaches, but there was no one there. You can't go swimming without a lifeguard, so I was looking for someone when I found you. Can you tell me why nobody lives on the surface anymore? And where I can buy sunscreen?"

"Query: clarification, not-I presence alone?"

"Of course! I always travel on my own. It's much more fun that way."

"Query: knowledge of previous biped?"

"I never saw him before in my life! I don't even like other . . . bipeds. Why do you think I came to the planet of the octopi?"

"Order: statement of name!"

Chekov hesitated for a moment, before finally gasping out, "Cyrano Jones."

Kirk had to smile at that.

"Query: purpose of presence? Order: truth!"

"As I said, I like nice beaches. Swimming is my favorite pastime, and I—aah!"

"Feeling of disbelief. Confusion, annoyance. Anger! Order: biped cooperation! Alternative: fatality!" The Farrezzi who was interrogating Chekov motioned to the one holding the ensign. They set off for the enormous structure that dominated the cavern. "Order: task completion high-speed. After merchandise transfer there, start of takeoff procedure now."

They were running out of time. If they didn't act, they'd lose Chekov *and* Yüksel. What was the first-contact protocol when the first members of a new species encountered were criminals?

The captain asked Rawlins for his tricorder. "Commander, make sure you keep everybody safe." There was confusion on Giotto's face, quickly followed by a sequence of astonishment, shock, then finally determination.

"Sir, this is crazy! I won't let you—"

"You will. Take them back to the shuttle and contact Spock." Before anybody could try to stop him, Kirk was speeding along the row of cryopods.

As he ran, the captain considered his dilemma. If they wanted to get Chekov and Yüksel back unharmed, he needed to act. He'd never been able to sit back and watch while others risked their lives. This was how he'd been raised by his parents, how he'd been trained at the Academy, and—most important—how he defined himself.

The rest of the Farrezzi had disappeared inside. Kirk ran across the open space between the last row of pods and the building. He put his back to the wall and began skirting along toward the door. He reached the open door and peered around the edge. What he saw made him wonder if he *should* wait until the *Enterprise* was here. The structure was a hangar, a large one, at least a hundred meters deep. Filling the vast space were either simple aircraft or something more complex.

Two of the larger craft had big bellies and were in the process of being loaded with pods. The other three were smaller and looked like they'd be nimble in the atmosphere. They all shared a common design. The central fuselage was short and narrow for the three smaller ones,

long and wide for the bigger two. Five armlike booms
jutted out, connecting to ventral protrusions that Kirk assumed were the engines. From the engines, landing gear
extended that supported the craft. As Kirk studied the
ships, it struck him that there was a similarity to those of
Orion raiders.

Kirk had to wait for an opportunity to get past the Farrezzi who were loading pods onto the two big ships. There
was no trace of his men, no clue as to which of the craft
Chekov and Yüksel had been taken on.

He wasn't letting them fall into the hands of slavers.

Today hadn't been a good day for Salvatore Giotto. He
couldn't just leave without attempting to get the captain and
the others back. Orders be damned. Only Tra had combat
experience. Their chances would improve if he took Tra
with him, but Giotto could not leave Seven Deers and Rawlins to fend for themselves.

"Listen up." Giotto had trouble keeping his voice even.
"Tra, you take Rawlins and Seven Deers back to the *Columbus*. Move quickly. No matter what happens, get them
to safety."

"You can't be serious!" Seven Deers said. "Commander,"
she added after a pause. "They'll catch you, too."

"You'll do as ordered. Once you're in the shuttle, seal
the hatch and take off. Hail Commander Spock, hail the
Enterprise, hail whoever you can, just get help."

Giotto nodded at Tra and headed off after the captain.

He rushed toward the big metal structure that the
aliens had been dragging the pods into. Giotto peeked
through the open door, careful not to show too much of
himself. There were various craft and a number of aliens

moving pods and other devices. Ceiling-mounted lights bathed everything in an intense orange glow, leaving few shadows to hide in. Taking everything in, Giotto picked a route, staying close to the wall on the left, where a stack of small containers afforded him a spot to assess the situation.

Where was the captain? He must be in here. Hopefully he hadn't already been caught.

It seemed reasonable to assume the captain might be hiding. Giotto performed a quick visual search of the likely spots. Nothing near the two big craft. Nothing on the other side of the hangar, where some shuttle-sized vehicles stood. From the corner of his eye, he spotted a flash of gold in front of the closest craft's landing legs. Giotto turned his head to get a better look. It was the captain, but Giotto had no idea how to get to him unnoticed.

The captain was apparently looking for a way into the transport. He was now hiding behind the landing leg, doing his best not to expose himself to the continuous line of aliens moving pods into the ship. However, if Giotto had seen him, it was likely some of the aliens would, too. Giotto breathed deeply, preparing for a sprint across the hangar floor. What he needed was an opportunity, something that drew the aliens' attention away from his position.

Three Farrezzi pushed a large cart loaded with pods over to the ramp and into the gaping hole in its belly, only to reappear moments later with an empty cart. They were strange-looking beings, with their gangly legs like elephants' trunks that constantly rolled up and extended, a motion that made him dizzy. Once they left, Giotto expected more to follow, but none came. This was his opportunity.

He'd barely crossed half the distance when squeaks and screams assaulted him from all directions. His heart stopped for a moment. Had he been discovered? Momentum carried him to the transport, where his sudden appearance gave the captain a nasty shock.

"Commander—" Kirk began, but stopped when all hell broke loose on the other side of the hangar. Giotto peeked past the landing leg, which was wide enough to give both of them cover.

Giotto expected a barrage of weapons fire to hit them. What were the slave traders doing? He couldn't see much from where they were, but the traders weren't coming over. They had stopped and now were talking to each other in hurried bursts of high-pitched squeaks, their attention focused on the door.

Hell, Giotto didn't like not knowing what was going on. A look at the captain told him Kirk felt the same. "Sir," Giotto whispered, "we should get out of here. They'll spot us soon."

Kirk shook his head. "I'm not leaving, Commander. And I remember ordering you to leave."

"Crew, captain, ship. The crew is safe. My next duty is to you, even if that means disobeying your orders, sir."

"I don't like it, mister."

"The situation calls for it." Giotto had to divide his attention between Kirk and the Farrezzi rushing toward the door. They weren't coming for them. He faced the captain grimly. "I had to, sir."

"This isn't over." There was a hardness to Kirk's voice. "Let's free our crewmen."

"Aye, sir." Giotto changed the subject. "What do you think got them all riled up?"

"It better not be anything to do with the rest of the team," said Kirk.

■ ■ ■ ■

On his way back from auxiliary control, McCoy found he was pleased with himself. It was his idea to push back at this other universe.

One problem solved—well, almost—one still left. His five patients were still in comas, and he hadn't gotten any closer to finding a solution. Nothing he tried caused more than a blip on the monitor, before every reading resumed its descent. If what was happening to the ship was related to their comas, maybe the engineers' solution would work.

Not likely. Between Padmanabhan's theory about this other universe's nonquantum nature and the paper by Harding-Cyzewski about telepathy as a form of quantum entanglement, perhaps he himself could find a solution.

"Deck Five," McCoy told the turbolift. The turbolift doors swished open to reveal a dark corridor. The lights were dimmed in this section, either because of a malfunction or to conserve power. The corridors were a mess, with chunks of support material pushed to one side. The bulkheads were scorched.

The doctor made his way to Sulu's quarters; the acting captain had been discharged there. Recalling what Chapel had said earlier about Specialist Ryerson, McCoy had come to visit. The mind was important to the healing process, after all. McCoy found him at his desk, collecting data slates in front of him. "Feeling better already, Mister Sulu?"

"I think so." Of the multitude of injuries the lieutenant had suffered, the most serious was the trauma to his head. Sulu would have to stay off duty for a while and give his body time to heal.

"I need to get back on duty, Doctor," the lieutenant said. "We're still in danger."

"The best thing you can do is rest." McCoy gestured toward Sulu's bed. "Or *you'll* be in danger." He was determined not to be talked into letting a barely healed man back on duty.

"I'm useless in here. All I do is think. Second-guess myself. Try to come up with solutions." Sulu clutched the desk and stood.

"Your reaction is natural," said McCoy. "But you need to give yourself time."

"But there's no—"

"Don't make me order you. Do yourself a favor and rest."

Sulu wasn't happy, but he got the point.

The quarters closest to sickbay had been turned into recovery rooms for over twenty patients, whose injuries were no longer life-threatening but still grave enough to require attention. The doors of these quarters all sported adhesive labels with the names of the patients inside. McCoy stopped at the first door he passed: GOLASKI-LAWRENCE, ISBELL and HAINES, JANA. When it opened, the doctor stepped inside. The younger woman was sleeping, but Ensign Haines—a woman in her early forties—was awake.

"House call," he said, holding up his medkit. "Everything okay?"

Haines nodded, then uttered a strained, "Yes." She was the one who had suffered a collapsed lung and some fractured ribs. Her grimace belied her words.

"You shouldn't be in pain," McCoy said.

He checked her chart. "This says you're maxed on painkillers."

"I know," she said, wincing.

McCoy scanned her. Nothing. "Where's the pain?"

"Everywhere. It's like a dull ache throughout my entire body, but it just keeps on building. I can't ignore it."

"Physically, there's nothing wrong with you." He flipped off the tricorder. "I can give you another dose of painkillers."

"Maybe I'm just imagining it." Haines lowered her gaze, as if she was ashamed of herself.

"Let's do something about it." He smiled his best smile. "Have you been sleeping?"

"No," she said. "It hurts too much."

"I can help you sleep. Would that be good?"

"I think so."

McCoy filled a hypo with a sedative. "You can rest easy now, Ensign. Sleep, and forget your pain." A hiss, then the hypo had emptied into her bloodstream. Within seconds, her eyes closed, and her regular breathing told him she'd fallen asleep.

"If only you could solve your own problems like that," he heard a familiar voice say, startling him. "You don't have a magic cure-all for this one."

Raising his head, he spotted somebody standing on the other side of the bed.

It was Jocelyn, standing right there in front of him, looking just the way he remembered her.

Another shot caused sparks to fly off the cryopod just ahead of them. Seven Deers thought she felt them on her cheeks. Tra had succeeded in taking them almost to the elevator. Before they could reach it, a host of armed Farrezzi had turned up, chasing after them, firing powerful projective weapons. With his training, Tra was faster than

Seven Deers and Rawlins, but he adjusted his pace to theirs. They were sticking close to the pods to reduce the chance of being hit. But the slavers kept on firing, with no regard for the lives of the sleepers.

There were ten Farrezzi closing in on them. On the elevator platform they'd be sitting ducks until they'd gone through the hole in the ceiling.

"Watch out," Tra said, "there's two of them on the left." Seven Deers strained to see in the gloom, only briefly improved by phaser fire and bursts from the Farrezzi weapons. Two attackers were trying to sneak up on them.

"I see 'em," Seven Deers said. Of her two shots, only one hit its mark, making the leftmost Farrezzi stumble and then collapse. The other continued unaffected—until Tra fired.

"Got 'im," Tra barked. The Farrezzi staggered, dropping its weapon.

"Onto the platform!" Tra shouted.

Seven Deers wasted no time and raced to the elevator. Rawlins followed right after her. Tra held off the Farrezzi with wide sweeps of phaser fire. Once on the platform, Seven Deers turned to see they were all still approaching.

Rawlins was close enough to grab the elevator's metal cage, but then he screamed and let go. He slid down, clutching his right shoulder. Blood seeped out between his fingers. The ensign knelt down and pulled him onto the platform. There was no time to examine his wound. From Rawlins's contorted expression, it must be pretty bad.

Five of their attackers were still standing. Hiding behind the cryopods, they were firing rapid shots at the Starfleet party.

"Get on!" Seven Deers yelled, straining to make herself

heard. Tra stayed where he was, as if he hadn't heard her. "Crewman, get the hell on the platform!"

"You need somebody to draw their fire!" Tra shouted back. "I'll keep them distracted."

"Don't be dumb! Rawlins has been hit. That's an order!"

His phaser in his left hand, Tra stretched out his right arm behind him to feel for the cage. He took another Farrezzi down. The return fire showered the elevator in sparks. Seven Deers felt something hot on her forehead, a burning sensation that wouldn't go away. She put her hand to it but yanked it away when the pain got worse. Her fingers glistened.

The air was smoky from the Farrezzi weapons. But Tra was on the platform.

"Hold on," Seven Deers said, getting up from her crouch to crank the lever upward. Her head began to swim, and a wave of nausea engulfed her. The elevator began to move, rumbling strangely. It hadn't made that noise before. Unconcerned about the weapons fire, Seven Deers slumped to the floor of the cage and began to consider problems that could have caused the irregularity. It was hard to focus.

All she wanted to do was close her eyes and sleep.

She closed her eyes.

NINE

The next year of Leonard's medical studies starts well. But things gradually deteriorate as his work begins to overwhelm him again. He spends less and less time studying in the apartment, doing his work in Bradley's, a café near campus. This reduces the friction between Jocelyn and him, but whole days go by where the only time he spends with Jocelyn is when they're asleep.

As his clinical work wraps up, Leonard begins planning for his internship. "We'll have more time together, then," Jocelyn says one evening when he comes home early. He falls straight into bed, clothes still on, worn out from a grueling day. She sits on the edge of the bed—it's the first conversation they've had all week.

"I don't know about that," Leonard says. "I've been talking to Armstrong, and when he did his, he—"

Jocelyn interrupts him. She wants a baby. Having a child will bring them closer together. Lying there on the bed, holding her, Leonard can't think of anything he wants more. They begin trying the day he graduates from medical school.

After four months, they succeed. Leonard isn't able to spend as much time with Jocelyn as he'd like to—he's hip-deep in his internship—but they're spending more time together than they have before, and things *are* better.

Joanna is born as Leonard's internship ends, and she's wonderful, beautiful, gorgeous. Leonard is absolutely in love with her. He and Jocelyn have decided that it's best for him to wait a year before beginning his residency so that he can help with the baby. He'll spend the year working part-time at a local hospital. It'll make things better.

Although Leonard loves every moment he gets to spend with Joanna, what he realizes is that he and Jocelyn have changed over the past seven years. Medical school has made him more serious, more driven than he was as an under-graduate. Jocelyn is less tolerant of Leonard's crabbiness.

Leonard spends the year pining for the job he should be doing. He wants to be a doctor, he wants to make people better. He's seldom at home helping with Joanna, but often at Bradley's, hanging out with the Emory medical students.

That is where he meets Nancy.

Stardate 4757.9 (2105 hours)

The Farrezzi who had been loading carts were gone. Kirk nodded at Giotto. "Time to go, Commander."

The gray-haired man grimaced. "You're sure we'll find our men in there? Pardon me, sir, but I'm not."

"Neither am I," Kirk replied, "but this is our only chance. We'll board that ship and look in every storage closet if we have to. If Yüksel and Chekov are there, we'll free them. If not, we'll do everything we can to stop those slavers." The captain wasn't sure when he'd decided on this action, but if it was a violation of the Prime Directive, he'd sort it out later.

He had lives to save—both his own men's and innocent aliens'.

Giotto relented. "Aye, sir."

The captain was aware of how his crew saw him, but he didn't think of himself as reckless. He did what needed to be done, even when that meant putting himself in danger. It rankled him that after serving under him for a couple of years, Giotto hadn't accepted this about his captain.

The pair waited a few seconds to make absolutely sure that no Farrezzi was going to get in their way. The ramp into the nearest spaceship was twenty meters away. Shaded from the hangar's bright orange light by the ship, their uniforms didn't stand out. Phaser in hand, Kirk sped up the ramp. He tried not to think about what would happen if they were caught.

The ramp led into a cargo bay as spacious as the *Enterprise*'s. It was circular, with a giant column in the center connecting it to the upper levels of the ship. Glancing around, Kirk was surprised to find only a few pods. He'd seen dozens moved inside. It wasn't a storage area, then.

There were five doors on the central column that he could see. "We have to split up."

Giotto's expression clearly showed how he felt. "Be careful, sir. I don't want to tell Mister Spock that I let you go to your death."

"I don't plan on dying any time soon."

"Few people do." Giotto looked around the bay. "There's one open door—you take that, sir, and I'll cover you."

"Good luck. Let me know when you find them." Kirk headed toward the open doorway.

"You too, sir."

McCoy had no idea what was wrong with him, but it was getting worse. Now he was seeing people. If this had been happening to anyone else, he'd have had them relieved of duty.

"Ah, but you'd like to think you're too essential for that, wouldn't you?" Jocelyn followed him as he headed back to sickbay. He needed to look at that research on quantum entanglement and telepathy, and at Ensign Padmanabhan's data packet.

Jocelyn looked exactly the way she had all those years ago, on the last day of the divorce proceedings. A head shorter than McCoy, she had long, dark brown hair tied in a ponytail. The simple truth was, she looked great. He, on the other hand, looked twelve years older. He wondered what she thought of him.

No, that was nonsense! Jocelyn didn't think anything of him, she was a hallucination, damn it!

McCoy headed straight to his office. Odhiambo looked at him as he passed her, but said nothing. Of Chapel, there was no sign. Good—maybe she'd gone back to her quarters to rest. He sat down at his desk and called up the Harding-Cyzewski paper. He was going to read this, and he was going to save those espers—

"Only *you* can do it, that's right," said Jocelyn. "That's the way it's always been. That's the argument you've always used for shutting out everyone around you."

No, it was true! He was the only person who could save the patients who were lying in sickbay, unhurt yet dying. He wasn't going to let her—

"If you'd just admit the truth about why you're here, then you could admit that you can't save them," Jocelyn continued. "You're not here because this is what you want to do. You're not even here because you're good at it. You're here because it lets you get away from me. And what kind of reason is that?"

She had him there. So many people signed up for star-ship duty because it was their calling. Look at Jim—that man was at home on the *Enterprise* bridge. But for McCoy, it was because he didn't fit in anywhere else. That was why he'd moved from assignment to assignment. This ship was beginning to feel like a place where he could stay . . . so of course it frightened him.

"Never anywhere long enough for everyone to find out that you're a fraud. You stayed here too long," she said. "Your third year here's just ended—you haven't been in one place this long since we met. And now it's done you in. You should have kept running, Leonard."

If he hadn't known that there was no way for Jocelyn to be in the depths of deep space, he'd have sworn she was here. A light fixture on the wall shined straight onto her, giving her complexion a weird, otherworldly look, and she had a shadow.

She wasn't there, and McCoy knew that. He wouldn't let himself think she was really there. His ex-wife was a fig-ment of his overstressed mind. If he ignored her, she'd fade away. He was going to read this article, he was going to fig-ure out what was wrong with those espers, he was going—

"The problem with you, Leonard, is that you didn't choose to be here." Jocelyn crossed the rest of the room, sit-ting down on the edge of McCoy's desk.

Hell, he could even smell her. She'd never been one for perfume, but when you live with someone long enough, you remember how they smell. His reaction was curious: a mixture of comfort and anger. If only they'd been able to make it work. If only *he'd* been able to make it work. Then he wouldn't be here right now, trying to solve this blasted—

"You merely chose to get away from me. That's all you've ever chosen."

McCoy switched off his monitor with an angry jab. *Physician, heal thyself* was the old saw. If he couldn't figure out why he was hearing voices and seeing people, then there was no hope for his patients.

He left his office, Jocelyn trailing behind him, peppering him with questions. How did he expect to stop his patients from dying if he wasn't able to do anything about it? Determined to get to the bottom of this, he fetched a psycho-tricorder from the equipment cabinet. The device was designed to gather relevant neurological and physiological data. It could tell him if there was anything wrong with him.

It could tell him if he was going insane.

After a few seconds, the tricorder reported heightened brain activity, but nothing else. A good CMO would relieve himself of duty. It was the right thing to do.

"Then do it!" Jocelyn said. "Do the right thing for once in your life!"

Chapel and the others then would have to face this crisis alone. No. The *Enterprise* needed a doctor. A neural suppressant was called for, something to clamp down on heightened brain activity. Jocelyn needed to disappear.

If there'd been another way, he'd gladly have done it. Time was running out. McCoy loaded up the hypospray and injected himself.

"Drugged up," said Jocelyn. "Oh, very professional for a medical practitioner. You'll be in top form with your brain slowed down."

"Shut up, Jocelyn." Back in his office, McCoy reopened the article and began reading, waiting for Jocelyn to add another biting comment.

Nothing came. When he looked up, there was no trace of her anywhere. He gave a relieved sigh. It had worked.

McCoy continued his reading, but to his dismay he quickly found it was hard going. Not because of voices, but because his body could no longer ignore the effects of exhaustion. Every sentence posed more of a struggle than the one before it. He'd used too much neural suppressant, McCoy realized with dismay.

Pulling himself together, McCoy was able to hold on until he finished reading. He decided he should rest his eyes for just a moment. That would be fine, wouldn't it? He'd earned it.

The darkness was so wonderful, and within seconds McCoy could feel himself relaxing.

He didn't open his eyes again.

With the shuttle safe inside the warehouse, Spock was using its computer to assess all the data they had collected. After changing its course repeatedly, the storm was now again headed for the city district the *Hofstadter* had landed in, more powerful than ever. It behaved like no known weather system. Its course was erratic, its power spikes unpredictable, and its speed highly improbable. Spock had no theory that would explain all of the storm's unusual features.

The Vulcan had begun reading Ensign Saloniemi's report on alien texts when the computer announced an incoming signal. Crewman Tra sounded exhausted and tense. *"Commander Spock,"* he said, *"Ensign Chekov's also been taken by the Farrezzi. The captain and Commander Giotto followed him, hoping to free him and Yüksel. We were ordered to leave. But* Columbus *is being followed."*

Spock limited himself to asking, "How many are there, and how close are they?"

"*Numbers unknown. We're faster, sir. As we took off, we were hit before we raised our shields. Our phaser emitter is damaged. They're out of range right now, but we can't fight back.*"

The presence of other craft changed Spock's priorities. "Are there any injuries?"

"*Rawlins has been shot, and Seven Deers is unconscious. They need immediate treatment.*"

"What is your shield status?" asked Spock.

"*Fully functional, there was no external damage. They just got the phasers.*" Tra sighed. "*Lucky shot.*"

"The *Hofstadter*'s shields are damaged. It is unable to fly through the storm," Spock said. His scans had showed that the interference pattern was growing worse. "How long will you need to reach our location?"

"*If I go suborbital, about half an hour.*"

"Acceptable. Crewman, I will need every piece of information you and your team were able to gather about the natives. Send us the data, complete with your latest tricorder logs."

"*Aye, sir,*" Tra said.

"*Hofstadter* out."

While Spock had been entertaining the theory that the population had not disappeared, as that would have been a logistical impossibility, he had not expected the other team's discoveries to be so incident-ridden.

Spock began powering up the shuttle as he awaited the arrival of the data packet. Once he had read it, he flipped open his communicator. Some of the landing party were exploring the warehouse.

"Spock to *Hofstadter* party. Return to the shuttle immediately."

M'Benga was back first. "What's going on, Commander?"

"Doctor," Spock said, "the *Columbus* is incoming, carrying two casualties."

"Who?" M'Benga asked.

"The wounded are Lieutenant Rawlins and Ensign Seven Deers. Captain Kirk, Commander Giotto, and Ensign Chekov are missing, in addition to Specialist Yüksel."

M'Benga's voice was shocked. "How did this—"

"I will send further details to your tricorder." He sent the data packet to the rest, who had come aboard while Spock and M'Benga had been conversing—with one exception. "Where is Mister Scott?"

"He said he had something to finish up," said Kologwe. "He's working on the shields."

"Continue the preflight checklist, Lieutenant." Spock stood up.

The Vulcan stepped out from the brightness of the shuttle into the relative dark of the warehouse. He could hear the whistling winds outside, much louder than only a few minutes before. The thunder—and, by extension, the lightning—seemed to have momentarily abated.

Scott was busy working on top of the *Hofstadter*. Spock could hear the buzzing of a hyperspanner. The engineer yelled down, "Give me just a minute, Mister Spock."

Spock stepped up onto the warp nacelle of the *Hofstadter*. The engineer's hands were in an opened access panel. "The *Columbus* is en route with wounded," Spock said. "A combat situation may be imminent. Is the *Hofstadter* capable of flight?"

"I've fixed the damage from the lightning strike," Scott replied, "but I want to adjust the shields. You canna fly up through the storm if the shields dinna work."

"The shield malfunction is due to external interference," Spock pointed out. "Can you remedy it?"

"Aye," he said. "Give me a few minutes. We canna help the *Columbus* if we're torn apart."

Spock considered. "Continue your work."

The engineer lifted his head and smiled. "I'll do my best, sir."

"The data from the *Columbus* indicates that its shields are unaffected," said Spock. "This suggests that the *Hofstadter* is more susceptible." Spock knew some of the differences between the G-class *Hofstadter* and F-class *Columbus*, but not as thoroughly as Scott.

Scott paused his work for a moment. "The *Hofstadter* is a later model," he said, thinking aloud, "and the power conduits that feed the shields are larger—leaving less room for insulation. The interference *could* be through . . . That narrows it down, Mister Spock." The engineer resumed his work.

Spock returned to the pilot's seat to examine the report from the *Columbus*. It was not unheard of for a planetary population to go to great lengths to save itself, including mass migration and climate modification. It was an unorthodox solution to place the entire population in hypersleep. It appeared to have worked. The atmosphere of Farrezz was near normal levels for the life-forms the *Columbus* team had found.

The shuttle was ready for takeoff. However, Scott continued to work on the shields. Spock conferred with Jaeger about the storm system. If the *Columbus* was still being followed, the *Hofstadter* crew would need to leave this location as quickly as possible, and he did not want to incur any more damage from the storm.

Spock's discussion was interrupted.

"Hofstadter, *this is the* Columbus. *We're five minutes out. Can you ready the door?*"

"*Hofstadter* receiving," answered Spock. "Which door?"

"*The southwestern, sir.*"

"We will be ready."

Spock closed the channel and called for Kologwe to join him. They headed back into the warehouse. Mister Scott was no longer on top of the *Hofstadter*, but bent over a nacelle, adjusting his hyperspanner.

"What's going on, sir?" asked Scott. "Are they all right?"

"We will know in a moment."

Spock quickly strode across the warehouse. He noted Lieutenant Kologwe was carrying a phaser rifle. "A logical precaution, Lieutenant." Spock activated the door's opening mechanism, and Kologwe pointed the phaser rifle through the growing aperture. The wind raged through the opening, carrying gusts of rain, clumps of dirt, and bits of debris. When the door had retreated fully, Spock was barely able to remain standing.

The noise made it impossible to be heard. Spock resorted to flashlight signals. The *Columbus* was hovering half a meter above the ground, moving slowly forward, when a strong gust of wind hit its side and threw it off its course.

It struck the building wall at a height of four meters with a crash that managed to permeate the howling wind. The considerable force shattered part of the wall, and pieces of various sizes began to fall.

Broken pieces blocked all their escape routes. Spock and Kologwe had nowhere to go.

Scotty was watching as Spock guided the *Columbus* into the warehouse. When the shuttle slammed into the wall, he jumped into action. He grabbed his phaser in one quick flick, set it to a wide spread, and fired.

The beam disintegrated most of the debris. Spock's Vulcan reflexes did the rest, pulling himself and Kologwe to safety. The engineer looked up to see that the *Columbus* was moving forward again. When it had cleared the entrance, Spock immediately closed the door, keeping wind and rain out.

Scotty rushed over to the *Columbus*, M'Benga right behind him with his medkit. The others quickly joined them. What had gone wrong?

When the hatch finally opened the doctor rushed in. Scotty hoped Rawlins and Seven Deers were okay. He knew Seven Deers had a family on Alpha Centauri. Her two children were adults, but they still shouldn't have to lose a parent.

Scotty moved off to the aft section of the *Columbus* to see if there'd been any damage from hitting the side of the warehouse. As he began to examine the shuttle, a loud crack made him jump and drop his phaser. It sounded like thunder mixed with an explosion. Had that been caused by the storm? What was it? Scotty looked around but saw little outside the beam of his flashlight.

Something small dropped on his head, and he looked up. A cloud of dust engulfed him, and his eyes began to burn. More small bits pelted him, in the face, on the forehead, chest, shoulders. Squinting, he pointed his flashlight at the ceiling above him, just in time to see a large piece of it race down.

His legs moved of their own accord, but then his world collapsed, causing waves of pain to smother everything. Blackness was the only thing his eyes registered before giving up.

So far, Giotto hadn't encountered any hostiles, but he knew his luck wouldn't hold. Even if the Farrezzi had no sensors to tell them that intruders were aboard, he'd cross paths with them sooner or later. The commander had his doubts that they would ever find Yüksel. The botanist had been gone too long. There was a slim chance they might locate Chekov—a very slim one.

Sweat covered his brow, caused by the humidity. The air was warm and smelled like the rich soil of a garden. Distracting, but nothing he couldn't cope with.

The floor suddenly shuddered. In the distance, Giotto could hear sounds. He sprinted to the nearest alcove and shoved himself in. Judging by the sockets and cables, its purpose was power distribution.

The sounds in the distance were barely audible. They became fainter, then disappeared altogether. Giotto waited another minute, just to make sure that they'd gone. Was it really possible that neither he nor the captain hadn't been spotted? If this had been the *Enterprise*, and intruders had found their way aboard, they wouldn't have remained undetected for long. It was possible, however, that this ship was not a military one. Giotto's scan of the exterior had not shown any weapon emplacements.

So far, he'd found nothing that would help him in his search for two missing crewmen. He'd seen no brig, no holding cells, no torture chamber. He'd inspected every side corridor, every alcove, along the way. Nothing.

His instincts told him he was going in one big circle. He had good orientation skills, normally not needing a tricorder or a map, but the slaver ship was turning out to be a challenge. It all looked the same, just one big tunnel, like the ones they'd seen below the city.

Giotto checked his tricorder, which had been automatically mapping the interior. The map told him he was *not* going in circles, but it was of little help otherwise. He remembered what Chekov had said about the unique physiology of the aliens. No front or back, so it stood to reason that their vehicles wouldn't have them either. Perhaps it was like the *Enterprise*'s saucer section, where everything important—bridge, sickbay, life support systems—was at the center. Common sense, right? At least, it was to humanoids. He was about to find out if the same was true for five-limbed squidthings.

"Now lift them up, slowly," Spock said.

The weight of the large block that had fallen from the ceiling and narrowly missed the *Columbus* was considerable, so he had ordered it cut in two by precisely modulated phaser beams, to minimize the danger to Engineer Scott, who lay trapped beneath it.

If the Farrezzi pursuing the *Columbus* had caught up with them, there would have been more than one strike. Could it have been lightning?

Mister Scott had been the only one hit by the ceiling piece. Spock regretted that his conversation with Tra had distracted him from noticing the ceiling fragment until it was too late. The lower half of Scott's body was covered by the larger chunk, making for an unsettling sight. It was fortunate that he had been standing close to the port nacelle's aft end, as it kept the concrete from crushing his legs completely.

The engineer required immediate attention. Doctor M'Benga had interrupted the treatment of his other two patients, who had been moved to the *Hofstadter*. Spock had given the order to remove the concrete block. After cutting it in two, Lieutenant Kologwe and Petty Officer Emalra'ehn had attached all the antigrav devices from both shuttles to the pieces and removed them carefully as Spock and the doctor supervised. At a safe distance, they disengaged the antigravs, sending the block of concrete to the floor with a resonating thud.

"What now, sir?" Lieutenant Jaeger asked, standing beside Spock, wide-eyed. "He needs a sickbay."

"I have every confidence in Doctor M'Benga's abilities." Spock's statement was not wholly true. Having Doctor McCoy present would have increased Scott's odds of survival by four full percentage points.

"I wish I had your confidence, sir," Jaeger said. For a moment, he gave the appearance of wanting to say something further but stopped himself. The geophysicist looked up at the ceiling. Through the gaping hole, they could see dark clouds lit by frequent flashes of lightning. "The rain is getting stronger."

A steady stream of drops had been pelting Spock's face, but their intensity and frequency was increasing.

"Ow!" Jaeger's hand shot up, covering the top of his head.

"As is its solidity." The rain had turned to hail. Spock stepped backward, out of reach.

"It's cooled down surprisingly fast," said Jaeger. "I don't think this place is going to be safe much longer, the way this storm is going."

"I agree," Spock said. "Tell the doctor we have to move Mister Scott."

Jaeger stepped over to the *Columbus*. Spock knew that with the wind gaining more strength, they would soon be caught in a deadly trap. The structure had been weakened by the ruptured roof and would not be able to withstand the onslaught.

Spock had to perform a quick reassignment of the shuttle crews. "Lieutenant Kologwe."

"Aye, sir?" The security officer stopped and turned, her hair and face covered in a wet sheen.

"Conditions are expected to deteriorate, so we must be prepared to leave in a hurry. You have the necessary experience; I need you to pilot the *Columbus*. Be prepared for protracted turbulence once we take to the air."

"Aye, sir," she said somberly. Spock knew very few humans who had such a tight grip on their emotions. He told Kologwe to take Ensign Saloniemi with her. M'Benga had moved Lieutenant Rawlins to the *Hofstadter* where he could keep an eye on him.

Spock returned to the *Hofstadter*, where Saloniemi was gathering his materials. The Vulcan sent out a highly focused signal to the approximate location of the *Enterprise*. With no contact for nearly twelve hours, it was difficult to say where the ship would be, but he was confident in his selection. However, he received no indication that the signal had arrived at its destination.

The increasing interference had affected both their

sensors and their shields. If there were distortions in subspace impairing the *Enterprise*'s journey, it was possible that there were similar ones much closer to Mu Arigulon. Mister Scott had isolated the interference pattern to create his countermeasure. Spock ordered the computer to map the interference, noting the levels.

"Fascinating."

"Sir?" asked Saloniemi, leaning over the back of the navigator's seat, tricorder in his hand.

"The computer has determined that the subspace distortion is strongest near the 'projector' at the hub of the reactor network," Spock replied. "This explains our inability to obtain precise scans."

"Is it creating a warp field?" asked Saloniemi.

"Possibly. The Farrezzi were clearly in the early stages of warp flight."

"But if there's a distortion reaching into deep space, they must be advanced." Saloniemi shook his head. "That doesn't fit."

"It is not a matter of advancement so much as sheer power," said Spock. "There were numerous reactors in the Farrezzi network, the equivalent of five or six times the *Enterprise*'s power. If we are to end the distortions, the logical conclusion is that we must deactivate the ractors."

The rain had returned and was increasing in strength. The shuttle's sensors told him that the wind had increased. Just then, a sensor blip caught his attention: three moving objects had been detected.

When they opened fire on the warehouse, it became clear what had caused the earlier explosion.

■ ■ ■ ■

Ahead of Kirk, the tunnel took a sharp turn to the right. He slowed down to listen. Nothing. That was a relief. He'd hate to run into—

Two Farrezzi stood near the next junction, roughly twenty meters ahead. They were large, impressive beings. Kirk stopped as soon as he spotted them, but it was too late. With their five protruding eyes, it was impossible for them *not* to have seen him.

They were fast, almost impossibly so, given their legs didn't contain any bones.

Instinct took over. Kirk ran, fervently hoping that his memory of the tunnel maze was reliable. When he passed an alcove, he hurled himself into the recess. The impact pushed the air out of his lungs, and his left shoulder hurt like hell after hitting the wall.

Two blurry shadows sped past him, which was good.

They stopped almost immediately, which was not.

In one quick motion, he grabbed his phaser, sped out of the alcove, and fired a rapid sequence of shots at the Farrezzi without waiting to take aim.

When one of them toppled, Kirk had good reason to fear being squashed, heavy as they were. The Farrezzi he'd hit collapsed on itself, legs giving in like cooked pasta, before its body fell backward and hit the floor with a thump.

One down, one to go. Before the captain could get off another shot, two of the Farrezzi's limbs shot out, grabbing Kirk's arms with their prehensile ends and pinning him to the deck. As the being came closer, two of its other limbs wrapped themselves around his legs, and the fifth made for his throat. His phaser was just a half meter from his right hand. It might as well have been on the other side of the planet.

Up close, the wrinkly, fur-covered alien torso resembled a large, fleshy bulb that expanded and contracted rhythmically. The legs' ends—not actually feet—split in two, then again in two smaller ones, to leave the Farrezzi with a total of four thin tentacle-like digits per leg, capable of wrapping themselves tightly around objects.

The grip on his throat was not that tight, but he was beginning to feel its effects. His vision started to swim, his heart pounding. Kirk summoned all of his energy to buck and thrash wildly beneath the slaver's heavy body.

Pinned down like an insect in a specimen collection, he had no chance. The more he resisted, the stronger the grip became. To top it all off, Kirk knew it could get worse. If another Farrezzi came to this one's aid, he'd be done for.

What he needed now was a plan—before he passed out.

TEN

Fourteen Years Ago

Nancy Bierce is a couple of years younger than Leonard. She's attending Emory for an off-world certification. She has a degree in anthropology, but wants to work off-planet for the Federation Ministry of Science and Space Exploration, which requires a semester of training courses, one of them in basic space medicine. Leonard notices Nancy when she joins a study group that meets at Bradley's Café.

Leonard likes Nancy almost instantly. She is capable of giving as good as she gets. She understands his complaining is just in fun. In fact, she rarely takes him seriously even when he *is* serious. Nancy doesn't know his name at first, but nicknames him Plum after an embarrassing incident with a disgusting smoothie. She knows Leonard hates it, which is why she keeps using it even after she learns his name.

He loves listening to her talk about space. She wants to immerse herself in alien cultures. Next year, she'll be a civilian specialist in a Starfleet survey crew to the Baten Kaitos sector. It sounds amazing. Leonard remembers how much he liked his time on Dramia II.

Things at home are growing worse. Joanna has provided him and Jocelyn with *more* things to argue about. Jocelyn is jealous of the time he spends at Bradley's. He's careful not to mention Nancy, even though he hasn't and wouldn't do a thing with her.

It seems that every night Leonard spends at home degenerates into an argument. He tells Jocelyn that he loves her, he tells himself that he loves her, he wants to stay together for Joanna's sake. But nothing works. He begins spending nights at his friend Armstrong's place, just to avoid arguments, but that only makes things worse.

One night he returns home and finds that the apartment door is locked. Jocelyn's changed the code. He hits the door chime again and again. "Let me in!"

After a few minutes of this, he finally hears an answer through the door. "You're going to wake Joanna."

"Then let me in, dammit!"

"If you're only going to come home when it suits you, then maybe you should find another place to live."

He stomps off in anger and ends up spending that night at Nancy's, falling asleep almost instantly. The next day he begins researching the possibilities for medical service in Starfleet. It's the easiest way to get off-planet; he can take the courses he needs while he does his residency with Starfleet. The recruiters are thrilled—he's a top-notch candidate, with his high grades and high performance evaluations.

He just wants to go.

A couple months after Joanna's first birthday, Leonard reports to Starfleet Headquarters in San Francisco. He wheedles an assignment on the *Republic*—the same ship Nancy is on.

She doesn't have her own quarters, but as a medical officer, he does. Nancy spends the night in his room, Jocelyn nothing but a distant memory.

Stardate 4758.0 (0058 hours)

"Doctor! Doctor McCoy! Wake up!"

McCoy felt his shoulder being jostled back and forth. His eyes snapped open, revealing Ensign Messier leaning over the desk to look in his face. Damn, he felt awful. He hadn't fallen asleep in a chair since he was a junior medical officer on the *Koop*.

"Wake up before someone else dies!" That wasn't Messier. McCoy swiveled his chair around to see another figure in his office—a man, sitting on the bench in the corner, old and frail. It was his father, looking as he had in the months before he died.

"What is it, Lieutenant?" McCoy stood up and immediately let off a pained groan.

"There's been an accident in one of the science labs," Messier said. The med tech's expression was grave. "Energy spike: A device overloaded and injured Specialist Huber. He's on his way here. Third-degree burns."

McCoy's mind was still fuzzy. The suppressant had done its job too well. It took him longer than normal to wake up. "I'll be right there. Prep for surgery and get me a nurse to assist."

Messier nodded and sped out. McCoy grabbed a clean surgical uniform. All the while, his father watched him. "I hope you can do more for him than you did for me," he said. "Just don't give up on him, and you'll already be ahead of the game."

He didn't have time for this, not now! Determined not to be drawn into a futile argument with a figment of his overactive imagination, McCoy brushed past his father into the main sickbay. McCoy examined the man, who was only half conscious and moaning loudly.

"Why hasn't he been sedated?" McCoy asked.

"He has been," Messier said as she approached, pushing a cart with a surgical arch on it. "As soon as I got to him, I gave him a dose. He should be out. I gave him the correct dosage."

"I don't doubt that, Ensign." This was the second patient who apparently felt immense pain despite sedation. More than a coincidence, but McCoy had no explanation.

"Take your time," advised his father, who'd followed him in from the office. "Don't rush into a decision or a diagnosis. You wouldn't want to take action prematurely like you did with me."

He bristled at his father's accusation. "You two," he said, pointing at two shaken-looking blueshirts standing next to the bed—doubtless Huber's colleagues from astrophysics. "Could you lift him onto the bed?"

Third-degree burns covered the majority of Huber's upper torso and forearms. His face was less affected, which told McCoy that he'd shielded it with his arms.

"Nurse!" he shouted. "I need some help here!" Then, to Messier, he said, "Please get them out of here."

Nurse Thomas hurried in. At the same time, the door behind him opened, and Chapel said, "Doctor, I got a call from Messier—"

"Christine," he said, interrupting her, "where have you been?" Then, realizing that Thomas was standing there, he nodded at her. "Nurse Thomas, thank you. Please look after the other patients. We'll call you if we need you." He trusted that Thomas wouldn't take this personally. The simple truth was that he and Chapel worked well together.

McCoy and Chapel promptly started treating Huber's wounds.

"At least you just didn't give up on him," David McCoy said reproachfully. "That's very determined of you."

The first step was the careful removal of the burnt dermis, large whitish-brown patches, leathery to the touch. McCoy drew his laser scalpel along the affected area, lifting the dead flakes with tweezers, while Chapel applied lab-cultured pseudoskin onto the raw flesh and deftly sealed the wound with her protoplaser.

It was slow work, due to both the nature and the size of the injury. The longer it took, the more McCoy found himself returning to the conundrum of the sedative-resistant pain. What could be the cause for this? Was it really possible that there was a connection to the distortions and, by extension, to the comas?

The Farrezzi holding Kirk down had started to emit strange shrieks that the UT couldn't translate. If it was a call for help, Kirk had to act now.

The Farrezzi's size and strength were its advantages, so the captain had to use them against it. He couldn't throw someone so big from his present position, but perhaps he could force it to come closer. The Farrezzi's tentacles were wrapped around his upper arms, leaving his hands relatively free, so he grabbed the tentacles and pulled with all his strength in one quick move. It was difficult to tell how heavy the alien was—at least twice his weight. The immense effort of throwing it off balance caused searing pain throughout Kirk's body, as overtaxed muscles and tendons complained.

The sudden force made the Farrezzi fall toward Kirk, and with no other option, the captain slammed his head into its abdomen. It fell sideways, landing on the deck. The weight constricting his chest immediately lightened. He could breathe now.

The grip on his arms and legs was still there, but now he had a fighting chance. It was lying on its side, all its limbs occupied, with no way of stabilizing itself or even getting up again—except by letting go of Kirk.

It didn't. Instead, it kept its grip on him while emitting more of those unsettling shrieks. They made Kirk think of animals in distress. Determined to put an end to this, he kicked and punched. His foot connected with a soft spot in the Farrezzi's abdomen. The alien emitted an ear-piercing wail, but it still wouldn't let go. Another kick had the desired effect: two appendages released him, the one around his throat and the one holding his left arm at the wrist.

Where was his phaser? In the melee, he'd lost track of it. It had been close before, but now he had no idea where it was. Kirk gave the Farrezzi another kick, then risked a quick look. Thinking back to where he'd seen it before, he remembered that the phaser had been just out of reach of his right hand, which was still underneath the whimpering Farrezzi.

He brought his left arm around to grope underneath the slaver's body. The Farrezzi didn't let him do that unhindered. It tried to grab him again.

He repeatedly punched with his left hand—at the alien's abdomen, its upper body, its head. The wailing increased, as did the intensity of its grip. His right hand was tingling, the tentacle-like fingers impeding his blood flow.

However, his opponent moved just enough for him to shove his hand in between body and floor. Kirk felt something wet and sticky and could only hope that it was the alien's blood. He thought his fingers had touched the phaser, but then the Farrezzi moved again.

Its eyestalk-like visual organs were—like those of most beings—bound to be highly sensitive. Kirk directed his next punch at the nearest one.

Another series of shrieks and wails followed, so loud that Kirk felt everybody on board could hear them. The tentacles on his legs retracted as the Farrezzi waved them at his hands to ward off further attacks. Kirk could see the phaser, still half-buried beneath the Farrezzi's bulk. The captain made a quick, carefully aimed grab and then held his weapon once more.

If Kirk fired the phaser on a high setting while touching the Farrezzi, he'd be stunned too, but as he dialed the power down, the injured slaver hit him on the upper arm, making him drop the phaser.

Kirk reached for it, and when he finally had his fingers clasped around it, fired.

The alien let go of him, unconscious. Kirk took a couple of deep breaths.

Celebration would have to wait. First he had to find his two men.

When Scotty woke up, he felt like he'd been hit by a caber. His legs wouldn't move, his head was fuzzy, and breathing was painful. Even worse, he had only the vaguest idea what had happened.

He tried to sit up. The pain told him he should reconsider. All right, then. Best to find out more.

"Hello?" he said. "Anybody there?"

From the corner of his eye, he saw a shadow move somewhere off to his left. With everything so blurred and out of focus, it was impossible to say who it was. The person was wearing a blue uniform.

"Don't get up," a male voice said. "You're not ready for that yet. Let me do my job first." Doctor M'Benga.

"Doc, I dinna remember much of what happened."

"That's only natural," M'Benga said. "You suffered a concussion, coupled with numerous fractures to bones in your legs. Memory loss is the least of your worries."

"Thanks for your concern, Doc." The little Scott could see told him he was in the *Hofstadter*. Despite his blurry vision, there was no mistaking the repositioned power nodes of a G-class. "So, what happened?" he asked.

"We were attacked."

"What?" Despite everything, Scotty was sure he'd remember an attack. "How—" A loud rumble interrupted him. Everything shook. "It sounds like the world's ending."

"Right now, we're dodging three fighter craft as we try to find a gap in the storm pattern so we can get up into space," M'Benga said. "Mister Spock says that before they located us, they flew all over the city, taking random shots. That's what got the roof."

"Well, I need to get up there!" shouted Scotty. He had to do *something*.

"Mister Scott," Spock's voice interjected, coming from the shuttle's bow, "we are aware of the situation's requirements. I suggest you let Doctor M'Benga take care of you."

"What's the problem?" asked Scotty. "Why canna we get up above the clouds?"

"The problem is twofold," replied Spock. "The *Columbus*'s phasers are still inoperative, and the *Hofstadter*'s shields are still impaired." Scotty could hear the whine of phasers.

"What?" That didn't make any sense. "I fixed the shields. My countermeasures—"

"—were an effective remedy," interrupted Spock, "and are contributing to our shield strength. Unfortunately, the intensity of the interference continues to increase."

Scotty sighed. There was just no winning. Three enemy craft and two shuttles, both of which were impaired—it would be nearly impossible to get through any gap in the cloud cover. One fighter could harass each shuttle while the third could block off any escape route. "Are Rawlins and Seven Deers going to make it?" he asked the doctor.

"Seven Deers is fit for duty. Her temple was just grazed, thankfully. But it's Rawlins and *you* that I'm worried about. I'm doing the best I can with what I have, but what I really need is a fully equipped sickbay." The deck rumbled, some of the energy of the Farrezzi weapons reaching the shuttle through its weakened shields.

"Doc, is there something you're not telling me? What's wrong with me?"

"Commander Scott, when the ceiling fell on you, your legs were very badly injured. Most of your bones from the femur on down are broken, a lot of tendons are torn. Your knees . . . I'll have to rebuild them."

Scotty tried to take in what M'Benga had said. Why wasn't he feeling any pain? M'Benga must have shot him full of suppressant—a staggering amount. No wonder he was feeling woozy.

Another rumble, much stronger this time. "How are our shields?" Scott asked.

Spock spoke up. "At the current rate of fire, they will fail in ten minutes."

"What's your plan?" asked Scotty.

"Ensign Seven Deers is working to repair the *Columbus*'s phaser system, at which point we will not need to fly cover for them."

Another boom, louder this time. The whine in the background, which his trained ears told him was coming from the shield generator, increased in intensity for about two seconds. "We need to get out of range. Let me help Seven Deers. Doc, do you not have to look after poor Rawlins?"

M'Benga said nothing, but his face spoke volumes. In a way, Scotty understood how the doctor felt. He'd feel the same way if his engines started complaining about the way he'd repaired them.

"Mister Scott, I appreciate your eagerness to be of assistance," Spock said. "Do you have an idea?"

"Mister Spock, I've got two of them. Link me up to the ensign."

Christine Chapel held her breath as Doctor McCoy glanced back and forth between Specialist Huber and the medical monitor above his bed. The surgery had gone well so far, and they were almost done. Just a few more patches of dead skin.

The doctor was working intently, beads of sweat forming on his forehead. He hadn't said a word during the past hour, apart from requests for surgical tools. It was as if he couldn't afford even the slightest distraction. Chapel decided not to ask him what was wrong. Once the surgery was completed, she'd get it out of him.

The last of the damaged skin was gone, and artificial skin had taken its place. Chapel ran the protoplaser over the new skin on Huber's arms, stimulating its growth.

Once Huber woke up, he'd find himself healed, and in a few weeks' time, there would be no trace of the accident whatsoever.

The doctor put away his tools, then turned off the surgical arch. "Good work, Doctor," Chapel said, smiling encouragingly at him.

McCoy mumbled, "Thank you." He was clearly preoccupied.

"Can you clean this up?" he asked, his eyes fixed on the life-sign monitor above Huber's head.

"Yes, Doctor." There was little to do besides disinfecting the medical devices. Huber was no longer in critical condition, although he would require at least a couple of days of supervision.

"Good," McCoy said. "Good." He disappeared into the ward to check on Bouchard, Petriello, Santos, Fraser, and Salah. Their condition had not improved, but at least it hadn't gotten any worse. The doctor's treatment was keeping their brains' deterioration at bay.

What if the espers never came out of the coma? What if they remained in this state until their bodies gave up?

The doctor doesn't know what to do. He always makes up things as he goes along, but now it's not working. He's rapidly reaching the end of his knowledge—maybe he's already exceeded it. Maybe you should stop idolizing him.

That wasn't true. She didn't idolize him . . . why would she think that? And she was sure he still hadn't tried everything he could come up with. There had to be something he could do to save these people. There had to be.

Her thoughts were interrupted by Huber's sudden scream. She almost dropped the protoplaser. What was going on here? During surgery, he'd been calm, just like every other sedated patient. Was he regaining consciousness? He shouldn't be, not so soon.

"Doctor!" she shouted, to be heard in the ward. "Doctor McCoy!"

By the time he arrived, Huber had started to spasm, so violently that he was in danger of falling off the biobed. Luckily, the surgical arch over his chest kept him sufficiently restrained. Chapel couldn't imagine what the cause was.

"Just what I feared," McCoy said, his lined face grim as he studied the biosigns. "I don't understand this," he said. "He shouldn't be experiencing any pain. The readouts tell me that he isn't. Not *pain*, at least. He's clearly experiencing something, though. Readings indicate high neural activity." He shook his head. "It's almost as if his body doesn't know it's sedated."

"Mister Scott." Spock cast a quick glance backward at the supine engineer. "Are you ready?"

"Just a moment," Scott replied. He was checking his tricorder, as he spoke into his communicator. "Did you switch the couplings, Ensign?" M'Benga hovered nearby, keeping an eye on him and the still-unconscious Rawlins.

"I hope luck is on our side," said Jaeger, manning the navigation console. "We'll need it." With his right hand he worked the scanner controls, and with his left he kept a tight grip on the bottom of the console. The geophysicist had never been in a firefight before.

"We do not require luck, Lieutenant," replied Spock, "only efficiency and aptitude." He swerved the *Hofstadter* to avoid weapons fire from a Farrezzi fighter. The fighters were more agile in the wind.

"All the same, I'm going to cross my fingers." Spock noted that Jaeger did not actually do so.

"*All done, Commander,*" the voice of Seven Deers came through Scott's communicator. "*Ready when you are.*"

"Good to go, sir," Scott said.

"Acknowledged." Spock's attention was devoted to the controls, as he worked to keep the *Hofstadter* from suffering any more hits. The shields were nearly depleted. It appeared that the fighters knew, because they were becoming bolder. The Farrezzi pilots had also realized the *Columbus* had no weapons, as they crossed in front of the other shuttle.

Spock activated the shuttle's comm to contact Kologwe on the *Columbus*. "Lieutenant, prepare to match my course."

"*Aye, sir.*"

Spock looked at the scans of the cloud layer. There was a gap in the storm, being blocked by one of the Farrezzi ships. This was exactly what they needed. "Now."

As the *Hofstadter* began to climb toward the hovering fighter, *Columbus* slipped underneath it, bringing the shuttles as close as was safe. "Engage on three," Spock ordered. "One. Two. Three."

Spock flicked off the *Hofstadter*'s shields. The gap in coverage was less than a second. *Columbus*'s shields extended out to cover the beleaguered shuttle. Spock turned the *Hofstadter*'s shield power back on, its power reinforcing the *Columbus*'s shields.

The other two fighters came up from below, firing at the two shuttles, but their weapons had little effect on the combined power of both shuttles' shields.

The Vulcan returned his attention to the third fighter. It was still hovering in position, apparently unconcerned. Its pilot knew one shuttle did not have phaser power.

"Fire," Spock ordered. He activated the weapons system. A bright blue beam lit up the darkened sky, striking the Farrezzi fighter, which shuddered under the impact.

He waited for a second phaser beam to join it from below, but nothing happened. Under Scott's direction, Seven Deers had replaced the *Columbus*'s damaged emitter crystal with one from a phaser rifle. It should now be capable of firing. "Lieutenant?" Spock asked.

"*Something's wrong, sir.*" Kologwe's voice evidenced a nearly imperceptible rise.

As Scott began barking orders into his communicator, Spock glanced at the navigational plot. They were twenty-one seconds from reaching the hovering fighter, which showed no signs of damage.

"Mister Jaeger," said Spock as he considered their options, "it appears we have a situation which calls for your crossed fingers."

McCoy was at his wits' end. Specialist Huber was yet another mystery. Would Huber also be experiencing pain like Haines's, pain that didn't go away? Would others be affected before long? Would he?

The thought made his knees tremble. Death had never been an issue. Dying was an essential part of life.

Since his father died, McCoy had feared pain. In the final weeks of his father's illness the agony had overwhelmed the painkillers.

"Doctor? What's wrong?" Chapel asked.

Glad for the interruption, McCoy looked her in the eyes. "Nothing, Christine, except that I'm getting older. I can't see what's in front of me." Something was eluding him, a link between Huber's state and everything else that was going on.

"We need to get Huber's brain to calm down. Right now, there are fireworks going off in there. I need a neural suppressant."

Chapel had the hypospray ready for him in the blink of an eye, and he injected it in Huber's neck. The effect should have been instantaneous, but it took half a minute. It was as if every fiber of Huber's body was fighting unconsciousness. Eventually, his thrashing ceased, and his breathing leveled out. McCoy glanced at the readings, which were returning to normal.

"Well done, Doctor," Chapel said.

A small victory, but he was still glad about it. "Thank you."

Aware that work was waiting for him in his office, McCoy decided to leave Huber in Chapel's capable hands. When he got there, the research was all still on his computer screen, but he checked on the medical computer first. Nothing yet. It concurred that there was a possible connection between the espers and the distortions, but it hadn't figured out what the connection was.

"Damn it all," McCoy grumbled. "There's too much uncertainty for my taste."

"Nice to see you recognize your limits. Makes a change." McCoy didn't look up. He could tell that Jocelyn was hovering over his shoulder, reading his reports, not that she'd understand them herself.

"What's that supposed to mean?" he asked, annoyed.

"You always thought you could do everything, heal every single one of your patients, but you can't. While we were together, you'd always complain and moan about your inadequacy—or worse, aim your anger at me," she said. "I'm not the problem—you just don't know how to deal with stress."

"I know perfectly well how to deal with it," McCoy replied pointedly, trying to tune her out as he sifted through the medical computer's data. "This starship has seen worse, and so have I."

"Is that really true?" asked Jocelyn. "Is yelling at your wife really an effective way of dealing with stress?"

"I don't yell!" he snapped, looking up from his screen. There she was, her face drawn into a taut frown. Arguing about arguments. As absurd as it seemed, it was a fight they'd had one too many times. "If you wouldn't stick your nose in when—"

"Is something the matter, Doctor?"

"Don't interrupt—"

The different voice gave McCoy a start. He turned to see Chapel hovering in the doorway. "No," he said, hoping she hadn't heard enough to think he was really losing it.

With a start, he realized that he'd been talking—*talking!*—to Jocelyn, and it had felt like the most natural thing in the world. He turned his head to see where she was, but she was gone. "No," he said again. "I just need to clear my head. I'm going for a walk."

Flipping off his computer, McCoy grabbed his medkit and headed out into the corridor. Jocelyn and his father were there waiting for him.

Ahead of Giotto, the tunnel curved to the left. At the end, it glowed orange, like all the lights on this damn spaceship. The tricorder told him that he was rapidly approaching the end of this particular tunnel, which led to a room. The tricorder also told him that the room was being guarded by one of the aliens.

Phaser in hand, Giotto slowly closed the distance so he could see without being seen. He didn't hear anything other than a big creature sucking in air. Giotto waited until he was sure the guard was just standing there.

He charged around the bend, took aim, and fired. The Farrezzi guard—a particularly chunky specimen—dropped like a bag of rocks before Giotto had even stopped his sprint.

He took a scan of his surroundings. He almost let loose a cry of victory when one of the life signs he detected behind the door was human.

The other one was Farrezzi.

Giotto inspected the big, semicircular door that the Farrezzi had been guarding, but it didn't have the usual release mechanism. This was either a cell or an interrogation chamber; the way to open it would be well protected.

Giotto went back to the unconscious guard. Straps of beige leatherlike material wound around the limbs, with pouches hanging off some of them, and the lower torso was covered with more faux leather, but in a darker shade. He went through the pouches, ripping them open and shaking their contents onto the floor. As he did so, he wondered briefly if he'd know what he was looking for once he saw it.

A metal ball rolled out of the pouch he'd just opened, hitting the floor with a loud clang. He grabbed it before it could roll away and studied it. Heavier than it had any right to be, and cold. Its surface was segmented, with colorful pictographs.

Was this a remote? Which pictograph should he press? He couldn't waste more time, so he decided to press every one. This might not be a good idea. But he had no intention of staying here any longer than necessary. Open the door, get whoever was in there out, leave. After four attempts without any result, the fifth did something. The door remained shut, but something inside it clicked loudly. A locking mechanism? On a whim, Giotto pressed the symbol again. This time the door slid open, retreating up into its frame.

He waited a few seconds, then he heard something big move. A Farrezzi was approaching the open entrance, holding something that looked very much like a high-tech version of an old Earth musket.

Giotto waited until he had a clear shot, and fired. Set to maximum stun, one short beam was all it took to drop the guard.

Stepping into the room, Giotto saw a man tied to a pole: Chekov. Was he alive?

Alive, but unconscious. He had been severely abused—numerous wounds covered his face and hands. There were bound to be more beneath his uniform. He was tied to the pole with a cord, but the phaser cut through it easily. Chekov fell into Giotto's arms and was lowered to the floor. Carefully, Giotto turned Chekov onto his side to ease his breathing and keep him from choking.

Giotto needed to wake Chekov up. They had to get out of there. He pulled out his communicator to contact the captain.

"*Kirk here. Report, Mister Giotto?*"

"I've found Chekov, sir. He's injured, but alive."

"*Good work, Commander.*" The joy in Kirk's voice was plain. "*I'll lock onto your signal with my tricorder and join up with you.*"

"We might have to move, sir, but I'll keep this channel open so you can follow me."

"*Copy that. See you soon. Kirk out.*"

He'd give Chekov five minutes, and if he didn't wake up, he'd sling the ensign over his shoulders in a fireman's carry. He went over to the door, facing the tunnel bend he'd passed mere moments before, his tricorder on active scan. If the Farrezzi came, he'd spot them before they spotted him. He checked the power level of his phaser.

Let them come.

ELEVEN

Thirteen Years Ago

The more time Leonard spends with Nancy, the more uncomfortable he gets. Initially a carefree release from his troubles, the affair starts to weigh him down with guilt. He's stopped wearing his wedding ring, and he tells everyone that he's divorced, even though he's still married to Jocelyn.

He's busier than ever, working in *Republic*'s sickbay and taking the required Starfleet courses. Jocelyn begins sending him messages, telling him that she's returned to work and Joanna misses him, asking him to come back. She insists that they can make it work. He sends back vaguely supportive messages, but nothing else.

Near Joanna's second birthday, Jocelyn serves him with divorce papers. He takes leave, goes back to Earth, and tries to reconcile with his wife. Jocelyn knows he's there only because of their daughter, and not because he still loves her. He's already made his choice. It pains him to leave Joanna behind, but he can't raise a daughter on his own. He's in Starfleet—a starship is no place for children. He leaves Earth, cursing Jocelyn for being right; he *has* made his choice.

However, once he makes it back to the *Republic*, Leonard realizes he can't stay. He puts in for reassignment, and takes the first posting that comes up, on the *Feynman*. He never tells Nancy that he's leaving. They step out of each other's lives without even saying good-bye. Later, he realizes that he's displacing his anger onto Nancy.

When Leonard has time for introspection, he begins to grasp just how awful a person he could become. He can't undo what happened, but he makes a promise to himself to change, to never again be that person.

Stardate 4758.1 (0151 hours)

The *Enterprise* had been through a lot these past hours. As McCoy walked through the corridors, he was struck by how much debris and clutter was still lying about. For the ship to be torn to pieces without an enemy to fight made him feel uneasy. Would things have gone better with Jim in command? Or would he also have insisted on pressing ahead?

"That would have relieved you of the responsibility, wouldn't it?" asked McCoy's father. He was following him like a well-trained dog. "If someone could just solve this problem by getting the *Enterprise* out of the distortion zone, then maybe you wouldn't have to do anything."

Dad . . . no, he wasn't Dad, he was an illusion, a figment of his imagination. Why was his mind doing this to him? Why did it torment him, reminding him how helpless he'd felt, watching his father waste away, ravaged and weakened by that damned disease?

In the end, his father had weighed so little. McCoy'd had nightmares the whole time, and they'd only intensified when his father died. To see the elder McCoy in that wasted state, here and now, was like being punched in the stomach every time their eyes met.

"That's what you like, isn't it?" Jocelyn said. "Shifting the blame for your problems elsewhere."

"That's not even true!" McCoy snapped, unable to avoid rising to the bait. "I've always accepted responsibility for my actions."

"Oh? Is that why you enlisted in Starfleet rather than stick it out on Earth?" asked Jocelyn.

"And is that why you always blame *me* for my death?" asked his father. His voice was becoming hoarse; every breath sounded labored, like it had been back then. Toward the end, he'd been unable to speak, merely giving barely perceptible nods or shakes of his head in reply to McCoy's questions.

"You asked me!" McCoy said, unable to help himself. "You *begged* me! What else could I do?"

His father looked at him reproachfully. "Leonard, I wasn't in my right mind. You should've known that. How many people have asked you to let them go when the pain got to be too much?"

He'd refused that request so many times . . . but not that time.

"And you had no better idea than to run from that, too," Jocelyn pointed out. "After you'd gone back to Earth for the first time in years to help your father . . . the first thing you did after he died was to run to Capella IV."

"And then, you ran here," added McCoy's father. "Not because you believed it was the best thing to do, but because Jim Kirk asked you to take Mark Piper's place and you thought—"

"And I thought out here in space, I could finally get away from it all," McCoy said, glad that nobody else was using this corridor.

"But you haven't!" Jocelyn wore a victorious smile, like when she won an argument. "I'm here, your father's here . . . even Joanna's here. You can keep on running, but you'll never make it."

They were right. He had never chosen to do this, he just ran . . . That's why he was wandering the corridors instead of working his ass off to find a cure.

His aimless wanderings had brought him to a turbolift junction. He stepped inside, Jocelyn and his father following closely. But where should he go?

It occurred to him that sickbay hadn't heard anything from auxiliary control. It was worth a visit, to make sure everyone was doing all right.

And hell, he wanted to know if his idea had panned out.

Jocelyn and his father didn't say anything on the trip to auxiliary control. They stood there, watching him, accusing him with their eyes. Their presence was a reminder of why he was out here, why he was about to fail the five comatose crew members and probably the entire crew. He felt sorry for poor Bouchard, Petriello, Santos, Fraser, and Salah. They deserved better. They deserved a doctor who knew what he was doing.

When McCoy and his entourage stepped into auxiliary control, things were relatively calm. Uhura was standing over Singh's shoulder at the main console, while Padmanabhan worked off to the side. DeSalle was nowhere to be seen—likely somewhere in engineering.

Uhura looked up as he entered, and smiled faintly. McCoy estimated she must've been up for more than eighteen hours. "I thought you might need a house call," he said, removing a hypo from his kit and loading it up with a fast-acting stimulant. "This'll let you do your job."

As he injected it into her arm, she let off a sigh. "Thanks, Doctor."

"Last one," said McCoy.

Uhura nodded. "Understood."

To her right, Singh looked up from his controls. "Lieutenant, we're set."

Uhura hit some buttons on his console, watching as readouts popped up on the main screen. "It looks good to me," she said. "Tell Lieutenant DeSalle that we're ready to go."

"Is that real-space bubble working?" asked McCoy.

An eager, high-pitched voice jumped in from the starboard alcove. "Really well!" Ensign Padmanabhan said. "But it's making it hard to get data on the other universe—we're overwriting it with ours."

"Things have stabilized, Doctor," Uhura said. "We're going to try to move forward again."

"Is that wise?" McCoy didn't particularly fancy plunging into another reality.

"Ensign Padmanabhan had the idea of extending the real-space bubble forward of the ship by a few thousand kilometers," Uhura said, sounding confident and optimistic. Apparently, the boy's relentless enthusiasm was contagious. "It should smooth our flight path enough to make travel safe."

"We're not going to warp again, are we?"

"No, Doctor," Singh grumbled. The lieutenant struck McCoy as being uncomfortable with so many people around, filling up the control room. Uncomfortable and tired. Like Uhura, Singh and the others could probably use some stimulants.

"It would be *impossible*," Padmanabhan pointed out with surprising fervor. "We can't use the warp drive—not for propulsion—when we're using it to make a real-space bubble!"

McCoy injected Singh, who simply *humph*ed in response, and then Padmanabhan, who nearly leapt out of his chair. Maybe the kid was a little too excited to need the stimulants. He made his way back to Uhura. "*Is* it wise?"

"We get a signal out; everything just bounces back. It'll be a week before anyone at Starfleet realizes we haven't reported in." Uhura took her chair. "It could be a whole month before they can send a starship to investigate."

"What are the risks?" McCoy asked.

Uhura pursed her lips. "It'll still be rough, and we'll still experience some computer problems."

"A euphemism for explosions?"

"We hope not. It should be like the earlier distortions— a little rough, but not terrible. The computers might flicker, but they should be fine."

McCoy reflected that Uhura didn't have a choice. It was this or wait for the ship's power to dwindle away. So going forward it was, then. "What about my patients?" he asked. "How will it affect them?"

"Have you figured out why they're ill yet?"

"No," admitted McCoy reluctantly.

"Then I don't know," Uhura said. "I've got Padmanabhan focusing on how this affects the ship."

"These are the lives of five men and women we're talking about."

"I have to think about the lives of four hundred. I'm sorry, Doctor."

This was just more impetus to solve the problem. As if he needed it. "Well, I'd better get back to sickbay."

He began to leave, but Uhura stopped him, her hand on his arm. "How are you doing?" she asked.

"I told you," he replied. "I haven't been making much progress."

"That's not what I asked," she said. "How are *you*?"

For a moment, McCoy wanted to tell her everything. Tell her that he'd started hearing things and moved on to seeing them. Tell her that he was having conversations with people who weren't there. Tell her that he had no idea what was happening to him, no idea at all. He smiled but was pretty sure it looked fake. "I'm just tired. But I'll be fine."

Karen Seven Deers had seconds. Kologwe was at the helm, with Tra beside her at navigation. Saloniemi sat next to Seven Deers, but he was an anthropologist. It was up to her to restore *Columbus*'s phasers.

She'd opened an access hatch in the deck to the phaser components. The emitter crystal from a phaser rifle was wired into a slot much too large for it. The connections were sound. Why wasn't it working? Commander Scott was listing possibilities over her communicator, but with her head still a little woozy, his constant stream of information was making it impossible to think. "*—the circuits through the whole shuttle, it could be a simple short or—*"

"Ensign," called Kologwe, "any time now."

Seven Deers snapped the communicator closed. She could do this. Think. How did the emitter crystal of a phaser rifle work? Energy accumulated in the prefire chamber and then—

Ah! The crystal's embedded safeties were rejecting the amount of energy the shuttle's phaser systems were sending it. It was more than a phaser rifle could generate. If she could convince the crystal that she was setting a rifle to overload . . . Seven Deers programmed the tricorder to override the safeties. "Now, Lieutenant!"

The crystal lit up as energy passed through it to the phaser rifle. Seven Deers looked out the viewports. Success. The Farrezzi fighter tried to dodge out of the way, but it was not fast enough. Sparks flew off the fighter, and it began to tumble. Both shuttles kept their phaser fire focused on it as they flew ever higher.

"*Engines to maximum,*" ordered Spock over the comm.

As the fighter plummeted, the two shuttles streaked by it, free to climb into space. Seven Deers let out a breath she didn't know she'd been holding. The clouds were parting, and stars were beginning to make themselves visible.

The phasers shut off. The emitter crystal was dark black, burnt out by the shuttle's phaser systems. Replacing the damaged crystal with one from a phaser rifle had been Scotty's brilliant idea. Phaser rifles weren't standard issue; each shuttle had been issued only one. Their phaser system was done for.

Her communicator signaled. "Seven Deers here."

"*Ensign, what do you think you're doing?*" demanded Scott. "*Switching off your communicator like that?*"

"Sorry, sir, I just needed a moment to think," she said.

Scott sighed. "*Sorry. I'm just frustrated, lass. I canna move!*" She was irritated he'd called her "lass," but she knew it was a sign of fondness. "*How's the crystal?*" he asked.

"Burnt out," she said. "We can't use it again."

"Shouldn't have to," said Kologwe. "We are clear for orbit."

Saloniemi whooped, and Tra punched the air with his fist.

"*Affirmative,*" said Spock. "*Plotting a course to bring us to the hub of the reactor network from above.*"

A pinging noise drew Seven Deers's attention to the front of the *Columbus*. "Ensign," said Tra, "something's coming up from behind us."

"What?" she asked, checking her own readings.

Tra shook his head in frustration. "It looks like those fighters are space-capable. They're right behind us."

Following Giotto's signal turned out to be more difficult than Kirk had anticipated. The spiraling layout of the Farrezzi ship meant that it was impossible to move in a straight line. The captain came to a wider section, like an anteroom, with a large opening at the other end. Stepping closer, he risked looking in. It was dark inside, but as he got closer, there was a familiar pale blue glow.

Kirk stepped inside. It was a storage area, filled with hundreds of the hibernation pods. The sight of so many innocent beings about to be exploited shocked him to the core, especially because they had no idea what was going to happen to them. The sleepers needed to know about their fate.

The captain decided he would wake them. Kirk picked a capsule far enough down the line to be outside the view of anybody approaching the opening. The controls on the pod were a small display showing six icons. He pulled out the tricorder and activated the translation program. It quickly displayed the meanings of the pictographs. The first four were settings for temperature, pressure, nutrients, and recycling. The last two read "power activation" and "purge." "Purge" hopefully would empty its interior of water. It seemed like the best option. Kirk pressed the sixth icon.

At first, nothing happened, but then a whirring noise could be heard, and bubbles rose inside the pod. Looking down, he saw water rushing out along the pod's entire circumference—a trickle that quickly grew into an impressive flush. It was all over in a matter of seconds. The Farrezzi stirred, first its eyes, turning, retracting, and extending, then its limbs, and eventually it pushed the capsule top up.

It let out a terrifying shriek that threatened to pierce Kirk's eardrum. The universal translator activated, and he was treated to an equally piercing, "Assistance! Assistance! Assistance requirement!"

The captain had to get the situation under control. "Please calm down," he said. "I'm not here to hurt you. My name is James Kirk. I am a visitor from another planet."

"Assistance requirement here now!"

"There's nobody here to help you except me. I'm sorry to tell you this, but some of your people want to sell you into slavery."

The Farrezzi had stopped screaming, but now it was trembling. Suddenly it was out of the pod, heading away from him, surprisingly fast for somebody who'd just come out of a century-long sleep. Kirk knew he needed to be patient, but he couldn't afford to be discovered. He had no choice but to run after it.

"I'm here to help you!" he shouted, desperate to be heard over the alien's wailing. "You're on a ship that belongs to these slavers. They've taken you from your underground refuge and intend to sell you to the Orions."

The Farrezzi was fast; he'd lost sight of it already. After a while the captain realized that he could no longer hear the loud thumps it made when running. It was hiding somewhere. He had to convince it of his intentions, but would it listen?

"My name is James Kirk. I am the captain of a

starship that belongs to an interstellar organization called the United Federation of Planets. We are explorers. We thought you had disappeared. We came to Farrezz to find out why. We discovered that you had not left. We were surprised. Then we saw the slavers. They were members of your own species. They took advantage of your sleeping state to put thousands of your kind on ships to be sold into slavery." He let that sink in.

Silence. From nowhere, shots rang out. Kirk ducked instinctively.

Where was the fire coming from? How had the Farrezzi got its hands—tentacles—on a weapon?

More shots, some of them ricocheting off the pods closest to him. Kirk realized that the shots were coming from the entrance. He held his breath, waiting for the next impact. There was somebody over there, probably a slaver who'd heard him talking, or the scared Farrezzi wailing.

The captain grabbed his phaser and leaned out from behind the pod. He couldn't see the doorway from here, so he'd have to move carefully. He waited for a lull in the shots and went into a roll, coming up behind another pod. Cautiously, Kirk leaned out and immediately jumped back as more shots rang out. But he had spotted the shooter. He leaned out and squeezed off a quick shot. His phaser hit the edge of the doorway, showering sparks everywhere.

A sudden wailing from the side of the room diverted his attention. "Assistance requirement here! Assistance requirement! Alien presence! Hostility! Hostility!" It was Kirk's sleeper, rapidly moving in his direction.

"Identity request! Identity request! Individual family location!" It was the shooter.

"Compliance: I name statement Horr-Sav-Frerin."

"Explanation: pod nonimmersion! Explanation! Explanation!"

"Sleep disturbance. Awakening with surprise, presence of unknown alien. Assistance requirement!"

"Identity class: sleeper?"

Kirk could see the wailing Farrezzi now. It had reached the doorway. "Affirmative. Assistance requirement immediate!"

A shot impacted a pod right next to the sleeper. "Direction: pod return! Alternative: fatality!" The shooter shot at the sleeper again.

A loud wail emanated from the sleeper as it began moving—*toward* the shooter. "Assistance requirement! Assistance requirement!"

The shooter slipped through the doorway, pointing its weapon right at the sleeper. "Alternative: fatality!"

Kirk leaned out, hoping that despite the fact that his opponent had five eyes, its attention was elsewhere. His luck failed him. The shooter began to aim its weapon his way, but Kirk got off two good shots, dropping the Farrezzi.

The sleeper ran toward Kirk and stopped short, then slumped against a pod. It emitted a strange, otherworldly wail that the translator didn't process.

"So," Kirk said, "are you ready to believe me now?"

The Farrezzi inclined its head slightly, to let all its eyes look at Kirk. He didn't mind being the focus of its attention; perhaps this meant it was no longer so afraid of him that it wanted to run away. "That person over there is one of the slavers."

Eyestalks turned and contracted, a limb curled upward, parting at the end to reveal two appendages that scratched the skin under the fur. The Farrezzi made a noise that sounded like a heavy sigh. "Not-I here defective youngchild repeat low-speed."

At last, a first-contact exchange with a Farrezzi that wasn't a slaver. But what was the alien saying?

Giotto heard thumps in the distance. This was it. He raised his phaser, ready for whatever they were about to throw at him. It was difficult to tell how many individuals there were. He'd just have to wait and see.

The first one was already coming around the bend. He didn't give it a chance to get very far. A slight contraction of Giotto's trigger finger released the energy that vaporized the target upon contact. He'd deliberately set the phaser to maximum because of the psychological aspect. When you saw a body drop in front of you, that was bad, but when it vanished, that was bound to even get to combat-trained warriors.

The Farrezzi didn't immediately follow their unlucky comrade. They stopped just short of the bend, out of sight, but not out of hearing. The commander could make out some of their strange squeaks: "Order request" and "Unknown assailant."

The shadows changed, there was a brief flurry of movement, and then something small and round came rolling along the tunnel, emitting a steady whine. Grenade!

He threw himself back into the room and grabbed the remote. He wasted precious seconds fumbling to find the right icon. Cursing himself for taking so long, Giotto squeezed the button as far down as it would go.

The grenade had almost reached him. Desperately, he stabbed the icon again. The door descended in a painfully leisurely fashion. It wasn't going to make it. Giotto sprinted to the back of the room, throwing himself over the still unconscious Chekov.

He heard the *thud-clang* of the metal door hitting the floor. Then an enormous roar drowned out every thought.

Slowly, he stood up and opened his eyes. The door had closed just in time. However, the grenade had bowed the door. It wasn't going to open again. Giotto didn't mind—he and Chekov were safer in here.

He turned his head to check on Chekov. The ensign was still lying there, but his wide-open eyes bore a scared, pained look.

Giotto moved over to Chekov. "Hey, Ensign. You made it." He noted with apprehension that he was barely able to hear his own voice. Hearing lost, hopefully only temporarily.

The ensign didn't reply. He simply lay there, seemingly mulling something over. Eventually, he opened his mouth, forcing out, "Papa?"

Giotto leaned forward, making it easier for Chekov to take in his face. "I'm not your father, Ensign. Take a good look. Recognize me?"

"I . . . what . . ." the ensign stammered.

"Easy, now. You're safe," Giotto said. "I don't know what they did to you, Pavel, but they're not here now. We just need to be patient. The captain's on his way."

Chekov stared at him with glazed eyes.

A sound made Giotto whirl around. The heat coming off the door was considerable, but judging from the small crack at the bottom, the Farrezzi were trying to wedge it open.

He knew he had to do something. It would make things difficult later, but he had no choice. Grabbing his phaser, he quickly adjusted the setting and fired a continuous beam at the door edge. It didn't take long for the door to heat up and seal them in the chamber.

Giotto looked over at the unconscious Farrezzi guard. He set his phaser on stun and fired, just to make sure the guard wouldn't wake up. Then he pulled out his communicator to hail the captain. Hopefully, he would be able to do something. If not, Giotto and Chekov were done for.

On his way back to sickbay, McCoy checked on his patients. Not surprisingly, Sulu was still eager to go back on duty. His tricorder readings were almost good enough for McCoy to let him. Almost. One more day of rest, and he could take back command of the ship. Haines was still sleeping, and the other outpatients were doing well.

As soon as he entered sickbay, he called out for Chapel, Odhiambo, and Thomas to come to a staff meeting, hoping that they would be able to suggest a treatment he hadn't thought of. A long shot, certainly—but occasionally, a long shot hit its target.

"Doctor?" Chapel said as she entered his office. "What is it?"

"Christine, Zainab, I need your help." He motioned at the two to sit down. "Where's Nurse Thomas?"

Odhiambo spoke up. "Getting some rest. Cheryl's been up since yesterday."

"Ah," was all McCoy replied to that. He hadn't noticed that, which showed how oblivious he'd become. "I need your suggestions for treatments you think might work for our coma patients. Something out of the ordinary— unusual, even unorthodox."

Neither of the two nurses said anything. The doctor imagined he could see their brains shifting into high gear.

Odhiambo turned her gaze away from the display case behind him, her face taking on a hopeful expression. "I'm not sure . . . it hasn't been done for years . . ."

"Yes?" said McCoy.

"Well, why don't we try deep brain stimulation?" Odhiambo looked embarrassed. "I know it's really ancient . . . like suggesting osmotic eels . . ."

"Interesting idea. I don't know enough—" McCoy interrupted himself. "Let's see if we can get all the literature on it."

Odhiambo seemed very interested in the deck. "I've done all the research. It had mixed results, but it wouldn't harm them, and it could help. The procedure is on your computer."

McCoy reviewed the data. It wasn't much to go on, but if there was even the slightest chance of success, he'd try it. "Well done, Nurse. This may be just the sort of left-field suggestion we need."

There was no device designed for this ancient therapy on the *Enterprise*, but a good doctor knew how to improvise. McCoy took a simple somnetic inducer and within a quarter hour he'd reconfigured it.

The nurses wanted to stay and observe. "I get all twitchy when you stand there behind me, looking over my shoulder," he said. So he sent them off to look after the patients elsewhere on the deck.

The modified device in hand, McCoy stood at Bouchard's bed. This was the moment of truth. The small device gave off a low hum, which was all the indication he got that it was working. There was a small but insignificant spike in brain activity. He didn't want to give up yet and continued moving the device over Bouchard's head for another minute.

No change.

Damn it!

His frustration was growing. McCoy knew himself well enough to take a break before he had to vent his anger at something. Or somebody.

The bosun's whistle sounded for a shipwide announcement. "*All hands, this is Lieutenant Uhura. The* Enterprise *is going to be advancing at impulse speed, accelerating gradually. We've currently stabilized our position by using the warp engines to project a bubble of normal space. Our goal is to smooth the path before us. We anticipate only minor turbulence, but all hands should continue to be alert, because automated computer systems may fail without warning. Report any and all unusual occurrences to your section chiefs. Uhura out.*"

Chapel reported discharging three more patients, leaving only two serious cases—in addition to the espers—for them to care for. Those who had been discharged were able to go back to their stations. McCoy ordered Odhiambo to go around with Abrams, checking on the crew to see if they needed stimulants. He didn't particularly like the idea but it was necessary if the *Enterprise* was going to free herself.

Discouraged, McCoy had injected himself with a neural suppressant again, to keep away his visions. But it was only working intermittently. He was still seeing Jocelyn or his father. Worst of all, they were joined by Joanna, who just stood there, staring at him accusingly. It was as if every guilty thought, every pang of his conscience, had been given substance, taking on the form of the three people in his life that he'd hurt the most.

McCoy would have welcomed some new data to distract him. The damned computer was still humming merrily away, but it had yet to figure out anything usable. He pinched his nose in frustration.

"Since when were you dependent on computers to solve your problems?" Joanna wanted to know, in a tone that allowed no opposition. "You always told me that a physician's best tools were compassion and insight."

McCoy fought back the instinct to reply. It was hardest with Joanna, because she was right. He *had* left her behind. Immediately after the divorce, he'd been so focused on getting away from it all that he'd spent barely any time with her.

"Don't desert these people like you deserted me."

It wasn't fair. He wanted to rail at her, to tell her that he was working his damnedest to save his patients. She was a distraction, a reminder of his failures.

"Like always."

This he couldn't let stand unchallenged, but when he opened his mouth to say something, the deck began to vibrate beneath his feet. His tricorder skittered across his desk, and the objects on the display shelf behind him rattled in place. Uhura had been right; the distortions weren't too bad.

"Don't let them down like you did me."

McCoy didn't recognize the voice. It was a man's, but it wasn't his father's. Too young and too strong. He looked behind him to see a man in a blue uniform. His torso was twisted at an unnatural angle, and blood was oozing down the side of his shirt. The face was familiar . . .

"I don't even know who you are," he said. "I've never talked to you before in my life."

"And certainly not in *mine*," said the man, and he laughed. It was a deep, rasping sound that made McCoy's spine shiver with guilt and cold.

Spine! It was Hendrick, the one who had died last night.

"Thanks so much for remembering me," said the man. "Senior Chief Petty Officer Luke Hendrick. Twenty-three years in the service, all over. And you can't even remember my name."

McCoy was about to argue back, but he snapped to his senses in time. That man shouldn't be here. *None* of them should be here! There must be something wrong with him, something he could detect and treat. Uncertain what else to do, he grabbed the psycho-tricorder from his desk.

His face fell when he studied the readings. Still nothing. How was that possible? McCoy was losing his mind, and he had no idea why.

TWELVE

Twelve Years Ago

After less than a year on the *Feynman*, Leonard lands an assignment on the *Koop*. His residency, jumping from place to place, can't look good on his record, but he's getting deep-space experience. The fact is, he couldn't stand it on the *Feynman*, but the *Koop* isn't much better. When he stays in one place too long, he begins to think too much. When he learns that Joanna and Jocelyn have moved to Cerberus, he requests a starbase posting in the same sector. He ends up on Starbase 7 in Sector 006, close enough to visit.

Joanna is almost three. He realizes that she thinks of him as a visitor, and not as her father. Pretty soon, she will have grown up without him. She throws awful tantrums, and he has a hard time dealing with them. Jocelyn has to step in to calm her down, which makes him feel even worse. It hurts him that he can't be an integral part of Joanna's life. Even if he wanted to give it another go, Jocelyn wouldn't take him back.

Frustrated, he transfers off Starbase 7 to the *Constitution*, where he finally finishes his residency. Despite his record, he lands a plum assignment as a junior medical officer on the *Newton*. After two years, he hears from his father. He's dying of pyrrhoneuritis, a rare offworld disease that's made its way to Earth. Leonard asks for a transfer back to Earth, where he becomes an instructor at Starfleet Medical. Weekends he spends in Forsyth, taking care of his father.

After two years of constant pain, his father dies. Jocelyn sends him her condolences. He doesn't answer the message, and hopes she doesn't come to the funeral. She stays away. Nancy doesn't come either. Leonard learns that she's married and has joined her husband on a survey mission. He isn't disappointed by the news.

The day after the funeral, he requests the deepest space assignment he can get. He spends six months on Capella IV, a planet near Klingon space. It's a welcome relief. He enjoys getting to know the Capellans and their rituals.

As his assignment ends, Leonard hears from Jim Kirk. He's met Kirk a couple times before. *"Bones!"* Kirk's comm begins. *"I need you."* Kirk is the new captain of the *Enterprise* and is just setting out on a five-year mission away from the Federation core worlds. He's looking for a chief medical officer.

"Jim, do you think I want to look at four hundred people's tonsils?" But he accepts the offer. Leonard has realized that he loves practicing interstellar medicine. He enjoys pushing himself, learning. He's at home in Starfleet.

Stardate 4758.1 (0230 hours)

Spock monitored the *Hofstadter*'s sensor display. The shuttles needed to elude the two remaining fighters only long enough to engage their warp drives. They then could jump to the other side of the planet, out of the fighters' detector range, and return safely to the surface. He began performing calculations on the minimum safe distance for engaging warp drive—the deeper a ship was in a gravity well, the greater the danger. The shuttles should be clear for warp drive in four minutes, before the fighters were able to catch up. The Vulcan turned to assess the situation in the shuttle.

On an improvised stretcher, Mister Scott was holding a tricorder and checking on the status of both shuttles. Doctor M'Benga was tending to Lieutenant Rawlins, who had just regained consciousness. "Your patients' status, Doctor?"

M'Benga didn't look up as he continued to run a device over Rawlins's shoulder. "Rawlins will be fine. I've repaired the damage." He paused. "It's Mister Scott I'm really concerned about, sir."

"I'm sitting right here, Doc," interrupted Scott. "I can wait."

Spock examined the immobile engineer. They needed to get Scott to the *Enterprise*'s medical facilities. That required deactivating the device on the surface. "Very good, Mister Scott."

The computer had confirmed his calculations and was now attempting to verify his assessment of local subspace disruptions. Analysis indicated this area of subspace was filled with distortions, rendering it nearly impassable.

Jaeger was reading the report as it came up on the central console. "What does that mean, sir?" asked the geophysicist.

"It means that going to warp is not an option," replied Spock. "We will have to defeat the fighters before we return to the planetary surface."

"Commander, I'm in a bit of a situation right now." Kirk looked at the Farrezzi in front of him, who was trembling as Kirk spoke into his communicator.

"*Sooner would be better. There's a lot of them out there, and I don't know how long we have before they get some cutting equipment.*"

"In that case," said Kirk, "I'll need reinforcements. I'll keep you informed. Kirk out." He slipped the communicator back onto his belt. What did you say to an alien that didn't think like you? How could you gain its trust? Start with the basics.

"My name is James Kirk of the *Starship Enterprise*. What is your name?"

"Acknowledgment. I inclusion thoughtspace now. Name statement: individual family location. Statement: Horr-Sav-Frerin."

Did it mean that its name was Horr-Sav-Frerin, or that Horr was its name, Sav its family, and Frerin its home? He said, "I am here to help you."

"Assessment: lie. Demand: explanation truth objective."

"I'm not lying. We were both shot at. That should be enough proof. You have been kidnapped by some of your own people. I want to free you."

"Assessment: deception possibility. Goal: revelation of secrets."

"Is this a Farrezzi ship?"

The Farrezzi looked around. "Design affirmative."

"Why were you all in stasis? Was it to escape your world's environmental collapse?"

Horr-Sav-Frerin waggled all of its tentacles at once. "Scenario affirmative. Awakening shipside: plan component negative."

Progress. "An alien wouldn't take you aboard a Farrezzi ship—only another Farrezzi would do that. Do you want to look at your attacker?" The captain gestured at the shooter, lying unconscious in the corridor.

Reluctantly, Horr-Sav-Frerin moved toward the slaver, Kirk trailing behind it. Horr's eyestalks wriggled as they examined it, though it always kept one pointed at Kirk. "Recognition!" it shrieked. "Recognition: affiliation!"

"Who?" asked Kirk.

"Group affiliation. Name: New Planets Cousins!"

"Who are the New Planets Cousins?"

"Function location ethics. Traders in interstellar space . . . morality dubious! Rumors! Slavers!"

"The New Planets Cousins are rumored to be slave traders?"

"Affirmation! Exclamation of woe! Repetition!"

"Do you know who the Orions are?" asked Kirk.

Horr jerked its tentacles. "Identification role ethics. Aliens traders morality dubious."

"I think the . . . New Planets Cousins were planning to sell some of your species to the Orions, taking advantage of the fact that your people were all in suspended animation. They must have set it up so they would wake first." Kirk gave Horr an expectant look, hoping his deductions made sense.

"Affirmation. New Planets Cousins past status: hibernation-opposition. Rationale: destabilization trading relationships."

Everything in the room began to tremble, vibrating at an intense rate.

"James-Kirk-*Enterprise*. Assistance requirement! Phenomenon identification!"

Was it a groundquake? No. Kirk recognized the feeling

of a ship's engines gaining power. "Horr-Sav-Frerin, the ship is about to blast off."

"Still stable," Singh reported from the helm.

Uhura's left hand flicked up to her ear instinctively. Nothing there. It was not very often she sat in the big chair, and each time she felt the weight of being responsible for the *Enterprise*.

An hour into the distortion, and the deck was still rumbling. However, there were no other problems. Sensors and lights had gone out a few times, but they'd always come back on. It would take the *Enterprise* approximately three days to clear the distort-zone at this rate, but they would make it. Uhura hoped the landing party was safe on Mu Arigulon; Ensign Padmanabhan had run simulations assessing how these incursions would affect a planet. She hoped he was wrong.

"Ensign Padmanabham, report."

"We're getting some amazing stuff on this new universe, Lieutenant," he said. "Too bad we can't send a probe through one of the deeper distortions."

They'd had this discussion earlier. Singh had pointed out that if the distortions reacted to warp fields, dropping a probe into one was probably inadvisable. Padmanabhan had insisted that an automated one had skirted this region before. Ultimately, Uhura had decided not to launch one of their own.

"Flight path, Ensign?"

"Everything looks clear," Padmanabhan reported. "The other universe is at eight percent permeation ahead of us."

The lights flickered out, then came back on.

"Nine percent," Padmanabhan amended, "but still steady."

The unreliability of the ship's systems made even the simplest task a challenge. Computer failures had been intermittent. The crew had switched off almost every automated system, relying on human control.

Another low rumble, then the lights flickered off again, along with all of the displays. After a few seconds, the lights came back up—but Singh's console did not.

"No engine control," he said.

Uhura pressed the comm button for engineering. "Lieutenant DeSalle, keep the bubble steady—"

She was interrupted by a chorus of alarms from Padmanabhan's controls. "Total collapse!" he shouted over the racket. "Other universe at seventy-five percent!"

Uhura felt the explosion, then the entire ship shook as though it had been hit by a giant's fist. The force of the tremors was so immense that she was tossed out of her chair. She landed hard on her knees and hands, her head just missing the base of Singh's chair.

Singh was quickly back in his seat, apparently unharmed. "Massive explosion, portside," he read, panting. "Trying to stabilize." The stars on the viewscreen spun past quickly as the *Enterprise* careened through space.

"Engineering, I need that bubble!" Uhura shouted as she got up, holding on to the chair.

"*We're trying, Lieutenant,*" came the voice of DeSalle.

"What happened?" she asked Singh.

The engineer didn't answer. He was too busy trying to bring the ship back under control. The deck trembled underneath Uhura's feet, but with both arms gripping the console's edge tightly, she remained upright.

"The computer system that was keeping the bubble balanced shut down," Padmanabhan jumped in. "Just for five seconds, but it was enough. Part of the ship was thrust entirely into the other universe before the explosion pushed us away." He checked a set of readings on his controls. "Still at fifty percent permeation," said Padmanabhan. "These readings are amazing."

Uhura wasn't inclined to agree. The ship was in danger of being ripped apart. "Engineering, what was that explosion?" asked Uhura. "I need a damage report."

"We don't know yet." This voice, Ensign Harper's, was a little more apologetic. *"Lieutenant DeSalle's still working on getting the bubble reestablished."*

Uhura had to wonder: How did Captain Kirk endure the knowledge that with one mistake, his entire crew could die?

When the alarms started blaring, McCoy tried to bring sickbay's lights back up to full, anticipating casualties. He couldn't—main power was out and they were on backup.

"Great," he groused to Chapel as they waited. Leslie had informed sickbay that his security team was on the way with casualties.

"Why don't you just give up, then?" Jocelyn demanded. "Run, like you do every time things get too tough." Had the real Jocelyn ever been so cruel? No, the woman he'd married hadn't been easy to be with, but at least she wouldn't rub salt into an open wound. This . . . hallucination, ghost, or whatever it was seemed intent on getting a rise out of him.

"We can handle it." Chapel didn't sound as if she believed it.

Less than a minute later, the door hissed open. Leslie and his squad were carrying two unconscious people on stretchers. McCoy steeled himself: more coma cases? As the security people drew closer, however, McCoy got a better look. Hematomas, evidence of multiple compound fractures. "What the hell happened?"

"Artificial gravity and inertial dampers shut down," explained Leslie, his voice shaken. "Repeatedly." Few things were more unnerving to a spacer than the thought of life-support failure. Technology was what allowed you to explore space.

They were computer technicians McCoy only knew by sight. Had they been in that section when— No time for speculation. A simple visual inspection of the two women told him they needed to be operated on at once. He sent Chapel for the drugs and tools they needed. He directed Leslie and his squad to place the technicians on the beds in the examination room.

All the while, his ghosts were following him closely. "I hope you can save them, unlike me," Luke Hendrick said, sneering. "Don't dawdle this time."

"I think you should move on," said McCoy's father, "just stop trying and leave everything like you did with me."

"No way," said a woman's voice. He looked to his side to see Crewman Santos standing there, with the four other comatose patients. What was this supposed to be? "He can't save us, so he's got to demonstrate he's capable of saving *someone*."

"Leave them all behind!" shouted Joanna. "Isn't this too much responsibility, just like I was?"

McCoy ran his hands through his hair in frustration. How was he supposed to get anything done?

"What happened to the safeguards to prevent this?" he asked Leslie. With so many voices vying for his attention,

McCoy found it hard to focus on the new patients' bio-readings.

"The bubble collapsed, the port computer bank exploded," said Leslie. "It breached the hull, and most of the life support in that section went offline."

McCoy hadn't considered it before, but there were duotronic circuits in every part of this ship. If they plunged fully into one of these distortions, there wouldn't be an *Enterprise* left.

"We can't find three people. Lemli is searching the area, but . . ."

If they hadn't been found yet, chances were they'd been sucked into space. What a gruesome way for lives to end. . . .

"Well, at least *these* deaths aren't your fault," said McCoy's father. "Other people let them die."

"He's about to let these die, though," said a new voice—Petriello. "Just like us."

McCoy wanted to tell them all to shut up. He couldn't work like this, with a crowd of imaginary people around him. He tried to focus on the patient in front of him. He turned to the equipment tray Chapel had brought over and grabbed a hypospray. In one quick, well-trained motion, he loaded it with a drug routinely used in percussive injury treatments. He had to admit he'd never seen a case as serious as these two.

"Just leave them," advised Joanna. "Move on and don't think about them any longer. Just like you abandoned me. Do you really need all this responsibility weighing on you?"

He bit down on his lip to curb his instinct to reply.

McCoy was reaching for a protoplaser when he realized he wouldn't be able to do this alone. No, that was wrong, he wasn't alone. Chapel was here. But they could work on only one patient at a time, while the other might be getting worse. He needed more help.

"You don't even want to be here," added Bouchard. "If you had your choice, you'd still be on Earth, practicing medicine like your father."

"Like me, the quintessential country doctor." McCoy's father coughed. "You went and ran away, though."

"Stop!"

It took McCoy a moment to realize it was Chapel who had spoken, not one of his visitors. His hands held the protoplaser, centimeters away from the first technician's skin. "What?" he asked, confused.

"You didn't take any scans," she said. "How do you know where the fractures are?"

She was right. He took the Feinberger she was holding out to him and moved it over the patient's head. Any injuries there needed to be dealt with immediately, while the others could wait, at least for a few minutes.

Chapel read off the result, and he modified the protoplaser accordingly. The trauma to the woman's skull had caused a hematoma that was putting pressure on the brain tissue. McCoy needed to reduce that pressure as quickly as possible.

"You can barely even handle a couple of compound fractures?" asked Jocelyn.

McCoy wanted to rail that it wasn't his fault, that he'd done everything he could. Why didn't they just leave him alone?

No, not alone. "Call in Thomas and Brent. We'll have to do this simultaneously." Cheryl Thomas was good at treating difficult fractures.

After taking readings on the second patient, McCoy tried to think what to do next. If he kept his mind on the task, the ghosts stopped harassing him. If he answered back, even internally, they replied. But if he didn't say anything, they grew quiet eventually. At least for a while.

Scotty wasn't a tactician, but he understood the shuttles' problem. If the *Hofstadter* split off from the *Columbus*, the other shuttle would be an easy target without a functioning weapons system. But by staying together, they were one target for two enemies. They needed a way to even the odds. Scotty tabbed through the displays on his tricorder, examining the readouts of the shuttle's sensors. Within the ring of satellites, there was a tiny energy blip.

"Mister Spock," he said, "one of the Farrezzi satellites is still active." He glanced to the aft of the shuttle, where the one they'd pulled out of orbit still sat. "If we get closer, we could get a good read and figure out what it's for. If it *is* something like a weapons platform . . ."

"We shall alter course," replied Spock.

The shuttles veered off in a new direction, dipping toward a satellite orbiting above the southern hemisphere. As Scotty watched on his tricorder, the fighters matched course with them, slipping ever closer. At this rate, they'd be in weapons range in fifteen minutes.

Scotty looked over at Emalra'ehn. The Deltan security guard had remained quiet. "How are you doing, lad?" he asked.

Emalra'ehn shrugged. "Passable. I am glad the ship has stopped bouncing so much." He shook his head. "It was disrupting my concentration."

"Aye. I dinna like roller coasters."

"I wish my ground combat skills were of use here," added Emalra'ehn. "I've never cross-trained in shipboard weaponry. This mission makes me think I should have."

The engineer knew the feeling. The Academy trained Starfleet officers to be in the thick of it at all times. He hated being forced to stand around with his hands in his pockets. Metaphorically speaking. His tricorder beeped. It had a clear read on the active satellite, which was directing a particle field at the planet's surface. "Is that a weapon?"

"Negative, Mister Scott," replied Spock. "The particle field is diffused energy—"

"What's it being directed at?" interrupted Scotty.

Jaeger replied, "The ocean down there. But—" He paused for a moment. "There's a storm down there—a small one, but it's definitely there."

"There are storms everywhere down there," M'Benga mumbled.

"But before there weren't," Jaeger responded. "There was the big storm over the continent. That was it! Mister Spock, can you plot where this satellite was when we made planetfall?"

"It was over the southern continent. I believe your hypothesis is correct," Spock replied evenly.

"What?" asked Scotty.

"That satellite," said Jaeger, "caused the storm down there. It's a weather modification device."

"Fascinating," said Spock. "The Farrezzi hid themselves because they were near the point of environmental collapse. They needed to leave an infrastructure capable of returning the planet to its original state. Approximately one thousand weather modification satellites could accomplish the task in one hundred twenty-six years." He paused. "Plus or minus two-point-seven."

"We should shoot it down," said Emalra'ehn. "We don't need any more weather like that."

Scotty held up a hand. "Wait," he said. "I want to know *exactly* how that thing works."

"Your curiosity is admirable, Mister Scott—" began Spock.

Scott cut him off. " 'Tisna curiosity, Mister Spock. A device that can shoot one beam of particles can shoot another."

"And a phaser beam is made up of charged particles." Emalra'ehn's face lit up.

"Exactly." Scotty looked over at the inert satellite sitting in back of the shuttle. "If we can figure out how that thing works, we've got ourselves another weapon."

Kirk held on to the nearest cryopod as tightly as he could as the transport ship surged upward. It had been a long time since he'd flown aboard an old-style ship. As every ounce of his body was pulled downward, Kirk decided that he much preferred inertial damping, to hell with the romance of early space flight.

Horr was even more agitated. Its shouts had degenerated into squeaks the universal translator couldn't decipher.

"Calm down," Kirk shouted, "it's almost over!" In actuality, he had no idea, but Horr quieted. Kirk continued to hold on to the pod just in case. The captain felt himself become lighter, his feet coming off the deck.

Horr was screaming again. "Assistance requirement! Assistance requirement!"

Moments later, Kirk's feet dropped back to the deck. So Farrezzi technology had progressed enough to have artificial gravity. Impressive. "We're in space now," he said, knowing that Horr required an explanation, "probably on our way to the Orion market where the New Planets Cousins are going to sell you and your people. My people are on the surface. Horr, I need your help, and the help of your people, to stop these slavers."

Horr quivered, but it stood upright, its eyestalks straight. "Request: orders. Demand: liberation!"

Kirk smiled. Perhaps with an army of liberated Farrezzi, he could rescue Giotto and Chekov, find Yüksel, and put an end to the slave trade.

The odd pair worked their way down the line of two dozen pods, pressing their "purge" buttons. Kirk doubted that this random collection of citizens would be combat-trained. If the New Planets Cousins were smart, they would have avoided stealing military personnel and justice officers. Kirk figured he probably had an army of expense accountants and kindergarten teachers.

"Horr, my friend," he said, "I think you should explain."

"Affirmation!" said Horr, turning to address its people. "Greeting of joy and sorrow! Fear and surprise! Status: perpetrator location purpose. Betrayal by New Planets Cousins, spaceship slavery-commerce."

The sleepers began to squeal, all at once, too much for Kirk's universal translator to keep up with. But Horr kept talking, trying to calm them down.

Eventually, after a few minutes of agitated squealing and gesticulating, the noise level decreased significantly. Horr shuffled back over to Kirk. "James-Kirk-*Enterprise*. Partial belief/disbelief. Requirement: superior proof."

How could he convince a group of Farrezzi that they were en route to an alien slave market? A thought occurred to him, and he grabbed Rawlins's tricorder, tabbing through it until he found what he was looking for: DATASOURCE REPLAY. He selected it, and the device began playing back the UT's first encounter with the Farrezzi language, from the slavers in the underground chamber. It seemed like ages now. "Play them this," he said, handing the tricorder to Horr.

The Farrezzi took the tricorder back to the group of Farrezzi. "Horr!" Kirk called after him. "How did you calm them all down so quickly?"

Horr wriggled one of his tentacles. "Experience calm-induction agitation surplus. Specialty: crowds."

"What did you do before you went to sleep?" Kirk asked.

"Occupation: educator. Specialization: youngchild age-group."

Apparently Kirk had underestimated the uses of a kindergarten teacher.

"There." McCoy switched off the dermal regenerator and handed it to Nurse Chapel. "All done." They had finally finished their treatment of the compound fracture cases.

"Which is good," Santos said, the most recent addition to his chorus of distracting voices. "Because you're not getting anywhere finding us a cure."

McCoy turned to snap at her, but stopped when he remembered Chapel was right there.

"Is something the matter, Doctor?"

McCoy looked back at Chapel, the others forgotten. "Nothing, Nurse. Why?"

"You seem distracted."

The compound fractures hadn't been difficult to treat, but Chapel had had to bring his attention back to the patients on more than one occasion. "Just tired, I suppose," he said. "It's been a long day *and* a long night." It was after 0500. It had been twenty-one hours since he'd reported to sickbay.

"It's more than that," Chapel insisted. "I've seen you tired, but this—"

The door of the examination room hissed open, and they both turned to see who was coming in now.

It was Lieutenant Uhura and Ensign Padmanabhan with an antigrav cart, on top of which sat a pile of portable computer consoles. They pushed the cart right past him and Chapel.

Uhura stepped over to him. "Doctor, a moment, please." McCoy followed Uhura through his office into his lab, which was unused at the moment. Padmanabhan began setting up the consoles on the central table, while Uhura started switching them on. "What is this?" McCoy asked.

"This," said Padmanabhan, pointing, "is a mobile sensor . . ."

"Ensign," Uhura snapped.

"Why are you here?" McCoy asked.

"We're setting up a tertiary control room," said Uhura, checking the status of each computer.

"What happened to auxiliary control?"

"When the portside computer banks exploded, we were lucky—" Uhura paused.

"Lucky?" McCoy offered.

"The waveform from the explosion bounced back from the other universe."

"And—" McCoy prompted.

"The backlash established a permanent rupture between the universes," Padmanabhan said quickly. "The other reality is slowly leaking into ours. The readings I'm getting—I've never seen anything like them before! They are simply amazing."

"Homi . . ." Uhura took a deep breath. "We got the realspace bubble back up. Our equipment isn't working around the edges of the ship. These distortions keep on getting stronger even though we've shut down any power they can feed on." Uhura's voice grew grave. "There must be some force pushing the distortions into our universe. We thought it was our engines, but it's something else."

"We've shut everything down that's close to the hull," Padmanabhan said as he programmed the computer in front of him. "I'm ready here, Lieutenant."

"Connect all systems," Uhura ordered.

"Sickbay is the most shielded part of the ship," McCoy said. "The safest place on the ship." That was the idea behind its location, at the center of the saucer section. Never before had there been a need to set up the control systems here.

"Anything else, Doctor?" Uhura asked.

"No, no." McCoy headed back to his office.

Uhura was certainly qualified to command the ship, but she was running on stimulants. Maybe it was time to release Sulu for duty.

"Sulu isn't going to fix anything," said Joanna. "Admit it: you know this is it."

"Shut up," he said, not very loudly in case somebody overheard him.

"What's going on?" Chapel asked. "What . . ."

"They've turned my lab into a command center."

"I didn't know things had gotten that bad," Chapel said.

"It looks like it, Christine. Can you give me a hand? They could use some chairs over in the lab," McCoy said.

"Yes, Doctor," she said and followed him, each of them with a chair.

When they arrived in the lab, Padmanabhan chirped his thanks. They quickly returned to his office. Now chairless, McCoy sat on the desk.

"You should get some rest," Chapel said. "I had my sleep, and you seem like you need it now."

McCoy shook his head. "What I need is to get back to work on the espers."

"I am perfectly capable of doing my job!" Chapel shouted. "Now leave me alone!"

What? He hadn't said—

With rising dread, McCoy realized that Christine hadn't been looking at him when she'd said that.

She'd been looking off to the side, past him.

"Christine . . ." he began, uncertain of how to phrase it. She looked anxious, but he plunged forward. "I just want to say . . . is there something going on?"

Her eyes locked onto his in apprehension. "What makes you say that?" Careful, just like he'd be if somebody had asked him the same thing.

"We need to be honest with each other," McCoy said, aware that he was forcing her to make the first move, to admit her mind was playing tricks on her, to make herself vulnerable in front of him. "Christine, who do you see?"

"Oh, Doctor," she said, relief washing over her features.

"It's him. I see Roger." McCoy was aware of only one Roger, her long-dead fiancé.

As Chapel began to sniffle, he pulled her into a hug, all the while shouting out for joy inside himself.

"I thought I was going crazy," Chapel said with a sob.

"So did I, Christine. So did I."

THIRTEEN

Stardate 4758.2 (0540 hours)

The damnedest part of it all was that Scotty couldn't do any of the work himself, stuck on his back. Mister Spock continued to dodge weapons fire from the Farrezzi fighters, while trying to protect the *Columbus*. Scotty was reduced to being a manual, cross-referencing scans of the recovered satellite and the working one while directing Cron Emalra'ehn and Jabilo M'Benga.

"Yellow wire to green wire," he directed.

"Which yellow wire?" asked M'Benga. "There are three."

Scotty looked again at the screen of his tricorder. "The medium-sized one." M'Benga moved to connect the two wires, but Scotty caught him just in time. "Not that one—the *medium* one."

"Damn," M'Benga murmured, reaching into the guts of the machine. He grasped the correct wire easily; he might not have an engineer's eye, but he had the sure hands of a surgeon.

"Easy, Doctor," said Scott, turning his attention to Emalra'ehn. The security guard was using a hyperspanner to reactivate the defunct fusion microreactor. It needed an initial charge, and the preternaturally calm Deltan could hold his hands steady long enough to do it. "You're almost there, lad."

Emalra'ehn nodded. "This is trickier than that time on Argelius . . ."

"Concentrate," interrupted Scotty wearily.

The *Hofstadter* rumbled as it took another hit. Spock had used some of the weather sats for cover, but the fighters had blasted straight through them. Two well-placed shots by Spock had hit the engine of one of the fighters. The effect was minimal—the shuttles were still being chased.

"Got it." M'Benga looked relieved.

Scotty checked his tricorder. The particulate energy had increased a hundredfold. "Thank you, Doc."

M'Benga nodded. "All things considered, I'd rather stick to medicine."

"Are you ready, Mister Scott?" Spock called from the front of the shuttle. "Our time is limited."

"Almost, Commander." Scott checked the charge of the microreactor. "We're good enough."

The worst part of the plan was that there was no way to remotely control the satellite. Someone would have to go out there with it. Emalra'ehn had volunteered.

"Ready, lad?" asked Scotty.

M'Benga was helping Emalra'ehn check the seals on his EVA suit. "Ready," said the young man.

Spock flipped on the comm. "*Columbus*, are you ready?"

"*Aye, sir,*" answered Kologwe.

"Accelerate to full impulse," ordered Spock. "Linear course."

Scotty felt the overtaxed engines of the *Hofstadter* surge. Once Emalra'ehn was outside the shuttle, they needed to have him set up just right.

"Open hatch now," commanded Spock. M'Benga tapped the hatch control, and it swung open.

Emalra'ehn climbed up onto the recovered sat, putting his feet on one of its projecting emitters. "Ready."

"Maximum impulse," reported Spock.

"*Matching speed,*" said Kologwe.

"Stand by," said Spock.

Scotty caught the eye of Emalra'ehn, who gave him a thumbs-up.

"Go."

All the Farrezzi had been awoken. They had been horrified, but once they saw the playback, they believed Kirk. None were trained in combat. Horr had suggested that the New Planets Cousins had deliberately gathered laborers, hoping to obtain passive slaves.

Kirk raised a hand to get the Farrezzi's attention, but their reaction was difficult to gauge, since no heads turned. "Attention requirement!" he shouted. "If this ship goes to warp, it will be impossible to keep you from being sold. You know what the New Planets Cousins plan to do. We have to stop them."

He walked over to the unconscious slaver and picked up its gun. Holding it up, he turned to the crowd. "Who knows how to use this? We need to arm ourselves."

A dozen Farrezzi were each waving two limbs in the air and saying something. Kirk could only make out the closest one.

"Statement: I possession ability of weapon use. I hunter training completion."

The others squeaked in affirmation. Maybe they'd be successful after all.

■ ■ ■ ■

Cron Emalra'ehn gripped the satellite as tightly as he could while M'Benga and Rawlins picked it up from either side. Cron saw Rawlins wince as the weight pulled at his shoulder. The doctor counted off, and they shoved it—and him— out the hatch. The force field crackled around him.

The Farrezzi fighters were coming up fast. Behind the *Hofstadter,* the *Columbus* flew cover, interposing itself between Emalra'ehn and the approaching fighters.

He reached inside an open panel on the satellite, twisting a dial. His tricorder told him that the satellite was locking on to a target. Using his tricorder, Emalra'ehn could adjust the direction.

"You okay, lad?" Scotty asked.

"Calibrating sights." Emalra'ehn was stunned by how calm he sounded. He hoped he had understood Scotty's instructions.

"Ninety seconds," reported Jaeger. Time was running out.

"Power looks good," said Scotty.

Emalra'ehn's visor lit up—the *Columbus* was taking fire.

"I'm lined up. Let's do this."

"Affirmative," Spock said. The *Hofstadter* dipped down slightly, then disappeared as Spock threw its engines into reverse.

This was it—Petty Officer Cron Emalra'ehn alone in the cosmos, with two enemy fighters.

"Now."

"Copy that," said Kologwe.

Seven Deers took one of the back seats in the *Columbus* to monitor the shield systems. They were taking quite a pounding, but they were needed if this was to work. Glancing forward, she could just make out a purple-and-silver dot ahead—Emalra'ehn hanging onto a Farrezzi satellite.

The *Columbus* slipped to one side. A moment later, a beam stabbed out from the satellite, hitting the closest fighter.

"*Hofstadter* is also firing," reported Tra from the navigator's seat. It had come up from behind.

An alarm chimed on Tra's controls. "Other fighter is firing!"

The *Columbus* lurched to one side, intercepting the Farrezzi fire before it could reach Emalra'ehn. The shuttle's deck rumbled as it took the direct hit. Seven Deers shivered at the thought of what those things could do.

Seven Deers didn't envy Emalra'ehn out there one bit.

McCoy called the rest of the medical staff in to compare notes. Now that he knew he wasn't the only one hallucinating, he wanted to find out who else had been affected.

Initially reluctant to say anything, Cliff Brent admitted that he was hearing people, too: Ensign Laverne, who'd died while he was treating her wounds, and his aunt Marys, who'd always blamed him for anything that had gone wrong. Nurse Odhiambo's only voice was her brother Vijay. Ensign Messier reported only a niggling doubt—nothing that she'd classify as a hallucination. However, Abrams and Thomas weren't experiencing anything out of the ordinary. Only McCoy and Chapel were seeing people.

"We've all been idiots. I thought the stress was getting to me," McCoy confessed.

The progression had been similar for everyone who was suffering from hallucinations. First a feeling of doubt, then a voice that became specific, and finally the images of people. McCoy had heard the voice the earliest, and he'd started seeing things first, too. Chapel hadn't seen anything until a couple hours ago.

"This gives me four times the data," McCoy said, "if not more." He sent Chapel to ask Uhura and Padmanabhan if they had been seeing things. Meanwhile, McCoy took readings of Brent, Odhiambo, and Messier.

"What do you think is causing it?" Brent asked, concern etched into his face. "Is it the same as what's affecting the coma patients?"

"I think it is," said McCoy. "Four of us experience hallucinations at the exact same time five people drop unconscious? If these cases aren't related, I'll turn in my license."

Chapel returned, reporting that Uhura and Padmanabhan had not been affected. Uhura had been concerned when Chapel explained what was going on, but Chapel had assured the lieutenant that everything was under control.

"It will be," said McCoy. He asked the medical computer to check for correlations with the espers. McCoy studied the results with satisfaction. "Exactly what I suspected—there is a connection. Our brainwaves spike just after theirs do." He pulled up the espers' readings. "They're deteriorating faster than before."

"Are they influencing us?" asked Chapel. "Or are we looking at two effects with the same cause?"

"What are your esper ratings?"

"Zero-four-nine," she said.

Brent thought for a moment. "Somewhere in the high thirties, I think."

"Zero-three-four for me," Odhiambo said.

McCoy's was 046. "None of us have any real extrasensory abilities. But we're the only ones affected . . ." The doctor let the sentence trail off.

"It has to be something specific to sickbay," Chapel said, finishing the thought for him. "Abrams and Thomas have been working outside of sickbay for most of the day."

McCoy said, "I think the espers are behind it. Are they trying to contact us?"

Chapel gave him a doubtful look. "Why this way? What kind of message are they trying to send by amplifying every little self-doubt?"

McCoy stared at the readings, but the longer he did that, the clearer it became that there was only one option. "I've been using neural suppressant," he said slowly, "but that's the wrong approach. What I need is a neural stimulant."

"You can't!" Chapel exclaimed.

"Oh yes, I can," McCoy said. "You're going to put me under, Christine. I want to talk to them."

"Hold her steady, lad," Scotty said. "More power to your target lock."

"*I'm trying, Commander!*" Emalra'ehn's voice was heated.

As Scotty watched on his tricorder, the energy beam hit the Farrezzi fighter. The *Hofstadter* drew closer from behind as the fighter's engines failed.

"Sixty seconds." Jaeger sounded nervous.

Finally, the fighter began to glow red as the energy proved too much for it.

"Cut your beam, Petty Officer," Scotty ordered the Deltan.

"Yes, sir."

Seconds later, the phaser beam from the *Hofstadter* lit the fighter up white-hot.

"Break off!" shouted Jaeger, but Spock was already doing it. As the *Hofstadter* veered, the fighter exploded, rocking the shuttle. Scotty felt the deck lurch beneath him.

"Fighter destroyed." Spock checked his controls.

The last fighter was closing in on Emalra'ehn. "Fire, lad!" shouted Scott.

"Power's too low! I have to wait for it to recharge."

Damn. If only he was out there—he knew a few tricks, but they were too complicated to explain to Emalra'ehn. "Hang on, lad. We're coming."

Spock brought the *Hofstadter*'s phaser to bear on the last fighter, but it was getting perilously close to Emalra'ehn. Without weapons, there was nothing *Columbus* could do.

Suddenly, the other shuttle split off. *"Maybe if we ram it—"* began Kologwe.

Spock cut her off. "Unwise. Try to envelop the satellite in your shields."

"Fire now, Cron," said Scotty. The microreactor was up to twenty-five percent, enough for several seconds' firing.

Emalra'ehn muttered something. Scotty couldn't make it out. "Repeat that, Petty Officer."

"What if I dumped all that energy out one of the projectors at once, instead of in a sustained beam?"

"It couldna take it," said Scotty. "You'd blow up for sure."

"I thought so."

"Well, then fire!"

The *Columbus* was trying to match the sat's speed, but its engines were near burnout. Emalra'ehn did nothing as the fighter gained ground.

"What are you—" Understanding dawned. "Oh no, laddie."

Spock had figured it out, too. "Fire, Petty Officer. That is a direct order."

"Ten seconds," came Jaeger's voice. The engines of both shuttles were on the verge of overloading.

"Sorry, Mister Spock. I'm—"

"Just do it, laddie! Dinna be suicidal!"

A split-second pause. *"Aye, sir. Firing."*

Scotty breathed a sigh of relief.

The beam stabbed out from the satellite, joining *Hofstadter*'s phasers. It wasn't enough. Spock cut the engines, and moments later, the *Columbus* was dead too. The fighter was right on top of the satellite.

The explosion threw Scotty violently across the shuttle before his head hit something, and everything went black.

Giotto hated waiting. The aliens had not given up, pausing only during the blastoff sequence. Now they were using some device to cut through the door—a kind of plasma cutter, judging from the way it sliced through the metal. He wondered if he could take out an entire assault squad.

Chekov was awake now. He was seated with his back against the wall, silent. He was trying to process, looking first at Giotto, then at the unconscious Farrezzi, then, finally, at the door.

Giotto's communicator sounded. "Giotto here."

"Kirk here. We're on our way to you."

"Chekov and I are trapped in a sealed room, with a lot of angry Farrezzi outside. Any sign of Yüksel?"

"Unfortunately not. Right now we've got to stop this ship from going to warp. I'll be there as soon as I can."

"Good luck, Captain."

"Same to you, Commander. Kirk out."

"We"? Had Kirk said, *"We're* on our way"?

Back to waiting. Perhaps the key to keeping Chekov from revisiting the horrors he'd lived through was to engage him in conversation. "So, Ensign, do you still think I'm your father?" Not the best opening.

Chekov was still glassy-eyed, not focusing on any object longer than a few blinks. "No, sir. I am sorry about that," he said, his voice as distant as his gaze and completely emotionless.

"It's fine, Pavel. Can you tell me something about your father? What does he do?"

"Do, sir?"

Damn, his mind was slow now. "I mean, what is his job? I assume he's still working?"

Chekov shook his head slowly. "No, sir. He retired."

"Ah? What did he do before, then?"

"He was a teacher, sir."

"Oh. Did he like his job?"

"Um . . . I suppose he must have, at first. Later, he complained more and more . . . about the children. They didn't know how to behave anymore, he kept saying."

"Sounds to me like he'd become disillusioned."

"Maybe, sir," Chekov said.

"There must've been something about it that kept him going."

"I suppose so, sir."

Giotto needed to get Chekov to focus on something else, like getting out of here. Anything but what he was obviously still thinking about.

"Chekov," he said, "tell me about your time at the Academy. Did you like it there?"

"Yes, sir. It was very educational."

"You sound like Mister Spock. I asked if you *liked* it there. As in, did you have a good time? Make many friends?"

"Ah, sorry, sir." Chekov was still as distant as before. "I made a few new friends. I even met somebody I fell in love with."

"Oh? Tell me about that."

"Her name is Irina. She attended the Academy for a while, and we spent some time together."

"The fact that you don't say more leads me to think it didn't end well."

Chekov looked pained. At least he was thinking about something else. "We . . . separated. She dropped out, there was an argument, we discovered that each of us wanted something different, and there was no future for us together."

"Do you regret splitting up? Excuse my prying, Ensign, but you sound like you do."

"Then, I did. It was all a big mistake. I doubt you're interested."

He was right, but Giotto wasn't going to admit that. "I am. You seem uncomfortable talking about it. Wounds still raw?"

"You could say that, sir. I mean, we both knew it wasn't going to work, but that didn't change how I felt. And still do."

"My dad used to say you weren't a man if you hadn't had a broken heart." What Giotto didn't say was that he'd always thought this was a load of bullshit.

Chekov didn't reply. With his beaten face—the left side of it was starting to turn purple, and there was an open cut on his chin—his matted-down hair, and bloody uniform, Chekov looked like a man out of options.

Even if they made it out of here alive, which now seemed at least within the realm of possibility, Giotto was kicking himself that he'd let the situation unfold so that the captain had to come to his rescue. This was something a good security chief just didn't do. And despite—

"They hurt me."

Chekov was once again staring straight ahead, with wide, empty eyes. Giotto decided to wait, to see if anything more followed that revelatory statement. He knew it was a first step on a very long and difficult road.

"They wanted to use my phaser, but I wouldn't tell them how . . . so they used their own devices."

"They—" Giotto interrupted himself to glance at the door. The plasma cutter had made it halfway along the bottom. He couldn't let them continue. He fired at the spot where the cutter's beam was coming through. There was a hiss, followed by intense light, and then the beam was gone. Giotto hoped he'd destroyed the tool, but he'd at least slowed them down. "They're outside, they can't reach you."

"Commander, they wanted to know everything I knew. I gave them nothing, but they wouldn't stop. They kept asking and hurting me, and I wanted to stay brave and silent and courageous, but . . ." He broke, then. It was terrible to witness—even for Giotto, who'd had his share of traumatic experiences. A young officer, reduced to a sobbing heap.

"They can't hurt you now." Giotto stretched out his hand to pat Chekov on the shoulder, but he caught himself.

Chekov didn't need superficial consoling gestures, he needed actual help.

The sound of a plasma beam being switched on made him turn again. It would come down to a final showdown. He was up for it. The anger he felt was fueled by what they had done to Chekov. Giotto watched the small, thin flame cut across the remaining section of the door. When it reached the side frame, it was switched off. Any moment now, he knew, the door would open, and they'd be outnumbered.

Outside, he heard muffled noises that sounded like weapons fire, interspersed with high and low squeaks. Chekov was lying on his side, sobbing violently, his arms slung around his knees.

Then, the noise outside died. Giotto raised his phaser, waiting for the door to open. Something was stuck in the thin gap in the door the cutter had left. He heard clanging noises, followed by a strange, multipitched groaning. Slowly but surely, the door rose. Before long, Giotto could see the ends of tentacles, but then, he spotted a pair of black boots.

"Ensign, everything's going to be okay," Giotto said. "The captain's here."

Much to his surprise, McCoy found himself wishing Spock was aboard. The Vulcan could have mind-melded with the comatose patients.

The doctor spent half an hour running simulations, trying to determine the best way to reach the coma patients. McCoy believed if he was awake when he took the stimulant, he'd simply see more hallucinations. If he was unconscious, he wouldn't be able to control what happened.

The computer confirmed that putting his brain into a heightened state while deprived of outside stimuli was the best way.

When McCoy told Uhura what he planned to do and why, she was stunned. "You're telling me the medical staff has been seeing hallucinations, caused by the comatose espers. And your solution is to place yourself in a coma to find out why, thereby removing the only doctor the *Enterprise* has?"

"Uhura, I believe that they are trying to tell us how to free the ship, but I'm too distant. This way I go to the source."

The lieutenant studied McCoy, shaking her head, finally saying, "Permission granted." Before McCoy could leave his transformed lab, she added, "Leonard, this better work. I'll never forgive you if it doesn't."

"I'll be fine." McCoy turned and headed to the ward.

"Here's your chance to get away from it all," Jocelyn said pointedly. "Talk about duty in the far-off reaches. Are you looking to kill yourself? That's certainly going further than anyone has ever gone before. And if you don't come back—oh, well."

"Jocelyn, I have to."

"You 'have to' do this, don't you, Dad?" Joanna asked. "Just like you 'had to' leave me on Cerberus. How convenient that all the things you 'have to' do let you abandon your responsibility."

McCoy was stung, because there was a kernel of truth in what they said. It wasn't the first time he'd volunteered for an incredibly dangerous mission.

He was lying on a biobed, one over from Salah. The medical computer had suggested that proximity would be best.

"Are you done yet, Nurse?" he asked.

Chapel was adjusting the bed's monitors, taking far too long. "Almost, Doctor. We can't be too careful."

McCoy shifted uncomfortably. Was it just him, or had the beds gotten harder? Maybe he was just tense.

"Is this really you? The Leonard I know gave up when things got difficult," muttered Jocelyn, somewhere to his left, but out of sight.

"Is it impossible to imagine that I've changed?" he snapped.

Chapel looked startled. "Was that—"

"Yes," he said. "Sorry. Sometimes I forgot they're not really here."

Chapel adjusted the controls. "We're set, Doctor."

"About damn time," muttered McCoy. "You'll need to knock me out with sonambutril first—"

"I was paying attention when we rehearsed this five minutes ago, Doctor." Chapel was on edge, but then they all were.

McCoy stared up at Chapel, who was holding a hypospray in her hands. "Would you do me a favor, Christine? In addition to the one you're doing me right now, I mean?"

"Of course, Doctor. What is it?"

"Sulu," he said. "Check up on him, will you? We need all the senior staff we can get, and unless he's falling over, release him for duty."

"I'll do that," Chapel said. "Now, are you ready?"

Was he? Was he ready to have his mind plunged into who-knows-where to try to contact people they weren't sure were looking for help?

"That's right, son. Run away from it all again."

Hell, yes—he was ready. "Put me under."

"Here we go." Chapel took one last look at the monitors, then plunged the hypospray into McCoy's upper arm.

Relief flooded through McCoy's body, penetrating every organ. He felt himself relax, *truly* relax, for the first time in weeks. "Well, I'll be. This is almost better than—"

FOURTEEN

"—better than a mint julep."

McCoy looked around him. He was standing in the waiting room of a doctor's office. Garishly colored plastic chairs all around him, a pile of data slates on a table, no doubt containing out-of-date downloads.

Wait a second—this wasn't any ordinary doctor's office. This was his father's.

His eyes flashed to the sign next to the door. "DAVID A. MCCOY, M.D."

He was back in Georgia—Forsyth, to be exact.

He'd only ever seen the waiting room this empty after hours, yet all the lights were on. The counter, where there would be a receptionist, was unoccupied.

A noise from behind McCoy made him turn around. In a little niche, where children's toys were kept, the hovertrain was running.

"This wasn't exactly what I was expecting."

"What were you expecting?"

McCoy spun around, immediately spotting his father at the reception desk. His father looked as he did when McCoy was a boy. Above a proud face with dark gray eyes, his dark brown hair was cut short. He was dressed in scrubs. A little black bag sat in front of him on the counter.

"Contact," McCoy said. "A welcoming committee. Hell, even a party. Not more of the same."

"Maybe you should stick to medicine," his father replied. "This place needs you—you left it behind. Leave the space stuff to the professionals."

"I *am* a professional!"

"That's why your cure for my suffering was death?" asked his father. "You stopped being a doctor."

"Never!" He turned around and headed for the door to the waiting room. "I have some patients to find."

"Running away like always!" his father shouted after him. "This place needs you, son! Stay here!"

McCoy swung the door open, expecting to find West Chambers Street. "The only reason I'm running—"

"—is to help people."

The first thing McCoy saw was a group of muscular humanoids, dressed in colorful clothes decorated with fur, all significantly taller than the doctor.

"This is Capella IV." The planet where he'd spent six months learning the local medical traditions and teaching the natives some new ones.

"Of course it is," his father said. He was standing in the center of the group of giants, the tallest of them. He had suddenly grown to almost two and a half meters. "This is where you went to get away from me, isn't it?"

"I didn't run away, I was posted here." McCoy crossed his arms in a defensive stance.

"Who selected the assignment?" demanded his father, sneering. "The outsider must be put to death!"

He reached out with the spear in his hand and stabbed McCoy through the chest.

For a fraction of a second, there was nothing. Then, pain filled McCoy, welling up from where his pierced heart still beat, working its way out to his fingertips. Every inch of him screamed in agony. His legs weakened, he fell to the ground. McCoy tried to inspect his chest, but there was nothing there, no blood, no wound. But the pain remained.

McCoy wished it would stop. The humanoids were standing all around him, more than he could count. He knew them all. They weren't Capellans. They were his father, SCPO Hendrick, Ensign Rellik, Lieutenant Rizzo, and others, too many to name. They were everyone who had died under his care.

A communicator appeared in his hand—his own, judging from the scratches and dents on the cover. With what little strength he could muster, he flipped it open.

"*Enterprise*, one to—"

"—beam up."

The pain was gone. He was standing in a darkened transporter room. The only light was coming from the lit-up circle beneath his feet.

"I never thought I'd be glad for that blasted thing."

The pad next to him lit up, illuminating the person on it from below. "Don't kid yourself, Bones. The transporter has saved your skin more times than you can count."

McCoy felt his mouth broaden into a grin. "Jim, am I glad to see you!" He tried to move toward the other man, but he couldn't get past the column of light. "Why can't I move?"

"You're safe here, Bones," Jim replied with a shrug. "Isolated, protected."

"That's not what I want!" insisted McCoy. "I went into space to do good, not to save myself!"

"If you had wanted to do good, the logical thing to do was to remain at home." With a flash, the next pad lit up. It was Spock. "Perhaps you should have enrolled in medical school. I believe the space-focused course of study is a mere four years."

"You blasted Vulcan, I'm perfectly qualified!" He moved toward him, but again was stopped. Was it his imagination or was the edge of the beam getting closer to him?

"That's not how it seemed to me." Nurse Chapel had appeared. "I may have gone into space to look for Roger, but with a degree in bioresearch, at least I know about space medicine."

McCoy tried to turn around, but he was trapped within the glowing column of light. He couldn't escape, couldn't run from here. This was his safe haven, dammit! He'd fled to the *Enterprise* to be safe.

"Bones, you *are* safe." Kirk smiled. "Within that column, nothing can touch you ever again."

"I don't want to stay here! I want to save my patients! They need me." The beam contracted as he talked, getting smaller with every passing second.

"That cannot be the case, Doctor, otherwise you would not be here," said Spock with an arch of his eyebrow. "If you are on the *Enterprise*, you must seek safety."

The espers had been reaching out to him by making him feel pain. If he wanted to meet them, he needed to go *toward* the pain.

"Beam me back down there."

"Are you sure, laddie?" Scotty was standing at the transporter console. "You want to go back to Capella IV?"

"Yes," said McCoy. "No, wait." He needed to go back to the pain's original source. "Send me to Jocelyn. She's at the center—"

■ ■ ■ ■

"—of this whole mess."

He found himself hunched over the computer in the office of the apartment he and Jocelyn shared in Atlanta. There was a stack of data slates, medical texts and articles and notes. His eyes hurt, reminding him that he'd been staring at this monitor for hours. He had an exam tomorrow and didn't feel prepared. Damn, it looked like it was going to be another all-nighter.

He felt a hand on his shoulder. "Are you ready for bed?"

"Not yet," he said, suppressing a yawn. "A few more minutes."

"You always say that," she said. "I'd rather you just be honest and admit that—"

"I *am* being honest!" He knew it wasn't true. "I'll be there in a few minutes."

"I want you to come *now*."

"What does it matter?" he snapped, turning his chair around to face her for the first time. "We'll be asleep."

Jocelyn was wearing one of his old oversized T-shirts. This one bore the words "OLE MISS." She stood there, arms crossed. "Leonard, if I wanted to spend every night alone, I wouldn't have gotten married!"

"Maybe you wish you hadn't!" he replied, astonished that he was shouting.

"That's not what I want!" Her expression was one of anger bubbling dangerously close to the surface. "Is that what *you* want?"

"All I want to do is pass my exam tomorrow! Not all of us have an easy office job."

"I like how you always make it about me."

"I like how *you* just made it about *me*."

They stared at each other, not saying anything for a moment.

With a start, McCoy remembered when he was. This was the first night he'd stormed out, a liberating move at first, establishing a pattern. The next day he'd come back, and the two of them acted like nothing had happened. Until the entire scene had repeated itself, again and again.

McCoy knew he needed to stay to make the pain *worse*.

"Maybe if you were supportive of what I do," he said. "Med school is the hardest thing I've ever done. It takes time."

"It takes *time*?" Jocelyn's eyes were angry. "The only *time* you spend is with *her*."

"Nancy helps me," said McCoy. "Which is more than I can say for you."

"She 'helps' you, does she?"

"I didn't mean it like that—"

"I know full well what you meant!"

They stared at each other for a moment. "If you're just going to shout at me, why do you *want* me to come to bed with you?"

"Maybe if you *did* come to bed with me, I wouldn't be shouting at you!"

"Well," said McCoy, turning his chair back around, "I'm staying here and I'm studying. I have patients to save." He looked at the text on the monitor—Harding-Cyzewski's paper. He was getting somewhere!

"Leonard McCoy, you look at me when I'm talking to you!"

He sensed it coming before he saw it. A data slate went flying by his head, straight at the computer screen. It connected with a *crack* and threw the thin device off its base and onto the table.

The monitor wasn't shattered, but a gaping black hole had appeared in the middle of it, growing as he watched. For some reason he couldn't fathom, McCoy felt drawn toward the increasing blackness.

"Look at me!" Jocelyn yelled.

The hole was enveloping the table. It would soon swallow the entire room. He could feel it reaching out to him.

The doctor knew he had to touch it. He extended his hand toward it. "I have patients to help, Jocelyn."

"You could help *me*." She sounded hurt rather than angry. The hole was pulling him in. He could feel it, a whole new universe beckoning him.

With a great deal of effort, McCoy turned to look at Jocelyn. She was crying. Regret coursed through his body. Could he have done it differently? "I wish I could, honey."

With a gigantic jerk, McCoy was pulled out of his chair. "But not—"

"—today."

McCoy was alone in the darkness.

There was nothing here. As far as he could see, there was inky blackness, featureless and empty.

It felt *real*. The places he'd passed through before had felt insubstantial and weightless. He opened his mouth to call out, but no sound issued forth. McCoy reached for his throat, only to realize he didn't have any hands.

He didn't have *anything*. No hands, no feet, no head, nothing.

Instinctively, he tried to speak. Again, no sound. The only evidence that he still existed was his thoughts. And he was alone for the first time in two days.

Welcome.

A chorus of voices came from everywhere and nowhere.

He formed a question in his mind, as if he were talking to them. "Is that you?" No noise, yet McCoy felt a normal conversation was appropriate. The doctor wasn't trained in mind matters. "Who am I speaking to?"

Olivier Bouchard.

Gaetano Petriello.

Hanna Santos.

Nanase Fraser.

Rammal Salah.

Then, as one: *We are here.*

"I made it."

Thank you for coming.

"What's the matter with you all? What happened to you?"

We reached out and we found Nothing.

"There's not always going to be a mind for you to touch."

We didn't find nothing. We found Nothing.

"What are you talking about?"

We hadn't noticed it before. We are low-level telepaths, none of us can read minds. And yet we always heard something. A buzzing, a crackling, a knowing. There was always something for us to hear.

"Quantum entanglement," realized McCoy. "All your particles were linked to everyone else's."

We could hear the universe.

"But not anymore?"

No. Our minds reached out as they always do, to feel the other universe . . . and felt Nothing. A whole reality of Silence, from end to end.

"And that's what caused your comas?"

We didn't understand. Our minds didn't understand. They shut down, drove us into comas. We reached out and found each other. We took solace in each other's minds, falling together. Pushing against the Nothing. We needed to hold it back. But there was nothing we could do.

"Why has the medical staff been seeing and hearing things?" McCoy demanded.

We sought other minds, ones that might show us a way out. We found you and the others. We worked our way in.

"Why the hallucinations? Who thought it was a good idea to appear as our worst doubts and fears?"

The only way we could gain access was via the weakest point of everyone's minds. Doubt. Your doubt was the strongest . . . your mind was the easiest to enter.

It was hard to deny. He had been restless, thinking about moving on. His doubts had opened him up to outside interference.

A thought stirred at the back of his mind. Weak . . . defenseless. "Did you try to reach Lieutenant Haines? Or Specialist Huber? They were in pain despite being sedated."

We tried to contact them. It . . . did not work.

"You caused unbearable agony."

We were desperate. We still are.

"You still haven't explained how you were able to do this."

We reached out and found each other. Together we are stronger than we ever have been alone.

"Five panicked minds working in concert . . . that could be enough to overwhelm even Spock."

It's difficult to control our power. We didn't want this. We didn't seek it out. Because of the Nothing, our lives are in danger. We can't survive here, so close to it. Help us!

"What am I supposed to do? Tell me. I've tried so many things, but none of them have worked."

Get us away. It's killing us.

"It's tearing the *Enterprise* apart. Don't you think *we* want to get away, too?"

WE MUST GET AWAY FROM THE NOTHING.

The thought blared into McCoy's mind from every direction, reverberating and rippling. The whole emptiness was defined by that one idea.

"How do I cure you? Your bodies are all about to die out there."

The only way to save us is to get the Enterprise *out of here. The Nothing will destroy the ship if we stay, everyone will die.*

"How?"

Power is the key.

"What do you mean?"

The Enterprise *can't move. Her power will be the ship's death. The Nothing will consume us all.*

"Don't be so cryptic. What do we have to do?"

Find another power.

He couldn't help but laugh at that. "And how am I supposed to do that?"

You will come up with something. We depend on it.

"Thanks. Will you let me go now?"

There was no answer for a long time. When an answer came, it was almost too weak to be heard. *We don't know how.*

"What? You called out to me because you wanted to talk to me, but now you can't let me out of here?"

We don't have control over this . . . We are not keeping you here.

"I need to wake up. If I don't, we might all die. There must be a way."

The blackness did not answer this time. No voice rose out of it, no thought or word came to him.

McCoy was alone in the darkness.

Stardate 4758.3 (0639 hours)

With growing concern, Chapel watched the readout over the doctor's biobed. He'd been under for fifteen minutes. At first his readings had been high due to the neural stimulant, but they had steadily dropped. They were starting to match the level of the espers'—their readings had sunk so low that they were all in danger of brain death.

"Why don't you stand there and stare some more. I bet that'll help."

The insulting sarcasm was something she had trouble ignoring. Roger knew that. He'd been observing her and commenting on her actions, pointing out how unsuitable she was. She found it hard to concentrate. Hopefully, the doctor would find a way to banish him and the other unwelcome visitors.

Doctor McCoy had been adamant that Chapel not wake him up unless she absolutely had to. He needed to wake himself up. "The last thing I need is to be learning what's going on and then have you tear me away. Let it go as long as you can." But McCoy's readings were sinking.

"I remember when you were a bioresearcher," Roger said, relentless in his taunts. "We were pushing at the frontiers of medicine together. Now you just stand here holding people's hands as they give up the ghost. What happened to you?"

"*You* happened to me!" Chapel replied before she could

stop herself. "I went into space to find *you*. Starfleet needed nurses, not bioresearchers." Fortunately, there was no one to hear her outburst.

"Well, that was stupid. You should have replaced me—just like I replaced you." Roger held out his hand and suddenly Andrea was there—the android woman he had built. She never said anything in Chapel's visions, she just stood there. Was she Roger's perfect woman?

Her ruminations were interrupted by the sickbay door hissing open. She heard Assistant Chief Engineer DeSalle storming in, and knew he was headed for the control center.

The *Enterprise*'s situation was directly connected to the patients' state. Chapel reasoned that she might be needed.

"I'm sure everyone really values the opinion of the ship's *nurse*," sneered Roger.

Roger could be such an ass. Chapel wondered why she'd never noticed it while he was alive.

She checked Doctor McCoy's readings—they were holding. She called in Odhiambo to stay with him and quickly made her way to the lab/control room.

DeSalle was in the middle of his report when Chapel entered. "—position, the power systems are a patchwork of fixes. The real-space bubble is draining our power reserves."

"We can't move," Uhura replied. "We know—" She stopped when she noticed Chapel and gave her a tired smile. "Hello, Christine. Is anything the matter?"

"No," Chapel said. "It's just that . . . with Doctor McCoy out for the moment, I thought I should keep myself up-to-date, as our patients are linked to whatever is out there."

Uhura nodded. "So, we know what will happen to any duotronic system entering an area of high distortion. This entire ship is loaded with duotronics." Chapel was struck by how exhausted she looked.

"*Pow*," said Padmanabhan, miming a miniature explosion with his hands. "Like a nova."

Uhura gave the overly enthusiastic young ensign a withering stare. "Thank you, Mister Padmanabhan. Why are we losing power so quickly?"

"The other universe is affecting all our systems," said DeSalle. "Not always catastrophically, but it's definitely draining them."

"Once we get out of the distort-zone, they'll be fine." Uhura made it sound like a certainty, but Chapel knew her well enough to spot the doubt underneath.

"Exactly," DeSalle said.

Uhura turned to Padmanabhan. "Ensign, any progress in pushing back the other universe?"

"The edges of the ship are getting worse and worse," he said. "It provides for some fascinating scan results, though. How does matter from our universe cope with one without quantum physics? I can't even conceive of it. The stuff I'm seeing just on ten-percent permeation—"

"You're getting off topic, Ensign," said Uhura.

"Oh, right, sorry. No progress."

"I want a way out of this thing," said Uhura. "We can't just sit here pushing back if in the end it won't do any good. We need to shut these distortions down, and get out of this zone."

"We barely have power," protested DeSalle. "And if we move—"

"Solutions, not complaints." Uhura cut off the engineer. "We are not going to lose this ship."

"Lieutenant—" began Padmanabhan.

Uhura cut him off. "I want the two of you to come up with options to get us out of here."

Padmanabhan and DeSalle looked at each other.

"We'll move the crew to the core," she said. "We'll shut down as many systems as we can, too. I'll coordinate it from here."

"I'll be in the spatial physics lab," Padmanabhan said. "Maybe Bellos has new information."

"I'll be in engineering," DeSalle said curtly.

When the door hissed shut behind them, Uhura headed back to her chair, but she stumbled before she could reach it.

Chapel rushed over, grabbed her, and guided her to the chair. "Are you okay?"

Uhura was breathing heavily, clutching her chest. "It hurts," she said. "All of a sudden."

Chapel grabbed a medical tricorder and aimed it at Uhura. As the readings began to come in, she frowned. "All of a sudden?"

"All of a sudden . . . a couple hours ago."

"There's a sliver of metal in your chest, working its way further in," said Chapel. "It's been there for a while, probably since the explosions on the bridge."

"I've been . . . trying to ignore it," Uhura said. "I've got to keep on going."

"Well, do *something*." It was just like Roger to add a snide remark when this was the last thing Chapel needed. "Standing here ruing her actions isn't helping. You're not turning out to be much of a nurse."

She ignored him and looked at the readings. "We're going to need to operate to get that sliver out," she said. "If Doctor McCoy doesn't regain consciousness in the next half hour, I'll do the operation myself."

Uhura nodded, grimacing with pain as she spoke. "Very well."

Chapel helped Uhura into the exam room. Carefully she helped Uhura onto a biobed.

Before the communications officer passed out, she said, "Christine . . . tell the captain I'm sorry."

"I will, Nyota." And then Uhura was unconscious.

Chapel checked to see who the senior yeoman on duty was. She got in touch with Lawton, telling her about Uhura's plan to evacuate the crew to the core and shut down sections near the edge of the ship. Lawton said she could implement it.

"You've lost your boss, and now you've lost your commanding officer," said Roger. "Just like you lost me. You're not doing too well, dear."

"Shut up!" Chapel snapped. She didn't have time for this. Determined to do her job, she flipped the comm. "Engineering."

"Ensign Harper here."

"Ensign, this is Nurse Chapel. I need to talk to Lieutenant DeSalle."

"He's busy with the warp circuits right now. I don't think he can—"

"That's an order, Ensign."

Harper sounded unconvinced. *"Aye."*

"DeSalle here. What is it?"

"Lieutenant Uhura is unconscious, pending surgery."

"So?"

"That puts you in command of the *Enterprise*."

"Not if we ever hope to get free. Is Lieutenant Sulu well enough to do it?"

A good question. "I'll check."

"*Look, I can do more good down here. Engineering out.*"

Chapel found herself wishing that Mister Spock was here. He would know what to do about the distortions, how to save the ship—

"Oh, that's *right*," said Roger, snapping his fingers. "You *did* replace me. With a man completely incapable of reciprocating your feelings. What does that say about you, I wonder?"

"I don't— It's not like—"

One blink later, a figure was standing next to Roger— Spock, as lifelike as could be. But unlike Roger, he didn't say a thing. He simply stared at her, a judgmental look on his Vulcan features.

"I've moved on, from both of you," she said at last.

Roger snorted. "That seems likely."

Spock just raised an eyebrow.

Spock set the *Hofstadter* to head back to the planet and the source of the subspace distortion. The explosion had sent both shuttles reeling, and Spock had just regained control. The *Columbus* was stabilizing as well. He ordered Lieutenant Kologwe to match his course.

"What . . . what happened?" Engineer Scott asked in a shaken voice.

"We were hit by the explosion of the satellite," Spock said. "Petty Officer Emalra'ehn was killed."

"How?" Scott asked.

Spock kept his eyes on the screen ahead of him, but he could hear Scott attempting to sit up, followed by M'Benga admonishing him. "Once it was apparent that the *Hofstadter* would no longer be able to assist, Petty Officer Emalra'ehn triggered the power dump. He died instantly."

"The poor lad . . . And the fighters?"

"The remaining fighter craft was destroyed. The shuttle sustained considerable damage. Shields are almost depleted."

"Should we land?"

"Rest assured that this is what I have in mind, Mister Scott. We are heading to the hub of the reactor network, the cause of the subspace distortions."

"Sir," said Jaeger, who was at navigation. "There's a Farrezzi ship in orbit. Over the northern hemisphere. It's bigger than the fighters."

Spock checked the readings. "We need to land before it notices us," he said. "We cannot enter another firefight."

"Are we still going to deactivate that weather satellite?" asked Jaeger.

"We will destroy it on our way down," said Spock. "How long will it take the anomalous weather system to abate?"

Jaeger checked his readings. "A few hours at most."

Spock nodded. "Setting course." His fingers danced over the console. Simple, too simple. He had protected his crew, he had done his duty. But it was too easy, too easy to kill. Of late, Spock was troubled that he was forgetting what it meant to be Vulcan.

"Mister Spock," said M'Benga, "do you know how the *Columbus* fared?"

Spock turned his attention to the physician. It appeared that he had sustained a cut on his forehead when the shuttle had been hit. "Kologwe reported that their shields held," Spock said. "There were no injuries."

M'Benga closed his eyes for a moment, then opened them to glance around, in search of something. "I need to look after Mister Scott."

"Perhaps you should look after yourself."

"No, sir, I'm fine. I can—" M'Benga wiped the blood off his forehead. He headed aft.

Spock swiveled around to face the console, resolving to increase their speed without overtaxing the engines.

Stardate Unknown

McCoy pushed upward, but the darkness swirled around him, dragging him back down.

stay here stay here stay here stay with us don't go stay here stay here

The voice was Jocelyn's.

He tried to shut it out, but it was almost comforting. Outside, all that waited for him was an insoluble problem. In here, he was safe.

that's right stay here stay here don't go stay here stay here

The voice was his father's.

Safe? No! When had he ever thought this way? He'd been dogged by doubt his whole life. Was he doing the right thing? Was it for the right reason? But he'd always been able to keep on going.

you can't you can't you don't want to you're scared you're frightened stay here stay here

The voice was Joanna's.

He'd spent his adult life on the move, escaping the past.

no no no no stay here stay here

The voice was everyone's. Everyone he'd ever left behind, everyone he'd ever let down.

Suddenly, he was out of the darkness, tumbling through . . . through what?

Thoughts peppered his consciousness from a dozen different directions, worries and anxieties, joys and triumphs.

The feel of sheets on the first night he'd spent with Nancy. The taste of Jocelyn's lips. The grateful smile of a patient he'd saved on Dramia. His hand switching off the monitor over the first crew member he'd lost on the *Republic*.

McCoy had never been as hard on himself as he had been today. This wasn't natural. It was because of the espers. It was because they had reached out to him. It was because they were desperate. It was because they needed his help.

How? The espers didn't know what was happening. They didn't know how to get him back to consciousness. He was trapped.

McCoy felt himself falling backward, sinking back into the blackness.

come back come back oh yes oh yes stay here stay here

He stayed.

Stardate 4758.3 (0708 hours)

Chapel watched the doctor's readings. They'd gone up for a brief moment and then slid back down. They now matched the coma patients'.

She had decided against a neural stimulant. Administering a stimulant had caused this, but waking him was just as dangerous. His mind was hovering on the precipice, not able to pull itself out. He wasn't dying, not yet.

"You can't do anything for him?" Roger asked, unwilling to leave her alone. "Nothing at all?"

She looked at her fiancé. It was an entire lifetime ago that she'd loved this man.

"He's beyond the abilities of our medicine to reach," she said.

Roger knelt down in front of her. "Here's the thing, Christine. It's all about self-doubt, isn't it? Yours, his. The constant thought that we're faking it, or that we don't do things for the right reason. We spend our lives ignoring our doubts because we want to accomplish something. But what do we do when we feel the worst?"

"We . . . I don't know." What was he getting at? How was he trying to undermine her this time?

Was he trying to undermine her this time? If Doctor McCoy was right, these visitors were the espers' way of communicating. Maybe he wanted to tell her something. "Talk to someone else?" she ventured.

Roger nodded.

A bleep from McCoy's monitor drew her attention. His life-signs were sinking. She turned to face Roger, but he was gone.

Chapel knew what she had to do. McCoy could be quick to criticize, but just as quick to praise. He was a caring, devoted physician who'd do anything to save a patient. Chapel wondered if he knew that.

"Doctor McCoy . . ." she began. That wasn't right. "Leonard. I know you're there somewhere, but you need to come back. Your patients need you. Only you can save them. You can't give up. Come back to us, Leonard. Come back."

Captain Kirk, Horr-Sav-Frerin, and Neff-Bironomaktio-Frerish—a Farrezzi with hunting experience—had taken the lead. With the element of surprise on their side, the fight against the slavers outside the interrogation room had been short. Several Farrezzi had been shot. Fortunately, several of the group knew first aid. The captain had been hit on the arm. He was keeping pressure on it as he watched the Farrezzi wrenching the door open with metal poles.

Only a few minutes more, and the New Planets Cousins would have gotten in.

The heavily damaged door had been raised only halfway when Kirk slipped beneath it. The captain felt the heat coming from the lower edge and took care not to touch it.

Giotto was standing near the ensign, looking tired but relieved. Chekov was a mess but alive. At the back of the room, a pole reached to the ceiling, beside an unconscious Farrezzi slaver. There were dark red smears on the wall.

"The cavalry's here." Kirk smiled to reassure his crew.

"Just in the nick of time, sir," Giotto said. "We'd almost given—" He cut himself off. "You're wounded!"

Kirk waved it away. "It looks worse than it is. How's Chekov?"

"Hard to say for sure, sir. He needs a doctor."

"We need to turn this ship around. The Farrezzi have collected the guns from the slavers we knocked out. They're ready to fight. . . . We'll have surprise on our side."

"How did you manage it, sir?"

"Diplomacy, Commander. And a kindergarten teacher."

Giotto gave the captain a curious look. He ripped off a piece of his sleeve for a bandage. Wrapping it around Kirk's arm, Giotto said, "Thank you, sir."

"Let's get Chekov out of here." Kirk could only guess at what Chekov had gone through. "We'll head for the command center."

Stardate Unknown

McCoy was on his own in the darkness, with nothing to do but think.

"Pains you, doesn't it?" a voice said from nowhere. It didn't belong to one of his ghosts, nor to one of the espers.

But whose was it? "When you have to stay in one place and can't hide from what's bothering you. You're not used to that. You always ran rather than face your problems."

"Who are you?" McCoy asked.

"Don't you recognize yourself?"

It *was* his own voice. He shouldn't be surprised—after engaging in conversations with hallucinations, talking to yourself was the next logical step.

"You sound like me, but that doesn't mean anything."

A chuckle in the dark. "Always the skeptic. Everybody lies, at least when they're dealing with you. Isn't that your opinion?"

"I never say that."

"But you fear it, don't you? Oh, I know you do. I'm you, after all."

A figure appeared, a couple of meters away, but it was as if it had been there all along and he only just noticed it. It looked like him.

"Can't you put away your doubts? Hell, I had no idea talking to yourself could be so aggravating."

McCoy chose to get to the heart of the matter. "What do you want?"

"To help you. And me, of course. We're in this together, you might say."

"How do I get out of here?"

His mirror image raised an eyebrow. "You don't know?"

"I wouldn't still be here, playing your damn game, if I knew, would I?"

"You can't run away. You have to face it. Make a choice."

"I've always made choices."

His other self shook its head. "But you always picked the easy choice, didn't you? The choice that let you leave anything behind that troubled you, that inconvenienced you, that limited you. Your wife, your daughter, your dying father. The list goes on. Even right now, you want to leave the *Enterprise*."

"That's not true," McCoy replied, but without conviction.

The other him snorted and took a step closer. "You may fool the others, but you can't fool yourself. You left because it was easier than staying. In space, nothing could touch you."

McCoy wanted to protest, to say that this wasn't true. But there was an element of truth in it.

"You thought if you could be out here," the other McCoy said, "where nobody knew you, you could avoid making connections with people."

"I *like* people. I have friends." He forced the words out. "And they like me."

"Do they? Or are they just claiming to like you? It's hard to tell, isn't it? You can never be sure if their affection is real. You'd have to be a mind reader to find out, like old Pointy Ears."

"Shut up."

"What?"

"Shut up, I said." McCoy could barely contain his anger. Instead of venting it aimlessly, he chose to focus it on what he'd come here to do. He wouldn't let himself be derailed, not even by what claimed to be a part of him. "I'm a doctor. In here, I can't do anybody any good. I have to leave."

"You can't."

"Let me go!"

His other self laughed. "You don't want to go, not really. Or you wouldn't have to ask for my permission."

"I need to allow myself to leave," McCoy said, in order to make himself believe it. "I can't stay here. I'm needed out there."

His double waved the comment away. "So what?"

"I'm a doctor. Saving lives is what I do. I used to run away. But I haven't run away in a long time, I've chosen. I've run to where I belong—Starfleet. I've saved lives that never would have been saved. I've chosen to stay."

From somewhere above his head, a beam of light engulfed McCoy. Very quickly, everything was getting brighter and brighter, until he could see nothing.

When the blinding brightness receded, he could make out shapes. A bed. A monitor. Sickbay. At first, everything was silent, as though he was looking at a recording with the sound turned off. Gradually, his hearing returned.

Was this another illusion? Everything told him it wasn't.

McCoy knew that his patients needed him, that only he could save them. They were all waiting for him. He couldn't give up, not this time. No matter how bad it was, he had to return to them.

Determined to save his patients, McCoy took a deep breath, and plunged ahead. He looked ahead as he always did—

FIFTEEN

—as he always did.

McCoy opened his eyes and inhaled deeply as he sat up. The sickbay air rushed into his lungs. Nurse Chapel was standing in front of him, her face lit up in delight. "Welcome back, Doctor."

McCoy shook his head, trying to shake off the numbness he felt. "Hello, Nurse," he said, a grin growing on his face. "How long have I been out?"

"Almost an hour," she said.

"Wow."

"Longer than you thought?" she asked.

McCoy frowned, thinking about how it had felt. "Yes . . . and no. It seemed like I was there forever . . . but time stood still."

"*Where* were you?" asked Chapel. "Your readings fell, but once I started talking to you, they began creeping back up."

"You were talking to me? What were you saying?"

She blushed. "I told you to come back, that you were needed."

"Thank you," he said.

She smiled. "I'm glad to have you back."

He grabbed Chapel's hands in his own. "No, thank you. You put up with a lot, and you never say a thing. Thank you for *everything*."

"You're welcome." Christine sounded profoundly grateful.

"It can't always be easy."

"No. But it's worth it."

There was a discreet cough from the doorway to the ward, where Lieutenant Sulu stood. McCoy quickly let go of Chapel's hands. God . . . now *he* was blushing, too. "Welcome back, Doctor."

"Thank you, Mister Sulu."

"Good to see you back." Sulu smiled wanly. "There have been developments."

"Such as?"

"Lieutenant Uhura's injured and needs surgery. I'm back in command."

"What happened to Uhura?" McCoy asked.

Chapel gave him a brief summary. McCoy tried to read the medical monitor. "How am I doing?"

"Fine."

McCoy leapt off the bed. "Excellent. We're going to save Uhura, and we're going to save these people."

Sulu said, "You're in a good mood, Doctor. Did you learn what you needed to?"

"Not really," said McCoy. "But we're saving these people. Every last one of them."

A Farrezzi was able to point out the tunnel that led to the command center. Kirk broke into a run, eager to make it there before the ship went to warp. Not everyone could keep up. When Kirk stopped to check his makeshift team, he saw that Giotto was in the rear, keeping Chekov company, talking to him in a low voice.

"James-Kirk-*Enterprise*," said Horr, "preparation lawbreaker attack now. Danger!"

"I know," Kirk replied. "I'm prepared. When we get there, we'll blast the door open and take them by surprise." Giotto had liberated some grenades from the slavers.

A few minutes later, they reached the command center. The door was open. In an instant, they were under fire from slavers unleashing particle weapons at them.

With its smooth, featureless surface, the tunnel offered no protection. "Fall back!" Kirk shouted to the crowd of Farrezzi around them. He and Giotto lay down covering fire with their phasers. This discouraged the shooters, but there was still chaos around them. Some of the Farrezzi were slow to retreat, while others were overly eager. A slaver's blast hit the wall next to Kirk, leaving a sharp odor of burnt plastic.

The group finally reached a bend in the tunnel that shielded them from the slavers' fire. Kirk motioned Giotto over to him. "Not the welcome I expected," Kirk said.

"A little too warm for me," Giotto quipped.

"Well," said Kirk, "maybe we can return the favor." He wished there was time to talk to these Farrezzi, get them to stand down. "You and I will go back, phasers set on wide beam. Incapacitate them, and mind the equipment."

"Stun everyone, keep the controls intact." Giotto smiled. "Easy. We'll need some covering fire."

"Horr and Neff," said Kirk. The captain checked his phaser. "My power's almost out."

"Mine, too," said Giotto. "If we fire on wide beam, that'll be it for them."

Kirk explained the plan to Horr and Neff. Chekov seemed to be recovering his strength. He was talking with the Farrezzi about their unusual physiology. For now the captain would leave the ensign with them.

"They're not going to expect us to try again right away," said Kirk. "Let's go."

Kirk and Giotto advanced cautiously up the tunnel, with Horr and Neff behind them. A shadow in the tunnel. The captain motioned to Neff, who fired up the corridor. There was a high-pitched squeal, and then a thump. They continued up the curving tunnel, Horr and Neff firing to deter anyone from coming at them.

A blast whizzed down the tunnel. It hit the tunnel wall, sending shrapnel in all directions. Some pieces hit the captain's face, feeling like hot needles piercing his cheeks. They were almost to the command center. If the slavers were shooting at them, the doors had to be open. "Go!" Kirk said to Giotto.

The two Starfleet officers charged up the tunnel, running straight into the command center. "Your shot!" Kirk shouted.

Giotto fired his phaser on wide beam, and Farrezzi slavers at the control panels fell to the floor. Kirk counted four down—there had to be more. A second later, three popped up in one corner, bringing their weapons to bear. Before they could fire, Kirk pulled the trigger. They collapsed as well. The captain checked the power level on his phaser—dead. He continued to brandish it, as he searched the room. Cowering behind a control panel was a slaver.

"Put down your weapon," Kirk ordered.

"Noncompliance," said the slaver with a sneer. "Lack of victory." All its eyestalks trained on Kirk as it raised its weapon.

Removing the sliver of metal from Uhura's chest had been a relatively simple task, and she was now recuperating in the examination room. The doctor didn't want to move her. McCoy now knew the only hope for the coma patients was to extract the *Enterprise* from the distortion zone.

While he was reporting to Lieutenant Sulu, McCoy wondered if he had learned enough to free the ship.

"So because this other universe has no . . . quantum entanglement, their minds found nothing and shut down?" asked Sulu.

"That's how it sounded to me," said McCoy. "None of them said quantum entanglement, but yes. They also kept going on about the Nothing."

"Why did they make the medical staff hallucinate?"

"They weren't thinking clearly," McCoy admitted. "They're desperate and confused, so they tried whatever worked. They never had abilities like this before—they're only this powerful working together."

Sulu had his arms crossed, a frown growing on his face as he listened. "Again, why?"

"At first, I thought they wanted to tell me what was wrong with them," McCoy said. "They told me the Nothing would destroy the ship and that the *Enterprise* had to get out of here. They said, 'Find another power.'"

Sulu was looking pale, as if he was about to keel over. "We're dead in the water." He called up a diagram of the *Enterprise*. Some sections were marked in green—SAFE—and others in red—EVACUATED. "We're slowly losing the ship. The longer we sit here, the worse it gets. The other universe is leaking into ours, causing our equipment breakdowns and our power failures. I'd give it a day before we lose power entirely.

"Stay and die. Move and die. We get to choose between catastrophes."

McCoy considered the espers' cryptic suggestion. "Sulu, they said, 'Find another power.' Could they have meant one different from the *Enterprise*'s engines? When the portside computer banks exploded, they sent the ship spinning out of control. There was a *lot* of power there. What about the torpedoes?"

"We can't use the computer to control them, too dangerous."

"I suppose we couldn't toss them out of the shuttlebay?"

"Doctor McCoy, you're brilliant. A shuttlecraft. It's a reasonably big mass of duotronic circuitry. And then there's the matter/antimatter engines."

"Wouldn't an explosion that close to the ship be devastating?" asked McCoy.

Sulu shook his head. "Not if we angle the deflectors right. We absorb the blast's kinetic energy, and then shut *everything* down before we hit a distortion. The momentum should carry us through the distort-zone."

Kirk pointed his phaser at the Farrezzi's head and coldly said, "I can kill you with a single shot. Drop your weapon."

The slaver hesitated, and in that moment, Giotto threw his phaser at the alien's eyestalks. As it recoiled, Kirk leapt and grabbed the gun out of its tentacles, aiming it at the Farrezzi.

"Is that all of them?" Kirk breathed a sigh of relief.

"That's all."

Kirk called Horr and Neff in, asking Neff to take custody of the last slaver. The captain looked up and saw that the overhead was a transparent cupola. Impressive. The ship was still in orbit above Farrezz on autopilot. Neff marched the slaver off at gunpoint while Horr went to get Chekov and the rest of the sleepers.

Another time, Kirk would have wanted to take his time and explore the command center. As he stood there, he realized his face hurt. He touched it gingerly. There were sharp metal spikes embedded in it. When he pulled one out, it felt like half his cheek came with it. He was not surprised to see it covered in blood.

"Sir," said Giotto, wearing a worried expression, "are you hurt badly?"

Kirk shook his head. Bad idea. "You know head wounds. Make you bleed like hell."

"Make you look like hell, too, sir."

The captain laughed, then immediately winced. "Damn you, Sal, that hurts."

"Sorry, sir."

"We need to find Yüksel. You round up the slavers."

"I hope there's a brig on this ship," said Giotto, looking at the unconscious Farrezzi around them.

"I was thinking," said Kirk, "that we could put them to sleep. Those empty hibernation capsules are waiting to be used."

Giotto grinned. "Aye, sir. I'll get some of the freed Farrezzi to help me."

As Giotto left the room, Kirk looked up and caught sight of something through the transparent cupola.

The second transport.

They had no way of keeping that ship from making off with their cargo.

Not yet.

The two shuttles successfully avoided the ship in orbit—or ships, as it turned out—and took out the weather satellite. Scotty discovered that it had been activated when they removed the other satellite from orbit, evidently in a misguided effort to "compensate" for the missing satellite. There were no other Farrezzi fighters, which Scotty took as a good sign. Spock had tried to raise the captain, but his communicator wasn't picking up anything.

"I still think you should sleep," said M'Benga, "now that the immediate crisis is over."

"I'm needed," said Scotty, "for when we get to the distortion projector." He was unable to move, but his mind was still working. "And Mister Spock agrees."

"It's against my medical judg—"

"Doctor," Spock said, "we have arrived at our destination. Mister Scott, you will monitor the situation and provide us with any insight you might have. Doctor M'Benga, you will observe Mister Scott and administer a pain suppressant should it become necessary. Understood?"

Chagrined, the doctor said, "Yes, sir."

"The device at the center of the reactor network is directly below us," Spock said, "but it is built into the side of a mountain. There is no adjacent landing area. There is still a strong wind. The shuttles will have to hover above the structure, while the landing party will rappel down."

"Ensign Seven Deers, Ensign Saloniemi, and Crewman Tra, do you copy?"

"*Aye, sir,*" came the reply from the *Columbus*.

Spock made his way aft. "Mister Scott, I have configured a tricorder to let you observe the energy levels. If you discover a danger to the shuttles, take them to a safe distance." He handed a tricorder to Scotty. "I have set up an autopilot program that can be activated with one click."

"Aye, Commander," said Scotty, looking at the device.

Spock had moved to open the hatch. "We will stay in contact." The Vulcan took out his communicator. "Spock here. Begin."

Spock exited the shuttle, rappelling in one quick motion, the strong wind just managing to ruffle his close-cropped hair.

"Good luck," Scott said. He breathed in deeply, hoping that the landing party would find something useful down there.

The command center was starting to fill up wth the freed Farrezzi. The inner part, below the cupola, was a large empty space. The control consoles were along the wall. Looking around, the captain noticed that there was no main viewscreen—then he looked up and saw symbols floating just below the transparent dome. A heads-up display made sense if you had eyes that pointed in every direction.

The consoles were unusual, circular and rail thin. Their displays were round screens that were mounted to a pole, three meters above the floor. Very ergonomic for a Farrezzi. Chekov was doing his best to cope with the design, Giotto at his side. Unfortunately, none of the Farrezzi had piloting experience, so Chekov was their best hope.

Kirk was scrutinizing the other transport on the dome display. The other ship was a twin to the one they were on. They hadn't found Yüksel—he could be over there. Regardless, they had to stop that ship. Both ships were ten minutes from powering up their warp engines.

But how to stop them?

"Horr-Sav-Frerin, I need your help," Kirk said, leaning against an unoccupied console to fight the fatigue.

"Assistance certainty. Argument: lack of ability. James-Kirk-*Enterprise*, I nonpossession of relevant skillset. Query: suggestions?"

The captain had accepted the communicator's failure to provide a better translation of the Farrezzi language. He understood that Horr-Sav-Frerin was happy to offer its help, but it didn't have the knowledge to operate the technology.

"I need you to tell the Farrezzi with space experience to take any controls even if they understand only vaguely."

Horr gestured animatedly. What did it mean? Or worse, had he said something insensitive?

"Correction, James-Kirk-*Enterprise*. People not-name Farrezzi. Agreement: planet name Farrezz. People name Community-of-Children-of-Farrezz."

"Thank you for the clarification," said Kirk. "I have an assistance requirement."

Horr gesticulated again. "Agreement. Offer: information completion. Query: acceptance?"

"Acceptance."

Chekov was staring up at the display, his expression intent, a smile on his lips. Kirk crossed over to him. "Ensign, I see you're enjoying yourself. Good."

"Oh, yes, sir," Chekov said, nodding eagerly. "This is amazing technology, completely alien—and yet intuitive."

"Go on."

"Let me show you, sir. Here, this is local space." Chekov pointed up at the display. It changed to Farrezz, covered in thick swirls of clouds and green-blue oceans. "I accessed the sensors in less than a minute. I am confident that we'll have complete control very soon, sir."

"Any weapons?" the captain asked.

Chekov shook his head. "No weapons, sir."

Kirk gestured at a large bank of indicator lights. "What are those?"

"Incoming transmissions," said Chekov. "Status reports from the satellites *Hofstadter* found in orbit. I believe this craft deployed them."

"Can we get a signal to the shuttles?" asked Kirk.

"I have been trying," said Chekov, "but our communicators cannot penetrate the ship's hull, and I haven't discovered how to link the ship's systems into our—" Suddenly Chekov gasped. "Captain, the other ship is going to warp!"

"Damn!" Kirk looked up at the transport, whose engines were beginning to glow.

"They probably got scared when they lost contact," Giotto said. "Can we go after them?"

"I can activate warp drive," said Chekov, "but it will not be good for the engines."

"I plan on trading this ship in for a better one, Mister Chekov." Kirk moved to the center of the room, back to Horr. "Are your people ready?"

"Affirmation. Query: current action?"

"The other transport is about to go to warp, and we're going to follow it."

"Exclamation of woe!"

Horr began to wriggle his tentacles again, but Kirk turned his attention back to the ship on the heads-up display. "Are we ready, Mister Chekov?"

"Warp speed at your command."

With a flash, the other ship was gone.

"Now, Mister Chekov!"

SIXTEEN

Chekov's finger stabbed down on the button he had identified as ENGAGE. The console thrummed beneath his hands as the ship jumped to warp. Once again, the other ship was back onto his sensor plot, only seconds ahead of them.

"Warp one," he reported. "We have matched course and speed." Chekov moved his hands to increase speed, but found that they were shaking. Not now! He was feeling better, he really was. He wasn't thinking any longer about—about—

"Are you okay, Ensign?" Giotto asked the question so quietly, only he could hear.

Chekov wanted to tell the security chief that he was fine, but he knew he wasn't. "I am trying, sir, but it is very difficult. I just wanted to put things—"

Giotto grabbed Chekov's shoulder and leaned in to whisper. "Focus. When you make a mistake, you don't need to atone for it, just don't make the mistake again. You can fly the ship." Giotto let go.

"Aye, sir."

"Good."

Chekov could not believe it. He had impressed "Stoneface" Giotto somehow.

The other ship was slightly ahead of them. Chekov increased the speed. The ship didn't feel right. He was flying a ship whose warp engines had been sitting for a century without maintenance.

A green indicator light began to blink. The forward sensors.

"What's that?" asked Giotto.

On a Federation starship, the results would come up automatically, but here someone needed to operate manually. "On the next console. Please press the orange glyph," Chekov said. That would display the forward sensor reading on the heads-up display.

Giotto activated the readouts, and a detailed plot of the surrounding region of space appeared, The lines were squiggled and twisted, not the standard lines of subspace.

"Subspace distortion!" Chekov reached for the controls to dial back warp power. Too late.

Spock had rappelled many times, both in preparation for his *kahs-wan* and during his Academy training. However, he had never rappelled from a hovering shuttle to a partially smashed alien structure built into a steep mountainside while being buffeted by a jet of air.

Quite agreeably, Spock found that he still possessed the skills.

Standing on a narrow ledge, Spock considered the building—a tall, narrow spire. He had not expected it to be so severely damaged. A rockfall had struck it, destroying a smaller annex completely and tearing away a considerable part of the main structure, including what could have been a landing platform.

Ensign Saloniemi was the last off *Columbus*. It took him longer to rappel down, but he did so without assistance.

"This way." Spock pointed to a large semicircular door, almost twice as tall as he. Seven Deers went straight for the dark panel to the door's left, pushed it, and stepped back.

Nothing happened. "The mechanism must have been damaged in the rockfall," Spock surmised. "We will need to seek alternatives."

"Agreed," Seven Deers said. "What do you suggest, Commander?"

"Brute force."

"Phasers don't work on these doors." Saloniemi's fatigue was evident in his voice.

"That is correct, Lieutenant," said Spock. He looked up above him, at the two shuttles doing their best to hover in position. "Time is of the essence. A phaser rifle on overload should supply the necessary force."

Sickbay was quiet, with nurses and med techs out there, going from one temporary recovery room to the next. McCoy stood at the foot of Bouchard's biobed, studying the man. There was no way to know how their plan would affect the five. The ship had to plunge through an affected area, before it would be free of the distort-zone. A course that would involve the shortest possible time spent in distorted space might still prove deadly to the espers.

"We are ready to leave this zone. Prepare for more jolts," Sulu announced on shipwide comm. *"Once we start moving, we're going to shut down every system we can, with the exception of inertial damping and life support. Five minutes. Stand by."*

McCoy's eyes ran over the espers' empty features: Bouchard, Petriello, Santos, Fraser, Salah. Five men and women exposed to a horrible mental trauma. He could only hope that this would work.

Chapel came into the ward. "I've finished my rounds, Doctor. Everybody's recovering well. Lieutenant Haines wants me to tell you that she's fine now. No more pain."

"I'm glad to hear that," McCoy said, and he really was. Haines didn't deserve the torment the espers had caused her.

"Are you ready?"

"Am I ready to be whacked across space like some kind of galactic piñata?" he asked. "Sure. It's too late to say no, anyway."

She smiled. "Well, if this works, you'll have saved the ship."

McCoy paused for a moment. He hadn't considered that. He'd saved the lives of the crew time and again—but saved the ship? That would be a new one. To be honest, he felt pleased with himself.

The intraship sounded, and Sulu's voice reverberated throughout the room. *"Attention, all hands. We will begin the operation designed to remove the Enterprise from this zone of spatial instability. We will eject a shuttlecraft into one of the distortions. The resulting blast from the shuttle's explosion will push us free. It won't be a smooth ride. Please stay alert and brace yourselves. With a little luck, we will come out of this safely. All sections, report."*

"Lawton here. Crew centralized in safe locations."

"Harper here. Main systems ready for immediate shutdown."

"Leslie here. Inertial dampers set for maximum."

"Padmanabhan here. Distortions plotted and course set."

McCoy hit the comm button himself. "McCoy here. Sickbay ready."

"DeSalle here. Shuttlecraft ready for automated launch."

There was a brief pause, then Sulu spoke again. "You are go for launch, Lieutenant DeSalle."

"Aye, sir. Shuttlebay doors opening under manual control . . . open."

McCoy looked at Chapel, whose face was creased with worry.

"Shuttlecraft launching . . . now."

Chapel noticed McCoy looking at her and smiled.

"Shuttlecraft away. ETA to distortion, seven seconds."

McCoy smiled back.

"Six."

He grabbed the closest fixed object to prepare for impact: Petriello's bed.

"Five."

Chapel did the same with Salah's.

"Four."

He thought of how brusque he was to her. He'd have to make it up to her.

"Three."

He'd have to make it up to the whole medical staff, really.

"Two."

He wondered how Jocelyn was doing.

"One."

He tried to remember the last time he'd talked to Joanna. He'd have to contact her.

"Zero."

McCoy couldn't hear the explosion, but he could feel it. The impact shook the deck, and despite holding on to the biobed, McCoy had a hard time staying on his feet. He thought he heard the ship itself scream, its metal wrenching and twisting as it hurtled through space. The lights went out and then came back on, dim, when the battery backups kicked in.

As McCoy watched, Petriello opened his mouth. The medical monitor began squealing in alarm. Petriello began to scream.

Moments later, they *all* did. All five voices slammed into McCoy's psyche, pushing their way into his mind. He'd never heard anything like it. The screams penetrated his most private defenses, tore down the walls he'd constructed around himself, and slammed into the core of his being, shattering him into a million tiny pieces.

McCoy's knees gave way and he collapsed onto the deck.

Stardate Unknown

McCoy found himself on a biobed, white, empty space all around him. There was nothing else. From out of nowhere, a voice came: *This is your solution?* Santos—materialized next to him, as if she had been transported here—looked confused. *Subject us to the worst of it?*

"I had to," McCoy said. "It's the only way." All five espers were now arrayed around him, peering down like he was a museum exhibit.

It's worse than ever before, Fraser said, her face lined with pain. *The Nothing. It's all we can feel now.*

Far away in the background, outside the emptiness he was in, McCoy could hear Fraser screaming as she spoke. He could hear all of them.

The Nothing and you. Salah's burly form loomed over McCoy.

"Our options were limited," McCoy said defensively.

We wanted to get away from the distortions! Bouchard said.

McCoy was determined to find a way out of this for all of them. He sat up on the bed and picked one of the espers—Bouchard—and looked him in the eye. "I've had enough of this." They recoiled from him, surprised by his sudden resolve. "Any doctor knows that there are times you have to confront your pain. There are times you have to grit your teeth and push through it."

McCoy gave them all a hard look. He thought they understood what he was getting at, because they nodded, despite the agony on their faces.

As one, they opened their mouths, uttering once again a shared scream that overwhelmed his senses. McCoy covered his ears, but he might as well not have bothered. It was impossible to block out the sound. It was everywhere at once—in his mind, in his heart, in his bones.

The entire ship tilted. It happened so quickly that McCoy wasn't able to grab the bed's edge in time. He rolled right off the bed, and then his head hit something.

He told himself that this was only an illusion. He'd barely finished the thought when he passed out.

Stardate 4758.4 (0914 hours)

Kirk felt the entire ship slip underneath his feet, the stars whirling in circles in the display. "Mister Chekov, what's happening?" he shouted.

"Attempting to stabilize, sir!"

Kirk watched as Chekov manipulated the controls, giving occasional orders to Giotto at the next console. The stars stopped swirling and the deck leveled itself out. Kirk let go of the pole he'd been holding on to. "Wormhole effect?" he asked.

"We have run aground into normal space, sir," said Chekov. "This is very similar to the phenomenon Lieutenant Uhura reported."

"And the other ship?" There was no sign of it.

"A little bit ahead of us. They did not cut power as fast as we did, and their warp drive suffered greater damage."

Neophyte space travelers—like the New Planets Cousins—wouldn't recognize a spatial distortion, and they certainly wouldn't know how to deal with it. Thankfully Chekov had his wits about him. The captain asked, "How far did we get?"

Giotto hit some buttons. "About a hundred light-seconds." A new view on the heads-up display showed Farrezz behind them, now nothing more than a bright dot.

"James-Kirk-*Enterprise*!" Horr shrieked. "Report: engine damage. Functional impairment."

"The other ship is worse off," Chekov said. "However . . . they are resetting their engines."

"Are they insane?" Giotto asked.

"No," Kirk said, "just inexperienced. What will that do?"

"If that ship tries to go to warp in these distortions with a damaged warp drive," Chekov said, "it will be ripped apart."

Killing thousands of innocent Farrezzi. Kirk needed to stop them, without weapons. He looked back up at the HUD, at the small dot of Farrezz. "How much time do we have?"

"Ten minutes." Chekov grimaced.

Something was stirring in the back of Kirk's mind,

even as he strained his neck looking at the tiny little planet. "Mister Chekov, can you magnify the planet?"

"Yes, sir."

The planet grew bigger, with only a slight jitter that told Kirk the computer wasn't entirely able to compensate for the spinning. "Increase magnification."

Now the planet took up the entire display, the continents clearly visible under the spotty cloud cover. Many island chains dotted the oceans, where submerged mountain ridges poked through the water's surface.

"Can you show me the satellites?" Kirk asked.

"That's a bit more difficult. They're small, and fast."

Kirk grinned. "My point exactly."

McCoy let off an involuntary groan. His body ached all over—he was acutely aware of the number of bumps and bruises it had taken over the past day. What had happened? Everything was still fuzzy.

He was on the deck. Blocking his field of vision was the broad base of a biobed. With what amounted to a superhuman effort, McCoy propped himself up on his elbows and scanned the room for other victims of the latest incident. Chapel lay on the deck across from him on her side, facing the opposing wall. She was unconscious but breathing steadily.

Gathering every ounce of strength, McCoy sat up and waited a bit before he tried to stand. His head was still fuzzy. It took a while, but eventually he was able to wake Chapel. Her eyes snapped open. She ran her hand over her face. "Doctor, what . . . what happened?"

"Our patients objected to our actions." McCoy's eyes flicked to the nearest monitor—Petriello's. The man's levels were improving steadily. Their plan had worked! For Petriello to rally so quickly could only mean one thing: they had put the distortions behind them.

McCoy inspected the others' readings. Fraser was improving, her readings climbing back toward normal. Santos, on the bed to her left, was doing the same, though not as quickly. Salah, too. And Bouchard—

Bouchard's were sinking. Fast.

"No, no, no, no!" McCoy shouted, hurrying over to the phaser control officer. Not *now*. Not after all this.

"Dalaphaline!" he shouted. Christine was already pressing a hypospray with the stimulant into his hand.

He'd have to inject it directly into the brain. The hypospray hissed as it released the chemicals.

"Come on, come *on*!" McCoy's eyes ran back and forth between Bouchard's blank face and the medical monitor.

Nothing happened. Bouchard was bottoming out.

His mind ran through all the ideas he'd had for saving the espers. Now that they were out of the distort-zone, maybe one of them would work, he just had to figure out which one—

The medical monitor gave one last *bleep* and then every readout was at zero: no heartbeat, no respiration, no brain patterns.

Bouchard was dead.

They'd moved the ship, but it had been too late.

Chapel grabbed his hand. "I'm sorry, Doctor."

"Computer, time of death: 0921 hours, Stardate 4758.4. Name: Olivier Bouchard, ensign. Cause: the Nothing."

SEVENTEEN

All Scotty could do was watch as the landing party positioned the phaser rifle. He was startled when he felt a hand on his shoulder. It was M'Benga's. "Relax," the doctor said. "There's nothing you can do."

Scotty merely nodded. There was a bright flash, then belching black smoke, which was swept away by an intense jet of air to reveal the remnants of the door. An alarm began beeping on his tricorder. "Commander, are you seeing this?" Scotty asked, as he was running a scan to make sure.

"Yes, Mister Scott." Spock's voice was grave. "*The power emanating from the tower is fluctuating rapidly. If we do not succeed in shutting it down shortly, it will explode, possibly forcing open a subspace disruption within the planetary atmosphere.*"

"Mister Spock, we've only got seventeen minutes," Scotty said, his voice rising in alarm.

"*I am aware of the situation, Mister Scott. We are moving with alacrity.*"

Captain Kirk's plan was simple. The ships were still close to the planet. If he reprogrammed the satellites, he could use them to overwhelm the fleeing slavers.

"A very ingenious idea, Captain," said Chekov.

"Let's see if it works," Kirk replied.

"I think it will, Captain." Chekov, working with Giotto, had connected his tricorder to a partially dismantled communicator that had been wired into the controls of their commandeered ship. "I've reprogrammed the control circuits for the Farrezzi satellites, allowing us to transmit to all of them at once. Their reaction control thrusters are under our command."

"Well done. Transmit now."

"Aye, sir," Chekov said. He began keying commands into his tricorder. "Captain, did you know that we are continuing a proud Russian tradition?"

"Do you think this is the time for that?" Kirk asked.

"Ah . . . no, sir."

Tilting his head back, Kirk could see that the satellites' thrusters had activated. "Horr," he called across the command deck, "can you pull the image back? And follow the satellites' progress?"

"Affirmation, James-Kirk-*Enterprise*," answered the Farrezzi teacher. "Intention of best attempt."

Small purple dots now flitted across the display. Horr asked, "Desire: explanation of developments." A couple of his eyes bent to study Kirk.

"We're about to hit the slavers with the satellites your people placed in orbit around Farrezz."

"Feeling of surprise. Query: chances of success?"

"Impossible to say. It *should* disable them if we aim them right."

"Feeling of disappointment. Lack of patience."

He wasn't alone there. "I know that it must be difficult, given that more of your people are—"

The ship shuddered, then flung him to the deck as everything tilted hard to port. Lights flickered; Farrezzi shrieks mixed with human curses.

In the darkness, Kirk could only wonder what had gone wrong now.

When McCoy stepped into his lab, he was surprised to find Padmanabhan and Rodriguez dismantling the computers, and Sulu nowhere in sight. ". . . we'll be working with the damage-control party on the bridge, if you need us, sir."

"*Very good. Carry on.*" The monitor showed Sulu in auxiliary control. "*Doctor, status?*" he asked.

"Petriello, Santos, Fraser, and Salah are getting better. Bouchard is dead." McCoy swallowed. "How's the *Enterprise*?"

"*She's fine,*" Sulu said. "*The ship's on course, and as we move from the center of the zone, the distortions lessen. There'll be some turbulence, but the worst is well behind us. We'll soon be clear.*"

Padmanabhan chimed in unbidden. "Amazing—there's so much out there, we've seen—even in just a brief squirt from the shuttle—it's just like—"

Rodriguez put a hand on the ensign's shoulder. "Okay, Homi."

"Can we make it to Mu Arigulon now?" McCoy asked.

"*There are still some distortions I'd like to avoid. I'd say we're two days out.*"

"Once we're on course, Lieutenant, you should get some rest. Doctor's orders."

Sulu smiled as he replied, "*We're only here because I listened to you, so from now on, I'll make sure to follow your orders, Captain McCoy.*"

· · · ·

The tower's interior thrummed with power. The room was small, barely large enough to contain the landing party. In the center of the circular chamber was an object resembling a cube, its faces covered with protrusions. Lights blinked, signaling the object's working state. It did not possess an input screen of any kind.

"How much time do we have?" Saloniemi asked.

"Eleven minutes, forty-nine seconds," Spock replied. "We must work quickly if we are to stop the overload. Ensign Seven Deers, have you determined the cause of the fluctuations?"

"No, sir," she said, working her tricorder. "It's almost impossible to get readings in here. Interference is strong."

"Ensign Saloniemi, report."

Saloniemi was running his tricorder over the glyphs on the device, moving from one to another. "It's all technical terminology," he said. "The UT is still working on it. This one"—he pointed to a prominent symbol on the top of the cube—"is marked 'playback.'"

Seven Deers was right next to him with her own tricorder. "It connects to a set of holographic circuits," she said.

"Press it," Spock ordered. Saloniemi did, and the lights on the cube dimmed as a hologram appeared above it.

"That's a Farrezzi!" Seven Deers exclaimed—unnecessarily, since the image matched the landing party's recordings.

The image of the Farrezzi was frozen, but a voice emerged. *"Occupants of this chamber have been identified as not of the Community of the Children of Farrezz. This message is for visitors to our world."* The voice stopped, and the image continued to hold still.

"That's not Farrezzi," said Saloniemi quietly. "It's one of the Orion trading creoles. Yrevish."

Spock nodded. It was logical to leave a message for off-worlders in a language that they would likely know.

The holographic Farrezzi began to move, its tentacles flexing slightly. A new voice, a little higher-pitched, began: "*I am Benshor-Ka-Morafe, head of the Deep Burrow Project. If you have analyzed Farrezz, you have discovered that its atmosphere has grown toxic after centuries of industrial pollution. We traveled into space to find a solution to this problem, but found nothing and no one to help us. We lacked the technology to evacuate our world. The only solution was to avoid further disruption, while returning the planet to its natural state. The entire Community of the Children of Farrezz has gone into hibernation while our satellites work to repair the planet's atmosphere. When it has been restored, we will return to the surface. We will take care of the planet from that point on. If you have—have—have—*"

The image paused, hanging in place. "It's trying to continue the playback," said Seven Deers.

"The statements of Benshor-Ka-Morafe verify our hypotheses," said Spock.

The playback continued. "*—have made it here, then you have bypassed the defenses we built before we entered our slumber. Knowing that a world of sleepers would present a tempting target for some of the species we have encountered, we designed a system—powered by warp reactors across the continent—that would project distortions in subspace, making it impossible for any vessel to approach this planet at warp speed. The projector is designed to respond to the warp bubbles it encounters; the more powerful the engines, the more powerful the distortions. We do not know how you* *managed it, but you have made it here. Please, let the Community of the Children of Farrezz slumber in peace. Do not loot our world. We have gone through much to ensure its continued survival."*

The Farrezzi raised three of its tentacles into the air, balancing on the two remaining. *"Please, go back to the stars. We are defenseless, we have only our pleas. I ask you to go back to your home so that we may keep ours."*

The image faded out. "This explains a great deal," Spock said to the assembled team. "The distortions the *Enterprise* encountered were caused by this device."

"Why is the projector so unstable?" Saloniemi asked.

"The warp engines of a *Constitution*-class starship are massive," said Seven Deers. "If the projector tried to match their power, the distortions would be enormous—far more than this system would have been designed to accommodate." The engineer shook her head. "It's reached its maximum, and it's now caught in a deadly feedback loop."

"Correct," said Spock. "The Farrezzi did not anticipate more advanced technologies. The power the *Enterprise* can generate would be enough to create distortions not only in subspace, but in normal space as well. Possibly even projecting into other realities. Fascinating."

"What about the overload? We need to stop this!" Tra was frantic.

"Correct, Crewman." Spock consulted his tricorder. "Additional ships have activated their warp drives, overtaxing the system—the two ships we detected in orbit. This system will overload in four minutes. We must stop it or the Community of the Children of Farrezz will no longer have a world."

■ ■ ■ ■

The lights flickered back on, but dimmer than before, making it hard to see. Kirk pushed himself up off the deck—and suddenly felt no resistance. The artificial gravity was out.

Kirk needed to remember to push gently to propel himself. He spun slowly toward what his brain was telling him was up, but now was just a surface like any other.

"Everybody okay?" he shouted.

"Aye, sir," came the somewhat strained reply from Giotto.

Kirk called out, "Chekov?"

"Yes, sir," said the ensign, sounding as though he was halfway across the command center.

The Farrezzi had fared better, their many limbs proving to be an advantage, but they were scared. Horr-Sav-Frerin had pulled itself into a ball, eyestalks retracted, two thin appendages wrapped around a pole to keep itself from floating away.

The captain instinctively hooked his foot on the ring that connected the computer display to the support poles. He pulled himself "down" along the pole, so he could take in the HUD. He needed to find out what had hit them. It turned out to be a swarm of Farrezzi satellites, floating outside. "Mister Chekov, you hit the wrong ship!"

"With only some of them," replied the ensign matter-of-factly. "Look, Captain!" He pointed at the heads-up display.

The viewer showed the slaver transport, bombarded by a swarm of satellites. Its warp nacelles were pitted with holes from the satellites' impact.

"Good work, Ensign," Kirk said. "Even if we did take a few hits ourselves."

"My apologies, Captain. It appears my targeting parameters were not quite specific enough."

"Are they dead in space?" Kirk asked.

Giotto answered, having floated back to the sensor controls. "Yes, sir. Unfortunately, so are we."

Ensign Saloniemi was studying the holographic projection above the control cube, which now displayed several rows of Farrezzi text.

"Status report, Ensign," said Spock.

"Well, sir," Saloniemi began, "I've managed to translate all the text."

Spock raised an eyebrow. "Problem?"

"It's very confusing. This is an incredibly complex system." He shook his head. "I'm matching it against what we know about Farrezzi technology from the matter/antimatter reactor we found, and information in the database, but it's going to take some time."

"Will you figure it out in three minutes?" asked Spock.

"No, sir." He slumped to the ground, but continued to pore over his tricorder nevertheless.

Seven Deers was working her way through the system. "I'm making small changes to the settings," she said. "With trial and error, we should be able to trace all the circuits." She sighed. "But it'll take too long."

"Continue working," Spock ordered.

The crackling energy was growing louder and louder, its pitch varying wildly as the system tried in vain to stabilize itself. Spock opened his communicator. "Mister Scott, have you been following everything?"

"Aye, Mister Spock."

"Mister Scott, the projector must transmit its distortions via subspace. If we can deprive it of access to subspace, we may be able to shut it down."

"Aye."

"Is it possible to configure the *Hofstadter's* warp drive to generate a bubble of normal space?"

"Well—"

"Mister Scott—"

"—it is, but it would take hours to put into practice. And I'm not rounding up, sir."

"Lower the millicochranes into the negative," Scotty ordered. "That should do it."

"You told Spock it would take too long," M'Benga called back.

"Worth a shot," said Scotty. He was going to do something, broken legs or not. "What's it doing?"

M'Benga tapped away at the controls. "I'm getting an error message."

"Hit 'ignore.'"

Scotty checked the tricorder. They had sixty seconds.

"There's no 'ignore' button!"

"Let me see that!" What was the doctor talking about? Of course there was an "ignore" button. "We dinna have time for this." Scotty couldn't remember ever feeling this helpless. "All of us will be *dead*—"

"Fine."

Suddenly Scotty felt himself being wrenched upward, M'Benga's arms around him. "This is going to hurt," he said. It did. Moments later he was lowered into the pilot's chair—gently, but he winced nonetheless.

There was the sodding error message. M'Benga was right, there was no "ignore" button.

How was he supposed—

"Fifteen seconds."

Scotty could figure out a way around it, but he needed time.

The Farrezzi scientists' miscalculations had doomed their planet. If only they had been logical— Spock stopped himself: what if they *had* been logical? The scientist had pleaded for visitors to the planet to leave. To impede the departure of visitors from the world would be illogical.

Spock scanned the "playback" button. It was connected to two circuits: the holographic device and an adjacent button whose connection had burnt out, a victim of the power surges running through the device. Sending an energy pulse from his tricorder, Spock activated the circuit. A single word appeared on the button: "DEACTIVATE."

He raised an eyebrow. Logical. His hand pressed it.

A loud crack rang through the interior of the tower.

Seven Deers said something, but not even Spock's Vulcan hearing could make it out. The crackling sound of the energy projector had become overwhelming. He glanced down at his tricorder. The projector was fluctuating wildly, climbing and then plunging.

Zero.

The crackling stopped. Everything shut down. They were standing in darkness.

Tra activated a flashlight, flicking it from person to person. All were present and accounted for.

Spock flipped his communicator open. "Mister Scott, we are still here. Were we successful?"

"Just a second, Mister Spock," came the voice of M'Benga. *"I'm afraid Mister Scott . . . One moment."*

While Spock waited, he consulted his tricorder. The tower was blocking exterior scanning.

"*Scott here, Commander. The whole thing is shut down.*" The engineer's exuberance was impossible to miss over the comm channel. "*The projector is deactivating. All the sensor and shield interference is gone, and so are the distortions in this system.*"

"That is welcome news," Spock said, suppressing the relief he realized he was feeling.

"*There is one strange thing, though.*"

"Please elaborate."

"*The satellites in the northern hemisphere are gone. I canna find any trace of them. It's as though they've been scooped up by some powerful force.*"

Spock was about to reply when his communicator indicated an incoming transmission. "Stand by, Mister Scott." He switched frequencies, calculating the odds that it was Captain Kirk. "Spock here."

"*Spock! Music to my ears.*" It was the captain, and he sounded almost as animated as Scott, which Spock took to be a good sign. "*Status.*"

"We have successfully eliminated a subspace distortion projector."

"*Succinct. I look forward to your detailed report.*" There was a pause. "*D'you think that you could come and pick us up? Giotto, Chekov, and I are on a Farrezzi transport ship we captured, and there are some slavers we need help with.*"

"The shuttles are damaged, but spaceworthy. We will leave as soon as possible," Spock said.

"*Try contacting the* Enterprise *again. With the field*

down, you shouldn't have any trouble getting through to Sulu. Tell him we need them here."

"Aye, sir. We will contact you when we are in position to board the Farrezzi ship."

"Good work, Mister Spock. Kirk out."

Four Hours Later
Stardate 4758.5 (1302 hours)

"You took your time, Mister Spock," Kirk said as he stepped onto the *Hofstadter*. The shuttle looked a little the worse for wear.

Spock looked up briefly from the shuttlecraft's controls and raised an eyebrow. The *Hofstadter* was sitting in the loading bay of the captive transport ship. The shuttle had dropped Giotto, Kologwe, and Tra on the other transport to round up the slavers and wake the sleepers. Neither ship was in any condition to land now, but Scotty and Seven Deers were confident that they could fix the vessels.

"Captain," Doctor M'Benga called from the stern of the shuttle. Kirk saw he was standing in front of a cryopod.

Yüksel. The exobotanist was floating in water, wires and tubes running from the rim of the large pod into his skin. His expression was frozen in agony as he bobbed up and down gently—a disconcerting sight.

Kirk turned M'Benga. "Doctor?"

M'Benga wore a somber expression. "The cryopod is designed to sustain a Farrezzi. It's slowly killing him."

"Can we get him out of there?" Kirk asked.

"I don't want to risk it without the facilities of the *Enterprise*'s sickbay."

"Thank you, Doctor," Kirk said. Would the ship arrive in time? "Mister Spock?"

"I have the *Enterprise* on standby, Captain," Spock reported. "The spatial distortions are closing now that the projector has been disabled."

"Good work, Mister Spock." Kirk crossed to the navigator's seat and sat down. "Kirk to *Enterprise*."

"*Enterprise here. Captain, this is Lieutenant Kelowitz.*"

"Lieutenant Kelowitz," said Kirk, unable to keep the surprise out of his voice, "what are you doing in command?" Rogelio Kelowitz was in tactical.

Kelowitz sounded haggard. "*Sir, I'm relieving Mister Sulu. The bridge is damaged.*"

Spock had estimated that the distortions were sizable, but— "Will you make it to Mu Arigulon?" Kirk asked.

"*Aye, sir,*" Kelowitz said, "*Probably another three hours of repair work, and then we'll be two days out. Is it safe to proceed?*"

"The spatial distortions have cleared almost entirely, Lieutenant," Spock replied. "Passage will be completely normal."

Kirk contented himself with, "We'll see you then, Mister Kelowitz."

"*Aye, sir. We'll keep you updated on our progress.* Enter-prise *out.*"

"Doctor M'Benga," Kirk called back. "Two days okay?"

"I can adjust the nutritional feed, sir—he'll be safe."

Kirk spun his chair to face Spock, who was still working diligently at his controls. "Well, Mister Spock," he said, "it looks like we're on our own for a while."

Spock only raised an eyebrow again. He really must be tired.

"Have you determined why the Farrezzi didn't wake up even though the atmosphere of their planet had been restored?"

"The information Neff-Bironomaktio-Frerish gleaned from the captured members of the New Planets Cousins indicates that they reconfigured the master purge mechanisms to release them first. They made an error and reactivated only when the *Enterprise*'s arrival triggered the distortion projector and an emergency reawakening protocol."

"The shuttles didn't do it?" asked Kirk.

"Negative," said Spock. "The power of the shuttles was below the threshold. Only the arrival of a starship could trigger the system."

"So if we'd never come here," said Kirk, "the Farrezzi would be sleeping still, unaware their planet was waiting for them to reclaim it."

"Correct, Captain."

"Lucky for them we came along," Kirk said, bringing up an image of Farrezz on the central console.

The first sight of a new world always offered him a thrill, but seeing a planet he and his crew had rescued was even better. "Let's get to work, Mister Spock. We've got a planet to wake up."

EPILOGUE

CAPTAIN'S LOG, STARDATE 4759.8

Waking the Farrezzi sleepers continues. The slavers on both ships have been detained, as have the ones on the surface. The actions of the New Planets Cousins have introduced complications into an unstable situation. The Federation has promised help. Supply ships and a team of special envoys will arrive in the next few weeks.

The thirteen of us who survived the ordeal are looking forward to the arrival of the *Enterprise*. Lieutenant Commander Scott and Petty Officer Yüksel are in need of medical attention in the ship's sickbay.

The entire landing party is due commendations for their exceptional actions during this crisis, but I would like to single out Petty Officer Cron Emalra'ehn, whose heroic action saved his shipmates at the cost of his own life.

Stardate 4760.7 (1738 hours)

McCoy stood next to Sulu in the transporter room, trying not to fidget. He'd brought a stretcher with him for Scotty. Over at the transporter console, Lieutenant Kyle was setting the controls. The two-day journey to Mu Arigulon V—sorry, Farrezz—had felt longer.

Sulu was looking good, McCoy reflected. You'd never

know that the helm console had exploded in his face. McCoy still hadn't come to terms with the loss of Bouchard. Being killed by the mere fact that the ship had gotten too close to another universe? That just wasn't fair.

"Ready to energize, sir," Kyle said.

"Beam them up, Mister Kyle," Sulu ordered, turning to face the transporter dais. The shimmering of the transporter effect, and then six figures materialized in front of them: Kirk, Spock, M'Benga, Scotty, Giotto, and Chekov. Scotty looked the worst, held up by Giotto and M'Benga.

"Welcome back, Captain," said Sulu, a wide smile on his face. "It's good to have you back."

"It's good to *be* back, Mister Sulu," Kirk said, stepping down off the dais. "What have you been doing to my ship?" His voice was light, but McCoy knew there was a bit of concern behind the question.

Scotty spoke up, clearly agitated. "I'll thank you for getting me to sickbay now, Doctor. I shudder to think what my wee bairns have been through these past few days. I need to be up on my feet so I can see what DeSalle has been doing to them."

McCoy pushed the stretcher over to the transporter dais, and with the help of M'Benga and Giotto, he transferred Scotty onto it. "Did you enjoy landing party duty, Jabilo?"

M'Benga smiled. "You can have every landing party from here to the end of the five-year mission, for all I care."

M'Benga wheeled Scotty out of the room, and McCoy went to join Kirk and Spock, who were talking to Sulu.

"—estimates it will take two weeks at Station C-15 to repair all the damage," Sulu was saying.

"So much for maintaining our schedule of exploration

in this sector," Kirk said. He turned to face McCoy. "Well, Doctor, I hear you saved my ship."

McCoy grinned, pleased with himself despite all that had happened. "Well, Lieutenant Sulu did the heavy lifting, but yes. How's that for an irrational, emotional ship's surgeon, Mister Spock?"

Spock's eyebrow went up. "Quite exemplary, I must admit, Doctor."

"Well, there you go, Mister Spock. Sometimes I—"

Spock cut him off. "Only once you abandoned emotional thinking and performed a dispassionate, logical analysis did you devise a solution to the crisis. I had no idea that you had progressed so far under my tutelage."

"Your—your tutelage?" McCoy sputtered.

Spock's face was as impassive as ever. "I have been maneuvering your thought processes towards a more enlightened, and logical, worldview. It seems that I have exceeded beyond my expectations."

McCoy looked to Jim for support, but the captain was smiling. "I think he's got you, Bones."

Of all the—! "You green-blooded computer! I save this ship, and you still can't let me have the last word?"

"Doctor, I offer you my congratulations." If McCoy hadn't known better, he'd have called Spock's expression downright smug.

Kirk laughed, slapping McCoy on the back. "Gentlemen, let's get to auxiliary control. We've got a ship to run." He walked out of the room, and they hurried after him. McCoy fell in behind Kirk to the right, Spock to the left.

For a moment, McCoy felt that he was being followed. Turning around quickly, he saw only an empty corridor. There was nothing there. He breathed out in relief.

"Something the matter, Bones?" Kirk asked.

"No," he said, "I'm just getting older."

Spock raised an eyebrow at McCoy as they followed the captain.

"You're not thinking of retiring, are you?" asked Kirk in mock surprise.

McCoy restrained a smile. "And leave all four hundred of you with no one to look at your tonsils? Jim, you couldn't get me off this ship if my life depended on it."

ACKNOWLEDGMENTS

When Steve was in high school, he coerced six of his friends into joining him in a *Star Trek* e-mail RPG affectionately known as "the sim," which lasted a few years before sputtering out—fellow participants are listed in the novel's dedication. But he would be remiss if he did not note that that RPG eventually spawned a series of amateur audio drama adaptations, one of which contained the seeds of this very story. Those audio dramas would have not gotten very far without the patience and assistance of a great many people, whom he would like to thank here: Josh Donaman, Nicholas Frey, Geoffrey Hamell, Adam Johnson, Lori Kinney, Bradley Knipper, Todd Kogutt, Timothy Moeller, Catherine Mollmann, Grady Owens, David Poon, Stephen Poon, Georg Rudorff, Harrison Sand, James Sand, Benjamin Stevens, Christopher Tracy, and Laura Waiss, not to mention Steve's parents, who put up with a dozen teenagers stomping into the house to use the microphone time and again.

Without DeForest Kelley's fantastic performance, Doctor Leonard McCoy would have been a much lesser character—and this novel would have had much less to go on. Credit must be given to Kelley for creating such a fun, irascible, enduring character. We should also acknowledge the many other actors, from big stars to background performers, who played the various other characters who populate this novel: Jeanne Bal (Nancy Crater), Majel Barrett (Christine Chapel), Michael Barrier (Lieutenant DeSalle), Booker Bradshaw (Doctor M'Benga), Richard Carlyle (Karl Jaeger), Frank da Vinci (Lieutenant Brent), James Doohan (Montgomery Scott), Victoria George (Jana Haines), Jim Goodwin (John Farrell), Deirdre L. Imershein (Lieutenant Watley), Walter Koenig (Pavel Chekov), Perry Lopez (Esteban Rodriguez), Cindy Lou (Zainab Odhiambo), Blaisdell Makee (Lieutenant Singh), Patricia McNulty (Tina Lawton), Sean Morgan (Ensign Harper), Nichelle Nichols (Lieutenant Uhura), Leonard Nimoy (Commander Spock), Eddie Paskey (Lieutenant Leslie), Naomi Pollack (Lieutenant Rahda), Bill Quinn (David McCoy), David L. Ross (Lieutenant Galloway), Barry Russo (Lieutenant Commander Giotto), William Shatner (James T. Kirk), George Takei (Lieutenant Sulu), Woody Talbert (Bobby Abrams), Maurishka Taliaferro (Yeoman Zahra), Joan Webster (Cheryl Thomas), John Winston (Lieutenant Kyle), and Grant Woods (Lieutenant Kelowitz).

We drew on the work of a few other authors when writing this novel, for both backstory and inspiration: Carmen Carter (*Dreams of the Raven*), Diane Duane (*Doctor's Orders*), Brad Ferguson (*Crisis on Centaurus*), Michael Jan Friedman (*Constitution* and *Shadows on the Sun*), David R. George III (*McCoy: Provenance of Shadows*), Vonda McIntyre (*Enterprise: The First Adventure*), and Howard Weinstein (*The Better Man*). Thanks for the bits we pilfered, and we hope you don't mind that there are bits we ignored.

Others here and there provided help where we needed it: fellow *Trek* scribe David A. McIntee gave us some assistance in Scottish dialect matters. Michael Bellos and

Christopher L. Bennett provided us with some much-needed quantum physics knowledge. Several books were also useful in this regard, especially *The God Effect: Quantum Entanglement, Science's Strangest Phenomenon* by Brian Clegg, *The Field: The Quest for the Secret Force of the Universe* by Lynne McTaggart, *Quantum Computation and Quantum Information* by Michael A. Nelson and Isaac L. Chuang, *Quantum Computation and Quantum Communication: Theory and Experiments* by Mladen Pavičić, and *Quantum Computing: A Short Course from Theory to Experiment* by Joachim Stolze and Dieter Suter. Of course, any errors were made completely intentionally for purposes of dramatic license, and not because these dense books threatened to do our heads in. Camilo José Vergara's *American Ruins* inspired some of the early scenes on Mu Arigulon V.

One book we must give thanks to above all others is Isaac Asimov's *A Choice of Catastrophes: The Disasters That Threaten Our World*, from which we brazenly stole a title. Someday we might even read it.

Special thanks must be given to Steve's fellow members of the Storrs Eight: Jared Demick, Gordon Fraser, Chantelle Messier, Hayley Kilroy Mollmann, Zara Rix, Christiana Salah, and Jorge Santos, plus auxiliary members Angela Demick and Phill Messier. Once again, without your recommendations, repasts, and rapport, this would have been a much lesser work.

Last of all, Steve must thank Hayley, whom he married between the first and second drafts of this novel, for her patience and support. Our own adventure is just beginning.

ABOUT THE AUTHORS

Michael Schuster is not owned by a cat, but he calls himself a writer anyway. He has co-written four previous *Star Trek* stories with Steve Mollmann, from the *Starfleet Corps of Engineers* eBook novella about Scotty, *The Future Begins*; to two short stories in the *Next Generation* anniversary anthology *The Sky's the Limit*; to *The Tears of Eridanus*, a short novel about an alternate Hikaru Sulu and his equally alternate daughter Demora in the third volume of *Myriad Universes*, titled *Shattered Light*. *A Choice of Catastrophes* is the duo's first standalone novel, and the first to feature all the classic characters. Michael lives in Austria, where he spends his days working in a bank and uses what's left of the week to think up stories. He has been making up stuff since childhood, but he never imagined he'd ever get to write about Kirk, Spock, and the rest of the gang. That just goes to show that life rarely turns out the way you think it will.

Steve Mollmann is owned by a cat, but he suspects the cat would prefer otherwise. In addition to the above-mentioned credits, he's the author of a short story in the anthology *Wildthyme in Purple* with a title too long to print here. He's also published academic nonfiction in venues such as *Sense of Wonder: A Century of Science Fiction* and

English Literature in Transition, 1880–1920. He lives in the "quiet corner" of Connecticut, where he studies science in nineteenth-century fiction, tries to finish his grading on time, attends talks solely for the free food, and tries to commit Robert's Rules of Order to memory. Most of all, he tries to carve out some free time to spend with his wife, Hayley.

Visit them both on the web at
http://www.exploringtheuniverse.net/

ANALOG

SCIENCE FICTION AND FACT

A full year of engaging reading delivered right to your door!

Discover the unbeatable combination of stimulating fiction, provocative editorials, and fascinating science articles in every issue of **Analog Science Fiction and Fact**.

Subscribe today and enjoy a full year of reading delivered right to your home for less than the cost of a single novel. You save 72% off the regular price!

1 year (12 issues*), only $12

To subscribe, fill out the order form below or call

TOLL-FREE, 1-800-220-7443 (M-F 8am–7pm, EST)

to charge your order. (We accept MC, VISA, AmEx, Discover.)

Mail to: Analog • 6 Prowitt St. • Norwalk, CT 06855-1220

YES! Start my subscription to Analog (AFF) right away. My payment of $12.00 (U.S. funds) is enclosed.

Name _____
(Please print)

Address _____

City _____ State _____ Zip _____

* We publish 2 double issues, in Jan/Feb and Jul/Aug, which count as four issues towards your subscription. Allow 8 weeks for delivery of first issue. WA Residents: Add applicable state and local taxes to your total order. For delivery outside U.S.A., pay $22.00 (U.S. funds). Includes GST.

XFAF67